To
Konrad,
Thank you s
much for
vo! It
great sign
Peter Pepper

BLUEGRASS

PETER PAPPALARDO

1663 LIBERTY DRIVE, SUITE 200
BLOOMINGTON, INDIANA 47403
(800) 839-8640
WWW.AUTHORHOUSE.COM

First published by AuthorHouse 07/15/05

ISBN: 1-4208-6709-1 (sc)

Printed in the United States of America
Bloomington, Indiana

This book is printed on acid-free paper.

Credits: Excerpts from <u>Bluegrass Breakdown: The Making of the Old Southern Sound</u> *by Robert Cantwell, Urbana Press, University of Illinois, 1984 © used by permission of the author.*

Cover Art: Bill Sterm, "Wildwood Flower" © 2003

≡ DEDICATION ≡

To Bill, Chris, Helen, Ken, Nina and Mona for their keen eyes, talent and insight, to all the players and Ramblers that made this book, and to my sainted wife Lynn for her patience and support.

⇒ PROLOGUE—CRISFIELD, MD ⇐

From the time he was two, Sterling Schiffler loved to read aloud. It came as naturally to him as birdsong, as smooth as a cool, mysterious, foggy fall morning, as definite as cedars burdened by shawls of snow, reeling ahead like ranks of defeated soldiers in the winter sun.

By the time he was five, he was a rapacious reader, big news in his hometown of Crisfield, Maryland, where most everybody either ran, repaired, built, stored, crewed, painted or stored boats or hauled oyster shells for fill or number one jimmies up to Baltimore for the pittance they gave you for risking your life.

Naturally the town was proud when he graduated at sixteen, the youngest ever in the history of the high school. They were equally proud when he was accepted at the same age to Yale, and pleased as pie when he graduated in three years with a soc degree and married a rich girl from Towsend.

His grandmother was mostly Lenape, and she was not so sanguine. She called his wife, not so secretly, "the trickster," and said that there was something about her heart that was not right. Sterling tried his best to ignore his grandmother's advice, but eventually there were two truths even he could not overlook.

First, he was unable to support her in the style to which she was accustomed. Even though she worked a bit organizing parties and functions—at which she was particularly apt—she was always broke, even when Sterling started commuting to Baltimore to earn more money.

Equally unfortunate was her discovery that she preferred her own sex over the opposite. They divorced, but she refused to leave Crisfield, leaving Sterling with nothing to do but move. He could not bear it to see them everywhere, and at all the best functions, too. So he answered the first ad he found, for a job as a program specialist serving mentally retarded adults. The job was in a place called Pigeon Forge, Pennsylvania, just on the fringe of the coal region, from what he could make of the map.

He was scared and upset, but determined to make the best of it. He was determined that she would not see him hang his head.

On the day before he left, he packed one suitcase and had all the rest of his things dropped off at the Salvation Army, to make a clean break of it––turned out that most of his possessions were simply books, and he had read them all, anyway.

But with the world yanked out from under him at the tender age of 23, he felt naked leaving the place he assumed he would always have. On his way north on 13, in a small bookshop in Pokemoke City, he purchased an odd book entitled "A Moderately Poetic Quasi-History of Pennsylvania."

"Fore-warned is fore-armed," the bookseller had said.

Odd as the book was, Sterling liked the way it sounded when he read it. It would come to remind him of the home he hoped someday he could win back, even if he had to haul oyster shells or paint boats to do it. As he rode, he read:

> States, like people, are defined by the lines that separate them from their neighbors—at least at first glance, they are. States like Wyoming and Colorado, the big Western states, are all right angles and straight lines. They say, "here it is, folks, what you see is what you get." There is nothing hidden here in big sky country, the color of which is a startling deep blue sometimes, and sometimes as dark as night, torn by gasping gobs and gouts of fierce light. Great ragged scuds and banks and twisted swirling worlds of black clouds blast along with rain so thick and hard it makes a place that will never be dry again, at least until the next morning when soft cotton-candy puffs of white clouds make shadows that chase across the miles of prairie all laid out for the eye to grasp, the sagebrush and grasses ululating in the gentle winds.
>
> There the landscape can be seen from fifty miles away, the sky in whatever shape or shade, the jagged mountains tearing at the sky, one could almost see the crystalline and white spray of the manic creeks and the lines they etch across the faces of the land,

growing into the rivers and the larger lakes. Up above, like a halo on a saint, the white splashes of snow in the cirques above tree line shine brightly. At times like that, if one listens with heart and soul and muscle and bone, one might hear the faint hiss of snow in the pines, just one tiny, minute, six-sided ice form multiplied, fractilized, transmogrified, until it finally buries the landscape in twenty feet of powder, pure, cold, haughty, silent.

1

≈ CHAPTER ONE ≈

Chat Dalton had just (finally!) gotten the muffler mounted on the manifold when he heard the bell out by the pumps. He pulled his glasses down on the bridge of his aquiline nose as he stepped out from behind the gleaming metal piston of the lift. It was Sterling Shiffler's banged up Nova, and Chat was tempted to go back to finishing old Mrs. Jerman's car. The afternoon sun nearly touched the small ridge on the other side of the swamp, brightly shining directly into the garage bays and making the oil burnished cement gleam silver.

This time of day was not Chat's best. In the afternoon, he couldn't ever sit in the cracked leather chair behind his desk in the small office that adjoined the bays. He would be out in ten seconds flat and wake up with drool on his shirt. And Sterling, God love him, required more patience than most, no matter what time of day or night. The car door slammed, and Chat watched Sterling's thin, elongated shadow creep over the floor, like a scene out of a grade B sci-fi flick. The misshapen shadow-head bobbled towards the back wall of the garage, touching first the Coates tire machine and then the half moon of the dip tank, full of rust-red ironized water.

"Hey!" Sterling shouted.

"Hey *yourself*," Chat said, walking out from beneath the car and squinting into the sun that reduced Sterling to an illuminated silhouette.

"Transcendental transmissions!" Sterling barked, laughing.

"What're you talking about now? Trans *what*?" Chat said, slowly wiping his hands on a rag.

Sterling walked far enough into the garage so that Chat could finally see his face, and Chat saw him pointing at the sign with the small happy yellow bear nailed against the back wall, advertising alignments and transmission repairs.

"Transmissions. That sign made me think. "

He ignored Chat's grunt.

"I was just re-reading <u>Walden</u>," he finished. "'Simplify, simplify, simplify! Why be in such desperate haste to succeed, and in such desperate measures?'"

Chat shook his head. He walked back under the car intending to begin threading the bolts correctly, tried the first, then stopped and pulled on his reading glasses. *Well begun was half done*, he said to himself, soon realizing that Sterling was still standing there, smiling, tall and lean, cheap tie and pilled collar, thin asymmetric nose, one unquiet green eye sparkling, with the other half-hidden beneath a cascade of straight dark hair. Waiting.

"Yeah, sure, that Thoreau guy. See, I *was* paying attention that year. Why'd he say it three times, then? Second, I'm far from desperate. That would be you at the end of a Saturday night. *And C*, as far as the haste goes, Mizz Jerman needs this car tomorrow, that's why the haste. I don't feature staying here past five again tonight," Chat said, muttering the last part and stepping back into the shade under the lift, intent again at the job at hand.

"You should lighten up, son," Sterling offered helpfully. "Excuse me if I get a funny thought from time to time. I mean, what would it be like if Thoreau had tried his hand at being a mechanic instead of making pencils?"

"That makes *no* sense, Sterling. They didn't even *have* mechanics then," Chat said, then paused, distracted.

His bushy eye-brows lifted slightly when he finally asked, "Pencils? Like, *lead* pencils?"

Sterling gave a so-smart nod and said, "Thoreau made pencils for awhile. From what I've read and heard, I understand that they weren't very good ones. I suppose it was because he spent so much time thinking of deeper and more meaningful things like truth and beauty. I have no idea why that Bear sign made me think of all this, but, I mean, what would that be like? Folks would drop their cars off and he'd say stuff like "Truth is Beauty" and all that sort of thing when he wasn't finished because he was out contemplating his navel or screwing around in the woods or something."

Sterling trailed off, then picked up a ratchet and spun it around a few times, chuckling.

Chat just squinted at him for perhaps ten seconds before finally shrugging his shoulders and snugging the first bolt home.

"*Generally*, people talk to make themselves understood, but in *your* case, Sterling, I guess that'd be asking too much." Chat paused, then said, "You should try reading a *good* book once in a while."

"Wow. Which book might that be, huh, Pop-eye?" Sterling said, laughing at himself. Suddenly he stopped and spun the ratchet around again a half dozen well-measured turns—like an old clock on the mantle: *click, click, click.* They both paused to look at each other.

"That book. I'm gonna break into your house one of these days and burn that thing," Chat said, miffed.

"That's not funny, Chat. You leave me alone about that."

Sterling paused for a moment, then said, "Anyhow, are you going down to the Bennykill early tonight? I think I might try to get down there and have something to eat before we start playing." He gave the ratchet a good strong right-hand snap and made it whir like the drag on an ultra-light when you get a three-pound brownie in some fast water.

Chat looked at Sterling and thought for the thousandth time about their dissimilarities. They were the same age, more or less. And they had the same tastes in music, again, more or less. But Chat was stout where Sterling was tall, steady where Sterling was flighty, had huge hands with thick little sausage fingers instead of the thin and elegant hands that fluttered around Sterling like white doves when he spoke. Sterling was never still, either mad or manic, always in an argument, great company one minute, a royal pain in the butt the next. And he ate like three men on the days that he actually ate.

"Someday I'll learn how you can pack it away like that and never put on a pound. I *swear*," Chat said, then, remembering the invitation, said, "Anyhow, I don't think I'll be there 'til it's time. I haven't seen Sue for more than five minutes this week, so it seems."

"We're playing too much."

"City folks like us now—that movie and all," Chat said, inattentive. He grabbed the torque wrench to check the tightness of each bolt, and for moment the only sounds were a light plane engine off in the distance and the click of the wrench.

Sterling cleared his throat to remind Chat he was still there and said, "Well, I just figured I'd stop and ask if you wanted to come down with me. I guess I'll see you later on, then."

"Hey listen, I'm sorry I'm not focusing here," Chat said. "I just really need to get this *done,* ya know? You take care, Sterling, ole buddy. See you down there. And put some new strings on that Gibson, huh? So you don't go *breakin'* em in the middle of a song all the time?"

"Mr. Perfection," Sterling scoffed. "Just remember, before you criticize a man, you should always walk a mile in their shoes."

"Ah, grasshoppa, so you can understand 'em?" Chat said, chuckling. He began putting away his tools, smiling and nodding as if he had just gotten done talking for hours.

"No, dummy. 'Cause then you're a mile away, and you have their shoes," Sterling said, laughing and looking over his shoulder on his way out into the sunlight.

He got back in the beater Nova and revved her up. Loose rings, Chat thought, but Sterling wore a prideful smile, as if it were the best-tuned engine in the world. With a nod, a wink, and a finger gun, Sterling peeled out of the parking lot, his wheels spitting gravel, arm pumping back and forth out the window as he sped up to make the hill towards town.

Chat cupped his hands to his cheeks and hollered, "That was *Keats,* anyhow!"

Chat didn't know if Sterling had heard him. He watched the Nova dwindle in the distance, Sterling's head bobbing from side to side energetically. Sterling was, as usual, happy with his own results.

"Never mind. Truth and *Beauty,*" Chat said, sighing.

He took his glasses off, bowed his head and pinched the bridge of his nose. To think—twenty years of playing together, longer than he'd been married.

Chat had only one sign on the place, two if the smaller one beneath it was counted. Both were bolted to a large sycamore tree at the edge of the parking lot and angled so they could be read from both directions. The bigger sign read: "Chat's garage". Just behind the sign, in the swamp that made for some powerful 'skeeters in June, the spring peepers were just beginning their spectral chorus in the fullness of the evening spring air. He lowered Mrs. Jerman's Colt down off the lift, globbing Go-Jo on his hands while it slid back to the floor silently. He wiped his hands again with the soft stitched cloth rags he paid twelve dollars a month to have.

Time to go home, get a shower and a good meal, and let the little rug-rats run over his legs. In the early days, he and Sue would sit on the back porch steps in the sunset. He loved the hint of winter that was left in the spring evening air. It made him grateful for the easing of bitter cold, the ice locking away the water, razor-sharp wind that took the breath away, the squeak of snow under hunter's boots in the deer woods, raw hands splitting wood or trying numbly to get loose a stubborn bolt. Although Chat was happy to have those things, he was just as happy that they were moving away from all that in this season.

Yes, before the kids had come to consume all their spare time, he and Sue would often snuggle under his Grandma's comforter, watch the big square of yellow the kitchen light cast on the greening lawn, and talk about small things, new wallpaper, the garden, maybe a trip they could take during the summer. They hadn't done that in ages. From time to time he wondered if it was that way with all the married folks—he had heard the joke about putting a bean into an empty jar for each time the woman was full of loving *before* the wedding, then taking one out *after*, and a man dying with a jar full of beans. On his tired days, he did have to admit he felt a little distance growing between them, as if her connection was half-hearted.

"She's just tired, that's all," he mumbled, still failing to move his worry any further away. He wanted to forget all about it and get home where he could do some good for it. She'd tell him if there was something he needed to know.

Chat knew he wasn't the most reflective man on the planet. That was why he was so good with cars: he was patient and methodical. He smirked at himself. A methodical Methodist. And in fact, his given name wasn't Chat at all. John Wesley Dalton: that was a little too much of a moniker to carry around a place like Pigeon Forge, where only the lonely were called by their Christian names anyway. Most folks were known as "Bud" or "Chooney" or "Slim", "Betty" or "Babs," depending on their given name and they way they looked or acted, or sometimes, because of their relatives.

He had gotten his name from Uncle Homer, early on, because Homer said that even though he kept his mind to himself, he could still chat anybody up when he wanted, which in those days was not too often. If it was so, Chat thought as he tidied up the three bays and swept out the two empty ones, *if* it was so, it was so because he found humans genuinely interesting, even when they were being disagreeable. In his mind they too often were. Even so, though, he would listen when they talked. He asked questions when they seemed troubled. He learned, and he remembered. More than one man tried to take Chat Dalton for a fool, he nodded to himself, and they generally wished they hadn't because he could be as simple and as hard as nails.

He tried that out as a line in a song:
Chat Dalton was a hard-drivin' man
driven' down the rails,
sweet to his women, to the men
as simple ...
    and as hard ...
        as nails...

with notes cascading smoothly down rich and full of heartache and maybe redemption like a Johnny Cash Folsom Prison song.

Then he remembered himself.

"Lord, sorry. About my pride. Work your will on me, Lord," he almost murmured, letting down the garage doors, remembering to lock them. *Making up songs to your own self.* Chat was pretty sure that was sacrilegious. He walked to the front, turned off the compressor, the lights. He supposed the peepers—a thousand of them?—trilled with no thought of anything but themselves, but in their combining Chat heard a music. He wondered if *they* heard how whole sections of the swamp would fall into cadence, then slightly out, then out entirely, and how they suddenly would be counterpoint to the shore half a mile distant, nearer the big road that ran through the county. Katydids were the same way, and the first birds of spring. There were days when it surprised him still, this bubbling of music all around him that he had begun to notice after all his younger trouble and when he had learned again to hear. It was as big a surprise as when he found out as a youngster that those hams he called hands played music just the same way they snugged a bolt, as if he were built for the job, as if he were born to it. Not a peep of slop in his work or in his music, either. All tight, all right.

Bluegrass. That was the way it was for him.

2

≡ CHAPTER TWO ≡

Jo-Jo Pasquale sat perched twenty feet up, smoking a Camel and waiting for the boy to fetch more lumber. He watched idly as the masons slogged around lugging ten pounds of thick clay on their boots. He considered his own: clean and dry. He could see the boy struggling with a twenty foot two by six.

"Hey you, Nappy! Get the lead out, huh? I want these rafters done before we get outta here," Jo-Jo said, barking like a junkyard dog.

The boy's pale face swung upwards, sweat-streaked, and then Jo-Jo lost sight of him until he re-appeared around the other side of the building. A moment later Jo-Jo heard the resonant *thunk!* of the board hitting the plate, and cat-walked nonchalantly over to grab it.

"Come on, will ya? We only got another hour of light yet."

"Jeez, Mr. Pasquale, I thought, it bein' Friday and all, and we did so good yesterday, maybe we'd, well..."

"Get the damned lumber and stop thinkin'!" Jo-Jo shouted.

The masons paused below and smiled. The boy scurried like he'd been whipped. Jo-Jo hoisted the board easily, balancing on the edge of the joists, and swung the board into place. The notched part of the rafter, the bird's mouth, settled exactly onto the plate, with the angled cut sitting flush with the ridgepole. Jo-Jo picked up his framing hammer and sent the twenty penny nail home in four swats, and tapping the angled point of the rafter flush with the ridgepole. Off by an eighth? What the hell! He nailed the rafter fast with four more spikes, then set the other end on the plate with eight economic *whacks*! that were like the opening of an opera. Not that he liked the damned opera. Not at all. He had to listen to it when he was a kid, all that screaming and what-all, and his dad never let him listen to rock and roll. "Bad for you," his dad had said. Even though he couldn't listen to his own music at home, there had been the old tube radio in his Grandma's house.

On Saturday nights he got to stay over, and on cloudy nights he could get WWVA, or that station down in Tennessee that he could never remember the call letters for, although he did remember that they had a knack for scaring the crap out of some little kid listening in at ten at night, with their tales of little boys who been sleeping at their gramma's house and had got thirsty and went to get a drink, and they thought it was fruit juice, but it was really their gramma's heart medicine, *and that little boy had...just...up...and died.*

Then the folks on the radio would play some music, real cheerful, too, with fiddle in it, and it made his young heart happy to hear it, especially after he had snuck in the bathroom *and* the kitchen when Gramma wasn't exactly looking, and he had checked to make sure there wasn't any medicine-y looking things laying about that he might mistake for grape juice in his sleep.

He smiled, remembering that, and settled back to wait for the boy to make it around the quagmire with another ball-buster of a board. And the kid was only, what, eighteen? A Hunkie or Polack, but a good enough worker, except he was always mooning over something.

Jo-Jo finished the Camel and flipped it expertly, as the coal glowed orange, fanned by its rush downwards, making a lazy arc and a *Spat!* into the mud pan of the mason below.

"Hey! Knock it *off*, would ya?" The guy hollered.

"Oh, hey, sorreeeeeeeee, " Jo-Jo said, then laughed to himself. Always so serious, these Anglos.

Then the boy was back with another rafter.

Thunk!

"Hey you, Nappy. Cut the last two an eighth shorter up top, huh?"

"An *eighth*?"

"What am I, talking, *Dutch*? An eighth. Hurry up. My ass cheeks is getting sore up here."

He imagined what the boy was muttering as he went to fetch the last two rafters, and smiled. From Jo-Jo Pasquale's point of view, life had very few shortcomings, unless you included death, which he personally would've figured out a better way if he'd been put in charge. But, okay, nobody asked him, so he figured he would go along, as long as he could control what went on while he was down here.

Or up here. Whatever.

Thunk!

He shook his head a couple times. He could hear the boy's muttering. Understandable. He'd worked the kid hard. He'd give him an extra twenty, then that night the boy would be the cock of the walk. That made Jo-Jo smile. He checked his nails: clean. He knew the girls watched the fingers as much as they listened to the notes, and it went a long way to excusing the too-large nose, the slight paunch, the olive circles under the eyes. Hey, what did you expect, Lawrence of Arabia? But it was good enough, most nights. Hell, they just loved a screwy musician.

The last *thunk!* made even the boy wonder; twelve hours on the job, and this old guy was slamming nails like it was eight in the morning, and singing, too. Not "Oh Solo Mio," either, but some crap about being high on a mountain. But the pink hue in the west, the curve of the Blue Ridge, and the exactly straight lines of their rafters and ridgepole in front of it all mellowed the boy somewhat. Maybe the old guy'd cough up some extra dough. Maybe he wouldn't quit after all.

Sue was listening to the kids in the next room. Bangs, crashes and damage—the boy. Recriminations, the long pause—the girl. She saw herself reflected in wavy obscurity in the oven door, her auburn hair now with a small streak of gray in it, and unconsciously she smoothed the apron over her still-flat stomach, half-turning to see if she is still as slender as she once was.

In the imperfect reflection, she noticed that her blue eyes appeared colorless. Her eye color wasn't the only thing missing from the picture: she could detect no hint of the fatigue she felt welling up around the edges at the end of the day. From the next room came another round of squeals and scuffles, and she took a half step towards the playroom, then decided against it and picked up the mixing bowl instead. She would give them to the count of seven, then see.

Still. I'm grateful, she thinks, emptying the flour. She begins counting.

One. Add flour and butter and mix without melting.

Two. They do love each other, my son and my daughter, his daughter and his son.

Three. Mix the cold water into the mixture, slowly, mixing gently and continuously.

Four. Fight like no tomorrow, then treat each other like kings and queens.

Five. Dot a greased pan with butter.

Behind that thought there is another: why the wildness? That question will not leave, and then the bookmatch: why put up with that wildness?

The inevitable wail from Megan:

"Mommmmmmmmmmmm!"

"*What* is the problem now?" Sue said, slapping her mixing spoon on the counter. Spots of batter spattered as she did.

"He took my standard!" Meg cried.

"She said my G.I. Joe was a doll!" Jesse said, pouting.

"I think you need to get your standards and your Mr. Joe and put them in the *quiet* box for awhile," Sue said, her voice thundering with frustration. The children looked confused for a minute, looked at each other, and then they shrugged shoulders and disappeared, whispering.

She wondered what the hell "standard" Meg was referring to when she heard Chat pulling in. She was just finishing the dough when Chat walked through the door. This moment always reminded Sue of the houses she'd seen in documentaries about Ireland—this one was titled "the house that had once been his parents." Like most folks in the country, Chat entered by the back door, which stood at the head of ancient stone steps that lead to the kitchen. The kitchen had remained unchanged since the late '40s, when his father's father finally installed some plumbing indoors. She wished that they hadn't forgotten the vent. The doors were too damned small, too, so Chat had to duck slightly as he entered.

He was grinning.

"Six…. seven," Sue said, and Chat responded, "Hey, Hon."

Sue put the bowl down on the counter.

"Honey," she echoed and let Chat grab her and give her a hug and peck.

"You got flour on yer cheek," he said, moistening his sleeve with his tongue and wiping it off.

"Eeeeewwww—Chat! I'm not one of the kids, you know."

She wiped at the damp spot with one hand, slapped at Chat with the other until he let go, laughing and covering his head with his arms.

"Well, I'm just so happy to see you, too, dear."

"You're a nice person. Go get changed and say "Hi" to the kids. Dinner will be ready in a bit."

"You're the boss."

"Hmmmfff."

She waved him off and frowned as he left the room, wondering when to talk to him about Homer. She loved Chat's uncle, odd as he is. Not that she was being judgmental, but.

Homer?

She thought she was patient. Didn't she put up with Chat being gone lots of weekends, kids all nuts and the driveway almost flooded with that insane rain they had in early June? And the all the phone conversations and practices the boys had? Always a practice when it snowed in the winter since Chad isn't getting any folks driving in the snow (well a couple brave or sheepish folks who forgot to get their snows put on). So practice was pretty much every three days, or every other Wednesday, or any combination that added up to three days— or nights!—a week.

And there she was, trying to get the kids to ignore all the action, get their homework done, maybe make some snacks or something, or a light meal. Like she was some kind of nanny.

She always does. She always was.

But Homer, he had her at the end of her extremely considerable patience. She frowned more deeply, thinking of the conversation she had with the Meals-on-Wheels people. She heard Chat's mock-roar in the next room and the kid's excited squeals, and decided to leave that discussion for after dinner.

She was frowning and studying the potatoes as she mashed them when Chat came back into the dining room. Ten-year-old Jesse was holding fast to his leg as Chat drug the boy across the floor, with almost-teen Megan draped over his shoulders like a mink stole.

"What's wrong?" Chat asked, nonchalant.

"Hmmmmm? Oh—nothing much. We'll talk later, 'kay?"

He gently lowered Meg to the ground and came over behind Sue, giving her a little kiss on the back of her neck. She thought, *he thinks I'm distracted.* In fact, she was. She was imagining Homer and Thelma, and the house up on the ridge, the way it must have been that afternoon.

Homer is peering out the window, the lace curtain flowing over his huge head, making him look like a pirate bride, sun-reddened face peering out into the yard, gnarled hands grasping the sill, and Thelma is standing nearby, stout in her housedress and white hair, blue eyes snapping with laughter that she dares not begin. Then, Homer begins crawling, crab-like, across the floor at the first sight of the car chugging up the hill, sidling over to the shotgun resting in the corner. Dark streaks on the wallpaper—they show the gun being moved and replaced time upon time.

And Thelma, a bit hard of hearing, shouts to Homer to leave up for a minute as the young man unknowingly gets out of the car with the white Styrofoam containers, and Homer barks orders to halt or be shot. And Thelma somehow manages to get him calmed down and the boy out of there without having Homer carted off by the Sheriff.

Sue watched Chat checking the mail, opening the fridge, taking off his work boots and washing his hands, and considered the man she has given herself to. With regrets? *Well, we're born with regrets, then, and maybe we might miss them if they were gone.* She thought then about Jo-Jo, then pushed the thought away, reflecting instead on the music and the children as she set the table. She hoped whatever got into Homer, Chat and Jo-Jo never gets into the kids. After all, she and Homer are also woodpile kin. Small wonder there; half the town is related to the other half, except for some new folks.

She hoped she wasn't carrying that bum gene.

3

⇒ CHAPTER THREE ⇐

Sterling decided against the Inn and went straight home. He hated to admit it, but Chat's comment about the book kind of spooked him, and he almost laughed at himself when he found himself thinking that he had better memorize it, just in case. His "hovel", as he liked to call his place, had no shower, a fact that discomforted him at first. But now he was used to the deep claw foot tub and enjoyed a hot bath at the end of a frustrating day. He particularly liked the acoustics in the high-ceilinged old Victorian rooms, and gratefully he lowered himself into the steaming water and began to read, not really listening to the words as much as the sound itself:

> Pennsylvania was no different than the rest of the country when it came to laying down borders. The continent was so new and untamed that folks were in a lather to carve all that majesty up, string barbed wire across it all and mark it with signs declaring INTERSTATE 80! and SPEED LIMIT: SAFE AND PRUDENT! and ONE HUNDRED MILES TO THE CORN PALACE! Folks slapped those lines down, east and west, north and south, unknowing worship of the old Indian ways, using not blue corn meal but sharp steel and indelible ink, staining the pale and vibrant land with lines that shouted ownership, conflict, broken bones, hearts, dreams, lives.

> And, East or West, those lines had nothing at all to do with the shape of the land, slicing mountains in two like a scalpel—but they told what would happen on the ground nonetheless: Bloody Kansas, The Walking Purchase, The Northwest Territory, this tribe exterminated, that one displaced, a third relegated to a few words

in a book: another study of bounding the world with lines so it could all fit into small minds and hard hearts.

The lines between states, perhaps like the ones between humans, are imaginary. Of course, Pennsylvania's lines are like that, too. Drive down from Binghamton to Scranton and tell where New York ends and Pennsylvania begins—try it just once. Start with that long line up top—the nub at the Western edge that includes Erie and Presque Isle, access to the Great Lakes and the sea—that was a series of battles with our neighbors to the north. Quakers would not be told how to live by a bunch of godless frontiersmen, not in that little corner of the world. How many go to meeting now, in the third millennium of the post-Christian era?

It turns out that Pennsylvania has always been bounded by the practical, the fiduciary and the secular. New Jersey lies across the pastel meanders of the Delaware, the last limpid glimpse into an era of water travel, a state of blockage-runners, slave smugglers, piney-woods pirates, mercenaries with thick German accents and the great thirst for beer and blood. New York is her northern neighbor, whose representatives sat drunk and disinterested at the Continental Congress, interested not in bold social experiments but in expediency, and abstaining in the votes which were sure to translate into money and opportunities lost.

And of course there is the Mason-Dixon line, thin tribute to trade and to the crazy attempt to keep a house of cards standing upright, the objectification of humans—800 dollars for a strong male Negro, less for a female or a cripple. It was a line between cruel and genteel planters, horse-racers and watermen, aristocrats to the south and the Plain People to the north. The northern zealots were bound to the reversal of the slave trade, secreting lives northward to Canada and the Northern and British idea of freedom from slavery, freedom to die from neglect instead of action.

And that cute little scallop down near Philadelphia—a radius scribed 22 miles from the courthouse at Wilmington. Delaware, the only state that beat Pennsylvania in signing the Declaration of Independence, the mighty mouse that roared, a little state that knew how to appreciate small bits of land. Those folks had their eye on the rolling hills of the Piedmont plateau nearest Philadelphia, city of brotherly love, cradle of liberty, once-capital of the United States, home of the horsy rich and the violent poor.

Sterling stopped reading for a moment, squirted some bubble-bath into the tub and turned the faucet with his foot to get the water warmed up, sticking his toe partway into the spigot and making the water shoot out faster, the better to bubble up the water. When it had warmed sufficiently and he could no longer see his feet, he settled back in and began again:

> For all the border wars—every state had them!—it really is just an afterthought now, an address to send in the money. Maybe the pavement changes color and there is a sign with a new slogan, or you can buy beer in a grocery market one minute and not the next, but for all of that, the great leveler of culture (or lack thereof!) has reduced state borders to an anachronism. The Cheyenne's magic and their White Ghost Shirts could not turn away bullets or defeat the endless supply of whites, and no border sign or muttered reluctant incantation can staunch the shrapnel of commerce.

Sterling put his mouth under the water and began blowing bubbles, turning the last word into a "put-put" sound, like a child playing with a motorboat, then put the book up and hoisted himself out of the now-tepid bath, wreathed in bubbles. He patted himself dry, wrapped a towel around himself and walked into the kitchen. He had lived here for almost fifteen years now "just as a temporary measure" after his divorce. He put a pot of water on for spaghetti and walked into the third room of the apartment, picking red boxer briefs and his cleanest jeans, then finding a T-shirt from last year's fiddle contest, he pulled it on and went back out into the kitchen. He unwillingly remembered his wife then, and shortly, one bad thought tied to the next like worry beads, he found himself thinking about his day at work.

That day had been the normal barrage of dull, pointless meetings designed to verify the boss' delusions, to make it seem like something was actually happening with his clients. Sterling knew better. In times like that he tried hard to imagine, above the human sounds, another sound— an auditory amalgam of wind on water, the tide rushing out through the sawgrass, the scrape of blue-claws in a bushel basket, the thin whistle of air through pinion feathers.

He longed for that sound, or the way it made him feel—longed for it like some men longed for God. And here, two hundred miles north of his beloved Crisfield, the closest he could come to any of that was on a Friday night, which mercifully this was. Friday night, a dozen cold beers, a banjo, and the high lonesome.

It was almost enough, even if he had to put up with preacher Chat Dalton.

4

⇒ Chapter Four ⇐

Johnny Shanahan looked around in the gloaming. The mahogany bar stretched like riches to a misty recess, interrupted in spots by elbows and glasses. He admired the punctuation of it: a long piece of nature cut by little chunks of dirtied flesh. Then he glanced at his glass, now only a third full.

Smiling, he drained his pint in two swallows and asked for another.

The barkeep jumped at his voice. At three hundred pounds and six foot seven, Johnny was daunting. He wished people would take things a little easier. He meant no trouble. He knew it is that way with most big men. They seldom made trouble; it was the little ones that usually started the ruckus.

The barkeep, pock-marked and compliant, set the cold, foaming black and tan in front of him and asked, "Another job tonight?"

"Oh, praise the maker fer beer and music. The money'll buy all the groceries for the week, and my beer to boot," Shanahan drawled, laconic.

"The pit's not producin', then?"

"It's been wet. You know how that goes. Fastest finish last. We got twenty clean tons out. That'll be enough to pay the bills. No steak this week," he said quietly. "But we'll live."

The barkeep suggested that wildcatting was a tough way to make a living, though, digging in the pit like that, and didn't old man Arlot sell his share out to the Lehigh, and get some pretty good bucks for it, too?

"Well, and now he's workin' at the Good Buy, baggin' groceries and bein' bossed by kids half his age. No, I don't think that's for me," Johnny replied, and drank down a great swallow of his beer, his blackened knuckles stretched tan over the huge protuberances, blue scars making a map out of his hands. He coughed a little bit, tasted the acrid coal dust even now, and thought of Caitlin and Andy, of his mother still living, of his father long dead, victim of a black pocket of airless dark after a cave-in, and with light and air only a yard away, as they discovered when they finally had exhumed the body.

He can imagine the maw of the now-defunct mine, the people huddled in knots of twos and threes, speaking hushed tones in the drizzle, standing with rank hair and soaked clothing in the late fall air. He can still remember, too, the sulfur smell of the fire down below that eventually would spread all throughout the veins of black diamond and spell doom to the little village on top. All that was left of it was now just shells of buildings with windows broken, and the cracks in the pavements belched plumes of smoke and vapor like the devil's own workshop.

He willed himself to steadiness. That kind of thinking never did a body any good at all, and so thought instead of Meg, the light of his life and the reason he went down to danger every day but Sunday. There had been a time, years ago, when Caitlin had been small, and he had been hammering away at that good vein of coal, seeing nothing but dollars going into the bucket beside him, the sky was a dime sized, jagged orb of light up above, and Johnny's eyes were all on the big black chunks of pure anthracite, seventy dollars a ton. Each big chunk that hit the bucket was about seventy five cents or a buck: a loaf of bread, a glass of beer. It was easy to see the bread, or the milk, or the beer in the black chunk of gunk, and whack away the only fist or head-sized chunk that stood between you and eternity.

And so he had: whacked away a tiny small piece of coal, maybe two hundred pounds, and half the chute had come down. If his partner Andy hadn't been up on top of the pit and on top of the job, Johnny knew he'd of been a long time coming up, and been in not too good a shape either, but at the first tremor (the earth, when disturbed, groaned and complained like any human might), two things happened at once: Johnny jumped for the bucket and Andy damned near stripped the gears bringing that bucket up, a cat's whisker ahead of ten tons of black chaos and death.

And didn't they get drunk that night, and weren't the wives happy they hadn't gone on to their reward?

Not that eternity didn't have something going for it, or so he'd been told. He'd heard it was a place free from worry, and that carried a lot of freight in his book. A place where there was—what did Chat say? He couldn't remember the word—something that meant a lack of trouble, deeper than peace and stronger than love. It was a place where they'd all be together.

That new road had come in. He'd been for it, not like Sterling, and surely not like Homer, but he figured it would be a better shot for his goods. And it had been so. He'd figured right. The price went up a couple dollars a ton, and at fifty tons a week, average, that made a difference. But what else had come in with the new road?

Well, the barkeep reminded him when he asked out loud about it, that the big road was half the reason they weren't still just playing on Chat's front porch, with ten cords of logs piled like giant pick-up-sticks out front, and the woods all 'round the back.

Said he, "The city folks like a couple local idiots, that's part of the package they bought."

And said Johnny, "So who's the idiot? The idiot or the idiot who's calling the guy the idiot? "

He sat a tad more upright, and looked down the smoky reach of the bar again. Megan would be waiting at home. His kids were hale and hearty. And for the next two days he'd be walking around above the ground, all in the air. What could be better?

"And another fine Yuengling if ya please," he said, and smiled again.

Megan Shanahan shook her blonde hair back from her forehead and glanced at the clock. It was almost six, and Johnny would just now be draining the last of his third beer, soon to be heading out the door. She moved lithely to the playroom to check on the kids, head-to-head on some conspiracy that involved two Mutant Turtles, Hans Solo, and a chunk of radiator cover that belonged in the living room and which she suspected would never find its way back again.

If that was the worst thing that happened this year, it'd be a damn good year.

They were mostly all good years as far as Meg was concerned, now that the perils of childbirth had been passed and she had escaped her parents. She'd learned how to deal with all that: she still loved them both, but she wouldn't let them reach into her life and stir the way that they had when she first married Johnny.

Her dad had a fit about that, perhaps sensing the loss of control he would suffer. No one would mistake Shanahan for a push-over.

Meg thought about it absently as she filled the tub. Johnny had been kind about her parents, very understanding about it all, and it wasn't until she herself had cut the cord, had drawn the line, that he stood between her and her father.

"You're welcome any time. Any time you're not drunk," Johnny had said, and her dad had screamed bloody murder at him, vile obscenities that raised a few windows in the neighboring shotgun houses by the tracks.

Her girl friends couldn't understand a bit of it, why a beauty like her would marry a hulk like Johnny.

On a summer's evening they would stroll down towards the center of town, him monolithic, his shirt sleeves riding up way past his wrists, since even the Big-Tall had a hard time getting shirts that fit him well, and her; barely five foot tall, blue-eyed, firm, young-looking, despite the children and her thirty-five years. She saw the smiles and comments they brought to strangers passing through, this mismatched pair. That did rile her a bit, their blatant rudeness.

"Just forget that, hon," Johnny would soothe her. "What do you think from people raised like a pig in a pen?

She was remembering this as she made her way down to Atbie's store earlier that day. The store was small by some standards, way smaller than the new Good-Buy's down in Fiesterville. She loved the tangy smell of old wood and fresh produce, and the slightly uneven tongue and groove yellow pine flooring the new folks called hardwood.

Well, the new folk would change, maybe. The rhythms of the country were pretty hard to ignore, Meg thought. And shouldn't they have a nice place to be, like everyone else? She swung open the door, hearing the jingle of the bell and looking instinctively for her best, nearest, dearest friend, Katie.

From the back of the store she heard a "Yoooohoooo. I'll be right up."

She cupped her hand and half-hollered "Just me, Kate! Relax!"

Meg grabbed a gallon of milk and a couple of boxes of Grahams before walking towards the back of the store. Kate was just finishing stamping a box of canned peas and stocking them on the wooden shelves.

"How are ya, Katie? Had enough of the public fer the week?

"Some of 'em, surely," Katie said, smiling, her green eyes with a look of fatigue in them.

"Working tonight?" Meg said.

"Yeah. Things keep up, I'll have next year's tuition saved by fall."

Both of them paused in their conversation as a thin woman, dark stretch pants, stacked heels, with too-black hair and too-red lipstick poked her head in the door.

"Youse know where the interstate is?" she demanded.

"Well, hi," Katie said. "Sure, I can tell you. Just give me a minute to ring Meg out here."

"Is this going to be long?" the woman demanded. Meg exchanged a mirthful glance over the counter at Katie, rolled her eyes and waved her away.

"Take care of her, Katie. Guess she's in a hurry."

She stood quietly while Katie went through the several turns needed to bring a traveler back to the Big Road. The woman was backing out the door before Katie had even finished.

"They need signs out here," she said, letting the door slam shut.

"Have a nice day!" Katie hollered after her.

They both watched the retreating figure with quizzical looks, and then laughed.

"Like hemorrhoids," Katie drawled.

"Huh?" Meg giggled.

"When they come down and go back up, they're not so bad. When they come down and stay down, they're a pain in the ass."

"You better go to mass, Katie! That's just too sinful!" Meg said, laughing out loud.

"Well, didn't Jesus throw the money-changers out of the temple?" Katie said, sweeping her arms to include the quiet afternoon store, and the soft, surrounding hills outside. Then she said, "Oh, and so is laughing at my sins, by the way, sinful. How are the kids?"

"They start soccer soon. I'm ready for some warm."

"No lie. Me too. How is Johnny?

"Best man this side of the border. Anybody new this week?" Meg asked.

"Usual suspects. Time's running out for me, I guess. Are you coming down to the inn tonight?" Katie said.

"Naw, not without a sitter. Hey. I better get. Don't let those idiots get you down, though," Meg answered.

"Water off a duck's back," Katie laughed, her slender fingers waving smoothly an inch above her dark hair.

"You say 'hi' to Jay for me, okay?"

"You bet. Let's get together Saturday, afternoon, maybe? Jay'll be playing and Sue said she'd take the kids for a couple hours," Meg said.

"Sounds good to me," Katie said absently, then made the "I'll call you" sign with her hand and walked back to resume her restocking.

5

⇒ CHAPTER FIVE ⇐

The sun was near the horizon. The glare it made off the silver water, trapped on various levels on the expanse of flat roofs, reminded Hugh McAdam of something. Below him, the rush-hour city was near orgasm as car horns blasted and vapors rose against the silky evening air. The scene never failed to stir Hugh's soul. The river in the distance was a deeper bronze; the barges on it left rippling trails of gold.

He looked east through the reflection of his own dark eyes. He imagined that he could see the shadows cast by his towers moving over the ant-people, scurrying to their warrens in the twilight of the day. That was a mixed metaphor, of course he knew that, but to Hugh, that was merely a detail.

He scanned the horizon. There, on the north end of the river, he could see his stadium lights flickering on. He had bet heavily during the strike when everyone said the sport was dead, conned the city council, coughed up the money it took to make it happen, kissed the asses of the million-dollar, steroid–infested crybabies who called themselves athletes, all to get the franchise and the new stadium.

Now, three years later, he could appreciate P.T. Barnum for the genius he was. Viewing the lines of headlights going in, he did the mental math. After expenses, kickbacks, campaign contributions, assuming four people per car, or really only three point seven, he was making ten bucks a *car*, for crissakes! *And* the best seats in the house. *And* the pick of any women he wanted, pretty much. Beyond that, he saw the Regency Towers. Each light in each window spoke to him: seventeen-fifty.

Next to the ocean, the Seaville landfill was a blue haze on the horizon. Each seagull, he joked to himself, seventy-nine cents. He had done that deal just to keep the gombas happy, although he was sure it was good for a couple hundred grand a month. Pin money, really. And yet, at the edge of all of this, a tiny regret. It was all used up. The big stuff was, anyway. Oh, sure, buy a couple blocks here and there, but it was nothing after the stadium deal.

In the midst of plenty, Hugh McAdam was jonesing.

He punched a button on his desk. A disembodied female voice rippled in the air.

"Yes sir, Mr. McAdam?"

"Get the 'copter ready, please."

"Yessir, Mr. McAdam. Any instructions for the pilot?"

"Tell him to make sure everything's topped off."

"Hunting again, sir?"

He paused. There was nothing overtly disrespectful in her question, but he didn't like her tone—it was far too familiar.

"You speak when you're spoken to, missy. You just put this down as a trip of indeterminate length. Yes."

He broke the connection irritably. It would be perfect, the conquest, the winning, if only there were more of everything. He watched the golden orb inextricably drawn towards the west. That would be the way he'd go. He did the mental math. At one hundred and sixty knots, he could delay sunset for perhaps an hour before he had to put down. Not, of course, that his ship wasn't equipped to run at night. Of course it was. But there was no point in it for him, rocketing above a landscape he couldn't see, couldn't possess with his eyes.

No mental math in the darkness. Just one of the unfortunate rules of life. Perhaps he could move to Alaska for the light half of the year. On his desk phone, the little red eye blinked twice, discretely. He punched the girl back on line.

"Sir? The pilot's ready."

"Good. Tell him I'll be right there."

He hurried up the stairs to the roof, where the sudden loss of walls was strangely invigorating. Perhaps he could add a few floors someday. His pilot hunched against the chopper, and as Hugh appeared, the smartly dressed man swung the steps down. Hugh stepped in without breaking stride, waving carelessly as he disappeared into the cabin. Not until the heightened whir of the blades had screwed them into flight did the intercom crackle.

"Good evening, Mr. McAdam."

"Yes, it is."

Hugh left the mike button down as they gained altitude and considered the city below, the sun now a finger's width from the horizon. Below, he could see the still-white ribbon of cement that was the Quickway, stretching towards the west.

"Follow the highway west," he said, leaning back and popping the button off *send*. He looked behind him into the dusk at his city, blinking awake after its slumberous daytime toil.

There was no way around it. His world was too conscribed. He had arrived in that large city with next to nothing, and he had made it his own. Seventeen years. He was forty- one. Was Boston too large a new target? He didn't know. He had no hunch. But, like a cat must scratch to keep its claws sharp, he couldn't wait for the knowing. He had to do something to keep himself trim.

Moments before, the damned buzzer had gone off, and Sarah had almost spit at it. What a freakin' week.

"Yessir, Mr. McAdam?" she had said, as neutral as she could manage.

"Get the 'copter ready, please," he had said. She looked ruefully at the clock. Even if Ty was quick, it'd be fifteen minutes before it would be safe for her to leave, and if the old bastard just wanted a bird's-eye view of the goddam stadium only to set it back down again, it could be longer.

"Hunting again, sir?" she said, miffed. She didn't care if he heard; she had about had it. His blast didn't surprise her any. She suspected she would've gotten it anyway, so it was better to get it out of the way. She punched Ty Herrington's button and was grateful when he answered quickly.

"Now what, darlin'?"

"Bastard wants the bird in the air, Ty."

"Be there in five."

Sarah looked out her window. She remembered how overwhelmed she was when she'd applied for the position, at the corner office, for her, a mere office manager, at the plush carpet, and the promise of reserved parking, not to mention the salary. God, it seemed like her friends were jealous for months. Now, five years later, she was past wondering. The door to the roof opened, and Ty walked in, trim, handsome.

"You ever read <u>Faust</u>? " she said, looking downcast.

"What the hell? All I read's the freakin' weather reports. Why so glum, chum?" he said.

"Why the hell is he so nasty?" she replied.

"It's Friday. He can't get anything done for forty-eight hours. Pisses him off."

Sarah put her finger to her lips and punched the bastard's button viciously.

"Sir? The pilot's ready," she said, throwing a paper clip Ty's way. He was crossing his eyes and prancing around silently with his hands on his hips in a caricature of an angry woman. Sarah pointed to the stairs leading to the roof. Ty blew her a kiss as he ran back up the stairs.

"Good. Tell him I'll be right there," McAdam had answered.

Sarah slumped when she heard the engines revving up for flight, and she thought of the phone call she had gotten the day before from her son, Josh.

"They got my Air Jordans, Mom," he had wailed, and Sarah knew it wasn't just the sneakers or the nasty shiner he was going to have from being tagged in the eye. She let him cry it out, only half-hearing the details of the three boys that had jumped him getting off the bus at school. It was the same thing as when she'd come home two weeks prior to find someone standing in her kitchen.

Did she see him? How tall? What hair? The cops, when they finally arrived twenty minutes later, had droned the litany to her, and she could only repeat, "only in silhouette, maybe six feet, it was only a second before he was out the fire-escape window."

Her wedding band. Her son's safety. Her privacy. Gone.

And the husband who wouldn't go away, who wouldn't let anyone else near. Bastard didn't even pay support. She picked up the paper. It was Friday, and she and Josh would bag the city and take a break, get a breath.

Suddenly, she needed a big, big breath.

Homer tried sitting on the porch, but he was having a bad time of it. He wound up pacing back and forth, trying hard to concentrate and remember. He heard the car first, he knew that much. And of course he did what came natural next—he got up and got ready.

"**Thelma!** Dammit, woman! Git the **Savage!**" he remembered bellowing, and then he grabbed the gun himself, unsure if she had heard him.

Then, when she saw him go for the gun, she started to chuckle! With a stranger rolling into the yard as bold as day!

"Whut the **HELL** you cacklin' about? Dammit all! They're a comin'!" he yelled at her.

"This ain't Waco, Homer. They'd leave ya alone if you'd stop writin' those stupid letters to the President all the time. 'Sides, that there is a Ford Pinto, ya numskull!"

Homer cracked the window a hair and spoke to her without taking his eyes off of the small white car.

"Like they'd be stupid enough to jest waltz in here with regular Government Issue."

They both watched out the window as the car came to a halt and a sandy-haired youth got out, slinging an insulated red packet over his shoulder.

"**HOLD IT RIGHT THERE, BUB!**" Homer shouted out, sticking twenty inches of nasty looking steel out the crack. "**PUT THE EXPLOSIVES DOWN!**" he shouted as the startled boy, turning white as a sheet and stuttering inanely, stopped dead in his tracks.

That much Homer remembers clear as a bell, but the rest got a little muddled in his mind. He remembered shouting out again to set down the explosives, and cocking the gun with a sound he knew the nasty red bastard could hear, and then the boy saying something about Honor Society something and chicken and spring vegetables. What other kind would you get in the spring, for crissakes? And then what on earth does that perverse woman do? She opens the door and strolls right out there in his line of fire! Here she is saying, "There, now, you just relax, son. He ain't been entirely right since…"

"Are you **NUTS? THELMA!** What're you **DOIN'?**" he knows he shouted. He remembers another part, too, him shouting at her, trying to stand, but his faithful Savage got wedged in the crack of the window, and he got all tangled up with it.

"I'm trying to calm this poor boy down, you idiot. Any fool could see he ain't from the government. Lord a'massey! Who killed the skunk?" she said then, waving her hand in the air to dissipate the sudden smell.

She just invited that boy in and bought that story about Meals-on-Wheels and him being from Sue, then helped him get cleaned up and gave him a big old helping of that good sponge cake Homer was going to eat on for the rest of the week to boot!

He finally got the shotgun extracted from the window and tried his best to keep from muttering, but he couldn't contain himself. Times like that, he always felt like a little boy who'd done something bad, instead of the grown man of the house.

"Put that thing away, ya damned fool," is what she said. "The way you wave it around, somebody'd think you was going to use it."

"Don't blame me when the gaddam reds jest stroll in and take over, mother. When they do I'll ask 'em to tea. Meals- on-Wheels? The lamest damned plot I ever heard. What's wrong with him bein' a meder reader, 'er a phone guy?"

"Homer, no meder reader's gonna come within ten miles of the place if they knew you was here. Hell, if it wasn't for me, we'd 'a been without electric ten years ago. Sue was just trying to be nice, is all."

"She's after the family money, Thelma," Homer said, then instantly regretted it. He hated to admit it, but he liked Sue.

He thought and remembered some more. She had been sassing him about the money.

"If **I** can't get it outta ya, precious liddle show **she'll** have, ya old goat. If you even *have* any," Thelma said to him.

And she let that boy just traipse on out of there like nothing ever happened. Now, sitting in the kitchen and watching the sun sink behind the swamp, all gold and silver, he kind of wondered how much of what he just thought he really remembered, and how much he might have thought about saying but never did actually say.

He knew that fall he took those years back trying to get at his brother hadn't done him any good. None at all. And so he got things a bit twisted up sometimes. That still didn't change reality, or the bitter tricks of it. He thought, *first Bill Monroe, then my brother, and now the Federal Government.*

His thoughts were interrupted when he heard the whapping of the chopper blades, coming fast. He scrambled off his chair, grabbing the Savage and a box of shells, then stumbled out onto the porch where Thelma was snapping beans. Before either of them could say a word the shining blue craft had whipped past them, and Homer defiantly pulled a bead on it.

"Sky-busting, Homer?"

"Gettin' old, Thelma. I coulda' had that bird twenty years ago. Damn Feds. Helicopters, now. Say. He's stopping other side of the swamp—down near Chat's."

"Best call, then. Odd thing."

Hugh pressed the button down.

"Set her down next to the swamp."

"That lot near the building, sir?"

"That lot. There's a town over there. When we touch down, get the Vespa out and we'll see what's what."

"Yessir." Wonderful. Podunk city. Ty wondered how much less American Airlines would pay, and if it would be worth it to make a change. He cleared the trees. Below him, a herd of deer jumped up and ran into the swamp, zigging crazily, trying to escape the noise above them. He set the aircraft down.

"Chat's garage," he read, muttering. "Wonder if they've got a pickle barrel."

Dinner was steaming on the table, the chicken fried golden brown, the stuffing flecked with plump raisins and golden bits of spices, and the biscuits steamed in nose-wrenching fragrance, while Chat, Sue, Megan and Jesse joined their hands for the evening prayer. Sue stole a glance at Chat when he started. He was a tad grayer, but still as handsome as he was the day she had married him. She bowed her head and thought guiltily that she hadn't been overly warm to him lately, had thoughts of the times before the marriage, even a few resentful moments when the never-ending list of chores was piled on the children's issues which was stacked on tiredness that was cemented all together with his own good opinion of himself, as if she had not saved him long ago.

Even when he talked to the Lord, something was not quite right.

She thought she heard maybe a little gleam of pride in his prayers. But of course a good Christian isn't one to go about taking stock of another's store, so she added a small prayer at the end of grace, just to herself and the Lord, for more patience and to know the right way.

When the phone rang, she motioned for him to sit and eat. She got up and picked up the receiver while Chat eagerly piled chicken and potatoes on his plate.

"If it's one of them sales people, I'm gonna get an address and pay a liddle visit first thing," he muttered. But he could tell from Sue's expression it was none of that.

"Homer," she said.

"Oh, Lord. What now?"

"He says there's a helicopter set down in your parking lot. Big one, he said."

"What? A 'copter? Whose danged thing is it, anyway?"

"Homer didn't say. Said he was gonna sneak down and see what he could see."

Chat groaned. He'd heard about the Meals-on-Wheels kid from a few of the boy's buddies, who'd come into the station for gas right before Sterling had stopped by. Maybe Homer was getting too far along? Chat gave Sue and the chicken a look.

He grabbed a couple pieces and stood.

"Better go out there," he said and thought to himself that the man who pulled him away from the people he loved—and the chicken!—had better have a damned good reason for interrupting.

He burned the road and chewed chicken, only half aware of the darkening landscape and of the sprawl of acreage he and Homer owned on the old road. His wheels left the road briefly on the last ridge descending the valley, and while airborne, he made out, with the ease of a man supremely accustomed to the scenery, the jarring angular lines of the chopper. He pulled up in front of it, leaving his headlights on, and got out.

Homer emerged from the bushes with the old Savage cradled easily in the crook of his arm, swamp muck smeared half way up his legs, and twigs sticking from his damp, matted hair.

"You look good, Uncle," Chat said flatly, eyeing the chopper with a scowl.

"Well, you're more than welcome, I'm sure," Homer said, panting from the walk and excitement.

"Where'd they get to anyway?"

"I hid down in the swamp there and listened. They jumped on a motorbike and drove off towards town."

Chat chewed pensively on what was left of the chicken, gnawing on the thin strip of crispy skin left near the end of the bone. The fact that it was still delicious made him suddenly angry.

"Who the, the, *heck* are they anyway?"

"You know as much as I do about that. No government, that's sure." The fact that Homer thought *that* somehow was more disturbing than if he thought they *had* been. Chat examined the chassis of the bird, admiring the smooth lines and the flawless shine of the blue painted metal.

"McAdam Industries," he said, reading the florid script near the door. He could see no sign of mechanical failure.

"They say anything, did they Uncle?"

"There was two of 'em. Stocky guy was in charge. Your age, maybe. Gray hair. Kinda flabby. Pilot was younger'n you. Twenty-five, thirty, tall. Looked like them muscle-heads down at the YMCA, sorta."

"Did they *say* anything?"

"Flabbo says, 'Let's go to town, see what's what.' Muscle-head says, 'How about the chopper? Jest leavin' it here?' and he kinda waves his arms around. He knew it was damned rude, all right. Flabbo goes, 'Well, we'll jest give 'em a couple bucks. Looks like they could use it. Maybe fill in that muck hole over there.' Then off they go, like a couple of drunk monkeys on that motorbike." Homer shook his head in disbelief. Chat looked down at his now-bare chicken bone, and remembered what he had left.

"We have to get that moved," Chat said, walking around the 'copter.

Chat swung his thumb towards the garage doors. All three were blocked by the chopper.

"How old are ya, Unc?"

"Shit, Chat. You know as well as I do I'm seventy-three *years* old," he said.

"What's that sign up there say, then?"

Chat pointed to the smaller of the two signs.

"Why, I believe it says. Well, hell. We both know what it says."

"Listen, Mrs. Jerman's comin' for her car tomorrow morning. Her nephew will be driving her out here to get it. Now just how's she supposed to get it out with that thing there?"

They stood about for a moment, puzzling it out. Chat got behind the machine and gave it a push with his hand. He was gratified when it moved the slightest bit up on the wheel chocks.

"We could push it into the empty bay, maybe," Chat said, doubtfully.

"How? With those blades?"

Chat went inside and fetched a stepladder, trying to rotate the blades by hand so they pointed in the same direction the craft was facing.

"Umppff. No good. I guess there's no sense in a clutch on one of these babies, huh?"

"Must be a way to take them off, eh?"

"Lemme see. Looks like the hydraulics work the mounting plates here. The blades are just bolted on. Can you get your backhoe down here?"

"Backhoe? Sure I could. What you gonna do?"

"Damned chicken'll be cold by the time I get back anyway. I'll see if I can't pop these puppies lose, use the bucket for a skyhook, and then we can use a come-along to get it into the bay."

"I'll be back in twenty minutes, then," Homer said, and began limping up the road.

Chat heard him began to sing "Old Home Place," as his old voice seamlessly joined the peepers' song.

By the time Homer had driven the old John Deere into the lot, Chat had the blades loosened, and, using the bucket of the loader, he and Homer had them off in about another twenty minutes.

"Not a scratch on 'em, now Unc," Chat said. "Don't want any cause for complaint."

With the blades gone, the chopper snugged right into the middle bay of the garage. They couldn't get the door shut, since the tail assembly was way too long.

"Get that scaffolding over against the wall there, Unc. We'll jury-rig something."

In another twenty minutes, they had buttoned up the garage using the welder, two blue tarps, the scaffolding, and some old blasting net Chat had around the back.

When finished, they stepped back and considered their work.

"Looks obscene," Chat said, chuckling.

"Naw, more like some of that stuff they slapped in front of the college down at Fiesterville. I swear. What *is* that junk anyway?" Homer said.

"Why, that there's art. Don'tcha know?"

"Well, old art better sober up," Homer said.

"Right as rain you are. Well, thanks, Unc. Lemme know if you see anything going on down here, okay? I gotta get ready."

"Down at the Inn again tonight?"

"Yeah, boy." Chat looked at his watch. If he hurried, he might be able to enjoy some cold chicken and at least some hugs and kisses. Her chicken was better than anybody else's, cold or not. Her kisses? Well, he saved that thought for dessert.

"Hey, Unc?"

"Yeah, Chat?"

"I heard about the Meals-on-Wheels kid."

"Awww, Chat. I didn't mean no harm. You know I can't abide strangers around me."

"Unc, give the Savage a break once in awhile. Okay?"

"Any other man, I'd tell him to go to hell right off."

"Me?"

"Thanks for yer concern. Go to hell."

6

⟫ Chapter Six ⟪

Layton looked at the ancient gray siding of the Inn, wondering idly what vinyl would look like. He'd had his house done with it earlier that spring, a nice beige color, and he thought it looked pretty good. Better, he thought, than the clapboard he covered, which seemed to need painted every year now that he was older. He picked at the barn boards as he looked down old Route 11. Traffic was down, but business was up something considerable from even just a couple years ago.

He held the thought of vinyl in his mind for a time. It'd make the place look more modern, but he wondered if that might not be a bad thing. He'd heard the newer folk showing off the place to their relatives up for Thanksgiving or a hunting trip.

"Can you *believe* this?" they would always ask. What they had such a hard time believing Layton just didn't understand, but he was getting used to that. He knew he wasn't the smartest guy walking. But he knew how to cook a good cheesesteak, and he wasn't against the boys using the meat slicer for venison, as long as they cleaned it good when they were done. He didn't care much for the state laws about that, or really about underage drinking, either.

That was just the way it was. After high school, if a guy had a job, maybe a family, Layton couldn't think of any reason why he shouldn't have himself a cold one after a hot day at work. Long as he behaved, of course.

So, all told, Layton did all right when last call was a foggy memory for his patrons and the receipts were tallied. He did so well that he could afford to have the Cold Spring Band play every other Friday or so.

Of course, before it <u>had</u> been every other Friday. But the rich folks up on Twin Lakes Road or some of the new developments often wanted them, for good dollars, too, and Layton didn't begrudge them that. Bluegrass was no way to get rich, the boys told him. The real serious money was in other kinds of music, like country and western or top-forty stuff, and they all swore they'd lay down their instruments before they whored themselves out that way.

Layton looked forward to those nights. He'd have hired the boys even if it cost him a couple bucks profit sometimes, which he suspected it didn't. And women did come in on a Saturday to find out more about Sterling or Jo-Jo. The boys would come down to the Inn after a practice or an afternoon pig roast from time to time, and sometimes he'd get a free show, along with whichever girls were after one of 'em at the time. Well, they had their rights, he guessed. That was none of his business, but he still wondered how a man could go on like that, Jo-Jo especially.

He sure missed his Rose, still, especially on these silky spring evenings when they'd be talking about what to plant in the plot out back that year. Why, times like that he could almost see the 'lopes and tomatoes the way he saw them when he and she had talked about it, way back in the long-ago warming springtime.

The sight of a tan Buick coming down the hill and trailing wisps of blue smoke brought him to. He examined the strip of clean, fresh wood he had mined from the edge of one of the boards as if wondering who had done such a thing. He dusted the old wood from his hands and overalls and went inside to check on the ice and beer for Kate before she started. She was strong, but Layton didn't like for her to be doing heavy lifting. She seemed to him to always heft ten pounds more than she was comfortable with.

"Make two trips!" he'd tell her.

She'd say, "What for? I need the exercise."

That much was baloney. He'd watched her more than once beat some drunk construction worker, first in thumb wrestling and then in *arm wrestling,* for goodness sake, although she did it more with timing than with muscle.

For the past year or so, he had been making sure that the heavy work was done before she got there, because he didn't want to be telling her what to do all the time. That wasn't the way. He smiled at her as she walked in the back door.

"Buick needs rings, Katie, looks like," he said, dumping the first of two buckets of ice in the well.

"I know it. School first."

"Rings are cheap enough. You know Chat'd work something out on the labor if you needed it."

"She'll last another ten thou. Then maybe I'll just have him do the whole show, bearings, valves. Like that."

"Burn much oil?" he asked, taking off his apron.

"Couple quarts a week," she said, putting her apron on.

"Well then. Better get the grill fired up. Boys'll be coming down pretty soon."

"Yeah, Mr. Pasquale himself," she said, smirking and moving behind the bar to change the water and put away the cleaned glasses. Layton chuckled as he wandered into the kitchen while Katie stretched to slide the glasses into their elevated slots on the ceiling.

She and Sue had talked about Jo-Jo, or, well, they had sniffed around that whole thing, even though it had been years and years since Sue and he had had their little thing back in high school. Kate was two years younger than Sue. In high school, that was a big deal. And Kate had to admit that Sue was a looker, and a really nice person, too. She'd do anything for you, and she never had a bad word to say about anyone, almost.

Katie was perpetually surprised that they were no closer, being with the band and with so much else in common. But Sue always seemed to hold back, particularly the few times that Kate sounded her for advice or some kind of insight into what made men tick, or, more accurately, what made one man tick.

Sometimes it seemed the only things Jo-Jo did know were wood, music and muscle. As a short list, it wasn't all *that* bad, she tried to tell herself.

She was sorry Meg wasn't coming tonight. It wasn't that Meg had much to offer in the way of advice about Jo-Jo, but Katie liked having someone close when the boys faded into the music. Sometimes when they disappeared into a song, it felt like whispered secrets on the playground—hurtful and nasty. It could almost be worse than being alone, if a person were in a needy frame of mind. Kate had to admit that she did not always achieve the independence she was so anxious to portray.

"There's two theories about men," Meg deadpanned, once, her one eyebrow tilted and her lips pursed.

"Really?" Kate had asked, interested.

"Yep. Neither one makes any sense," Meg joked, nodding her head and laughing.

Kate saw her point: either love them and do what had to be done, or forget them. Change wasn't in Jo-Jo's vocabulary, much. It was like pushing a rope: it was hard to do, and the rope didn't appreciate it.

Pensively, she cleared Layton's clutter to make a small area near the register for a half-dozen mugs, and then she turned the steaming water off. She looked at the empty bar and the head rail above it. The shelf was packed with old Shell gas pump heads, empty tins of Bisquick, wooden hay rakes, shotguns, fly rods, ladies' hats, wool underwear, old lumbermen's hats, rat traps, ski boots, ice tongs. In another place, it would've been put there for show. Here, it was just that Layton's garage was stuffed full of things like that. The overage he'd carry inside, not even knowing he'd done it. He couldn't bear to see things thrown out, even worthless stuff. And since he was related to half the county, when the old ones passed on, it was Layton who took the remainders home with him.

She smiled as she sliced the lemons and limes. There were some who wanted more than a beer occasionally. Outside she heard the crunch of tires on gravel, and the guttural laughs of the first customers. She saw the growing dusk in the small window above the back wall of the bar. She never knew exactly how the arrangement came about, but Layton opened only for lunch, shut down from two or so on, until sundown in the short days or until dinnertime during the summer. Then he'd open up again. It had been that way for so long that nobody even asked why. All Kate knew was that when she opened the front door, her customers would be waiting, usually a dozen or so guys, lounging against the wall or leaning on the huge wooden pillars that held up the porch roof.

And they were there. Some were grease-stained or covered with spackle. Those were the ones who had skipped the niceties of home and had moved straight from work to the inn. Those fresh out of the shower were the ones who had done their homely duties and were now officially on leave. In the back, two new faces in expensive clothes were evident. The younger one was tall and sandy haired, with a big square jaw. *Could've been a cop or a soldier,* she thought. The other had the negligent air of a big wheel. His lips pouted in what she guessed was a perpetual sneer, and his almost-black eyes darted around, never looking straight at her. She decided she didn't care for that one at all.

"Evening, gentleman," she said to them all, holding the door open. The younger of the two new ones regarded her frankly. Katie wondered if she minded that. The rest of the regulars streamed in, murmuring greetings and jostling up to the bar. She returned the greetings as she moved back behind the bar, then watched as the older stranger whisked himself past a few of the boys to get waited on out of turn.

He barked, "Give me a martini. Dry. Olive."

Katie could swear the younger one gave an imperceptible shrug.

"Just a minute, sir. I'll have to find some vermouth. Just let me take care of these fellas first. Only take a minute."

For a moment she thought the stranger was about to say something, but he kept still. She popped open several bottles of Bud, drew a few drafts, made a few small jokes, and went into the back to find the dusty bottle of vermouth she knew Layton used sometimes for his soups.

"Sorry about the wait, sir," she said when she returned, and gave the stranger a smile. "My name's Kate."

"Right. Hurry up with that drink."

"Your friend?" Katie asked, indicating the young one with a nod of her head.

"My dear, perhaps you could be so kind as to forgo the small talk and give me what it is that I want," the man said as he rocked back on his heels and smirked.

"Well, sir. I'd have been happy to comply a half a minute ago. But now, I think it would behoove me to tell you to kiss my ass. Take your attitude someplace else," Katie said loudly.

The two men stood there in a suddenly silent space that lasted only a second before the muffled snickers began.

"Now, now. Let's be reasonable, young lady. I would like a drink, and of course you would like to sell me one. Now doesn't that make sense?"

"If you weren't so busy being patronizing, you would have noticed that sign over there—the one that says you can be refused service for any reason or for none at all? So consider yourself flagged for life, mister. Your friend can stay and drink if he wants," Kate said, pushing a stray lock of dark hair nervously behind her ear.

"Where is your boss, sweetheart?" the older man said, unctuously. The silence was complete. This was better than the TV as far as the regulars were concerned.

Behind her Katie could hear Layton moving out of the kitchen. He would have his Louisville slugger in his hand.

"Best leave now, mister," Layton drawled, cutting him off with a palm of his hand raised. "Katie don't want to serve you, you won't be served."

"You're making a serious mistake."

"Made 'em before. Always survived. Now there's the door. Don't let it hit ya where the good Lord split ya."

Katie's face was aflame by now, her mad still up. Yet she grinned wide when the odd pair walked out the door and the bar exploded in laughter, hoots and catcalls. The patrons were buzzing about the two who'd just been thrown out.

"When was the last time that happened, Layton?" somebody asked.

"Hell, I don't know, exactly. Threw old Curtie out for cussing in front of some ladies once. Heck, ten years?"

"Curtie? He drinks here all the time. Don't he?"

"Well, he came back and apologized. So no harm done. It was just the beer talking anyway. He don't even cuss no more, so that worked out fine for all of us, eh?"

Another one of the regulars came sauntering in the door, grinning.

"Well, what was the commotion all about just then? That pair of yuppies that just walked out? The old boy was madder'n *hell.* Said he was gonna buy this place and burn it down."

"Can't if I don't sell it. And I don't aim to do that," Layton said simply. "No, I don't guess they'll get me out of here so easy."

7

⟹ CHAPTER SEVEN ⟸

By nine pm, the Inn was busy, and at a minute past nine, Sterling and Chat came through the door, cases in hand and arguing, if it could be called that.

"I'm telling you, that part's got an E minor in it, just for a beat. And you're not playing it," Sterling said, his voice squeaking.

"Well, so."

"Are you saying you *are* playing it?"

"No," Chat said.

"Then you *aren't* playing it."

Chat shrugged.

"Well, goddam it. What *are* you saying?"

"Sayin' I wish you'd clean up yer language some. But I guess that's too much to ask."

"What's my language got to do with it? Jo-Jo, doesn't that *New County Breakdown* have that E minor in it?"

"Hell's Bell's, Sterling. We haven't even had our first beer, and you're at it already."

"Well, doesn't it have that part? That's all I want to know."

"I oughta say no just to hear you sputter, Sterling, but, fact is, I don't exactly know. Could, I guess."

"Like a bunch of old married biddies," Katie said, giggling.

"The hell with you, then. Katie, give us a beer. If you guys don't want to trouble yourselves to play it right, then I guess I'll just have to live with it."

"Sterling, if you don't calm down, you won't have to worry about it," Layton said quietly, "because you'll be ten toes up. Always sounds good the way you do it, so I don't see the need to change it."

"It's got the E minor. And I'm gonna keep playing it that way 'til you can prove me wrong," Sterling muttered, taking a pull on his beer.

Chat held up his glass.

"Here's to you, Sterling. You just do what you need to. I think it gives that part just a little *tension*, you know. Like when we come out of it there, and it resolves into the D. Well, that makes my *hair* stand up. So, here's to ya, best danged banjo player in town."

"Thanks for nothing, old pal," Sterling said tersely, but Katie could tell he couldn't hold his mad for long, not with Chat hugging him around the shoulders that way.

"Come on, old buddy, get her out and let me hear what you're *talking* about," Chat said.

Sterling, still a little huffy, snapped open the case and got the Gibson Bowtie out, that great-sounding RB250 he'd got when he was just a shaver, too small even to lift it. Katie remembered that story. Chat always told it when another banjo player was around, bragging, sort of. Then Chat got out his '58 Martin—his baby, he called it— and Katie knew enough about guitars to know this one was special. A D-28 employee's model with snowflakes on the fingerboard and sides of beautifully grained Brazilian rosewood—the kind you couldn't get any more—the deep sound actually made the glasses by the register rattle when he did the church lick from the low G up to the D.

That was how they started, like it was just a practice, like they were still on Chat's front porch. For all they cared, they were. Sterling ran out the change he heard, Chat playing through it on a C chord, and then the next time ducking down to the E-minor like Sterling wanted him to do.

"See? Now doesn't that sound better?" Sterling said.

"I'm afraid to agree with you, ole boy."

"Why, 'cause I'm right?"

"Listen, play that over, and I'll hold on the C like I did before, only right before the bridge there."

Kate thought that made no sense whatsoever, but Sterling just nodded and they went at it again. When they finished, Sterling gave a quizzical look to Katie and Jo-Jo.

"That sounded better," Jo-Jo said. "See? Neither here nor there, was it? And why you two have to fight like that all the time, couple ole biddies."

"Well, being in a band *is* kinda like being married to three guys without sex," Sterling said, unsatisfied.

"And that's on a *good* day, too," Kate said, letting a smile tickle the corners of her mouth.

Sterling said, "Well, I don't guess it'll make much difference. We never play it the same way from one time to the next anyway. As they say, you can't step in the same river twice."

"I can tell you the same isn't true for dog shit," Jo-Jo said, and they all laughed.

"Well, that's settled, then. Soon as Johnny gets here, we'll get started," Chat said, still smiling.

Before long Johnny had come through the door with his old bull bass. His fingers gripped it anxiously, exposing white knuckles streaked with a black pigment in all the creases—stains that might never go away, like spiderous tattoos.

Just like that it was officially a Friday, and the show commenced.

Katie enjoyed it, although she hadn't cared much for bluegrass in school. It was rock and roll then, Three Dog Night and Cream, Hendrix and Joplin, Blues Project, The Who. She was pretty typical, she knew. Jo-Jo had listened to that stuff, too. Chat never had. Back in those days, he could be seen driving fast in his old red pick-up with Merl Travis or Roger Miller blaring out of what had to be one of the county's first 8-tracks. She pictured him sailing down the river road when part of it was still gravel with a plume of dust trailing behind and the windows open. The tape player Homer had bought him blared out "King of the Road" as his very cool long hair whipped around his dark and grinning face. Even then she had a feeling he was putting on some kind of show, and his face when he played was the same face as in her picture.

The boys would gather in a circle, tuning, saying "Give me a G" or "play that whole D chord," "again" and "again," and "again," they'd say, and they would turn the shining mother-of pearl tuners or the hammered brass ones. The notes all sort of circled around each other like birds of prey. They would sip their beers and laugh if they were ready and the other guy wasn't.

Fifteen years? Trying to imagine them without each other was impossible in her mind, like thinking about the Titanic without the iceberg. Katie had to admit that she'd have been a little jealous of Jo-Jo even if he were steady with just her, and of course she knew he wasn't. She'd have to have been pretty blind to miss that, although it did surprise her the times some young thing had come down after a festival. None of them seemed to know about Katie. Too full of themselves, she guessed, or too full of him, maybe.

But she was jealous of that thing they shared also. Folks laughed at male bonding, but to see those four, relaxed—well, except Sterling—joking, standing around oblivious to the folks who were taking tables or bar stools and waiting—that was no joke. To her, that was an antidote for loneliness. And even if she couldn't always get the cure, to see them have it, well, it made life just a little smoother, knowing a cure existed.

She made a game out of calling the first full note; the place where the clowning and tuning and sipping stopped and the sound began to whirl around itself, lifting them all up.

She never quite got it, even with the significant glances, the small head nods. She might get within a second. She'd say, "Now!" and a beat later they would all come in on that first strong chord, usually the first in a fast instrumental they used to tighten the tuning. Or she would just begin to think the "now!" and that first fat note, nineteen strings, or twenty three strings, all suddenly shuddering like they'd just let loose a volley of arrows.

She'd seen folks smirk at that first chord.

But she'd also seen them drawn into the music because the way the boys played it, it was damned hard to deny. Strangers would deny it with their lips, making the remarks she supposed passed for wit where they came from. But their feet betrayed them; you would have to be missing something in your soul to not be affected by it, at least for a time. Under the table, where their friends could not see, ten toes tapped. And smirk as they might, they would grow quieter when the four began to sing because they sang about true things that meant something in a matter-of-fact way that said, *here it is. Here's life. Here's what I make of it, and here's how I feel.* In fact, when the smirkers realized how true the words were, how sweet those voices were who had raised themselves in song all those years together, that was often when they'd leave.

Too close to the ranch, Chat said. *A lightening bolt too close to the hayloft.*

She liked that the band wasn't all sourpussed about it, not that they always goofed around. Sometimes they'd step back when they were finished with a song. The last note would fade into the background noise of laughter and glasses clinking and they would move apart like they were making room for something, like they could see the song out there in front of them. Sometimes they'd seem to bow to it, just a little at the waist, or they'd get that look in their eye, a surprised, pleased kind of look. *Was that me? Was that us?* But that tableau didn't last a minute until somebody, usually Jo-Jo, would crack a joke, and then they'd all take a little sip and Chat would say "Mountain Girls," and they'd be at the next song.

She'd been to some festivals with Jo-Jo, or with the rest of the girls, and she'd seen the headliners: Del, Ralph, Bill, Larry. Those guys sang it the same way, sound-wise, but boy, she thought, they were just as proper up there as possible, suit coats, a few aw-shucks jokes, and the rest was up to their fingers.

The audiences didn't seem to notice. 'Course, they hadn't seen Janis at the Filmore either, the way Katie had. That music, she tried to put her finger on just when she stopped listening to it, or why. When she heard the songs at a party or here and there, she remembered the words, remembered "Take another little piece of my heart" or "White Room." But it had become too much, that music and that life.

This was gentler and had more humor to it if you were bright enough to get past the surface of things. And these guys were way more relaxed, talking with each other and the audience like they were in somebody's kitchen. Well, the band was only a notch or two below the second-stringers, not bad for a band that only played a half-dozen times a month. And from time to time they were a notch above, also.

It all depended mostly on how much in love with each other the boys were at the moment, and somewhat on how much rest they had. They all had two mistresses, even Chat, and Katie had known Sue long enough to know that she understood how important that other mistress was. This was the First Church of Bluegrass, and anybody could attend if they left their little minds outside.

On any night, the regular mishmash of folks would assemble there. The locals, well, they'd have come even if Cold Spring was just a joke, since there wasn't a lot going on out there. And college kids came up from Fiesterville, to play darts, and if they were underage, to get served. Truckers would stop, older ones' usually, out of habit for the time when the old Route 11 was the only way, and Ellie's place, just up the road, was the place to stop for a cup of coffee and a flirt with the waitresses.

They were playing again, a bluesy thing. Johnny played a bass line like a man walking around, snowbound and getting a little crazy, and all four sang with no room for improvement that she could tell. *"Tell me baby, why you been gone so long, wolf is scratchin' at my door and I can hear that lonesome wind blow."*

She thought back to the two strangers and about how they'd take the music. She figured the paunchy guy'd make the same lame crack they'd all heard ten dozen times: "Hey, I'll give ya ten bucks to stop, har har har." She hadn't liked the look of those small, cold eyes.

She did regret the rangy younger one, though.

She drew a round of drafts for a half dozen kids in tie-dyed shirts as they finished, and Jo-Jo kicked off "Big Sandy," one of the songs that made Chat's Uncle spitting mad. The notes were soaring above the now-thin blue haze of smoke that would thicken like a good gravy as the night wore on. She patted her belly. Thank God that bluegrass church had room enough for women and children.

Hugh was not a man given to swearing; usually he had little need. But tonight he found himself bouncing along the wretched stretch of road with that young tart's words ringing in his ear and picturing the simple-minded idiot owner with the baseball bat, and he swore nonstop. The wind blew the spittle backwards against his cheeks as the Vespa whined back towards where they left the helicopter.

Ty wished he would stop. Between the cussing and Hugh's increasingly oppressive hug, he was beginning to feel, if not dizzy, then at least a little bleached out. This wasn't what he'd signed on for, not at all, not in the least.

"FRACKA FRICKA BATCHA BITCHCA," was what it sounded like to Ty, Hugh's goings-on behind him. He looked gratefully down the hill to the solitary light above Chat's Garage.

And he failed to see his chopper. Hugh was so absorbed by invective that he failed to see that things had changed drastically in just the past few hours. Yes, they had tooled around, seen the downtown. "With a goddamed Five and Dime? Puh-leeeze!" Hugh had cackled. They had asked about lodging and had been directed to the Inn.

"We'll just lay low a couple days, check out who thinks they're big shots, see what's what," Hugh had said smugly. "Steal some land. Hey, how about a Dude ranch? They still have them? That might be fun."

Now it was a different matter. Now Hugh couldn't wait to get back to the city, to spread some of his spleen, Ty thought, and lick his wounds.

"Let's get the Fricka fracka micka macka," he heard Hugh holler as they entered the parking lot, and then he heard a pair of plaintive yelps from Hugh. One came when he couldn't find the chopper, for the human mind, once it locates an object in space, wants badly for it to stay where it's been catalogued.

The second yelp came when Hugh finally located the chopper, or at least the nether end of it.

"What the hell? The shit. Why, goddam," Hugh sputtered.

"A note, sir," Ty said, almost reverently, pointing to a piece of corrugated cardboard pasted fast with duct tape. In the slight breeze from the swamp Ty could see the backside of it. "Prestone", was printed in yellow.

"A NOTE? A GODDAMNED NOTE? WHAT DOES THE GOD-DAMNED NOTE SAY?" Hugh screamed, pushed beyond his means of control.

Ty pulled it off and read the small, neat printing.

"It says: 'Next time, ask. Signed, Chat Dalton.'"

"That's *all*? That's *it*? *Ask*?"

"No, sir. There's ah, a bill, sir?"

Hugh tried to comprehend that and failed. Here was a blatant violation piled upon vile rejection heaped upon crass unconcern, and whatever coping skills he may have had lo these many years gone were simply not up to the task. He found to his surprise that what confronted him was so novel and so beyond his ken that his anger dissolved in a sort of bemused stupor.

"The bill. What's it for?" Hugh asked, sotto voce.

"Remove rotors, thirty-three dollars. Backhoe rental, one hour, seventy dollars. Storage, four hundred dollars."

"Here's a place where a tart refuses to serve me, and some bumpkin wants to charge me five hundred and three dollars for something I should have him arrested for?"

"Well, sir," Ty offered, buoyed up by this new and strange kind of calm, and he simply gestured to the smaller of two signs.

"No Parking!" That's what the sign said.

"I'll own this place, and I'll see these idiots get what they deserve!"

"What about tonight, sir? That inn's the only place in town to eat or sleep."

That was how, after Hugh drained himself of a last surge of obscenity, they found themselves shivering through the now-damp darkness, driving to the south until they found a cheap motel with no bar and only a greasy-spoon cafe opposite it. The thoughts of cold crab cocktail and an Absolute martini did little to assuage Hugh's rancor.

Tomorrow he would begin. Suddenly life had meaning.

8

$$\Longrightarrow \text{C{\small HAPTER} E{\small IGHT}} \Longleftarrow$$

The city at 4:30 in the morning isn't dead by any stretch of the imagination, but especially when the weather wasn't warm, girls were scarce. Even if they were out en masse, Tony mused, he really didn't have time to check out babes while he worked. The truck moved too fast, and if the schedule started falling behind, the rest of the shift was a bitch.

During the summer, he wound up pulling muscles because he couldn't take his eyes off a good-looking woman, the lack of which was one of the reasons he had left the pit of a town in Pennsylvania where he had been born.

He always thought it odd when it happened—but then, wasn't life odd?—that some lines of poetry might come to him. He never told the boys about that. They would have busted on him without mercy, even more than they already did.

People were always tossing out porn, and he might snatch up a few magazines to look at for the last three hours of the shift when they didn't really do much but sit around at the yard, play cards and bust on each other. Union work. It was sweet. He liked to cop the books, mostly, although he never made a big deal out of it.

Actually, he hid the books inside the porn.

One of them was a bunch of dead people talking about each other, and he had, just out of boredom, started his own little funeral conversation. It was kind of easy, and whenever one of the others started on him, it made him feel good that he could cook 'em down to a couple dozen lines, just like his boss—a big, muscle-bound idiot that read the *New Yorker* and thought it made him smart, except he never did get what he read right and wound up sounding even stupider than somebody trying to talk ball who had never played a day in his life.

Tony had cooked one especially for him that he called "Big Bubski." He smiled as he jumped down and grabbed a trashcan, flipping it expertly to the gate. He grabbed two bags, flipping them in as well, and then finally jumped back on the truck. In his head, he recited the poem, with the last word of each line punctuated by the sound of trash bags breaking open or garbage cans banging hollow on the odorous tailgate of the truck:

My body is my *temple*

My body and the mind that is *in it*

The temple where I worship *myself*

All I do is to my own *increase*

And every increase to the greater *glory* of me.

It would be perfect except that *I know*

The sun cannot reflect *itself*

And there are no *others* in my world.

He liked that one; it made him smile. So what was wrong with being a poet? He wasn't some kind of faggot, after all. He could still knock the block off of anybody on his shift. Almost.

Eliza Jane stood outside Chat's garage resolutely, with her small feet planted together and her gnarled white hands clutching her embroidered purse. She watched Jimmy drive back up the hill towards town. She shook her head and continued to watch up the hill. With the sun just coming up as it was, she knew that even her poor eyes would catch the glint of light off metal as Chat's car came over the breast of the hill.

She was early, and she expected Chat to be a mite late; he often was, by a minute or two. So the bright blink of light off a windshield she saw a moment later was a surprise. Eliza had figured on ten or fifteen minutes to relax and watch the sun come up, and to think about the old days of sled rides, skating parties and bonfires in the winter and of the milk wagon laboring up what they used to simply call "the big hill" in the rest of the seasons. She looked down on her hands—they always surprised her, even now, even after she had had them all these years. They were spotted and twisted now, and were no longer the sleek and winsome hands many boys fought to hold all those years ago.

She turned once more to face that thing she saw sticking out of the garage when her nephew had dropped her off. Jimmy had snorted when he'd seen it, just like he did when some kind of tomfoolery was going on with that idiot box he was always watching.

"Big Blue," he had sniggered. "Huh huh huh." She hadn't liked it much.

She was happy when he was gone, and even happier to see Chat, who was a nice boy, even if he had been a little wild after his folks passed on. Nobody minded it much. Wasn't any spleen behind it. Eliza gave a small wave with her gloved hand as Chat climbed out of his truck.

"Mornin', Mrs. Jerman. How are you today?" he said.

"Oh, fine. Thank you for asking. You look a bit tired, Chat. Hope this wasn't too early for you."

"No, no. Not a bit of it! I wanted to get here a few minutes before you, ma'am, but I can see it's mighty hard getting the jump on you, now, isn't it?"

Eliza Jane blushed with pleasure.

"Chat, what on earth is that, anyway?" She gestured at the chopper.

"Well, that's why I wanted to beat you here, Mizz Jerman. The fella who left it here—he's bound to come back for it, and I don't expect he'll be real pleased."

"Whose is it? And why'd he leave it here, then?"

"Don't know and can't say. That'd be the short answer to those questions," Chat said quietly. "But enough about unpleasant things. How's Jimmy doing?"

"Chat, I hope you don't think bad of me, and I know he's my kin and all, but I just don't care for that boy much. He gives me the willies."

"Oh, well, he's just young and a little wild, *that's* all. You know *I* was a little wild there for a time, too," Chat said, smiling down at her. The top of her head was even with his chin. God love her, she was so *short*, and she looked up to him with watery blue old-age eyes that had a hint of permanent pleading in them.

"Well, when you lost your folks that way—sorry to speak of it, dear—but, what would you expect? Besides, you got over that after a bit, too. Jimmy just goes from bad to worse, seems like. I wish sometimes he had a father or older brother to look after him, someone…" she said, her voice trailing off into nothingness.

"Well, maybe he'll soon meet a nice girl and that'll solve *that*. That's the way it worked out for me, God be praised! Now, let's get that car of yours out here," Chat said, and unlocked the garage door. Eliza Jane had been watching up the road for the last few seconds, and Chat soon saw why: a pair of men was coming down the hill on a motorbike that didn't look as if it should hold them both.

Chat backed the car out carefully, shut off the ignition and handed Eliza the keys. He turned and stood passively watching as the two men swung into the lot. Eliza heard Chat draw a big breath the way she used to when she was a kid. Back then, she'd beat out her brother-in-law, Jimmy's dad—also named Jimmy—when they were holding their breaths underwater down at the river. She could always win. She'd just watch for the thin trickle of bubbles that would always leak out of his nose just before he ran out of steam.

Chat's voice brought her back.

"You own this machine?" he asked the red-faced stranger, who had advanced upon them.

Eliza could see the stranger was trying hard to hold his anger, just the way big Jimmy had made fish-eyes trying to hold his breath under water all those years ago.

"Yes, it is. And I am very curious as to what kind of a man would treat a visitor this way, destroying his property like this." The older stranger waved at the thing sticking out of the garage.

He's putting on the dog, Eliza thought. What he *really* wanted was to strangle Chat. Even her old eyes could see that.

"Well, sir, there's not a scratch on that machine, so I can't say there was any harm done, first of all. And second, just sticking that thing in front of my place like that, with no cause, well, that was mighty inconsiderate. Here's Mrs. Jerman, waiting for her car, and how could I get it out? Now if you'd have had a care about us and just set it over by the side of the building, why, I wouldn't have been quite so upset. So I'll thank you to pay what you owe me, and I'll put it back the way it was for nothing. Then you can be on your way."

"You aren't even curious why we're here? Or if something was wrong?"

"No, sir, there's nothing wrong with that machine. Curious? I am that. But it's none of my business, so I intend to keep my nose out of it."

Eliza Jane knew it was wrong, unchristian, even, but she loved it when a puffed-up toad got brought up short. And *this* toad didn't fool her any with his smarmy way.

"Well, as far as the money, I think you'd better reconsider."

"No reconsider about it, mister. Five hundred three dollars, or I could always call my aunt Jenna. She's the district magistrate, and I bet she'd be happy to come down here, Saturday or not, and swear out a complaint on you. I'd rather not do that."

Eliza watched for the stranger to fold, to blow his own little stream of bubbles, and was surprised when it didn't come. The younger one expected it too, she could tell, but instead the stranger just shrugged like it made no difference at all to him and reached in his pocket for his wallet.

"I suppose you want cash?"

"Cash or check. I don't expect you're the kind of man that would write a bad one," Chat said.

And just like that the man scrawled one out, asked Chat how long it would take, and jumped back on his little motorbike by himself, leaving the younger one to make sure no damage was done putting the thing back together.

"Sorry about the unpleasantness," Chat said to Eliza, before she got in her car to leave.

"That man, why, I thought he was going to bust a gusset, Chat," she said.

And he had replied, quietly, "His kind don't, unless they can gain from it. We haven't seen the last of *him*, I bet."

He wished Eliza well, started the oxyacetylene torch with a loud pop, put on his welding hat and started cutting the heavy metal netting away from the door.

Jimmy Jerman was quite sure that work was not the path to happiness. He'd watched his old man bust his back and wind up with nothing. Hell, after the funeral he could barely afford to bury the old bastard, once his Aunt had made him pay for the refreshments at the fire hall for all the old farts. Man, they ate like they hadn't eaten for a week. He had watched in amazement as little blue-haired women packed it in like there was no tomorrow. Jimmy guessed that at least some of them might be right. And were any of his classmates there? That was a laugh! So he'd gone over to the Legion and spent the last seventeen dollars from the policy on beer and video poker, and wound up winning an even hundred, which was enough to get really toned the next night. Yeah, all his old buddies had been so busy worrying about the cheerleaders' shorts and cars and acne, and Jimmy had been going into the city and cultivating contacts. That's how he said it.

It went like this: "What'd you do this weekend, Jim?" "Oh, I was in the city cultivating business contacts." They'd always laugh, like he was joking. But where corn was three dollars a bushel, other crops would bring a guy a hell of a lot more in the right places. He gloated at the image of his aunt and old man Dalton in the rearview mirror as he pulled out onto the road. What would Mr. High-and-Mighty Dalton say if he ever found out he was helping ole Jimmy to a piece of the American dream?

He had to admit that getting up at dawn to avoid being seen and lugging heavy things over long distances did sound a little like work, but if it were work, it was the kind he could stand. He paused the car at the top of the hill to make sure there was no one coming the other way first, and then he took a left at the top of the ridge onto a dirt logging road that overlooked the swamp. The pulloff was hidden by mountain laurel and rhododendrons, and he eased the car to a halt. Whistling tunelessly, he opened the trunk and got out the shovel and the feedbag, placing them on the ground in front of him. He sat on the lip of the trunk to slide his sneakers off and his waders on.

In a moment, he was bounding down the slope towards the swamp in the half-light, and he made the hundred yards in about ten seconds, halting at the heavy fringe of brush that lined the swamp. His heart was pounding madly from exertion and excitement, and he took a moment to catch his breath. Once he was in the swamp—and even here in the brush at the edge of it—he was safe. He gazed out over the level grayness of the swamp, at what he liked to think of as his hundred-acre spread. He listened for an unusual sound, the rustle of leaves or the clink of metal, anything to indicate that he was not alone. But of course he was. Nobody messed around in there among the mud and skeeters. Actually, it was pretty easy to get turned around in there. A body could spend hours walking in circles inside and never get nearer the fringes, even though Jimmy figured it to be less than a mile from one end to the other.

He could hear Dalton on the other side of the swamp beginning to hammer on something. Old man Dalton. He was better than a freakin' watch, he was so predictable! The flatness of the ground and all the water made the sound seem much closer than it was, and the ringing sound echoed back and forth between the garage and the hill behind him like two men talking: *ka-CHINK!* the hammer in Dalton's hand said, then *KA-chink!* the hill answered. The conversations overlapped where Dalton hit out of time, every fourth or fifth hit or so. Jimmy watched the ragged wisps of his breath even out. He moved slowly until he found the deer trail, then ducked beneath the brush and eased into the swamp.

Off in the distance, he could hear the hum of semis on the big road that shaved two hours off the trip to the city. Jimmy loved the place. It was full of sex and drugs and money—and forget about the rock and roll! Nearer to him, he could also hear the rattle of dried leaves beneath a bare blueberry bush, and saw the white and black of a chickadee's cap sharply contrasted against the muted grays and browns of late spring. The bird perched on a bare blueberry twig, then flew to the ground and half-buried itself in the litter, wings and leaves flying for a second or two. A moment later the bird flew back to his branch and gave the *chick-a-DEE-DEE-DEE* call. He ignored Jimmy until only a few feet separated them, then flew off deeper into the swamp.

The skunk cabbage was up. The big green rolls of leaves looked like cabbage and smelled way worse than a skunk, more like road-kill, Jimmy had always thought. Hell, even the flies were fooled by it; when the plant flowered, it would be covered with flies buzzing around looking for the meat to lay their eggs in. Jimmy's feet crunched through the thin crust of ice that fringed the sphagnum moss and muck, and he sank in up to his mid-calves. That was good, he thought. The ground being partly frozen, he could muck up the hills faster, and it being a dry winter, the muck would stay where it was put, not run off in ropy gobs like it did later in the year.

He held a course for the big old dead tree on the other side of the swamp, trying to stay on the hummocks where he could. The fringe of last years growth sprouted from them like an old man's hair. Some of them would lean over when they were stepped on, so it was a delicate balancing act for Jimmy to keep from getting pitched on his ass in muck. Occasionally a footstep would put him in up to his thigh, and he would have to grab the top of his wader with both hands to pull himself free or risk losing the wader and getting crap all over him. He didn't crave having to wash his jeans, or explain to some busybody why he was all gunked up to begin with.

It took about twenty minutes to reach the patch, still camouflaged with dead branches and swampgrass, just as he had left it before the last hunting season started.

Auntie had been so happy when he had gotten his first hunting license back in junior high.

"Well, Jimmy! That's a good thing, surely," she said. "I'd so love a nice fat grouse to roast or a venison chop from time to time."

"Well, we'll just see what kind of luck we have, Auntie," was what he had said, using the name he knew she hated. What he was thinking was *I'd like to see you hold your breath waiting.*

Fact was, that was the only way to be out and about in the fall without having to answer questions. And Jimmy hated questions almost as much as he hated being straight. He'd even tried to get stoned before these runs, but he got so paranoid and cotton-mouthed that it actually was better to be straight long enough to do the hour or so worth of work first and then get blasted at his leisure.

He hummed as he cut the thick black muck from the edges of the pool, using his shovel as a knife to cut out blocks of the smelly gunk loose. When it dried and got some air to it, it would be almost all the fertilizer the plants would need to grow full and bushy. And he'd have a ready place to get water for the fertilizer mix he favored using. Just like the TV commercial said, it worked miracles.

The sun was beginning to warm things up a bit, and he thought back to when he had started planting. He figured to avoid work completely when he was green, and that's the way *High Times* made it sound, too. Just find a spot like this, throw up some islands in the middle of it, plant your seeds, visit once during the year to pull the males, and wait until the fall to harvest nice, fat, fragrant buds of sensimilla.

Twenty-five hundred a pound. That was how much good weed went for, and a good patch would yield five to ten pounds, easy. That was the math that got him started, but the problem that first year was that the slugs, the deer and the voles liked what he was growing as much as he did. Ironically, it was the tease of riches that taught Jimmy the idea of disappointment. Each year, he had losses, and every winter he made plans. When he figured one thing out, like rat poison for the voles, some new worry would spring up. One year he figured to have the crop of his dreams, only to discover bud rot, which made a beer-can sized bud dissolve into nothing in a day. Another season, he lost his best patch to a bear that decided it was just the place with water aplenty and lots of blueberries.

He figured he was a match for whatever Mother Nature could dish out. His daddy didn't raise no fool. He finished mucking up the hill, reached down into the feedbag and sprinkled lime to sweeten the soil and fertilizer to help growth, and then he folded both into the muck, which still oozed out thin streams of black liquid into the pool. He pulled out a bag of potting soil and coated the gelatinous mass to give the seeds a drier layer to sprout in. He'd tried it without, once, and the seeds that he had painstakingly separated from the good homegrown he had bought just turned white and slimy from mold.

He pulled the film canister out and carefully scattered seed culled from last year's crop. He had gotten scientific about it all, actually keeping records as to which females had been fertilized by which males. Sometimes he even painted the pollen from one plant onto another, to get the characteristics he was after, mostly to be kick-ass weed with big, full buds, but also to be resistant to the rot and able to take extremes of wet and dry weather. If you didn't like the weather in Pennsylvania, all you had to do was wait a minute, they always said.

Oh, how they loved those big huge tops in the city, tops they could wave around and brag about to their friends, like fine wine or fast cars!

He covered the mounds with a bit more potting soil, sprinkled slug pellets around, and set a half a dozen mousetraps with peanut butter for the voles. Then, he spent a good half an hour recovering it all with peat moss, sawgrass and sprigs of brush until he thought even a hunter walking over the ground would not notice that there was anything unusual, just another series of hummocks in the swamp.

Of course, later on when the leaves were out and he put up the fencing to keep out the deer, a blind boy would know what was what, but nobody came in there at that time of year. The skeeters, ticks, the heat, the thick brush, the poison sumac and the stinking muck were all the reasons a body would need to avoid the place. Some folks might walk the edges for blueberries, but that would be about it until bear season, when pretty every foot of the place would see humans.

By then, he would have the plants hanging upside down in his attic, spending his nights stripping the leaf from the bud and smoking, packing the buds in gallon pickle jars that he would set out in the sun on a hot fall day until the droplets of moisture disappeared from the sides of the glass and the air was thick with the smell of the herb. Then he would seal them up and hide them in the stone-row behind his house, to be cracked open when he needed a few thou or a big bud to smoke. Occasionally, he would find one he had forgotten about, and then it would be like Christmas, sort of, because each plant and each year had its own character, just like a person or a wine, he guessed.

It beat the hell out of working a real job. He finished that hill and worked his way towards the next one. Ten hills, at maybe five pounds per? He might make a hundred thou this year. Across the swamp he could hear the clatter of scaffolding being stacked, and the echo booming from behind him. He giggled and waved his middle finger in the air.

"Thanks a lot for the use of the land, Dalton, you old shit."

Chat concentrated on the job at hand, carefully guiding the oxyacetylene torch along the welded strands of thick iron rope that made up the blasting net. Being cautious meant that he would not have to grind down too much of the stubs left on his doorframe. While he worked, the pilot sat on a milk crate that Chat had dragged out for him. He didn't move much, just swiveled his head to take in the few cars that passed. Other than that, he sat stone still like a man who has been trained to wait for something that might only last a moment. Maybe like a hunter. Maybe like a musician. Chat finished taking down the netting and the scaffolding, and he paused to consider the pilot before he went inside to call Homer down with the backhoe.

"You care for some coffee?" he asked, finally.

For a moment the pilot did not stir, as if he had not heard Chat. But after a long pause, he turned to face him.

"Are you talking to me?"

He didn't ask with an attitude or with anger, no chip-on-the-shoulder that Chat could see. It was just a question that meant nothing more than it seemed.

"Yes, sir. No one else here, and I'm not one to talk to myself when there's others around. That might give you a bad name in some places, eh?"

"It might at that. I'd like that coffee, thanks. The past day or so hasn't been what I'd call a day in the park, that's for sure."

"Can't have been pleasant spending it with that boss of *yours,* I'd bet. No disrespect meant, of course."

The pilot stood and extended his hand, and said, "None taken. My name's Ty. Ty Herrington."

"Chat Dalton. Pleased to make your acquaintance, Ty."

"Likewise," Ty said. "That was a nice piece of work you did on the blades, there. You had training?"

" Training? On helicopters?" Chat laughed easily at that and said, " No, I just looked it over real careful before I started. Wasn't all that hard. So let me get my Uncle down here with the backhoe, and we can get you folks out of here, then."

"Sounds like a plan, Chat. Don't mind me. I won't break anything."

Chat grinned at him as he walked back inside. *The man wasn't half bad,* he thought. Darn shame he was keeping such bad company.

"Make yourself at home. I'll be back when Unc gets here with the backhoe."

Chat walked back inside to the small room off the bays that had the counter, the cash register and the bathrooms. He sat down on the cracked leather swivel chair and dialed Homer up, told him to come on down, and to bring some coffee with him. He had given up the fight about keeping a Mr. Coffee down here. Homer was petrified it would short-circuit and fry the place, and Chat had gone through three of them, all of which disappeared under odd circumstances. Of course Homer denied any knowledge of their whereabouts, but that didn't fool either of them.

"Unc," Chat had said, " I use a torch that pulls fifty *amps*, and you're worrying about a *Mr. Coffee?*"

"Made by the Asians to burn us to the ground!" Homer had howled, and so Chat had to call whenever he felt like a cup. Most days Chat didn't mind.

While he waited for Homer, Chat tallied the bills, looking up from time to time. Ty was walking about the bays, examining the chopper, the workbenches, the racks of fan belts and head gaskets, all items that had dimmed into nothingness for Chat. He wondered, *What would it be like to see this all for the first time, to actually see the nubs on the block walls, the one crooked window at the side, really any detail of the place at all?* Maybe it had simply become the backdrop for his life, the sort of thing by which a man defines himself, and not a place outside himself at all.

Chat shook off the thought. That sort of thinking was against the word and the book. Defining *yourself!* The idea smacked of the great sin, and he knew that he was prone to that. He came from proud stock, and that might be his undoing if he didn't mind his p's and q's. He went back to tallying the receipts and had just added the one from McAdam to the pile when he heard Homer's backhoe chugging down the road. That one check was as much as the whole week's receipts.

9

⇒ CHAPTER NINE ⇐

Cotton-mouthed and groggy, Jo-Jo awoke, a good hour later than usual, and stumbled into the bathroom to take a leak, leaning against the wall with his eyes closed while he relieved himself.

Something was poking around at the edge of his memory, some little bitterness in the fun he had last night, and he teased at that while he examined his eyes in the mirror.

Damn. They're redder than they ought to be, he thought, pulling one lower lid down to examine it more closely. In the mirror, his hand trembled slightly. He hadn't really gotten that drunk. He'd had, what? Ten or twelve beers, really a light night for him.

And there it was: Kate. They'd been "dating" for years now, a few, maybe three times a month, and the arrangement suited him fine. Low maintenance and no promises. Something was going on with her last evening, like she was close to doing the thing that would surely drive him away for good.

Joseph Theodoro Pasquale hated "the talk." He was—as he had made it very clear to almost every girl he had ever dated—not built for marriage. He wasn't cruel or ignorant, yet even he had to admit he was being selfish about the way he saw relationships. In the end, he just told himself that there was no sense pretending. He was what he was. He did treat women nicely while he was with them. It was just that, for him, a little woman went a long way. Maybe he was ADD or something, but he just couldn't get into the idea of one woman forever.

How the hell did anybody do that? It must be like eating nothing but hamburgers, breakfast, lunch and dinner.

He remembered now. Last night he had seen a look in Kate's eye, the little awkward pauses in between lines that wanted to be filled in with the beginning of a conversation that could last ten years and never be finished, and that surprised him. He'd never taken Kate for someone who would forget the basic truth of the relationship, of him. She had always been too sensible for that. What might have changed? He couldn't think of a single thing.

He shook his head and stuck his hand out in front of him, willing it to stop its minute vibrating. After a minute, he had it stopped, but a faint numbness still troubled him, as if he had fallen asleep on his hand. He'd dry out for a couple days, he guessed. Couldn't hurt; might help.

He went back into the bedroom, threw on a pair of sweats, and slumped down the out-sized stairs. Outside the huge atrium windows, the sun was shining brightly, and a soft west wind had stirred up the surface of the lake down below, chopping the surface into a million facets of silver and gold light, bending graceful arcs out of the slim green branches of the weeping willows that lined the far shore. He could make out flecks of bright yellow as well: some goldfinchs were flying from one tree to the next in great swoops. Closer to the dock he noted the ripples of a muskrat's head cleaving the water and leaving behind a shimmery wake that fanned out until it disappeared in the reeds.

He went out to the kitchen, snapping the coffeepot on and grabbing the paper. In ten minutes, he was in his chair, sipping good hot coffee, reading the slim local paper that detailed a few weddings, two or three state police blotters on speeders or accidents up on the big road. He scanned Ann Landers and the cartoons—what was funny about some of them? Some of them were really just drawn soap-operas, although he did like Dilbert and the Lockhorns. He turned to the community page and read about the meeting of the garden club and the Optimist's, about a tricky-tray to be held at the Elks to benefit a girl with cancer, Sunday's fire company breakfast, and the big tire sale over at the new Sears in Fiesterville. Jo-Jo twitched when he saw the picture of that geek Malchio glad handing a mock check for twenty grand to the United Way chairwoman, who looked to Jo-Jo like she could miss a meal.

He threw the paper down for a minute and looked out the broad windows. A flight of ducks came in to land on the bright lake, and Jo-Jo realized it would soon be time to put the boats in the water. He felt no hint of excitement about that, and it troubled him.

He took stock: leather chair with magic fingers, big-screen TV, a house that would run the average slob a half a mil, his own lake, couple boats, a bank account with lots of cash in it, and the opportunity to have fun most every weekend. He was doing all right for a kid who dropped out in the tenth grade. He was, however, beginning to get some flack about all the building going on from his friends and acquaintances. He was sure Chat and the rest were going to be right royally pissed when the news of the low-income housing project hit the fan, right down the road from Chat's old homestead. But, hey, at least it wasn't him who was building it.

It should have been, though. Malchio was a rip-off and a worm, screwing everybody and then not even building the damned things right. He eyed the picture in the paper again. He steals a few hundred grand a month building crap, and then he gives twenty thou back to some bunch of community swells and gets his picture all over the paper to boot. Big deal. Not that Jo-Jo was a bleeding heart or anything, but the people Malchio ripped off, dark as they might be, couldn't really afford to be donating their life's savings to build libraries or half-way houses or whatever.

Jo-Jo, uncharacteristically, sighed. He was not one given to morose thoughts, all gloom and doom, not usually. So why did he feel so thin this morning, so fragile?

He sipped more coffee. Probably just a touch of the flu or something. Or age? He hoped it wasn't that. Maybe the same kind of thing was behind Kate's looks as well. Perhaps it was that biological clock he kept hearing about. He hoped it was a passing phase. She was an old steady, and he would hate to lose her. Hell, cruising in Fiesterville was fun if it *was* fun, and not something that had to be done, and that was the way he wanted to keep it.

He tossed the paper on the chair, went into the kitchen, slugged down an OJ and a fistful of vitamins, and went back upstairs.

He'd go to sleep and start the day over. Maybe he'd get it right the second time.

Sterling almost succeeded in sleeping through the alarm, hitting the snooze button five times before he pulled himself out of bed. It was almost nine, and Sterling had a choice to make. He could shower and shave, or he could have breakfast, but if he was to be on time to pick up Bobby Lee, he couldn't do both.

Last night's spaghetti was long gone, and the sour stomach he had made the choice easy. Bobby didn't care what he looked like. He grabbed a book and pulled on last night's clothes, brushed his teeth hurriedly, and was out the door in five minutes. Overnight, the Nova had gotten another ticket for overnight parking. When he had first moved there, the secretary at the township office had waited until he had a few dozen, then she would call him up to pay them, so it was like having a parking pass, kind of. At a buck a ticket, it wasn't so bad at all.

Then, last winter, he had gotten a notice from the magistrate, Chat's Aunt Jenna, for $37.50. The tickets were five bucks now. The rest was court costs. That was the end of his nice little arrangement. Now he paid weekly and tried to remember to move the car over to the parking lot on the next block before he went to bed. He cussed a little under his breath, grabbed the ticket and jumped in the car, swung by the Wa-Wa that had just gone up by the highway to pick up a large coffee and hockey-puck breakfast sandwich, then zoomed over to get Bobby. Bobby might not know how to read or write, but he sure could tell time, and if Sterling was late, Bobby would be a pest all morning.

He pulled up to the group home with three minutes to spare. Bobby was standing on the porch, twenty ounce Pepsi in hand, a Saint Louis Card's ball cap on his head, New York Yankee jacket on, rocking back and forth on his heels. He was an odd Downs syndrome fellow: his parents were Chinese, and between the lack of epicanthal folds and the fact that he was borne in Taiwan, folks often didn't know that he *was* Downs, which of course Sterling loved best of all. Sterling pulled up and beeped, and Bobby came bounding down the steps, piled into the front, and handed the book to Sterling.

"You read 'em," Bobby said, a touch too loud for Sterling's comfort.

"What did we talk about, Bobby?" Sterling said, patiently. Bobby looked like he was trying hard to remember.

"What did we say about greeting people?" Sterling prompted.

"Ah! You say, '*Say Morning*!' Morning! Now you read 'em!" Bobby said, obviously pleased with himself.

"Alright, Bobbo. Wait till we get to the park, okay?" A few minutes later they pulled into the small strip of green, found a park bench and sat down in the warm morning sun, Sterling with his coffee and Bobby his Pepsi, and Sterling picked up the history and said, "Where did we leave off? Ah, I think I remember. Here it is:

> Plenty is hidden there in the almost-rectangle that is Pennsylvania, almost exactly twice as long as it is high, 310 average miles across, 158 miles top to bottom except for the pursed lips that suck at the breast of Lake Erie. One thing in abundance is coal, packed down in the Carboniferous Era. Over a course of some 200 million years, plants lived and grew and then died, being mashed into peat, then lignite, and then soft coal, covering at least one third the state at some depth or another, sometimes veins half a mile thick.
>
> Boatload after boatload of immigrants debouched in the cities; the more adventurous of them escaping as soon as they could to find the land of milk and honey they had heard about. They slogged over muddy corduroy roads into the hills of the Delaware Uplands, insinuated themselves into the smaller hills of Nazareth, farmed contentedly the rolling hills of Lititz. First the Dutch, then the Swedes, finally the English made homes, followed by the Irish, the Mennonites, the Italians, the Poles. They came to escape starvation, persecution, ignorance and poverty. They brought garlic and sausage and scurvy and the pox, pasta and potatoes, and valiant, desperate hope.

"Hope? Hope not home, nah. Not home!" Bobby interrupted.

"Not *that* Hope, Bobby. Not Hope, your care-provider at your home."

"No. Hope not home. Not home, nah. Hope go to town t'day!"

"Right. But this is a different hope, like when I say 'I hope you feel better,'" Sterling tried to explain.

"I fine. How you?"

Sterling laughed.

"I'm fine, too. You want me to read more, or should we take a walk?"

"Morning! You read 'em!"

"Alright. Now:

The only witch trial in the state occurred in February of 1683 when Margaret Mattson was tried and exonerated in Philadelphia. Apparently the persecution of the Quakers by the Puritans was an object lesson not lost on William Penn's progeny. The Mennonites came in 1683—by 1776 one third of the state was German— Pennsylvania "Dutch." In 1718, with the clearing of the highlands and the installation of the house of Hanover in England, waves of Scotch-Irish arrived, dispossessed when their British overlords discovered that they could make more money with sheep than with tenant farmers.

Besides, sheep never complain, nor do they arm themselves and fight back bloodily or corrupt the air with heathen fiddle tunes. The Scotch-Irish had nothing left to do but to jump on a ship with their fiddles and a hope-shaped heart, to search the small dells up in the hills where they could try to recreate some of what they had left. Not that the land was much similar, all wooded and hidden as it was, certainly not the somber heath that they loved.

But they survived. In 1737 a walking purchase was required to get more land from the Leni Lenape Indians, who called themselves simply "The People." The Lenape had the lived there some 10,000 years, so long that the other tribes called them "The Grandfathers". All the land bounded by the distance a man could walk in a day and a half, that was the deal, but Edward Marshall ran the full time, covering all the ground from Easton, where he started, to well beyond the limits of the Blue Ridge. Settlers called them the Delawares —misnamed from Lord De La Warr, the Frenchman who had been first to sail up the estuary that now bears his name. Imagine pasting your name on such a sweep of nature!

Eventually the Lenape lost patience. They went on raids, killing whites throughout the Eastern counties, until the good folks in Philly asked Sullivan to cut a road up to the Wyoming Valley, the valley that would eventually lend its name to a new state, one of the new, large, square ones. Tedyuscung, last of the Lenape chiefs, calmed things down somewhat afterwards. After all, the Lenape were forward-looking, in their own way. But that peace could not endure. What peace can when you covet your neighbor's goods?

The Brits invited the Shawnee from the Carolinas to come and supplant the Lenape, and as soon as they had, they were in turn invited by the Brits to leave. Follow "Shawnee" as a place name right across the country, where the big road now runs. Follow it all the way to Oklahoma and watch it disappear north into Canada, along with the last of them who made their way there at the close of the 1800s.

If they had known that the whites were like the buffalo and the fish that teamed in the rivers, the passenger pigeons that blackened the sky for a day at a time, might they have pushed them back into the sea? In the last days, many of them perhaps wished that they had.

The Italians came to mine slate, the Irish to build the railroads and the Poles to mine the coal. It was *the* ethnic state, proud of its kielbasa, prosciutto, corned beef, galumpkes, and scrapple as well as its peaches and pears and apples, fields of soy and corn and summer and winter wheat, sorghum, alfalfa and hay, proud of the first soldiers to fight the Brits, those intrepid "First Defenders."

But Pennsylvanians are largely silent about the only President that hailed from the Keystone State—really one of the nation's four commonwealths—silent because Buchanan was so abominably bad and delayed the Civil War only four scant years before more than a million and a half lads lay dead or wounded. We *were* proud, though, that we compelled the first use of force by the Feds to make the colonies and the colonists toe the line. The State motto should be "Try Us And See!" After the Feds' first use of force against a colony, the tax on corn whisky was a fact of law. The whisky rebellion was history.

"Hissssssssteeeeeeee!" Bobby said.

"Yes, hissssssstee indeed, Bobbo. Now listen. This part is just the way it is up here, far as I've been able to tell."

There is that stubborn side to the state: more small farmers that any other state, more municipal governments. Pennsylvania imports the most trash (Thanks, New York!), drinks more beer than wine, more whiskey than water. Drinking was part of the old blue-collar tradition: when a lad risks his life and limb in coal breakers or the mines, why not leave him have a beer or two? Up in "the valley" they would say "couple two-tree" in places like the Electric City, Dupont, Olyphant, Jim Thorpe, White Haven. The coal belt is a land of slagheaps and culm banks, and clear, sparkling streams dead as any moonscape from too much acid mine drainage.

Then there is the occasional mine subsidence. Ole Joe wakes up one morning and his house is cold, and he figures, "trouble with the furnace." Trouble it is, alright: the furnace and everything else in the basement is at the bottom of a thee hundred foot-deep mine shaft, and Ole Joe's basement is now without a bottom because his house is on top of a mine maybe his great-grandaddy worked. King Coal was supposed to leave the last pillars of coal in place to keep the roof up, but the supports looked too much like money now in the time just before the mine closed, and the last thing they did was to strip those supports out to leave ole Joe's house suspended all these years over a hidden void.

"Void!" Bobby said, then, making a race-car sound, said, "Vvvvvvvvvvoid!" A middle-aged couple who had settled on a bench down the way from Bobby and Sterling, looked at the pair again and began whispering feverishly.

"Probably think we're gay or something," Sterling muttered. "Old farts."

"Hehe. Derling say 'farts!'"

"Shhh. Bobby, listen, now:"

The collapse of King Coal! It's the 'Rust Belt' now—just listen to Billy Joel! 'The Steel' as Bethlehem Steel was known back in the day, is now just a memory! The Steel, the giant that ruled the teens, the twenties, the whole first half of the century. That mighty engine of commerce and trade used to make the Lehigh River gorge hum with traffic, built the iron that created the skylines of New York and Chicago, built the steel that made the ships that replaced the burned and bombed out hulks in Pearl Harbor, made the munitions and the guns that brought down the Axis.

Now it was miles of shuttered buildings, the gated entrances every ten blocks that saw thousands of men—during the war, women, too—walking in a dark and sinewy stream three times a day in both directions, those gates were now shut and silent. In those days, a coffee truck parked at one of the gates was a gold mine, something handed down from father to son.

All that is a dream now, just as the sons and daughters that proudly sacrificed their lives in the big WWII are little more than a dream. One in five that served in that war came from the Keystone State. That was right and just: Pennsylvania was once the third most populous state in the Union, even without many large cities. Now, the young folks slowly bleed out of the little dells and hollows, away from Delabole and Frackville, Hughesville, Altoona, Huntingdon, Bellefonte, Dubois, out of the hills and towards the third-world states. As hard as life was, to the old-timers it seems that was the time of glory.

Sterling stopped reading for a moment, took a sip of coffee, then looked at the leafless branches laced above him. Bobby tried mimicking him, the foam of the Pepsi shooting out the sides of the bottle as he brought the bottle down too suddenly. He wiped his face with his sleeve and moved his head backwards to look upwards.

"No leaves yet, Bobbo. Limbs are bare," Sterling said, pensively.

"Hehehe! Derling say '*bare*'!" Bobby said, loud enough for an older passing couple to stop an instant and scowl at them.

"Morning! " Sterling said to them, then he turned to Bobby and said again, "Bobbo….shhhhhhh. Don't bug them. Here, let me read some more, then, alright?"

"Morning! You read 'em!" Bobby nodded, happy.

Sterling began again:

All that rust, and then the landscape, too. Now, at this time of the spring *before* the greening fringes hills with hope, birdsongs lift the still-cold heart, the fecund smell of damp earth inviting the spade, fat trout in the restless brooks, the goose-bumpy caress of soft southerly breezes, no, *now*, the landscape is gray. From the road, all one sees is everyone's back yard, full of wrecked trucks, old car chassis, burn barrels, and mounds of wood that meant to be something more than a place for chipmunks but missed the chance.

Gray is the fact of the matter, top to bottom, sky, land, trees, all leaden, bare, desolate.

From the back roads and the back yards, the woods extend as far as the eye can see. All the trunks and limbs are etched out against the forest floor with sad hints of brown making that gray seem sickly, the great gentle curves of mountains fringed on top with the same color fringed—muted!—with silver. Skies are leaden, and scuds of clouds wrap around the tops of First Mountain, Kittatinny Ridge, Godfrey's Ridge, Tussey Mountain, Roundtop, the gray settling like shards of dirty wool in the crevasses of the Boulder Field, hundreds of acres covered with boulders the size of freight-train cars or houses.

The entire landscape was left negligently when the last glaciers receded, leaving long sinuous hills called escars and round ones called drumlins, or huge terminal moraines shaped like Camelback. The land is porous, too, and so water is everywhere, on the tops of hills and at the bottoms, squirting through rock-faces where local wags fool the new folks by sneaking out at night to color the huge icicles—come see the amazing natural phenomena!—the variegated ice bright translucent blues and reds, cold but festive.

Through the gray underbrush the insistent litter beams yellow, red, blue and white. Coffee cups, beer cans, once-red Marlboro packs and oil cans lay half-buried in the leaves and yellow plastic bags, snagged in the brush near the roads, snap in the breeze. Roads are covered with grit from all the anti-skid material that has built up over the winter.

The human debris is joined by bedraggled carcasses of deer skeletonized by months of the freeze-thaw cycle, the same one that makes the clay swell to twenty times its volume, heaving roads like they were paper, peeling off great chunks of banks and eventually roadsides—Monongahela—Indian for "Place where the steep banks fall"—popping up pot-holes like boils all over the Commonwealth's record-breaking miles of roads.

No, in a few weeks things might look hopeful, but the mud month of March gives little to hang onto except the warming air and the slightly-longer days. Perhaps the sound of bat and ball is enough, the excited squeals of a pick-up game in a sandlot or on the basketball court near the old school. Perhaps the eerie flashes of red lights arching across the lawns and golf-courses is cause enough for hope as the old-timers and the kids search for night crawlers, trying to get the five hundred needed to last the trout season. For some, just thinking about the shape of the garden-to-be is enough, summer sweat and 'skeeters all just a conjecture in the mind, not the for-sure thing they must become. In this state, much is hidden, and what is hidden is often forgotten until it is at last revealed.

Sterling stopped reading, glanced at his watch and realized it was almost lunchtime. He closed the book, anticipating trouble from Bobby about it, but all Bobby did was finish his soda, lean his head back for a moment to look again at the branches, then jump up and quietly say, "bare."

10

⇒ CHAPTER TEN ⇐

Homer pulled in with a stingy-brim Stetson on his head and a thermos of coffee in his hand.

"Morning, Unc. See you got the coffee."

"Morning yourself, Chat. See you got company," Homer said, hitching his head towards Ty who had moved to the edge of the parking lot and was peering into the swamp.

"Yeah, that's the pilot. Guy named Ty Herrington. He seems all right. Hey, Ty. Come on over. Meet my Uncle here."

Ty stood for a second longer, looking into the swamp, and then he turned and walked over to Homer and thrust out his hand.

"How do, sir?" Ty said.

Homer almost smiled.

"Fine, sir, fine. You like our liddle wildlife preserve there?" Homer said, pointing to the swamp.

"Somebody's in there," Ty said shrugging.

"Sure, sure. Mr. Turtle and Mrs. Deer and the huckleberry twins," Homer said, laughing.

"I know that sounds nutty. But I saw him in there, for a second here and there. Clear over the other side of the swamp. I saw the light flash off of something first. That's what caught my eye."

Chat and Homer looked at each other, then at Ty.

"So where'd you learn to see so much? Slicker like you," Homer said suspiciously.

Chat could see that Homer was getting to Ty. No wonder there. That was pretty much what Homer did for a living.

"Well, I can't blame you for being doubtful. But you might be surprised to find out that not everybody from the city is really from the city. I mean," he said, waving away Homer's attempt to make a comment, "I wasn't always from there. I grew up in Lexington."

"Oh, Lord." Chat groaned.

"Lexington? Oh, whooooo! Well ain't you something then? Mr. High and Mighty!"

"Unc, please. Ty, I'm sorry."

"Snotty so-and-sos. They invented everything. Hmmmppf," Homer said, hugging the thermos to his chest like it was a blanket.

"Never mind," Ty said to Chat. "Where the hell's he want me to be from?"

"Unc, please, fer goodness sake. Can't you see this fella's all right?"

Homer retreated to the backhoe. Chat pulled Ty aside for a minute.

"Listen. Not that I asked you to set this dang thing down here, but I understand a thing or two about how things happen. Unc was watching you fella's when you landed, and he claims you had a mind about trespassing. That true?"

"With McAdam, you do what you can, but it's usually damn little you can do. Like they used to say where I was from, you can always tell a McAdam. You just can't tell him much."

"Maybe him and Homer are members of the same tribe, then," Chat said. "They always used to tell me not to try to teach a pig to sing 'cause it's a waste of your time and it annoys the pig. Lemme tell you just a little about Unc. The whole story would take a book, and we ain't got that. But he got it in his mind early on that the good folks in Kentucky stole every last thing they took credit for, starting with the long rifle, Danny Boone, good race horses and bluegrass."

"You mean the turf grass? Bluegrass?"

"Yep. And the music. Most especially the music. Something about Bill Monroe and his guitar and harmonica player. He never makes any sense the few times I've tried to pin him down to what the real ruckus is about. Anyhow, when you said Lexington, that wasn't so good since Lexington is about as Kentucky as you get."

"Especially since he's got the coffee and the backhoe," Ty said, as if he didn't really care how this it all turned out.

The two men stood there for a moment, watching Homer leaning up against the machine and glaring at them.

"So we don't get the rotors put on today, then?" Ty said finally.

"Get 'em put on never, if he doesn't soften somehow. Although it seems like that wouldn't be just a tragedy from where you stand."

"Well, I do get an hourly rate. So this isn't so bad as I thought, relaxing here and enjoying the country, getting paid a couple hundred an hour to sit and watch the world. Hey, I was born in Wheeling. Think that might help?" Ty said, brightening.

"Well. Let's just try *that* out on Unc, then. Maybe that'll be enough."

Chat paused for a moment, looking into the swamp intently.

"You really see somebody in that swamp?"

"You don't get to be a pilot with bad eyes."

"Curious. Let's go see what we can do about Unc."

"Chat? One thing?"

"Sure. What?"

"You did a nice job of pulling those rotors. But if it's all the same to you, or even if it isn't, I want a hand at putting them back on."

"No breaks on the labor," Chat laughed.

"I was thinking to avoid breaks myself. They don't take rebates in heaven, huh?"

"Well, let's see what we can do with Unc over there."

When Homer heard that Ty had been a Wheeling issue, his tune changed, and he happily turned over his thermos to Ty. Ty winced when he saw the floor jacks coming out, but said nothing, and they had the chopper back out in the lot in a minute.

Homer pulled the backhoe into the garage, and with chains and blankets, slung the first rotor to the bucket and backed it carefully up to the chopper. Ty was at the workbench and grabbed up several tools it would have taken Chat a half an hour to realize he needed. With the ladder still padded, they got the first rotor mounted and then the second in only half the time. Chat watched as Ty worked the hydraulics first, sticking his head out the window to verify that they were behaving as they should.

"You all want to stand clear now," he hollered out the window, and he started the blades up. Chat winced at the dust and grit that was kicked loose when the blades first started, thinking that he had maybe better get a power washer in there and clean up the blacktop. After a few moments, Ty took the craft up a few hundred feet, backed it, made it go forward, and brought it in a lazy loop back to the exact spot it had started. He killed the engines and re-emerged, a satisfied look on his face.

"Well, she seems to be none the worse for wear. I have to remember that. Backhoe. Who'd have thought? I notice you didn't monkey with the hydraulics," Ty said, admiration in his voice.

"No sense doing extra work, huh? I could see I could pop the blade without messing with it. Besides, those fittings are metric. And *way* larger than any engine block plug I got. These things hard to fly?"

"Well, not when things are going right, no."

"So you work all your life for a *moment*, so you can make something *not* happen? Like that?"

Ty laughed.

"Something like that."

They were all standing on the edge of the swamp and peering into it and drinking coffee when McAdam arrived, wearing a sardonic smile on his face. He coasted the Vespa to a halt in front of the chopper, cut the engine and dismounted.

"Well, well. Nice little love fest there. Get this thing in the air," McAdam said to Ty, and walked up the steps, disappearing into the dark interior.

"Job market's gotta be good for a fella with your skills, eh?" Chat said, holding out his hand.

"Stranger things have happened. Thanks for the hospitality, Chat. Maybe we'll meet again, later days," he said, shaking Chat's hand firmly.

Chat watched Ty load the scooter in the storage bay. He secured it with webbing to hooks in the wall, snugging them carefully, and re-testing and tightening each strap after he had affixed another to the bike. Finally he was satisfied, and turned and waved.

"Adios, amigos, " he said, and mounted the stairs, pulling the door closed behind him. In a moment, the rotors had whirred into a blur of energy, and the chopper rose slowly, circling the swamp once before streaking off to the east.

Hugh began by mixing the martini so long denied him. He splashed the vermouth into the shaker glass, swirled it once, and up-ended the glass over the trashcan. After he had packed the glass with ice, he added the vodka in ritual slowness, finally spinning the stirring spoon a full turn to the left and once right before he strained it into the frosted glass he removed from the freezer while the drink rested.

Outside, the sky was so clear that Hugh could see the Empire State Building almost as soon as they were up to cruising altitude; there was not a single blot of white on the blue that stretched off towards his city. The ride was so smooth that not a ripple appeared on the surface of the drink, and Hugh daintily sipped it with eyes closed, sagging back into his posh seat with a relief like any traveler would feel returning home. He thought to savor the image of that cracker Dalton, and, like any good athlete, imagine himself with his foot upon the neck of the worm that denied him even a moment of control. But in the instant he saw Dalton in his mind's eye, standing there with wrench in hand, the image that was called forth made the sweet snap of the martini grow bitter in his mouth. Almost immediately, he was thinking about his father, and about Lexington.

It was a rule for Hugh that he should not think about those things, about his father's egregious lack of foresight in the way that he had handled things in Lexington. He was not bitter. He had to learn what not to do and how not to behave when the issue was conquest. So what was the message here? Never underestimate your enemy? That might be a good one. Hugh took a sip and found his taste returning. Forewarned is forearmed. Another sweet sip. The mountains were reduced to hills, and Hugh was already looking forward to returning to his perch high above the pestilent masses. And, finally, the third-time-is-a-charm clincher: To conquer, make your enemy your friend. Ahhhh. He set down his glass, the milky frost of condensation marked in three places where his fingers rested on the glass. Hugh rested his head against the cushion briefly, relishing the discipline that would be required to right this wrong and bring the cretins to heel.

He picked up the yellow legal pad and began scribbling furiously, punching up the computer and logging on with one hand and scrawling notes in haphazard order on the pad, connecting and ordering them with sweeping arrows and numbers until the page looked as if it would sink into oblivion from blue ink. To Hugh, it was growing clearer by the minute.

11

⇒ CHAPTER ELEVEN ⇐

Sarah awoke to the sounds of birds and the quiet murmur of the stream that ran behind the inn that she had stumbled upon the evening prior. It was a bit run-down, but the rooms were cheap at twenty bucks a night, and the music the night before, country though it was, was fun to listen to and to watch. She was especially taken by the fiddler, although she couldn't point to a single thing about him that was attractive, except maybe his music and the fact that he obviously had a very healthy libido. She could use some of *that*.

She stretched, feeling luxurious, and peeked over to where Josh lay. His head was buried in the blankets and he was snoring softly. *Just like his old man that way,* she thought. She pushed that thought away. No sense spoiling a perfectly nice morning with those kinds of things. She was surprised to find that her stomach was growling for food. She slapped it twice, and then sat up in bed. That woman last night? Kate? Kate. She had said there was a good diner up the road. A walk in the country, with probably no muggers. *Gimme a man and I'm complete,* she thought.

She sat up and put her feet on the floor, twisting her back to the left, and to the right until she heard the bones pop, and then she slipped off her sweats. She pulled her daybag up to the bed, sitting cross-legged in her bra and panties, and laid out her options. She picked jeans and her UNC sweatshirt, brushed back her blond hair and wrapped a scrunchy around it, then checked the whites of her eyes in her compact. They were clear right up to the pale blue irises. *Amazing what a good night's rest can do for a woman,* she thought.

She stood, put on her sneaks, scrawled a note to Josh, eased out of the room, but quickly returned to grab her jacket. There was still a bite to the air, although it seemed as if the day would turn out warm.

Going down the stairs, she minded her step, as her daddy had always told her to do, and began to laugh. Going up in the dark, she could not have known that no two steps were the same. Although it was apparent that the whole step was sturdy enough, no two steps matched any other for type or number of boards. She saw what looked suspiciously like a piano bench seat on one and that was the entire step. Another was strips of pallet material, a third, construction plywood. Sarah would recognize this, of course, because her dad had been, first and last, a carpenter. One step was made of something she supposed was a plastic, of some sort, in an annealed gray color that made her wonder where the owner had gotten his materials.

Perhaps she was still half-dreaming because of the early nature of the hour, but the old man she came upon suddenly when she rounded the corner of the building made her draw a deep breath. It was not apparent that she would ever let that breath go. It might be her last, for all a spectator would know.

"Oh dear. Dear, dear. I'm sorry about that. Sorry to have frightened you, Miss. Are you all right?" he said.

He stood with a wooden window screen in his hand, the metal of which was mottled with age. Next to him was a stack of them with burnished metal tabs on the top that were meant to slip into the mating tabs above each window.

"I'm fine. Fine," Sarah murmured.

"Well. I'm glad. Glad. My name's Layton. You must be the guest that came in last night that Katie left the note about.

"Yes," Sarah said, taking a breath. "My name is Sarah."

"Well, then, Sarah. How did you sleep?"

"Ohhhh, I don't think I've slept this late in years. What time is it?"

"Well, it's almost eight. Farmers are going to lunch right about now," he said, and his shoulders shook with a silent laughter. Then he got serious for a moment.

"What's your last name?"

"Ummmmmm. Percelli."

" An eye-tie? You don't look like no eye-tie."

Does she explain the marriage and the treatment she got? How could she explain the long hours left with a child while your mate is out doing whatever it is they have convinced you they must do to keep the walls from tumbling in, until you finally get the message that you are just a piece on the board? Maybe later you find out that it was all a matter of choice, and that you maybe wasted some of your years. Those years had looked like a railroad track when she was young, just stretching out to the end of the horizon.

"Ma'am?" When she came to, Layton's watery blue eyes were inches away from her own, and she jumped a bit.

"Oh. Sorry, Layton. I was just thinking, there."

"Not too damn happy thoughts, I'm thinking," he said.

"You own this place?"

"Or it owns me. We've been here since the first war."

"World War I," Sarah said, imagining it.

"No, no. The *first* war. The war for Independence. Actually, we were here a-ways before that. This whole place was Dutch then."

"Dutch? Like the Pennsylvania Dutch?"

"No, no, no. Those are German—and not too dang polite, neither. Dutch, like Peter Stuyvesant. Like the Bronks. Dutch. From Holland. You know, twenty-four dollars in beads for Manhattan? And that's about all it's worth, as far as I'm concerned."

"And you live here alone, then?" she asked.

Layton stopped and looked up the road for a moment.

"Well, my wife went on seven years ago. About this time of year, it was. But we talk most every day. She sets me straight yet."

"I'm sorry, Layton. You miss her."

"I do that. But we'll be together someday. Now, about that diner. You have to try the scrapple and eggs. This would be the last month for good fresh scrapple."

"Scrapple? That doesn't sound too appetizing."

"Most folks that are from away don't know it, but it is dang good, I think. You like bacon?"

"Oh, it tastes great, but..."

"Sure sure. All them health nuts got it in for what tastes good, but I say a little of anything ain't gonna hurt a body. It's mostly buckwheat anyway and good ham scraps. Tasty tasty. You try it, and if you don't like it, you tell Ellie to charge it to me, you hear?"

"Oh, that won't be necessary. I'll try it on your say-so."

"Now you have to do what I asked. You just tell her what I said, anyhow, and see what she says," Layton said, his shoulders shaking again and his gray eyes squinting mischievously.

"Is this some kind of joke between you two?"

Layton laughed for a moment longer, rocking back and forth on his cracked work boots. Heel to toe, toe to heel.

"This whole world is a joke, Miss. That's the way I see it, and I never met no teacher or preacher that could sell me otherwise. It's like the prayer I say every day."

"The prayer?"

Layton squared his shoulders and placed his hands at his sides, looking for the world to Sarah like a third-grader asked to recite.

"Lord," he said, "forgive my little jokes on thee, and I'll forgive THY, GREAT, BIG, ONE, ON, ME!" he finished with a shout and a giggle that was irresistible. Sarah laughed out loud at that.

"That certainly seems to be the case some days, doesn't it? Well, I guess I'll go on up there. If my son wakes up and you see him, let him know where I went. I wrote a note, and I don't expect he'll be up this early, well, for him, early. But just in case."

"Be happy to, ma'am. You just go on and enjoy your breakfast," he said and held out his hand. Sarah grasped it firmly, feeling the calluses and the sinews beneath the skin like taut wires.

"Thank you, Layton. Thanks."

She began the walk up the hill, turning to look back as the road began to curve away from the little stream. Behind her, Layton was back at work, swinging the glass storm windows out and hanging the screens in their place. The trees had just a hint of green to them, and Sarah wondered if that had happened overnight or if she had simply missed it the day before while she was so wrapped up in her own little world.

She walked briskly up the hill. The tangy morning air smelled like apples and loam—a rich, organic smell that made her want to plunge her hands into the dirt to plant seeds. As she walked, she noted with approval the neat houses and cottages. Most of them were white clapboard and some had rectangles of earth turned up and raked smooth with rows of onions already poking up through the dark brown soil. At the crest of the hill, she saw the sun glint off the stainless steel of the dining car, and as she drew closer, she could hear the clink of china and silverware, and the low buzz of conversations. She walked through the parking lot smiling.

She was about to initiate a conversation with a stranger named Ellie because of another stranger named Layton. The idea made her laugh.

"Thy great big one on me," she said, and opened the doors to the warm and fragrant room.

12

≋ CHAPTER TWELVE ≋

Megan bounced from foot to foot in the kitchen, anxious to begin walking towards the church. She liked the pinecones she found, especially the ones with the branch still attached. They looked like small pipes to her, like the pipe that the dark woman was smoking in the picture she knew about in the attic.

Megan was old enough not to talk about her knowing. The picture was stuck behind some loose boards in the attic in a place that most people wouldn't ever bother to look, and there must be a reason for that. There was a reason for everything, her Daddy said. The picture wasn't the only thing in what she liked to think of as her treasure trove. There was an old Bible, a small bag of grass seed, and some letters. She never even told Jesse about it because he talked too much. She bounced again.

"Meg, would you please?" Sue said. "How do you expect me to get this ribbon in your hair with you bouncing around like that?"

In the next room, Jesse was as close to ready as he was liable to get. Both shoes were on, with laces tied unevenly, and his shirt was buttoned, although one collar was up, the other down, and his shirttail hung out over his corduroys in the back.

"She jumps up and down like an ole SAWMILL!" he half-sung and half-shouted.

Chat, wearing a smile, appeared from the bathroom and answered, singing, "Turkey in the hay, turkey in the straw, roll 'em up, twist 'em up, take another chaw, sing a little tune called 'Turkey in the Straw'," then said, "Time to get going, here."

The kids bolted after him as he walked towards the door of his home, thinking, *how heavenly*! He stood on the threshold, waiting for Sue and sucking in the spring air gratefully, as the kids jumped down the steps and ran out into the driveway. Sue walked out of the back room with a sweater hugging her shoulders. She was a vision in blue: blue hat, blue dress, and blue gloves. She gave Chat a nudge in the small of his back. Before Chat and Sue had the door shut, the kids were down by the stream with Jesse throwing rocks into the small still pool just above the riffles that dumped into the cut banks.

There, where the stream finally emptied onto the soft loam of the river bottom, they would have a world of fun snaking native brownies from beneath the elms that had washed out, fell over, and now arched across the deep and foamy currents. That would happen just as soon as the water warmed and the season opened. Some of those trout were impossibly large for a stream so small. Chat knew they existed. The trick was to *catch* one. The few he brought to net were full-bodied with a gorgeous golden color underneath. Their sides were shot with flaming orange and pink circles like the capital of a state on some map. Catching one became the brightest moment in an hour shot full of light.

They began to walk towards the driveway to the church located down below where they lived. Even further below that, where the stream was bending around the last mountain between here and the sea, they could see the smoke coming from the chimney of the inn. A few cars drove up to the church entrance, and recognized them by honking the horn in a friendly tattoo or by waving out the window with calloused farmer hands or petite, white-gloved ones.

"I wonder what the sermon's gonna be," Chat said, distracted.

"Jesse! Get away from the edge there, I swear. You're gonna be all mud by the time we get up the hill. Megan, three is enough. And get that out of your mouth, for pity's sake. What you see in those dang pine cones is beyond me, but I am tired of finding them all over my darn house."

Sue checked her watch. It had taken them ten minutes to get about twenty feet.

"Hey, ma! Lookit! Look what I found!" Jesse screamed. In his hand, he held a small piece of flint. The deep gray surface was knapped to form a small arrowhead.

Chat bounded over and sang out, "Whoa! *Good* one, there, kiddo! This is an *old* one, see? It's got the little tail on it." He fingered the small bit of stone reverently.

"Some Indian, out for some dinner," Megan said dreamily. "He shot a nice fat grouse, and he brought it back to his teepee, right there. And then his wife made it with some wild grapes, and they had a feast."

"Maybe they did, punkin'. Maybe so," Sue said, noticing a stranger walking up the hill towards her. A smart-looking woman, dressed in what Sue guessed was urban casual. They didn't have those kinds of clothes where she shopped, and she had heard, although she did not necessarily believe it, that some of those poofy sweaters cost a thousand dollars. As for the black wool pea coats, who would have been seen dead in one of those when she was growing up? They probably cost three times as much nowadays. Sue figured this woman was probably not going up to church this Sunday morning. Perhaps she was headed up to the diner instead, although she was more than a bit overdressed.

Chat was watching her as well.

"She's pretty. Don't you think?" she asked Chat, mockingly.

"I couldn't notice, sweetie. Not with you in my eye like that. I saw her at the inn Friday night. Had a boy with her. She maybe stayed over at Layton's for the weekend then."

They watched as she walked towards them, and the kids both stopped for a moment to check her out as well.

"Who's she?" Megan asked.

"She's the squaw from your teepee," Jesse said, laughing, and ducked away from Meg even though she made no move towards him.

Meg eyed him and finally said, "Smarty-pants. You should mind your manners." She had Chat's own drawl and was a chip off the old block.

Chat made a soft shushing sound as the stranger approached, and then he bowed his head in greeting.

He and Sue murmured, "Morning." The woman, at first studiously avoiding their eyes, turned her head and awkwardly said "Hi."

"Fine morning, isn't it?" Chat asked, slowing. Jesse took this as a cue to begin a small excavation in the clay bank beside the road while Megan continued her search for the perfect pinecone pipe, sneaking peeks at the new lady while she did.

"Yes. Yes, it certainly is," the lady answered.

Meg smiled to herself and went back to her search, watching out of the corner of her eye as her mom came closer and extended her hand.

"My name's Sue. That's Meg and Jesse, and this is my husband, Chat, " she said. The woman took it and gave it a firm shake, looked them both in the eye.

"Glad to meet you, Meg. I'm Sarah. Chat, I think I've seen. You played Friday night at the inn, right?"

"Yes ma'am. Hope you enjoyed listening. I sure had fun playing."

"Oh. It was very nice. Even Josh stopped making fun of it after awhile, which is pretty good for a teenager," she said, and smiled.

"So where is your boy, then?" Chat asked.

"He's still asleep. I'm heading up to the diner. Ellie's diner? Layton told me about it yesterday, and I thought I'd go up there again this morning. Josh won't be up probably until ten or so, I guess."

"You all had a late night?"

"Well, we went to Fiesterville and caught a movie. Guess we're just unwinding."

"Hard to be wound up in a place like this, I agree," Chat said pleasantly.

Sue stood silently, a small smile on her face, half-watching the kids. By now Meg had joined in the digging, and small clods of dirt began flying out into the road.

"Kids! Save that for later. Come over here," Sue said finally, looking at her watch again. Chat said, "Guess we'd better be on our way here. The early service gets crowded."

Sarah nodded and smiled. "It was so nice to meet you both, and you too, Jesse, Megan. The company is as nice as the countryside." She continued on past them as the rising sun just touched the top of the hill, the little dell below, and Sarah's hair as she walked into the sunlight

"Bye!" Meg echoed, still for once.

"See? Not every stranger is all bad," Chat said.

"And it doesn't hurt she's blond and beautiful, I guess," Sue said, quietly.

"Ah, it's what's in the heart that's the real beauty. Why, you're the most bee-you-tee-ful woman in the known universe," Chat whispered, kissing her suddenly, not fifty feet from the front drive of the church.

"Mr. Dalton, you behave yourself!

Jesse groaned.

"Always, kissing. Yuk!"

"That's romantic," Meg explained.

"It's gross! Kissing girls!"

He made mock kissing faces that made him look like he was in pain.

"Oh. And frogs aren't gross?" Meg said, sticking her tongue out.

"See? See what you get them up too, Mr. Dalton? Now, let's *all* behave for the next few minutes, shall we?" Sue said sternly. Chat thought he saw the twinkle in her eye.

Inside the church, the pews were already half full, and the family made their way to the pew they habitually used, the second one on the left side. The kids tumbled in to the pew, sliding over the smooth rich oak while Chat closed the pew door, a piece of church architecture left over from the days when each family had their own pew as a matter of payment and would bring a bucket of hot coals in the winter to keep their feet warm.

Chat checked the program to see what the sermon would be and which hymns they would be singing. He was pleased to see the first listed was "Amazing Grace" since he knew the high harmony to that one. The theme of the sermon was to be "Brothers," and Chat looked it up in his indexed Bible. There he found a long list of references, and he idly flipped to the second reference, skipping the first tale of brothers listed and going to Joshua 1:14: "you are to help your brothers until the Lord gives them rest." That, he thought, would make a good sermon. He would start it by singing out, *Let me live in a house by the side of the road, and be a friend to man.* But he thought the chances of that being the choice weren't good. Reverend Donnelly usually liked something with a little piss and vinegar to it. He found the next reference in Psalm 133. He didn't bother to look that one up. That went " How good and pleasant it is when brothers live together in unity. It is like precious oil poured on their head, running down on the beard." Chat smiled a little at that image. He imagined Homer with some SAE-30 dripping over him like some Three Stooges movie. Definitely not that one. So it would have to be the fourth reference.

Chat had always loved to see the patterns in things, particularly the subtle patterns. It was what made him such a good mechanic. He was able to diagnose trouble based upon things that didn't seem related. And he remembered how delighted he was to discover the pattern the Reverend used to pick his scripture. It was never the first one listed in the study Bible, but it was always one of the following three. Sue had doubted Chat when he announced that he had cracked the code, but in the year that followed, Chat had proven time and again that he could predict the reading. In fact, Sue was even now looking over to see what Chat had discovered.

He passed the Bible over to her, with his finger marking Proverbs 6:19:

There are six things the Lord hates

seven that are detestable to him

haughty eyes

a lying tongue

hands that shed innocent blood

a heart that devises wicked schemes

feet that are quick to rush into evil

a false witness who pours out lies

and a man who stirs up dissension among his brothers.

Why did the Lord hate six and detest seven? Ah—well, six things the Lord hated, and the last in the list was not a thing. The last was a man, and the Lord would not hate a man. What a man did, maybe, but not the man himself. Chat thought that a good rule. It was one he tried hard to follow himself.

The Reverend, tall and rough-looking, strode to the podium and greeted the congregation. In the moment before Miss Eliza laid into the first hymn, Chat saw The Reverend scanning the crowd, marking who was and who was not there. In his prize-fighting days, he had a reputation for never quitting, and he was not above a touch of intimidation to improve attendance and the contents of the plate. And while years of pounding had not improved a voice that was probably average to begin with, the right Reverend made no apologies for his crooked nose or his edgy voice, singing as lustily as taste would allow or perhaps a shade above that.

Chat always tried hard to help balance that edge with some rounder tones. He listened carefully as the first hymn started while a small part of his mind worried over the sixes and sevens.

Sarah was halfway through her breakfast, savoring the meal and the scalding coffee, when Josh walked into the warm diner. He wore the smile of a relaxed man, at an hour he would normally still be deep asleep at home.

"My, you seem in a good mood," Sarah said, smiling back brightly.

He walked up to the booth and sat. "Those freakin'—oh, sorry—those birds sure are loud out here. What's that stuff?"

"That's scrapple. It's better than it looks. Ellie, can I have another platter, please?"

Ellie smiled and said, "I'd be happy to get you one, dear. And that's a fine looking boy you have there."

"Geeze, Ma. Two days here and you're a native, huh?" Josh said, reddening.

They ate and half-listened to the conversations going on around them from the continual "hey now" the locals exchanged to the oblique jokes that neither one of them understood, which got what Sarah now knew was a big laugh out here: a snort and a couple of silent shoulder- quivers, with maybe a guffaw thrown in at the end.

Later, they had driven around, saw the General Store and the gas station, and the school and several other churches. All were tidy and inviting. They came to the river on the outskirts of town, leaden and cold-looking from the spring thaw with logs, twigs and trash jammed helter-skelter on the islands that were visible from the road that ran along the shore. At a few bends, Josh pointed out black plastic trash bags clinging to tree branches and fluttering twenty feet above them from some prior flood. They stopped and talked about what it must have been like when that flood had come along, and how far back from the bank the water must have risen.

At one point, Josh asked to be let out to pee. Sarah pulled over, enjoying the sun and the quiet. The river took a steep bend away from them here, and nearer to the river in the slack water at the inside of the bend, Sarah noticed oddly stacked angular shapes that looked to her like slabs of concrete with odd streaks of an off-white color. Careful as she wanted to be with her sneakers and the mud, she could resist no longer. She was about to call Josh, but she stopped. He was still doing his business, so she resigned herself to washing the sneaks and eased down the bank through thickets of thorn bushes with petite turfs of green, grabbing and catching her skin and pulling loops from her sweater. She slipped and slid from sapling to sapling towards the shapes, which resolved into blocks of ice three feet thick and twenty or thirty feet across. Streaks of mud and leaves gouged from the bottom and banks camouflaged the ice perfectly. Only an occasional end was still anything resembling white, and on them she could see the layers of darker and lighter ice that must have been the various freezes or thaws, recorded like frozen tree rings.

"Josh," she called out. "Check this out!"

He jumped up on top of one of the huge cakes of ice, bounding from one to the next until he was fifty yards up river. Then his feet shot out from under him, and he slid off a chunk five or six feet above the ground, shooting off the end like it was a ski jump and landing, butt-first, in the soft mud.

Sue tried hard not to laugh for about one second, and then she let out a guffaw that echoed off the mountain cliff behind them.

"I wouldn't laugh too hard if I was you, mom," he finally said. "You look like you were shot out of a cannon, more or less."

Sarah stopped laughing.

"More or less?"

"Well, yeah. Without the less, I guess."

Sue laughed again.

"I think we need to get changed and get going, or we'll be late getting home."

He didn't make too big a scene when she demanded that he take his jeans off, offering her windbreaker to cover his legs until they got back to the inn. It *was* a Beemer, after all.

When they got back, she went upstairs and got him a change of clothes. They ate a late lunch, damned good burgers and fries, and even managed to get in a short nap before they had headed back, but not before Sarah had thanked Layton for the hospitality.

"Never you mind," he said. "You just come back soon."

13

≡ Chapter Thirteen ≡

Ted Malchio was tired of waiting. He had lobbied hard to get the interstate to come through Pigeon Forge instead of the more practical route twenty miles farther south. If he could have, he would have changed the name, too; it disgusted him. Pigeon Forge was provincial and small-town sounding. What he really wanted was far more than the country club, nice as it was. It wasn't nearly posh enough, nor was he rich enough.

Yet.

He leaned back and looked out his windows at the grounds of his corporate headquarters, savoring the Sunday quiet. This was sacred time and hallowed ground, and the time and place to plan all his coups. He'd heard the locals joke about the sign out front, or, more accurately, had the jokes reported to him by some of his eyes and ears. Ted picked nobodies for the job, people who would do anything for a few bucks, including dime on their own friends. He had them on his own crews, working odd jobs in the two schools that serviced the towns. All this effort was expended just so he could know the minds of the people around him. "Your friends close, your enemies closer," his father had always told him, and his dad was a man who should have known, losing friends as quickly as he had made the first Malchio millions.

"I guess the fruit don't fall far from the tree," he said to himself.

Sad truth was, a builder could only make so much constructing one house for one family, one at a time. He put his feet up on the desk and leaned back in his leather chair, arms folded behind his head, and thought about his next move. He was up to fourteen crews and clearing a mil a year. He would buy all the small lots for fifty miles around if he had to, or, better yet, cut deals with the owners to sell them at whatever price they wanted, as long as he could put his house up on it. They always bit, too. But it was happening too slowly. He was thirty-five, and he still didn't have a membership at the NY Tennis Club or the jet. Never mind that he had no place to jet to. It was the principal of the thing. Which, as another joke went, meant it really *was* the money. He studied the map of the county he had on the one wall that wasn't a glass window. The red pins represented his job sites; the larger areas ironically shaded green were pieces that were slated for development. He always named the places after what had been there before the D-9s came in: Red Fox Run, White Pine Way, Forest Hills. Marketing. That was what he trained hard at, like some men lift weights, and he was getting damned good at it.

The problem was the lack of land to be had: good, flat land. The farmers just wouldn't sell. And outside the valley where the Bennykill ran down to the river, all a builder could find were too many swamps and too many craggy hillsides where it would cost too damn much to build. Cost too much, that is, unless one could just blast the rocks and put them in the swamps. He chuckled. Flipping tree huggers. Well, the new governor was gutting the rules for wetlands and for mining, too. Out where the first exit was, Ted was gearing up to tear out an entire hillside, to make room for a Biggie Burger, maybe a strip mall and some gas pumps, and he wasn't intending to ask for any permits, either.

"Not mining. God, no. I could call it lot improvement," he mused, almost satisfied. He was glad the idea of zoning had been shot down time after time by the locals, who hated to be told what to do and what not to do. Hey, they got their burn barrels, and he got what he wanted, so that worked out fine.

He had the distinct impression that he was missing something, a larger picture. He studied the map again. His eye was drawn, as always, to the large sinuous plot of land that ran the length of the county on either side of the river, up the Bennykill and finally up to the first gentle ridges. What was left in the county was largely rock and misery when it came to building. Sure, back when he started, the local government let anyone put a cesspool right next to a swamp or something. Hell, maybe the sewage could sweeten up the damn swamp. Back then, building the second homes that only the rich people in the city could afford, it wasn't such a big deal. They came up for a "couple two three weeks," and then went back down again. The systems could handle that. It was when they started moving up and actually *living* in the homes that the trouble began, and now builders had to kiss the sewage enforcer's *ass* to put houses up.

He sighed. Maybe he should have cornered the market on elevated sand mounds. That was what they had to build on every new plot in the county. Those raised plots kind of looked like they are supposed to be a volleyball court or something, and it cost twelve grand for each one. All it was was a bunch of sand and pipes. It made him crazy to have people with fistfuls of dollars that he couldn't take, all because of the flipping tree huggers. What he couldn't do with the several Dalton pieces, and not something mundane, either, like houses or shops.

He fought the comfortable grip of his three-thousand dollar chair—worth every penny—and got up. Ted had no idea how long he had been sitting there, mulling and planning. In school, he had been prone to daydreaming—ADD, they'd call it now, no doubt—but of course now he could say with some satisfaction that much of what they had called dreams were now reality. That new complex down by Fiesterville, with six different kinds of fast food, three car dealerships, a Wal-Mart, a Kmart, and three strips with smaller shops, they had all said it was overkill, but wasn't he raking in the bucks? Small businesses couldn't even rent a place out down there anymore, and now the other big box stores were antsy to get in as well. He had the land down there all sewn up.

A twinge in his back announced itself and he stretched, surprised to realize it was growing dark outside. In the large dark windows facing the valley below, he could now also see his own reflection superimposed on the landscape like a some trick photography: balding on top, his face getting a little puffy and pale, brown eyes washed out, perhaps just the imperfect reflection did that, a bit more gut than he would like sticking out over his belt. Best get back to working out mornings and maybe buy a tanning bed for himself.

The Fiesterville project was all well and good, but too much was never enough for Ted. He had been trying for months to think of something the city wankers needed or wanted that they couldn't get in the city, something besides a crummy deer or an oak tree. Every place in the state had those types of things. What was it that they liked best of all? What was the difference between them and the chowderheads he had grown up with? The locals—well, he was one of them, once—called it rudeness, or thoughtlessness, but Ted knew his clientele. They weren't thoughtless at all. They constantly thought. They thought about things, about how to get more and better things, about how to get them cheaper than anyone else could get them.

"I got mine!" That was their motto, just like it was Ted's. And, like the man said, you can't cheat an honest man. That was at the bottom of all his business deals: *You stick with me and I can get you a deal, honestly, but you have to promise, I can't stress this enough, that you keep this just between us two. I see we're members of the same tribe, you and I, and won't the Joneses be sick when they see what you've got here, the vaulted ceilings and the 4,000 square feet of living space?*

Things. Those people were—what was the term that dweebie science teacher had used for the foxes and wolves?—consumers.

"Buy and buy and buy," he muttered, thinking it sounded vaguely familiar.

He would get it, eventually. For right now, he had other contracts to let on the piece next to Dalton's obscenely large tracts of land, and in the growing darkness, he moved his hand over the landscape like a pharaoh, imagining that he was the master of all he surveyed. He smiled at that. He and Chat had never gotten on, not since the day back in high school when Ted had tried to stiff him for some body work that Chat had done on his 'vette. Chat had knocked him flat, bloodied his nose, then said they were even.

Ada DeLeon sat on the bed in the dusk and listened to the streets below: always the quarrels and the breaking glass, the snarls of rage, the dull thump-thump of stereos in the low-riders playing gangsta, even on the Lord's day. It was bad enough to hear that all the day and half the night. And she would gladly have tuned it out, or tried to, and listened instead to the lyric sounds of the music she loved. She had been good on the guitar, the old style. It was music made for silky nights. It was a good way to let the wildness almost come out, to let it bubble underneath the chants and laughter until late at night, until she felt the urge of sleep, went back to the small huts, slept for a few hours. She awoke to the smiles of all the neighbors, grinding the corn and making the tortillas, gossiping about who in the village had their eye on whom, or perhaps which one had too much of the rum and let the wildness all the way out with someone just as wild. She couldn't imagine even one small part of the music, not a single song. Tonight she was listening to that sudden change of sound that usually came just before the one that made her catch her breath and panic. It was such a small sound, truly: gunfire.

Freddy was out there still despite her firm request to be in by five, before the shadows created havens for devils that would take a boy's sneakers for a ten-minute thrill of crack and leave the boy for dead. She twisted the rosary in her hands and watched Angelina playing quietly. What could she do? Lock them in all day and all night? Quit her job and go on welfare so she could walk them to and from school each and every day, and hope that all three of them would not end up as Paco had?

Paco. He had said that it must be better here, better than the starving and the midnight raids by the police. Better, he said, than the even more terrifying times when neighbors suddenly did not know their own any longer and laughed viciously at the carnage. Paco's work as a teacher and her's as a market owner marked them both the minute Samosa began his reign of terror. Educated people were so much harder to train "correctly," she guessed, and of course the government wanted any business that made money.

They had almost decided that she should stay, and that he would leave. At that point, the government had not yet begun to take businesses as long as the owner was still there to run it, although they did have to finally give up replacing the window glass, deciding instead to board up the windows with wood just as most of their neighbors had already done. It gave the small street a gaunt look that she couldn't get used to. Finally she had had enough. How could she stay there and hope to profit when her greatest treasures might be snatched from her?

So late one night, they bundled up a few possessions. They packed the crucifix, some pictures and jewelry, and the two very small statues of the virgin made by Paco's ancestors only a few years after they had buried the great Ponce DeLeon in Peurto Rico and made their way into the mountains. There had been a time, Ada thought sadly, when that lineage had called forth respect and reverence instead of suspicion and hatred. Malice was all that remained of the dream of El Dorado.

They had made the voyage with eighty other souls. The children constantly asked questions neither she nor Paco could answer, fleeing the only world they had ever known and giving up a life that Ada had thought would be forever when she had first wed. Seven did not make it past Brownsville, dying from the heat and from a month of hiding more than eating. She remembered grimly the joy they had felt when they had all managed to get over the border and they were dropped off a hundred miles away in the dead of night.

The trip to the north had eroded away the joy and left the familiar nugget of fear and anger in her heart. The people did not want them here. They made it apparent in every gesture, in every snub. In some places, it was done openly; they were refused service, or the waiter would take care of all the others until only they remained. All the time, Paco had said, "It's going to be okay!" in his big cheery voice, as he pawned first this piece and then that of their history to fat men in seedy shops. At last they had come here, to this city, at first relieved to hear their own tongue, and Ada began to hope that he was right, that all the fear and suffering, the image of the dead ones in the chaparral and of her home far away would fade in new goodness, Blessed Virgin be praised!

That hadn't lasted long. Too often the voices became the frightening night voices of the rebels in the mountains she had left, and the smells the same ones that had stung her nostrils when they had fled away from the village down to Leon; sewage, sweat, disease and despair.

Outside, it was nearly dark, and the laughter was becoming more riotous. Angelina had paused in her play to look out the window. Ada saw the same smooth contours of cheek, the thick, lustrous hair, the royal Castilian cheekbones haughty and strong, and her same dark eyes. She realized with a shock that Angelina was crying.

"Ouuuuu, come here, come here. Shh shh shh," she said, holding the small girl tightly and rocking her.

"Why do you cry, eh? Why do you cry?" she asked, and was afraid that the little one would answer her. Ada began to cry herself, quietly, so as not to alarm her baby.

They started to hear the front door slamming shut from downstairs, and the opening and shutting of apartment doors in the three-story brownstone.

People were checking to see if they needed to throw the second bolt or run out the fire escapes.

"Mom! MOOOOMMM! I'm HOMMMMEEEEEEE!"

Ada wiped away her own tears and took a deep breath to erase the ragged sorrow that had bubbled up in her throat.

"See, little one? See? I told you! There is nothing to worry about! We are all fine! You, Freddie! What will I do with you, eh? We are here worried sick, and you think of us not at all! You are an ungrateful child!" she scolded.

"Look, mamma. I couldn't come quicker! The store was robbed. I went to the Line and got the bread instead."

"So—you think bread with the meal is more important than obeying? Than your *life?*" She smacked his shoulder gently with her hand.

"Momma, I am sixteen! Look! I am bigger than you now!"

She looked at him severely. All she could see was Paco standing in front of her, saying that all would be well.

"And are you bigger than your Poppa, too?" she demanded.

Freddie dropped the bag with the bread on the counter carelessly.

"It is always that, isn't it?" he demanded. "He made one mistake, and now we all have to sneak around with our backs against the walls and scared all the time? That is no way to live, momma! No way!" he shouted, his face grimacing in anger and shame.

Instead of a tirade as he expected, his mother simply slumped up against the sink and put her head in her hands, fending off tears.

"Fetch for me the paper, Ferdinand," she said regally. It was her mother's voice she imitated in times like these, and her mother's attitude also.

When he returned, she opened quickly to the real-estate section. She still had a few thousand left; if she stayed, it would get eaten away little by little until they would be stuck here forever.

"We shall see what we shall see," she said quietly. And to herself she promised that the next night would not find them here any longer. Better the whispers and the snubs than a bullet in the brain while one slept.

14

≡ CHAPTER FOURTEEN ≡

"Hey Guido! How's the garbage business, eh? Picking up?" Hugh said, sarcasm oozing from his words. "Listen, piasano. I need a little something from your folks in the country. It's a clean job, nothing hinky about it."

Hugh winced a little at the volume of the voice at the other end of the line and looked out on the sun rising over the city. It had taken a few hours of thinking, a few hours of sleep, a few hours on-line, and then a cold shower to pull it all together. By the time he woke Guido, he had an idea about how to proceed.

Full frontal was not the way, especially since Dalton was involved. Hugh had learned his lesson in Lexington about that way of doing business. It would take a few weeks, maybe, to get the lay of the land. But when he finally had it, the job would be much easier. Daltonwoods. Yes.

"Jumping Jesus, Guido. Stop hollering! I know it's early. But I have an offer you can't refuse. Your boy, that nice-looking one that just got married? Tony? Yeah, him and his bride should really have a little time to themselves, get their marriage off on the right foot. Sure, sure, I know that leaves you short. I know, I know. I'll cover that. I'll have a man for you to use."

Hugh frowned and allowed the loud complaints to go on for a few moments. That was part of the price for dealing with the older Dagos. They couldn't do anything quietly. But Tony, well, he was second generation, born out there somewhere in the country, and Hugh thought he would fit in pretty well. He half-listened to Guido's litany: tipping fees were getting too high, and Hugh had let that large contract to the Irish for demolition wastes last year, on and on and on.

He looked at his watch impatiently, and then out at the empty desk in the outer office.

"I'll have someone pull that contract up, Guido. I'll make that right. It was just an oversight, a mistake. Really. That only runs until June, and then, well, best offer, I'll say, eh? Thanks, yeah. Sure, sure. Have him here at lunch. I'll have my people go over what I need from him. And, Guido? Get some rest. You sound like you could use it," Hugh said, laughing silently, and hanging up before Guido could start his next outburst.

He turned at the sound of the key in the outer door. The girl burst in, disheveled and breathless.

"Mr. McAdam, I'm sorry, the traffic, " she said, standing first on one foot then on the other. He gave her a flat look.

Hugh would never say it, but he hated when they cringed like that. Respect, that was one thing. But they screwed up, and then they thought that bootlicking was all they needed to make up for it. He wasn't stupid enough to kid himself; he loved being the big cheese. And he *dearly* loved to make the high-and-mighty types do the groveling. But these people made him nuts when they did it. On another day, it would have simply made him explode. But he hadn't time to train a new girl, not with what was in store for the next few months. It wouldn't take longer than that, he figured, so he wouldn't fire her ass. Not yet.

"Forget that. Pull the McIntuire contract and tell the legal beagles to find a way to bust it—and a black solution, not a red one, either. I don't feature making those spud-lovers any richer than they are."

"Yessir," she said.

He watched her trim figure hesitate as she neared the door, and he turned back to the map on his desk. He had a few more calls to make, and then perhaps he would take the day and walk around his city.

She walked out of the office and almost turned to tell McAdam to stuff it where the sun didn't shine, but resisted the urge. It was Josh she was really mad at. Maybe that was the problem with McAdam, too. Maybe he was pissed at somebody else all the time. She shook her head silently at the thought that they could have anything in common.

After such a pleasant weekend, this morning Josh had reverted to form. She had to threaten and bluster to get him out the door and off to school—not before he had screamed that he hated school, her, and life in general.

She pushed a stray lock of hair back into place and went to the computer, pulled up the contracts and pushed the print button. She dialed the legal department, telling her counterpart there what McAdam had in his twisted little mind, and sighed.

It was going to be a long week.

Across the city, in a pigeon-stained brownstone, Ada, Freddie and Angelica walked past what was left of a Dodge minivan, holding two shopping bags and the cheap suitcase Ada had bought before she had left the land of warmth.

"Momma," Freddie murmured. "I don't wanna. Really, I don't."

Ada shushed him, pointing to the girl with her eyes, and silently asking for his help: *don't make a scene—Angie will get scared and start crying, and this is hard enough.*

Ada stopped next to the ruined van, looking at her son and seeing her lost husband, and somewhere in the depth of his eyes, the possibility of happiness. She turned her eyes away from Freddie's and traced her delicate fingers in the smooth, shiny depression the bullet had left in the blotched metal.

"This is what we live for? You must let me try this, Freddie. We both know if it becomes a mistake, then maybe we try another city. But we must try. We must," she whispered softly, nearly in tears.

"Momma, please. I'm sorry. Please don't," Freddie said, for one moment a grown man comforting his mother. She patted him on the cheek.

"You say a prayer for me, then. Let's go."

They made their way to the subway, and by mid-morning, they had boarded the Greyhound, sitting in the front, as far away as they could get from the nauseating smell of bathroom disinfectant. The sun highlighted the faint green of the trees, and they rode in silence for a time, each lost in thoughts.

"Do we have a plan?" Freddie finally asked.

"See, here? There is land for sale and houses. I have some little bit of money left. Six thousand, I have. So we find whatever jobs we can. I cannot know what it will be until we get there, but we will find something. Jobs and a place to live," she said. She tried to sound firm, positive.

"We will?"

"You must work also, Federico. Until we get on our feet. And there is school."

"Mom. I'm sixteen. I could just work, if that's the way it has to be."

"I will not sell you for $5 an hour. You are worth at least $10, si?"

She smiled gently, combing Angie's lustrous hair with her fingers, as her daughter slept cozily in the corner of the seat while the bus rolled down the highway. Ada could see into all the backyards full of rusted trucks and odd pieces of farm machinery, 55-gallon barrels, birdfeeders, rectangular mounds of soil covered with grass in the middle of the woods, above-ground pools—half of them with a side caved in, no covering on them or water in them—woodpiles, mounds of saw-dust and the smoke curling up in a gentle curve downwind—not too much wind today, just a nice soft breeze. The faces around her were the ones she was still trying to get used to. White, distant, never making eye contact with her or nodding to say hello. That was just their way, not intentional rudeness, but always there, to her. Know your place, spic, was what she had heard some of them say in the grocery lines, loud enough to be overheard on purpose. She sighed again. She was from the country, and she was going back there again. Perhaps they would be nicer, calmer. She hoped so. At least tonight she did not have to fear death. The rest would take care of itself. It was in God's hands.

Chat wandered into his garage that morning, thinking about the week's schedule. As he turned on the compressor and flicked on the lights and the heater, he spied the milk crate Ty had used as a seat and remembered what he had said about seeing someone in the swamp. He hadn't seemed a man prone to making things up. He looked up at the clock. He had almost an hour before he had to open. Outside, the air was still and crisp, and Chat knew that the soil in the swamp would still be frozen solid.

"Well, it'll be a nice walk in the nature, I guess," he muttered, closing the bay doors.

He slid down the cobble and broken cinder blocks that edged the parking lot, which had been reclaimed from the swamp twenty years before. *Try and do that kind of fill these days*, he thought, *see what you get*. A few yards beyond, the twisted branches of blueberry and sedge made a barrier that seemed unbroken, but Chat simply bent at the waist and the deer trails became visible, small tunnels that found the best ground between uneven hummocks and thick muck. Several yards in, he kicked out three deer, their white tails flagging around the perimeter of the swamp and the thick cracking of brush making the hair stand up on Chat's head, even though he hunted less and less as the years wore on.

After the first hundred feet, the swamp cleared out considerably, and small islands covered with yellow birch and red maple made the going easier. Chat kept the garage doors in sight as he eased into the thicket, carefully choosing his footing and looking for signs. If Ty was right, it should be easy enough to tell.

Besides blue jays and squirrels, all he found was a shed antler from a nice 8-pointer, one beam of it gnawed almost through by some hungry critter. Chat could see the far side of the swamp coming up, and on the high ridge, he caught the movement of the three deer he had pushed out. They would probably bed down up there, and Homer's fields would be handy for grazing when the sun went down.

Chat stood on a flattened hummock and looked at his watch. He had half an hour left, just enough time to return, clean up a bit and get that truck's trannie pulled. He checked the bay doors again, and then the swamp in front of him. He stood upon the last place where someone in the swamp would be visible to another sitting in his garage. Nothing but this spot, no matter how sharp-eyed the fellow might be.

He shifted and noticed a thin ooze of swamp muck edging from beneath his boot, odd considering the rest of the ground was crispy with frost. He looked more closely at the mound upon which he stood. Idly he nudged a shoot of blueberry, small green leaflets and buds coating the shoot down to the ground. And below the ground as well.

He stooped and grasped the pencil-thick shoot, and it easily pulled from the ground, which, Chat noted, was covered, not with sphagnum moss, but with what looked like the humus found in the forest. And in amongst the soil, a small seed, like birdseed—the kind of seed he had seen some of his friends clean out of the nickel bags they were certain would be legal any day.

Chat had tried it, figuring he couldn't condemn something he had no knowledge of, even though part of his brain was making the connection between that and Genesis and the apple. But he hadn't much cared for it, and besides, it was against the law and could get a body in trouble. He noted that trouble followed many of the folks who went that way, since many didn't stop there, with loss after loss: wives, jobs, cars, even, once or twice, a life. He had stuck with beer and tried to ignore it when Jo-Jo and Sterling went outside during a band job to "check their hubcaps."

But this was something different. This was his land. And he didn't feature somebody doing this here.

He carefully smoothed away his one footprint and replaced the branch, critically examining the area for any trace that he had been there. He looked back to were he had last seen the deer. They were either laying down or gone. Chat remembered that area. An old towpath ran along the brow of the ridge up above. That would be how they got in and out. And Chat bet that he could see that pretty clear from his office with a pair of good binoculars.

"Good reason to buy a new toy," he muttered, leaving the swamp on the opposite end and walking the road rapidly back to the garage.

Tony was slumped in his kitchen chair drinking coffee near the window, his eyes even with the sill. He was watching the next-door neighbor's wife as she talked on the phone. She was a nice piece, and he had gone out of his way to be nice to them both, signing for packages and stopping at their tired little cocktail whatevers. He could be nice, and he could be charming, too. *Sure, sure,* the boys at work busted on him. *What the hell does a garbage man need with a college education?* If he couldn't go to college, he could at least read. He watched as she idly toyed with the charm around her neck. As if she would sack up with an ignorant goomba.

She was getting into the conversation, and Tony watched carefully what she did with her hands as she spoke, smoothing the fabric over her breasts, tucking the shirt in, and then smoothing, tucking again, and finally playing with the pendant.

Nervous hands are good hands. That was one of Tony's current rules of a hot lay. Of course, he was still doing the research, is what he joked about at the garage after the stink was washed off. He needed a larger sample.

When the phone rang, he cursed, sliding out of the chair and crawling past the window, and then muttering softly as he reached the wall phone at the opposite end of the room.

"Who the hell is this calling at six-freakin' thirty?"

On his day off, no less. He listened, frowned.

"Unc, listen. Sure, I remember. Yeah, but."

He listened for a long moment, frowning.

"Sure thing, Uncle Guido. Thank you."

He stood there, and he didn't care if she saw him. For months he'd been setting it up, the accidental testing of the waters with this babe, and he felt he was getting close. Maybe, he was thinking only this morning, it would be this weekend when her old man was at the office and Nancy was out spending the money like there'll never be an end to it.

Not that he had anything against Nan for that. He thought he loved her pretty well and took care of her, and he appreciated the little things she did for him, too, the backrubs and the small notes she put in his lunch. But he'd always been restless that way, and she knew that when she married him. Hadn't she joked about killing any woman she found him with, as if it would be entirely their fault?

He'd laughed at that and tickled her, and a minute later they were all over each other.

And now, Guido wanted him to go back to the sticks, back to what he couldn't wait to leave. He was in the family, and he never wanted any of the cousins to forget it. And he was as good as any damned one of them from the city.

That was something he was especially sensitive about, being from out of the city. God, how he looked forward to those family reunions back in the day when the cousins and uncles and aunts from Bayonne, Queens and Jersey City would descend on his folks place. Out "beyond beyond", as cousin Sal was fond of saying.

"What the hell your old man stick you out here for, anyway, Tony?" Sal would taunt him.

"What the hell you drag your ass four hours to bust me for, then?" Tony would snap back. After a few minutes of wrestling, a "smell my pit" and a squealed "awright! AWRIGHT!" they'd walk up the road to smoke cigarettes and flip pebbles at the chickens at the next farm up the road until the farmer, a silent old German that who had been born in eighteen-freakin' something or other would show up, never really saying anything, just kind of standing there and looking. Then they would slink back down the road. By then, the heads would be half-bagged or deep in pinochle. It was easy enough to hook a bottle and a couple packs of smokes, and they'd find a spot up on the hill to throw down the blankets.

When he had the chance to come to the city, he hadn't even thought about it. Leave that and go to Queens, work nights at his uncle's, and he'd have a job waiting for him. That's what the cousins all said.

"Hell, Tony, you'd do all right, buddy. The girls, Tony. Ohhh-yesssss. And the money!"

He'd put it to his old man like a businessman would. Chance of a lifetime. Expenses paid. Career path. He threw in every buzzword of success he could think of, watching his father's eyes carefully. He was close to empty, and he knew the look.

"What's the catch, huh?" his dad had droned, like it wasn't even a question.

"Catch? What do you mean? Angie said it was as good as done. I said I wanted it."

"You already talk like them," his dad said. Tony waited for the argument. One minute. Two.

"You don't want me to go, then."

His father had risen, walked over to the kitchen window, and looked out over the lush lawn embedded in the trees.

"Dad?"

When he turned, Tony was shocked to see tears in his father's eyes, and he waved his hand a few times, the way someone who is choking or laughing too hard to speak would do, a plea for a too-long moment to catch the breath.

"Why do you think I am here and they are there? Why do you think I put up with the snubs from the damned pig farmers and the little-minded shopkeepers? Why, Tony?"

And his father had shrugged his shoulders, holding one hand out in a silent plea for thought before he walked out of the room.

Tony had waited for his father to forbid it, but he never had. And one spring day, when the tittering farmgirls and the snotty debs had him at wits end and spending far too much time alone with himself, he steeled himself to announce his intentions.

He was ready for a fight, for recriminations, for the least resistance. Then he would put the foot down. He was not ready for what he got.

"Be careful, Tony," his father had said, shoulders slumping.

"You remember who you are," his mother had enjoined. Then they had hugged him and left the room.

They saw him off like they were going to a funeral. Tony knew some odd details of how his father had come to move to the sticks, really a gutsy move back in the '40s. Back then that part of the country was suspicious of anything foreign, let alone anybody that was a German ally like the eye-ties were. Tony had heard some rumors from the cousins about his dad and most particularly his Granddad, who had a huge tile and marble business in the city. He and Tony's Grandma would take cruises to Egypt and Sicily every two years, and later Tony found out that the person he thought was his Grandma was not his biological Grand mom at all. There were some very convoluted lines drawn on the old family tree right around there! Pop, as they called him, had actually *fled* to the country to escape the strong-arm the mob was putting on all the contractors in the city, especially the ones who might have had some trouble with immigration.

Tony didn't care for the country life. Hunting? The blood bothered him although he wouldn't ever say that to the guys. Fishing? You give a man a fish and you feed him for a day. You teach a man how to fish, and he'll sit in a boat all day and drink beer. He liked the beer part, but that got old. It was the same with spotting deer, which was fun the first couple of evenings. That got old pretty quickly, too.

Now Guido wanted him to go back. He stalked back to the chair, to the now-cold coffee, and looked out the window. The window opposite was empty.

Nan lay on her bed and listened to the conversation between Guido and Tony. They had only been married a few months, and already she was wondering if she had done the right thing. She didn't want the thought since that was exactly what her mother had told her she would think, but there it was.

Tony was still a hunk, and he treated her fine, not rude to her or mean like some of the older guys in the family. But she was still a romantic. That had won her over, all the flowers and diamond bracelets he gave her and the sexy looks over bottles of wine that cost a couple day's pay. She couldn't really tell the difference between them and the Dago red her old man had on the kitchen table, but it was the thought.

And the poetry. He had made her promise never, ever to tell anyone about that, had demanded that she cross her heart—she did!— but they were so sweet she did show a couple of them to her girlfriends, who she knew could keep their mouths shut. They were all practiced in the art of the silent lie, going to charity functions and donating money that came from who-knows-where.

Out on Long Island, she knew old married couples who had been together ten, fifteen years, driving to the mall with the men in the front and the women in the back. The conversation between them was more like a running argument sometimes, and they would get together with other couples, and then use that as an opportunity to put out those little zingers, about the spending, or the card games, or the chores. She fingered the satin sheets and wondered what *their* issue would be. She wondered if they would be like the other couples, with her and some friend talking about kids or house decorating while the boys argued about sports or lied about golf.

Downstairs, Tony was unhappy about what he had heard on the phone, she could tell that. She sighed. Now she had to be careful of what she said for the rest of the day, and had to take special care not to ask for anything: advise, decisions, permission. And then she ran the risk of him getting mad for her not paying enough attention, for being too distant. *Be all eyes and ears, and offer to do the little things when it seems safe.* If it was only a little deal, things might be all right by dinner.

She hoped so; angry dinners were worse than going hungry. Downstairs, the phone conversation was over, and she wondered what Guido wanted.

It seemed glamorous, in a way, Tony's connections. She knew that not every garbage man's wife lived like she was living. But she could tell the times that they yanked his chain because then he wasn't his own boss, and that was what Tony liked the most, being the big wheel. Sometimes she knew he was being told what to do, and he made it sound like it was his idea. She had to be careful then, to praise his idea, but not too much, since it wasn't really his. Then he would get mad, but he wouldn't be able to tell her why or do anything about it.

She got up and got dressed silently, putting on some light makeup. It wasn't even eight and she was tired already.

15

$=\!\!\!\equiv$ CHAPTER FIFTEEN $\equiv\!\!\!=$

Sterling was reading, only half-watching Bobby, who was sitting at his table and putting together the components of a roller bearing for the Osgood Engine Works. He was good at the repetitive work, and the job-training folks gave him a penny a bearing. Most days he cleared ten or fifteen bucks extra, enough money to get him the large Snickers bars he prized, and the big twenty-ounce sodas he loved.

Sterling was reading "Bluegrass Breakdown: The Making of the Old Southern Sound," nodding his head in agreement to the author and wondering if the guy played. One of the perennial mysteries to Sterling was people who didn't play music. An even bigger wonder was people who didn't play but still understood.

"Hey Bobbo! Wanna hear something?"

"Morning! You read 'em!" Bobby said quietly. He didn't pause in his work, but tilted his head to the side closest to Sterling.

"Okay. Here it is."

Syncopation is an art by which rhythmic tension is created, complicated, brought to a crisis, and finally resolved—not consecutively, but simultaneously— in an equilibrium of musical energy called swing. If syncopation divides rhythm and meter, swing brings them back together again: not as in the European tradition, at the foot of the music, through synchronization, but in the head, through what Gunther Schuller patriotically calls the "democratization of rhythmic values"—a "perfect equality of dynamics" among rhythmic forces which preserves the "full sonority of notes" as well as the powerfully explicit or "propulsive" quality characteristic of music doing service in rhythm and melody at once.

Sterling savored that thought: the democratic nature of bluegrass, where one player is not above another, except in the moment of their break, or the need to have the high tenor voice strain at the lyric melody line, or the bass thunder up from down below like an earthquake. Tonight was practice, and Sterling read the passage again, memorizing it easily. Let the preacher tell him the way to play a break or arch his eyes at one of Sterling's choices in harmonies, and he'd have something new to say about it.

Harmonies could be broken down six or seven different ways in most songs, but those ways were not created equal: some were mundane; some were beautiful. Sometimes just switching parts made all the difference, one voice soaring more effortlessly or blending down below more deeply. Sterling remembered some arrangements, ones that he had fought against— sometimes simply because they were Jo-Jo's or Chat's, he had to admit—wind up sounding fine when the execution got tightened up. He read the passage one more time. "Sonority of value," he muttered, and Bobby quietly echoed, "Norty va loo. Norty loo."

It was not the uncertainty that was the most troubling part of the journey: Where to stay, what would happen, what would tomorrow bring? Uncertainties could be tinged and colored with hope. Ada remembered what her mother had always said: "Hope makes a good breakfast, but a poor supper." It wasn't the unforeseen and the uncertain that made the sin of hopelessness so appealing; it was what was always certain: the looks, the sudden silence when she walked into a room, the small glances they made. One part of her hoped that this would be different, but sad as it made her— was sadness a sin also? She hoped not, or she was one of God's greatest sinners, then!—she had to admit to herself that this town of Pigeon Forge promised to be the same as all the others.

"Freddie! Come on, now! Get Angie and let's go over to that diner there. We'll have a nice supper, and we'll find a place to stay for the night."

"Why here, Ma? I mean, we could have stayed on the bus until Hazleton or Williamsport—someplace bigger than this," he said, hefting the sleeping child with one hand and a suitcase with another, and looking around at what might be his new home.

"It is still early, and there is another bus later this afternoon if we cannot find a place for the night. Those places have hotels, I know. But from one city to the next? It is the city we are trying to leave. We try here first and we will see what we will see," Ada said, resolutely, while opening a door of silver metal that matched the rest of the siding.

It was well into the lunch hour, and the counter was full. All the round leather seats, fastened atop stainless steel posts, swiveled as the owners considered the trio that had entered. Ada saw the heads ducking slightly, a few laughs, and the expected second glances. Most were looking at the suitcases more than they were at any of them. The older of two waitresses swept up to them from behind the counter.

"Hi, folks. How about a table for you today?"

"Thank you, yes," Ada said.

"Pigeon Forge rifle team?" Freddie softly asked no one, looking at a poster of twelve boys and girls with guns slung over their shoulders or cradled like a lover in their arms. In his own arms, Angie squirmed awake, let out a small bleat and jerked her head upright to see where they were.

"Look, Mommy! Horses!" she pointed out the window to three indifferent horses scattered about a small lot that was almost devoid of vegetation. One was a dappled gray, and the other two bays, all of them standing as if waiting for something.

They sat down. The woman followed closely with white placemats and a fistful of silverware, expertly making three places for them, and grabbing a pitcher of ice water at the service table to pour them all a drink.

"Coffee?"

"For me, yes. Thank you very much," Ada said. *No slyness about this one,* she thought.

"I'll have a Coke," Freddie said, and quickly remembering himself at Ada's stern look, added, "Please."

Angie tried to hitch her chair around so that she could see the horses better, and Ada put her hand on her shoulder to quiet her.

"What would you like to drink, Princess?" the old lady said. Angie was still craning her neck to see out the window, and the waitress had to repeat the question before she had her attention.

"Soda!" Angie chirped.

Ada added, "Sprite, please. No caffeine for her."

"Doesn't seem she needs it," the waitress laughed. "Name's Ellie. Yours?"

It was a simple question, but it took Ada by surprise, and she was furious with herself for the tears that almost welled up in her eyes.

Because of a kind word? Madre Mia!

"My name is Ada DeLeon. This is my son, Frederico, and my daughter, Angelina," she said, her voice shaking slightly. She blushed and hoped it was not as evident as it seemed.

"Well, welcome to Pigeon Forge, Ada. I'm Ellie. We have a nice meatloaf special today or a Salisbury steak platter. Both come with choice of potato and vegetables. Our soup is ham and bean or chicken and rice—homemade, too! And we have lemon chiffon pie and German chocolate cake for dessert. Or would you like to see a menu?"

"No, thank you. The meatloaf is fine for me. Freddie?"

"Salisbury steak?" he asked.

"It's a hamburger, hon. Fresh ground round. It's way better than those pathetic hockey pucks they serve at McDonalds."

"Okay," he said, then, after a pause, "Thanks very much."

"And for the Princess?" Ellie asked.

"My *name* is Angie!'"

"Ohhh. Sorry, hon. What do you like to have today?"

"I want what *he* has!" she said, happily.

"All rightee, then. We'll get that right up for you all."

As they ate, the lunch crowd thinned out. Most had places to go and work to be done, so by 1:30 the place was almost vacant. The three devoured the platters with homemade mashed potatoes and gravy, fresh veggies, and biscuits as light and fluffy as clouds—all so good! Ada decided to splurge and ordered dessert as well, and still lingered over the last of the pie, creamy and delicious, reluctant to leave.

"So. Forgive me for being a buttinski, but are you folks thinking of staying?"

Ada took a moment. Why not trust her? If she was wrong, they get on the bus and try a bigger place. What is the harm?

"We are looking for a place to stay and for work for me—in the city, I am, I am..."

She fought the blush and failed.

"Ah. Say no more, hon."

Ellie sat in the fourth seat, near Ada, and patted her hand gently. Angie scrambled away and jumped into a booth near a window to watch the horses, kneeling contentedly on the thickly padded window seat with her face an inch from the glass, watching intently as the horses did nothing. Freddie blushed as well and feigned sudden interest in the placemat, which was covered with advertisements for car washes, batting cages, canoe companies, ski areas, and a long list of appliance, feed, tack, grocery, fabric, and convenience stores.

"Well, as far as a place to stay, Layton has a nice apartment over the inn that I know is empty right now. Maybe a little small, but from what I hear about those city apartments, maybe not so small after all. And I could use a hand here at the lunch and dinner shifts. Chrissy is just helping out till she goes back to school. She has some kind of internship down in North Carolina she's got to start soon. So? What do you think?"

Ada sat, tongue-tied, while Freddie stared at the two.

"I mean, it's not much, but it would tide you over 'til you find something better. I know you will, too. So? What do you think?"

It was all too much. The trip, the struggle of wills between her and Freddie, the worry, and most of all the strong act she had to put up. Ada began to weep silently, finally remembering her manners and murmuring thanks over and over while the few remaining patrons looked frankly and curiously at her.

"There, there. Things are going to be fine, hon. I don't know what it was drove you here, but the Lord has his ways. You'll be just fine." Ellie handed Ada a napkin, which Ada used to wipe her eyes genteelly, while Ellie explained how to get to Layton's, when the buses ran to Fiesterville, when she had to be to work, and how she could find the schools to register the kids.

"You'll want something better than slingin' hash, unless I miss my guess," was how she dismissed Ada's thanks.

"Now, I don't think I forgot anything," she concluded, "but if I did, well, you know where to find me. Right here, 24/7, as the new saying is." Ellie smiled and patted her hand again.

"You are a saint. A saint. I will pray for you! And someday I will be able to repay you! This I promise!" Ada said, once again in control. She gathered the children, warned them that they would have a bit of a walk ahead of them, and grasped Ellie's hand once more before she left, smiling.

They were not even a dozen paces down the road when Ellie went back over to the register, pulled the phone off the cradle and dialed a number.

"Layton? Yes, sure I owe you from the Super Bowl. Layton, that's money in the bank and you know it. Why don't you ever come up to collect, then? Oh, sure, since when does it say 'loser flies?' Well, when you want it, you can just come get it, you old mud flap. Seems to me when I *won* the year before last you tried the same trick on me. Now, listen, that isn't why I called at all. In about twenty minutes a woman with a couple kids is going to be showing up down there looking for a place to stay. No, no, now, listen, Layton, I know it doesn't square up that bet. Lord, will you just hush for a minute? She's going to be working here, and I want you to treat her nice, now. I told her about the apartment, and I want for you to give it to her. No, there's nothing *wrong* with her, but. Just promise me you will? "

Ellie swallowed hard and said, "Favor to me?"

She listened for a long moment, said her good-byes and finally hung up the phone ruefully. This one would cost her. She watched the three until the bend in the road finally hid them from view. She trusted her heart. He'd get over it. Maybe even by the next World Series. Definitely by the next Super Bowl.

"Come on, ole bean. Time to close up shop," Sterling said to Bobby, closing the book and smiling.

He watched Bobby's fat fingers with the ends splayed characteristically. Bobby carefully picked up the ball-bearing sleeve with small metal tabs that pointed upwards, looking like silver fingers. Fat fingers or not, Bobby had the sleeve loaded with shiny, half-inch metal balls in a few seconds, then he smoothly placed the piece on the table press and pulled the handle to crimp the tabs down firmly.

"Va loo," he said happily, and tossed it into the half-full bin that represented that day's work.

"Nice work, Bobbo. Let's get you back to the house, huh?"

In the main room, Sterling heard the rest of the staff bundling up the rest of the clients and the noise level rising as parents came and went with their "children" of forty, fifty and sixty years old.

The trip through the main room always lasted five or ten minutes between the last-minute questions of the staff on some medication or protocol, and the sometimes bizarre "good-byes" of the clients to each other.

"Bob Bob Bob Bob," one of them chanted at Bobby, sticking out a lizard-like tongue that was as wide at the base as it was long.

"Norty Va LOO!" Bobby shouted back, waving his own tongue back and forth and laughing, his eyes squinting with delight.

"Okay, Bobbo. 'Nuff norty loos, there. Come on. Don't want to keep supper waiting, huh?"

At the mention of food, Bobby ran over to the door, and a moment later they were out on the gray deck that led to the street. The weather had taken a turn, and their breaths hung in the damp air, vaporous streams that quickly merged with the drizzle that had begun to fall. Sterling shivered and helped guide Bobby over to the van, hoisting him up by his elbow into the front seat. He thought about his dinner date with the new secretary that had started over at Retter's housing, the outfit that ran the group homes that many of the clients lived in. Not that Sterling was getting his hopes up; he knew all about the Chance Brothers joke: Slim and None, and Slim left town, haha. But it would be a nice diversion for an hour or two, especially since he could leave at the end of it with an excuse of something he had to do.

How long had they been at those practices? How many thousand beers had they drunk along the way, and how many hundred arguments had they started, and shelved, then rediscovered? Man, it seemed like it had been forever instead of twenty years or so. But Sterling had to admit that it was now as much a part of him as the little gnome on his shoulder whose heeltaps were, at this moment, so faint as to be almost unnoticeable.

He pulled up in front of the house, a house like any other on the block. The neighbors had fought tooth and nail to keep it out. Good thing for the clients there was no zoning to worry about, and now, after eight years, the folks didn't seem to mind them much, although they didn't exactly throw parties for them, either. They'd as soon ignore a body if they could; they were clannish that way, and Sterling knew all about that country kind of clannishness. It wasn't good and it wasn't bad. It was a parochial kind of thing, and he understood why it existed. It was the same way his mother's people had been: live and let live, on one hand, but do it someplace else, too. Xenophobia, sure. But then, look at what a lack of xenophobia had done for the Lenape, or the Bushmen, or the Inuit. So Sterling had ignored the harsh glares when he first came up with his court papers and his high-minded ways, staying pleasant, always being infuriatingly polite when he had a chance to greet them or speak to them. And after awhile, it gave them something to gossip about, gave them a target to pick on when they were feeling down about their little town, or who got the best seats at the church social the Sunday before. After awhile, Sterling and the rest of them began to serve a purpose, and then the neighbors let up a little. It was kind of a truce, now. That counted as a victory in Sterling's book.

He got out and helped Bobby to the ground, again stabilizing him by the elbow as he helped him up the stairs of the Victorian, then up onto the porch, where he could see someone peeking at them through the curtains on the old-style double doors.

"You behave yourself, you devil, you," Sterling said to Bobby.

"You the debble," Bobby said. "You, Norty loo!"

Dinner was fine. The girl's name was Amy Belinda—Amy B., she called herself—and she was from Knoxville, Tennessee. They had spent a pleasant time together, talking about the South and their own respective hometowns. She had just graduated from the extension at Fiesterville, and she was hoping that her first job would lead to a more responsible position with Retter's. She had picked that school because a few of her relations had wandered up that way during the depression, and she had visited there off and on from the time she was growing up.

Sterling gave her a polite peck on the cheek, a few words of encouragement, asked if he could call on her again, and tried not to be too self-congratulatory when he said she would enjoy that very much.

She was only 23, after all, and maybe she thought Sterling would make a good father or something. Stranger things had happened. He remembered that Canadian girl who he had run into some winters ago, when the ski area up north of there had started up. She had stayed on the whole ninety days that she had before she got on the bus for Montreal. Sterling still swore he had seen a tear in her eye when she left, but he didn't know if it was for missing him or her chance at a citizenship, which was something she had admitted that she wanted badly.

Sterling wasn't about to let himself get all balled up in emotions. He insisted that he had no clue what love was, at least when he got a chance, which was seldom. The boys usually avoided serious subjects if they could, as if saying something about love would make it come true. Sterling was fond of saying (when he could) that nobody had ever measured it, when it came and when it went was impossible to tell, that the symptoms of love and the flu were about the same, so if it did exist it was simply some kind of malady, like a sinus infection or athletes foot. One might reason about thought, and fear, gratitude, even loyalty. But love? He was taking a flier on that one. Maybe for good.

Sterling stopped at his apartment long enough to pick up his instruments and check his mail. He ignored the blinking of the phone machine: that would be his boss, Angie, with some instruction or another about tomorrow. Maybe he would listen to it when he returned, maybe not. The mail wasn't much, which was fine by him. No news. The latest issue of <u>Bluegrass Unlimited</u> had arrived, and he carried that out to the car with his banjo and his D-18. Fifteen seconds later he revved it up and was on his way down the road.

16

≡ CHAPTER SIXTEEN ≡

By the time he had arrived at Chat's, the darkness was complete, and the drizzle that had continued unabated since the morning had turned to a steady downpour. It was a relief to see the warm yellow lights behind the gingham curtains, spilling out on the twenty cords of firewood stacked like jackstraws in front of Chat's porch. Out front was Johnny's old red Chevy with a blue tarp over home-made ribs on the back, neatly stitched shut with some dirty old mine cord so Johnny could just open the tailgate and slide his bass in when they were done. Inside, Sterling heard the two of them talking and laughing, and he heard the idle note or chord that always comes when a fellow stands about with an instrument. *It was in their nature to be played, and it was in a fellow to play them,* Sterling thought.

He walked up the steps, and from the inside, he saw Johnny reach over and open the door in front of him.

"Hey, Sterling. How you been?" he said, as Sterling eased his cases through the doorway.

"Johnny, Chat. How's it going?"

Chat stood next to the counter that separated the front room from the kitchen, his 28 in hand, and smiled. Sterling could hear the TV going in the playroom as well as the rumble and thud of the kids playing.

"Going good, old son. How are you doing?"

"Fine, fine. Jo-Jo's not here again, huh?"

"He'll be here directly. He just called and said he had to stop over to Ziegenfus' about some lots. Want a beer?"

"Sure thing, Rev. The boy is pounding out the units, that's for sure. He's definitely not hurting for business," Sterling said.

Chat moved to the fridge and pulled two longnecks out, flipped the tops off them and handed one to Sterling.

"Well, good for both of them, I suppose," Chat said. "But I get worried, sometimes. I hear Malchio bought that piece next to my place."

"The Huffsnyder piece? I thought Junior was gonna keep that," Johnny said.

"Well, I guess he saw the tax bill," Chat said, frowning.

"You don't seem to be too happy about getting new neighbors, there, Chat," Sterling said, grinning. He took a pull on his beer.

"Well, it's *natural* for a man to like his privacy, isn't it?" Chat said, finishing his first and beginning his second.

"You just don't want any brothers moving in there, I bet," Sterling said. Chat stiffened.

"Listen. You just quit that right *now*. I got nothing against them."

"You've got nothing for them, either. Fact is, you don't like them blacks much, do ya, Rev?"

"Geeze, Sterling, why you gotta be so nasty like that?" Johnny asked. "Like to like. That's all it is. You want a bunch of niggers next to you? I don't believe you do."

"Johnny. Please," Chat muttered.

"And they say things about the South," Sterling said, rolling his eyes.

"Hey, listen here. God made 'em, and that's enough for me," Chat said, the color rising in his face.

"But that doesn't mean you like 'em," Sterling persisted.

"Heck, man, I can't *understand* 'em. I mean, the Johnson boys from Fiesterville, them I know. They're okay. But the new ones? When they stop at the shop, they treat me pretty poor, always *laughin'* at me like I was dumb as a stone, and talking that jibber-jabber. Course I don't like that. What man *would*?"

"A true Christian," Sterling smirked, leaning against the counter and chugging his beer.

"*Hell*, Sterling," Johnny spat. "You always gotta be so *snooty*, don't ya, from the big school and all that trash. God made us different for a reason. You see them inviting us in for dinner? No, we gotta go to them all the time. So I figure it's better to just leave the whole thing lie. Like to like. That's right in the Bible, isn't it, Chat?"

"I'm not sure, Johnny. Let's leave this be, okay? It's not like we can do anything about it anyway. Sterling, you must be horny or something, you got your blood all riled up. Come on, get that banjo out and let's work on a few things," Chat said, unstrapping the guitar and placing it on the couch. While Sterling unsnapped his case, Chat went into the kitchen, returning with three more beers, which he slapped down on the counter.

They began tuning, and were part way through the first song, teasing at a close harmony, when they heard Jo-Jo pull in. A minute later he walked in, black leather jacket half-open and his fiddle in his hand.

"Evening, evening," he said, smiling.

"Hi, Jo-Jo. Make your big land deal?" Chat said.

"Do I detect a note of crankiness tonight?" Jo-Jo said, throwing his jacket on a chair and placing his fiddle on the counter. He walked into the kitchen and opened the fridge, helping himself to a beer. Chat half-turned, noodling around with his guitar.

"It's in their nature to be played," Sterling said absently.

"What?" Chat said.

"Instruments. It's their nature to be played."

"That's—what do they call it?—personification. It's their nature to sit there until our nature makes us pick 'em up, more like."

Sterling stood irresolute for a moment.

"Well, try this for nature, then, Mr. Wise guy. The Big Ridge Bluegrass Association called me this week," Sterling said smugly.

"Oh? And what is it that *they* want? They call to tell us we gotta work a bit *harder* to make their cut?" Chat snapped

"Chat, Chat. Easy, boy," Jo-Jo laughed. "So what *do* they want?"

"They want us to play the festival this summer. But they said that they only book bands with recording experience."

"Oh, so in order to get a job that pays five or six hundred, we gotta drop five or six thousand on a CD?" Jo-Jo said.

"They're not that much, Jo-Jo. I spec'd 'em out last night on the 'net. We could do one for maybe 2,500, after the master was done. I made a couple calls. Studio time is between forty and eighty an hour, and, from what I heard talking with those guys, we should be able to do it in maybe ten or fifteen hours."

"Fifteen or twenty hours? Jumpin' jet boats. We can't even work out one tune an hour, and I bet you money that as soon as we tape it, somebody's gonna be unhappy about somebody, so that'll double the time. They just said that to get us in there. Like drilling a well. All they have to convince you to dig is the first fifty feet, after that, you go until you hit water, even if it's 500 foot down."

"Which the last one I had drilled was 543 feet, actually," Jo-Jo said, taking a pull of beer.

"What do you expect? You keep punching holes in the ground and sucking it dry like that," Chat muttered.

"Progress, my boy," Jo-Jo said, eyes narrowed.

"A CD would be nice to have," Johnny said. "It might make sense. It's not like we couldn't sell a few. People ask about it at jobs all the time."

"Get some more details, I guess. Those people bug me, though. Their attitude," Chat said.

"Ah, well. Big Ass Bluegrass, " Jo-Jo cracked, making a wolf-whistle on his fiddle. They all laughed a little.

"What about the Ice-Cream Man? I thought I heard he was starting to do some recording out near Williamsport someplace."

"Anthony? He's out in Wellsboro. He maybe would cut us a break on the recording. Old times and all that."

"The way you all are always going on about him and his old lady, I figure he must be too expensive for the likes of us," Jo-Jo said, smirking.

Chat said, "You're just *jealous,* Jo-Jo. I guess I can call him up and see what's what. Anyhow, where were we?"

"We were working on that 'Rank Strangers,'" Sterling said.

"Key?"

"Try it in A."

They stopped the chitchat, playing with the harmonies until they had a version where they were not doubling each other in any notes. After twenty minutes and several more beers, they had it down pretty well, Sterling thought.

"So that's the arrangement, then?" Sterling asked.

"Let's see. Hey Sue, com'ere, could ya?" Chat hollered.

She emerged from the playroom, her thick hair cascading out over the thick teal sweater she had knitted the first winter they had been together.

"You boys have enough beer?" she asked, eyeing the dozen empties on the counter.

"Plenty, thanks. Hey, give a listen to this, once, and tell me what *you* think," Chat said. They went over the song once more, and Sue stood staring at the ceiling joists, listening. When they were done, Chat raised an eyebrow in question.

"Not bad. I'd do two things. There oughta be more call in the call and response. Maybe once you could do it, Sterling, then once Jo-Jo, then maybe both together? That way you just did it is too predictable, A, B, A, B. Change it up a little, maybe," she trailed off and looked at Chat and Sterling, both nodding.

"What's the *other* thing, then?"

"You and Sterling could maybe switch parts for the middle chorus? Make a better balance and go with the switching calls?"

Both men nodded, and without a sign kicked the song off again, trying the two variants Sue had suggested. They stumbled a bit on the first pass, talking out the difficulties quickly, in bursts of words, "you take...here..." and singing, then, "do you, should I go," singing, "And then both of us," and singing, and with nods, grunts and snatches of phrases, agreeing or disagreeing until they had the new parts resolved.

By the third repetition, they did not need to interrupt the song. They played it through, from front to back, and Sterling had to admit it sounded very sweet indeed. He had a twinge of regret that he had busted on Chat so hard earlier.

"Sue, that's the cheese, all right," Jo-Jo said.

"I married above myself," Chat said happily.

"Thanks, Jo-Jo. And stop being a goofball," she said, slapping Chat with a very small smile.

"They're right. That gives it full sonority of value," Sterling said, in a manner he hoped was offhand.

The other four looked at each other and burst out laughing.

"Well, Mr. Sionara, whatever you say," Chat smiled.

"It means," Sterling began, but Johnny laid his hand on Sterling's arm to shush him.

"Yeah, we know. It sounds good. Can I get you another beer?

And they all laughed again, a happy family in that slice of time.

17

≈ Chapter Seventeen ≈

By the next week, Chat had gotten in touch with Anthony, who had an opening the week following. Chat imagined that they would be recording as if they were playing live, but the Ice-Cream Man had said that he'd rather lay things out in layers so they could put it back together the way they liked without the bleed-through from two mics.

"Oh, and listen, my guitar-picking friend, just you and Johnny the first time."

"Anthony, I don't think I can do the songs right without Sterling playing the banjo, at least."

"Well, against doctor's orders, then. And we definitely need to keep it down to you three. I haven't gotten the basement studio finished, so that's all I have room for."

"Umm, I.C.?"

"Yes, my tongue-tied brother?"

"Sterling wanted to know if he could bring his new girlfriend along."

"She will be bored and unhappy, I predict."

"I told him that. He says he told her that. Neither of them care, I think."

"Sounds truly like love. Well, she's more than welcome. I'm getting excited! I'll see you in a few days, then!"

So they piled in the van with tote sacks, sleeping bags and coffee cups, bags of pretzels and peanuts stuffed in all the cracks between the seats, generic bottled waters rolling around on the floor in the way back of the van beneath the tumble of guitars, banjos, mandolins and fiddles.

They drove down 611, then picked up 33 to Easton, dodging traffic, Chat driving taciturn and Johnny sitting shotgun and talking excitedly about a new vein they had opened up last week. It was a nice, fat one, he said, maybe twelve feet thick, plunging down at a 45-degree angle, and rich as Croesus. The Snyders in the next wildcat hole down the ridge—one of the six of them left out of all the dozens and dozens that had been operating when Johnny was a kid—were working on a new idea of a machine they were making from bits and pieces of breakers and some crushing equipment from the gravel pit down in the next valley. If it worked the way they hoped, Johnny might be interested in getting mechanized with the new vein and all. Then Johnny wondered out loud about the session out at Wellsboro and if it was going to be as much work as they let on it was.

"As *who* lets on?" Chat asked him, eyeing Sterling and Amy in the mirror. They were sitting in the back seat happily whispering in each other's ears and giggling.

"All the things I read about recording," Johnny said, shrugging.

"All the things you read about recording," Chat repeated.

After a long pause, Johnny said, "Well, Chat, I *can* read, ya know."

Chat looked at the mountain of a man beside him, and realized he had hurt his feelings, just with that little repeat.

"Johnny, 'course you can read. I just never thought about reading about it beforehand. Tell me what you read, Johnny."

There was no response for a moment, then Johnny told about how many hours it took Kentucky Thunder to cut just one song, and how the some other bluegrass band had spent twelve thousand dollars arguing.

"Twelve thousand *dollars?* Chat asked, genuinely awake.

"That was just the cash, too. None of the *hours*," Johnny said, "But then, that won't be us. I don't think."

"Guess we'll find out when we get there," Chat said.

In the back, Sterling now was cooing baby talk to Amy B., and Chat rolled his eyes at Johnny as they drove through a Sunday Easton, where stores were shuttered with curtains of steel, a few kids hung out on the sidewalks, and old ladies wearing old men's overcoats and too-large hats pulled two-wheeled carts. Chat cut across Pine Street, past the bocce courts and the back yards of the upscale restaurants that had sprung up over the past ten years.

Easton was a dying city no longer, not with 78 making both New York and Philly a hop, skip and a jump away.

Chat maneuvered the van into the alley, clearing the retaining wall on one side and the old factory loading dock on the other by inches until the driveway opened out a little. They could see the front of Frank's luthier shop painted like an Italian market with black background and gold trim announcing "Bella!" which was the name of Frank's guitars.

"Wait 'til you see this shop, Amy B.," Sterling gushed. "This guy is *incredible.*" He got out of the van as empty Styrofoam coffee cups rattled out of the sliding doors and onto the ground. Sterling bent to pick them up as Amy B. watched, and Sterling was talking a mile a minute now:

"And so he took that broken fiddle bow. It snapped right at the tip, and he went and carved a dovetail in it that had to be about the width of a pencil point. You couldn't even *see* the thing."

"Wow," Amy said, admiringly, although Chat was figuring she didn't know a dovetail from a Dove bar.

Johnny wasn't even out of his seat when the door to the shop flew open and Frank came bounding out, bear-like, face creased into a grin, his grey curly hair flecked with small curls of wood shavings as well.

"Hello hello! How are you, my friends?" he asked, giving Chat a hug that took his breath away for an instant.

"Took us *forever* to get down here," Chat muttered, eyeing Sterling and Amy B., who were checking out Frank's garden-to-be, outlined in huge blocks of gray granite that Frank had pilfered from the abandoned warehouse that sat catty-corner from his alleyway down near the Lehigh River.

"How in the world did you get this *up* here, Frank?" Sterling asked, spreading his hands over the largest one, a stone that was ten feet long and two feet thick.

"We used a come-along first, but we only moved it like three feet in an hour. I figured at that rate it would take twelve years to get them all moved, so I borrowed Curtie's Jeep with a winch on it."

"Off-roading in the middle of Easton? Nobody called the cops?" Chat asked, laughing in spite of himself.

"I take care of my neighbors, and they take care of me. Hey, you boys have to stop by when the garden is all planted. We'll have a fertility party."

"Ouch. Maybe a bit too, umm, pagan for me, ya know?" Chat said.

Frank's brown eyes twinkled and his face creased in an eager grin.

"We wouldn't sacrifice any chickens or anything, Preach. Strictly secular, this would be. Whaddya say? Sometime in June when the weather gets really nice?"

"Y'all might be waitin' 'til July at this rate," Amy B. offered, shivering a little bit as she stood in the shade of the wall. Sterling came over to her, wrapping his arms around her.

"Frank, this is my friend, Amy Belinda," Sterling said.

"Ah, you're cold! What am I thinking? Come in, come in! Warm yourselves up while I get Johnny's bass down here."

He ushered them into the shop, took down a sheepskin coat from the rack and draped it over Amy B. with a flourish, motioned towards a handmade stool for her to sit upon, and went into the back room to fetch Johnny's instrument. They stood or sat without saying much with Sterling standing behind Amy B., her leaning on him and patting him absently, and Chat and Johnny looking around at workbenches full of half-assembled guitars, walls festooned with wood clamps, forms for guitars, drawknives and block planes, shelves full of bindings and tuners, and racks and racks of aged woods. Sitka spruce, mahogany, rosewood, ebony and the highly figured maples, curly and tiger and birds-eye, lined the walls in racks and stacks, most of the wood going back to the first days of the Martin guitar boom in the late '60s and early '70s, when there was serious money to be made in the huge ageless hardwoods carved from the rainforests in Brazil. They had all heard stories about back when guys guarding skids of logs as big as a barge would turn up missing, the wood along with them, trees that took a century to grow and a minute to cut, deep rich grains swirling like the mists of time or like the fog in a wooded hollow just before the rains.

Frank returned with the bass in his hands.

"I had to take the fingerboard off, and there were all kinds of cracks in the neck below the fingerboard. I soaked that in thinned out superglue and put two graphite rods in the neck."

Johnny picked up the bass, eyeing the repaired part of the neck closely, running his fingers over the spline Frank had put in the crack between the heel stock and the neck. He ran a riff from "Tell me Baby" on it with the notes fat and round bouncing off the chestnut rafters of the old shop, and then he squinted and played a C scale from the top of the neck down to the lowest note, which made the windows rattle a little bit.

"Oh, that sounds sweet," Johnny said. But his face was a worry mask.

"But what?" Frank asked him.

"I can't get my fingers underneath the strings anymore," Johnny said.

"That was how far out the neck was, Johnny. Not much I could do about it this go-round and still have it ready for the session. We could put an adjustable bridge on it, or I could cut that one and put the wheels on it, next time. I didn't even get a chance to clean it up," Frank said, apologetically.

Chat said, "Johnny, it sounds awesome. You'll figure how to work it just fine."

"I don't have to play it as hard to get the sound, I guess," Johnny said, dubiously. But when Frank told him what the price was for what must have been several days' worth of work, Johnny and Chat both looked at Frank as if he had bumped his head.

"Frank, you sure about that? I mean, I'm not trying to talk you out of it, but that's a lot of work for the money."

"Eh, you'll be famous and then I'll get ya back. You just play wonderfully and tell everyone to buy Bella guitars. I'll see you all in a month or two when you get the record wrapped up."

Then off to the middle of the state they blasted, Amy B. requiring stops every 45 minutes to get more coffee or pee, while Chat was doing his best to keep from getting pissed and checking the clock every five minutes, calculating.

"We can't be stopping every ten minutes, not if we expect to get to this place before dark."

"Is that so important?" Amy B. said, squeezing Sterling's arm and smiling.

"You ever been out to Tioga County? There's a whole lotta ways to get lost out there, and not a gas station or a McDonald's on every corner. Last time I was up there, I got on some back roads, and I thought I was gonna come out in Canada. It was so freakin' desolate. So I think the answer is, 'Yes, it is so important,'" Chat said, his lips pulled downwards in a frown.

"Chat, you've got to loosen up, my friend. We won't get anything done if you're going to be all pissy about things," Sterling said, holding Amy B.'s hand. She was looking out the window, and Chat realized with a start that she had tears in her eyes.

He stopped talking and glanced over at Johnny, who was staring at nothing and thinking about having to change his style of playing bass, when time really was money.

"Okay," Chat said to the back of Amy B.'s head. "Listen, Amy. I'm sorry. Okay? I forget my ways sometimes. I just want this to go right, having to take the time off like this."

She said nothing and snuggled into Sterling like a small child. They road silently again, just the road noise of tires on concrete, the road sweeping among little bumps of hills on one side, First Mountain on the other, and not a house to be seen in the miles and miles of gray forest that were now being tinged with the warmer hues of sundown. Chat glanced at the sun setting out his window, estimated a handsbreadth of distance between it and the horizon.

"One hour. It's gonna be close," he said, and he brought the van up to eighty. They got off the interstate at Mansfield, picked up Route 6, the old road, and got into Wellsboro just as the sun touched the horizon. At the diner, they stopped, and Chat called Anthony, who gave them directions.

"Get his cell," Sterling was stage whispering to Chat, who shushed him with a look and a wave of his hand.

"No sense in getting a cell. There's no service out here at all," the owner said.

"All the more reason to move up here, then," Johnny joked. "No more rude cell-phone conversations."

Chat finally hung up and showed what he had written to the man behind the counter, who deciphered the lefts and rights into a kind of map that kept trying to crawl off the left side of the page.

"Then you take Ike's Road to Ding-Dang Road. That one isn't marked."

"Ding-Dang? That's a joke, right?"

"Nope," said one of the kids working the counter. "That's the name of it."

"How did it get that name, then?" Johnny asked, but nobody knew any answer. They said their "thanks" and went back outside as Amy asked if maybe they could get something to eat, but she was ignored. They got back in the van, took the rights and the lefts, missed a turn and saw signs for Charlestown, and turned back around in the dusk, slowing and stopping at the bottom of a broad valley with farms stretched out on all sides and the woods further up above.

"He said something about butter signs," Chat said, offering the flash of memory as if it were a signpost.

"I saw one of them back up the road a bit," Amy B. offered, and they continued on, discovered that the sign for Ike's Road was only printed on one side and was blank on the other, took the hill and bore left on the last turn they would have to make, and pulled up in front of Anthony's with only an ounce of light left to the day.

"Wow," Amy B. said. The three-story house was angled in the front like the prow of a ship and had huge windows that overlooked the valley below. The back of the house was tucked into the hillside and was surrounded by a broad deck that ran from the front to the back.

They parked and popped the trunk, each grabbing bags or instruments, and walked up to the back door, rang the bell and could hear music and footsteps from inside.

"Why do they call him the Ice-Cream Man?" Amy wanted to know. Before any of the boys could answer, the door swung open, and Anthony's wife, Sue, a radiant and beautiful dusky blond woman, stood in the lighted portal, grabbing Chat and giving him a kiss on the cheek while grabbing a guitar with one hand, pulling him in to the house.

"We were getting worried about you all," she said. "Come on in. Let me help you with your stuff. Anthony is out at the plant—he just called and asked if you were here. Sterling! Johnny, how are you both? And this must be Amy B. We're so glad you could make it up here."

For the next twenty minutes, they ferried bags and instruments in, paused to admire the sunset, delighted over the hardwood floors and the soft plush carpet, watched as several does came out into the field below the house to feed, carried the bags into whichever rooms they were assigned all the while, stomachs grumbling after a day of pretzels, cold kielbasa and coffee.

"Here, sit down. I made a chicken soup. Anthony will be here directly."

So they sat down at the heirloom cherry table, watched the darkness descend over the expanse of valley below and the moon come up full and large as they had ever seem it. They talked about music and things related to music, and Sue talked excitedly about an Australia tour that she and Anthony were scheduled to take in the coming months.

"Wow. Australia, " Amy B. said. "That must be cool."

"Better than Holland. We played there last fall. Rude," Sue said, shaking her head.

Chat was on his third bowl of soup and sixth homemade biscuit when they heard Anthony pulling up, jumping down from the SUV and running into the house.

"Another five minutes and I would have been out looking for you guys," he said, shaking hands with all of them, giving a small peck on the cheek to Amy B. and a much bigger one to Sue.

As they ate, Tony went over what he expected to accomplish over the next few days, beginning with getting the levels.

"We'll just lay down the rhythm tracks first, maybe with just Chat singing. We may have to lay down separate guitar and vocal tracks for you, Chat, later, if there are any fixes. Then we can lay in the harmonies, and the last thing is the instrumental breaks where you want them."

"That's gonna be tough, playing a break without hearing anybody playing the break," Chat said around a mouthful of biscuit. "At least that's what Sterling and I thought about it."

"I hear what you say to me, my biscuit-eating friend! Let us break biscuit together! I can play along and put breaks in you can play against. When Jo-Jo gets up here, we can scrap what you want and keep what you want. But that's not for tonight or tomorrow. We'll be lucky to get the basic tracks down the next two days anyway."

They ran mic cords into the respective bedrooms with headphones for each, set just one vocal mic up for Chat, had the levels wrung out by nine or so, and then relaxed afterwards, jamming for a few hours, red-hot licks from Sue on fiddle and Anthony on mandolin. They hit the sack after eleven. The next morning, it was time to get to work. Amy B. was excited at the beginning because she thought that she would be the photojournalist, but she became miffed when she realized that she could not see anyone or even talk to Sue because someone's mic would pick it up.

For the boys, it was time to go to their respective rooms and shut the door. Sterling's room had a computer desk in the corner, a fax machine with light blinking, stacks of mailers in bins on the desk, photos of Sue and Anthony with Vassar and Sam Bush and Byron Berline, Del and Charlie Waller, and pictures of them playing to thousands of tie-dyed hippie fans in big-tented venues. Sterling spent the idle moments (there were many) scanning the book titles or reading with the "cans" still on his ears.

On the other side of the house, Chat needed only ten minutes before he got a little buggy. At least there were woods out the windows where Chat could watch for movement when he had to stand there waiting while someone would have to redo an intro or break, sitting on a futon listening back. For ten hours he listened to Anthony saying, "We are rolling" and "We are live" and then Chat or Johnny or Sterling would interrupt by saying, "What am I doing here, trying to come in before the verse?" or "Which part are you playing it back from, just after the break or after the chorus?" and "The chorus is the same as the break" and somebody saying "Just play it from right after, 'My old hen,' okay?"

By the time the sun had set, all of them secretly knew that their ears were shot. Chat could hear phantom sounds that didn't even exist, and for all of them, the sounds in the headphones were the only real true thing; what the Ice-Cream Man was pumping into his head was the whole world, and with a twist of a knob he could make Sterling's thin and reedy voice fatter, Chat's occasional bellow mellow, Johnny's tentative singing certain and astute. Every sound was a facet of light in a beautiful stained glass window, the sound of fingers on strings, heavy breathing at a moment, the squeak of the leather on the guitar strap, and in between times the faint sound of real-time noises in the other parts of the house when Anthony would finally holler, "Stand by. Five minutes 'til I get his cued up right." And then the "Let's do it again" and "again" and "again!" until they all had no patience left. Their ears felt like they were stuffed with cotton and the boys were allowed out of the box for fifteen or twenty minutes every so often to keep them fresh. On the third day, Chat said to Sue that she must think they were terrible slackers because she only saw them sitting around and eating. She laughed and explained that she refrained from coming down until she heard their voices so she wouldn't mess up the recording.

"And here I thought it was just a coincidence that you always caught us goofing around," Chat laughed.

They left after three days of recording, silent in the van except for the thin and reedy sound of Amy B.'s voice whispering to Sterling. For the next six weeks, they followed the same pattern, one weekend even driving back and forth three times in two days to get the sessions in that they needed to make the master by the deadline for the Big Apple Bluegrass people.

Throughout it all, Jo-Jo had problems: problems with the cover art, problems with the song selection, problems being included out on the first session, even thought Johnny had tried to explain it to him one night at the inn.

"Stop being so smug and sanctimonious, you bastard," Jo-Jo had growled at him, and just blushed a deeper red when Kate had overheard him and reminded him that the last words on anyone's lips concerning Johnny would be those two.

"What are you, in love with him or something? 'Cause if you are, there he is. You're welcome to him," Jo-Jo snapped.

And just when they thought it couldn't get any worse, and putting on the headphones actually made Chat shiver with dread, Anthony played back a cut that they had tried to finish and on which Sue had laid down a harmony fiddle with Jo-Jo's stuff.

"What the hell is that?" he demanded, and when Chat told him, said simply that he was the fiddle player, and if there was any fiddle going to be played on the CD, it was going to be him and him alone, or otherwise he would quit.

Much as Chat wanted to call his bluff, he didn't have the nerve to test him or the heart to hurt his feelings, and they reluctantly agreed that, mandolin or not, only Jo-Jo got the nod for fiddle.

That was the way it went through the last stages of spring, through the onion snows and Saint Patty's day, the opening of trout season, beyond the first ball games and spring gobbler, hurt feelings, recriminations, dozens and dozens of cases of beer, chilly looks from Sue, a few jobs for doctors and lawyers and Indian chiefs. Finally, Jo-Jo softened and grudgingly let Sue lay down some tracks, all to save time.

Eventually, the master tape went out to Oasis and the CD was done. Even Jo-Jo, recently dubbed "The Master of Curmudgeon" by Anthony, admitted that the thing sounded pretty damn good, and the shipment was due three weeks before the deadline for the Big Ridge Bluegrass festival.

"Ah, it is a thing of beauty," the Ice-Cream Man said when the boxes arrived, and they had the CD release party at the inn, where their fans packed themselves in that night, not a seat or a square foot of room to move.

Everyone was laughing and drinking, buying CDs and T-shirts like mad and making even Chat's Sue smile with pride.

18

≡ CHAPTER EIGHTEEN ≡

Sterling tried hard to stay out of the fray concerning the CD. He was paying more attention to Amy B. these days, and he could swear (only to himself!) that at times Chat and Jo-Jo were jealous of them both. They spoke of that one night down at Ellie's after dinner.

"Just look at the trip out to Anthony's," she had complained. "I don't think Chat said five words to me the whole time."

"Hon. You're sensitive about that, I know. But he's all about the music, so I wouldn't take it so personal. He has his ways, same as I have mine."

She slid closer to him in the booth.

"I like your ways better," she smiled, and then kissed him. Ellie passed by, smiled and shook her head.

Amy's look grew pensive, and she said, "Besides, you didn't see him being like that to Frank or Anthony. No. He was all buddy buddy with them. He sure can turn it on and turn it off. I'll say that about him."

"Well. I'd deny it if I could, I guess, although I have no idea why. Best buddies and all that," Sterling said, shrugging his shoulders and finishing his coffee.

"Grr. Forget him. Let's go out to my place. I'll start a fire and you can read to me—give me a footrub."

"This is a dream, right?" Sterling said.

"A right good dream. So let's not wake up, shall we?"

They rode in silence through the soft spring air with their windows down, crickets chirping in the darkness, lost in thoughts of Tennessee mountains and Maryland salt marshes, of moonlight on the water and gentle mists in the hollows.

Sterling had been taken by the girl and especially by her place, a tidy garage apartment on the Wynasock Creek with a balcony in the back and a soft down comforter and stuffed animals on her bed. It was decorated in what he thought was fine style, the delicate glass figurines of animals and ballerinas (she was a dancer and a writer) and the prints of sunflowers and harvest fields on the wall. It was not that his place was a mess. It was more the case that he simply didn't pay much attention to outer forms. He was too busy looking for inner ones.

"Hey!" she said to Sterling finally. "Earth to Sterling! Come in, Sterling! The fire's ready. What does Bobby say? 'Morning! You read 'em!'"

She handed him a book, and they settled on the plush faux fur rug in front of the fire. Sterling thought of the ride down, took her small feet cocooned in soft flannel socks in his lap, leafed through the history and found the place he was thinking of. As he rubbed he read:

> The change from bleak earth tones to effervescent greens and golds is subtle, autumn backwards. Here the reds and oranges, the purples and golds are laid down faintly beneath the burgeoning green. One minute the landscape is all muted browns and grays, and then seemingly the next minute every hill and vale is covered with the soft beginnings of spring, the calming pastels of a hundred shades of color, pale, almost yellow fringes around the swamps, the winter wheat a stunning Kelly green, the high-lands so translucent it seems almost electric in the shimmering, shining sun.
>
> If the winter landscape is the bare bones of the picture—the broad and sometimes harsh brush-strokes of the skeleton that holds all up—then this blushing of life is the beginning of the shades and nuances, the playful mottles of color that will be reprised again in more dramatic fashion later in the year.
>
> In the woods and fields, the lone flocks of juncos and chickadees are supplanted by brighter groups of warblers, goldfinches and bluebirds winging up from unknown tropic haunts on their way to procreation, fate, and the vast northland. This ferocious fecundity is disguised as small, colorful bits of feather and bone.

Sentimentality aside, the song of the red-wing is a challenge to all the others. The trill of the red-eyed vireo is an iron gauntlet tossed in front of those who would be king. Although to some eyes the small tuft of meadow, the single oak tree in the hedgerow, or the cattails by the rushing brook are mean and pitiful kingdoms, to those harbingers it is the world entire, and they mean to save it by saving themselves.

Deer, gaunt and footsore from months of pawing through icy crust to find the too-scant acorn, are busy grazing, morning 'til night, and they are not shy any longer about who might see them. The hunt is over, and the coyotes are smaller danger than the ones that have plagued and chased the deer all winter—hunger first, then hunger's brother and sister: disease and death.

In spring, a young man's fancy lightly turns to thoughts of love, so says the poet. In the woods and fields, love is too kind a word. The robin smashes himself bloody against the phantom rival he sees in the window, the night woods are pierced by the shrill ungodly shriek of fighting 'coons, or the blood-curdling howls of ferial cats. To the victor go the spoils; to the vanquished, the void.

"I'm not sure I like that part," Amy said. "The void. Brrrr."

"It's just poetical," Sterling said. "At least the victor gets the spoils."

"Hey! Don't stop the rubbies! Make me a victor, Victor, and spoil me some."

"Move over a little. There—that's better." She scooched over and Sterling continued:

Superimposed on all the carnage is the conundrum of new life, order springing from the bowels of entropy and death. The shelf mushroom shouts "Life!" on the bones of the dying maple. The ragged v-formations of geese as they trumpet are mocking the memories of ice, foxes, and loads of chilled #4s ripping wing and breast.

In the rivers, shad struggle past rocks and riffs, pulled inevitably towards their mating and their death, only later to float in scores down the river, washed up in back eddies, food for huge catties and the occasional bald eagle, which had once been removed from the area, but is now very much back on the scene. The river has been cleaned up down near Philly now, stripers are making it up to the reservoirs that tap half the Delaware's water to run silent and deep through 8-foot tall aqueducts to New Yorkers, who cavalierly flush it all out to sea.

The old river is a memory—the days of the log rafts floating from upstate down to Philly, full of rough men, drunkards, thrill-seekers, running Skinner's Falls and Fowl Riff, the Ten Mile River, all for a few bucks and a long walk back home. Those days are over. Even the later invention of the canals and a boat ride powered by mules through Easton and Martin's Creek is a living long gone, every trace gone as well except for an overgrown ditch in a few spots between 611 and the river.

"Hey! I saw some of them on the way down to Easton that day!" Amy said.

"Saw what? The ditches?"

"Yeah! That's kinda cool, being in the book and all. You didn't see them?"

"Naw. Guess I was thinking of something else."

"Ummm hummm. Do some more."

"Otay, boss:"

It was always about moving the goods. The first railroad in the United States was a Pennsylvania line. The Stourbridge Lion replaced a gravity railroad near Hawley, and the twin ribbons of steel spelled death to the canals and the vast network of ponds, banks, and even bridges that supported the new technology. Imagine floating high above the Delaware on Roebling's first suspension bridge, a watery highway a hundred feet above the river, thence up the Neversink, across land to the Hudson and down the river again to the gaping maw of the city, coal for heat and for forging steel, to make the goods that the city folk demanded, the insatiable appetite that stretches out feverish tendrils to consume in larger and larger concentric rings, a crushing tsunami of hunger.

"They had a bridge with water going over the *water?*" Amy asked.

"Yeah. It's up there still, but with a road on it instead of the viaduct."

"Viaduct? Hehe. Wasn't there a Three Stooges movie—no! It was Groucho Marks. 'Viaduct? Vhy not a duck?' he said. I never understood that till now. No—hey, keep rubbing or no goodies for you tonight."

"All right! No more threats. Lemme just finish this page or two."

That makes the greening of the land the season of destruction as well as one of life. The D-9's belch toxic clouds of oily smoke into the air, ripping up forests, zigzagging across old fields that might yield twenty bushels of corn an acre. That's, what? Sixty bucks worth, then there is the price for the oil and the tractor, the tires, batteries, the barn to put it in, the insurance. So now with the price of everything going up all the time, a farmer might peel a few acres off the lower forty. It's wet down there, only good for grazing, really. And he gets a good price for it, too, even after the government helps themselves to a big old chunk of it.

What follows? Houses that house the children that need the schools and are owned by the adults who want a store nearby and a larger road to fit their faster and bigger cars and SUVs. Suddenly that nasty stuff the farmer is putting on the few fields that are left means there are actually days when the residents can't open their windows, use their pool or their thousand dollar barbeque on their massive decks and patios, and shouldn't there be a law?

A conservationist is somebody that already has his house built. The red-wing trills his limpid notes from the cattail, staking a claim to his universe, and when that universe is improved with the transit and the bulldozer, nature with a budget, the red-wing is gone, replaced by two-legged versions of himself, whose legs, as Thoreau's Acadian pointed out, had his knees on backwards. Those humans will also pound themselves bloody for the rights to possession and to trill limpid notes of conflict and victory.

"What's that mean, about the backwards knees?" Amy said.

"I thought you said no more interruptions."

"Women's prerogative. How am I supposed to grow up to be smart like you if you don't tell me these things?"

"Well, Thoreau wrote about this French guy, French Canadian, I guess, that chopped wood around Concord, and somebody was saying to him that humans and chickens weren't so different because they both walked on two legs. So the French guy thought it was a big deal that the chicken's knees work backwards from a human."

"Ummmmmm. Oh—that feels sooo good. Don't stop! I never thought about it. I mean, usually when I see chicken legs they don't have the knees onto them anymore, you know?"

"Yeah. It's like chicken lips. You generally don't see 'em much. Well, here, just a little more and then we could go to bed, maybe."

"Maybe," Amy said, then laughed. "You read 'em!"

In springtime, a young man's fancy turns the soil, not so lightly, to sow houses, roads, malls, fences, border wars of a different ilk, such as the man moving his fence six inches a year when the neighbor is away on vacation until the guy can't even get into his own backyard: adverse possession, the real estate people call it. A low-down, dirty double-dealing trick. All that is legal in some places. Anything that generates money is eventually legal in the United States these days.

All this happens even in the season of color, of new life, like a single cell that misunderstands, thinking that the world must belong solely to itself, finally killing the host. The most impractical parasite, it eats itself out of house and home.

Lines are drawn to be crossed, land is to be walked, papers are to be filed, and new hosts are formed to replace the old. Annie Dillard made like Thoreau and stalked nature one day, congratulated herself on her stealth when she discovered a large bullfrog nestled in the reeds—little Moses in his basket, more or less—then was astounded to see the frog deflate before her eyes into a husk of itself, and the dark form of the water beetle, four inches of death, darting away and leaving the frog skin empty and her pride turned into something more somber.

Did the trilling redwing make a note of that? Dillard did not say.

Sterling closed the book and stared at the dying fire for a moment, until Amy arose lightly with a dancer's move and took his hand gently, leading him to the soft warm bed.

19

≡ CHAPTER NINETEEN ≡

In June, they went to one of the smaller festivals at a fairgrounds near Fiesterville, which had once been a race track with the dirt tri-oval still apparent. The paved quarter-mile drag strip was the preferred location of those who camped with big units. Forty and fifty-footers were nothing unusual at festivals these days. Chat remembered when it was almost all pop-ups and tents or hard-side tag-alongs in the early days, and those folks were still there, scattered about in the twenty-acre field or up in the woods, nestled between rock oak, maple and scrub pine trees and the huge layered sandstone outcroppings that broke up the undulating hillside, so hard to deal with they called the rock "Pike County Diamonds". Building on a piece like that was a real pain, probably the reason the neighborhood was still undeveloped.

They had left work early on this Friday to help the Pigeon Forge Volunteer Fire Department— "To Serve and Protect!" their motto—specifically to help them "build" their stand out of a few hundred cases of beer and soda, which would be happily cannibalized, iced and sold during the course of the weekend. One of the fire company boys would sleep there to reduce the amount of pilferage, although at a buck a can, there was no good reason for theft.

In all the years he had played, Chat could only remember one theft at a festival up in New York when the too-anxious owner of a loud generator found his missing on a Sunday morning. He was fond of firing it up at six in the morning—one of the only three good hours to sleep between the heat of the sun and the insane picking that would go on until dawn. They found the generator later that day, tossed into the stream that ran through the campground, minus a spark-plug, but otherwise, none the worse for wear.

"The first thing we gotta do is build the walls," Chat said happily. "Then we can get our stuff set up."

"How's beer-drinking jive with the Bible there, preach?" Sterling asked.

"And why is that any of your concern?" Chat asked, carefully stacking the cases of beer one on top of the next, staggering the courses so the wall would be solid.

"Just curious." Sterling muttered, grabbing another case of beer and handing it to Chat.

Chat grabbed it, put it in place on the wall, sprang up on it, spread his arms out wide, and threw back his head.

"'I would give you spiced wine to drink, the nectar of my pomegranates!'"

Jo-Jo paused in his unloading and looked at Chat quizzically.

"Keep yer freakin' spiced wine. Hell, it's getting hot out here."

Chat jumped back down and moved to help Sterling with the stacking. He said, "I'm glad for hotness, then. You don't remember bitching about that deep freeze we had in January, then? And the quote is from Songs 8:2, for your information."

"Never heard of that one. Like the wreck of the ole '97 is it?" Jo-Jo cracked, wiping perspiration from his forehead and smiling.

"Bad form to poke fun at God, Jo-Jo. I swear, the bunch of you are godless as *Hindus*," Chat said, hoisting a case up on the wall.

"Actually, Hindus have way more gods then you do, preach. Hell, they got a god for every freakin' thing. Even sex."

"Wow. Maybe I'm a Hindu, then," Jo-Jo laughed.

"And to think that only yesterday you were a lesbian," Sterling said, mock pensive. "Hey, that reminds me. You hear about that new band? Lead singer is a guy named Slick Pete, and he has all these chicks behind him playing?"

"Oh, all girl band. *There's* a concept, " Jo-Jo sniffed.

"Well, remember that video with that guy, rock and roller, had all those girls with short black hair and red dresses, played behind the guy and then they all danced to the tune, kinda?" Sterling asked.

"Robert Palmer," Jo-Jo said.

"Right. Well, this guy has the same set-up, except they're all Indians."

"Nava-*hos*?" Jo-Jo smirked.

"No, dummy. Indian Indians. You know, dots?" Sterling said, poking his index finger at his forehead as he said it. "Anyway, this guy calls the band 'Slick Pete and Hindi Bimbos.'"

Chat laughed out loud.

"My God. Listen to you two. Where on *earth* would a band like that ever get *hired*?" he said, grabbing the last of the cases off the second truck.

"Where else? Califorinicata. But I hear the girls are really hot pickers, so maybe it isn't so wacky after all," Sterling said, hoisting the case up to Johnny.

"Well, no weirder than that bunch we camped next to last year at the big festival. What was it? The 'Gay Blades of Grass?' Those guys were nuts," said Johnny.

"I still can't believe you asked them what it was like to be gay," Jo-Jo said.

"How the hell was I supposed to know that they were gay *impersonators*, for the love of Pete? Hell, I don't even know what that means. I mean, I think they *were* gay after the way they acted after the beers and shine, " Johnny said.

"Well, they get the bookings. They were on *Oprah* the other day. I mean, imagine that, a bunch of bluegrass players on *Oprah*, for gosh sakes. Perversion pays these days, I guess," Chat said sadly.

"And there's no homophobe about you then, is there?" Sterling said to Chat.

All four of the boys were covered with sweat now, the beads welling up, then curving droplets would wash away the thin layer of dust that was beginning to settle on everything near the road. The units came rolling by in ones and twos with drivers with their arms out the window, waving as they passed.

"I'm not afraid of 'em. But they're sinners all the same, and being a sinner and pretending to be one seems to be the same thing to me," Chat said, frowning.

"Well, they do seem to have a blast, nancying around up there. And if they *were* gay, who would ever know, now? So this way, they can do what they like and the average guy can at least justify it all as an 'act.' Incidentally, isn't that what we all do act, to some extent?" Sterling said, pausing in his lifting to wipe his forehead with the back of his hand.

"No acting about me," Chat said firmly. "Or with Johnny, here, either. Right, John-boy?"

"That's right!" Johnny said happily. He never paid these talks too much mind. They were too complicated, and somebody was sure to get a little pissed about it, so keeping out was the best way he could think of to keep it down.

"What about me? You saying I'm some kind of *actor?*" Jo-Jo asked, staggering backwards with his hand palm out on his forehead and his face contorted as if in pain, fanning himself manically with his other hand. He stopped and looked at the three with sudden seriousness.

"Well, there was that other group I heard about. Does all the old cowboy songs. The Hanks, Jimmy Rodgers, like that, and they call themselves the Mad Cow Boys," Sterling said, straight-faced.

"That's pretty funny," Chat said.

"Oh. So diseased livestock jokes are okay, then?" Sterling said. Chat shook his head with the shadow of a smile still on his face.

"Well, I was thinking, with all the Indian craze going on, we could call ourselves 'The Troubled Utes.' Come up there with those funky hats on and act bad."

"Yeah, sure thing. We could raid people's camps, carry off their women," Jo-Jo said.

"Hindi Bimbos. That's funny right there," Johnny said, as he snugged the last case of beer into place. The "bar" was complete. The four stepped back and considered it: the cases of beer, neatly leveled on pallets, comprised three sides of a rectangle ten by ten and maybe eight feet high. Three large galvanized water troughs soon arrived, and the first ten cases of soda and beer were quickly iced down while poles were raised on the four corners. A blue tarp was raised overhead and down three sides, immediately plunging the inside into cool and welcome shade.

"Ah, a thing of beauty!" Sterling murmured.

"Like the tower of David! Pretty near. So, ready to get the cabana up, then?" Chat said.

From the hollow came the mournful sound of a recording being played over the PA system: Larry singing "Six More Miles." The four men bantered easily as they made camp, first setting up the cabana in front of the pop-up that Chat had hauled down the night prior—a ten by twenty-foot tent of white, complete with four sides, zippered door and by-gosh windows on the sides. They placed the sawhorses in the one corner nearest the tree line, then the plywood bi-fold door on top, then the table cloth, an old plastic one with pictures of pinecones and canoe-paddling Indians on it (not Indian Indians)—that was the mess area. On top of that went milk crates stacked one atop each other for the cooking necessities, and bungee cord hooks on the aluminum framework of the cabana made a convenient place to hang pots and pans.

They got out their half dozen chairs and an empty spool of wire for a table, and set up the fire ring out front near the pile of logs and construction scrap that Jo-Jo was stacking against a small pin oak out in front of the campsite.

The last thing they did was to string the huge blue tarp over the area where Johnny and Sterling were pitching their tents, forming a small compound with the cabana in the center. Rain or shine, they'd have a place to hang out and play when they got bored or tired of traipsing all over the campsite in the middle of the night.

They ran up the state flag and iced the beer. Over on the hillside, in the mid-way of the old dirt track and on up into the woods, small knots of people were doing the same thing. A steady stream of festival goers were driving in, slowly, usually making a circuit around the track once to lean out of their windows and greet those who were already there. After a minute, a new rig they didn't recognize slowed and stopped next to them, and when the door opened, there sat Red, as big as life.

Red was a long-haired biker with grizzled beard and a stomach too large to even be called a beer-belly. In fact, it wasn't beer at all that did it too him, at least not directly. It wasn't the calorie-laden, bubbly goodness that was at the center of most music, or beer's caustic relative, booze, either, that made Red look like he had swallowed a quarter keg. It was his liver that was failing after four decades of boozing it up, banging down a fifth of Jack a night and picking until the first bird chirped. That's when a fellow knew he had done it again, and that he would be suffering until the sun went down and the cool shadows laid their healing hand on the scorched summer hills. After a long afternoon "nap" and then a cheese-steak to settle the stomach, a real picker would be right back in the saddle again.

More than once the boys had seen Red flat on his back in the dewy grass of a festival site, seemingly dead to the world, or propped up in a chair near the fire-ring with head slumped on his chest, listened as the night became a thick stew of half-remembered licks and songs, and the small pauses between songs grew and grew until they annealed the night with silence. Then someone would carefully unstrap the Martin and put it to bed, leaving the picker to the cold and the dew in the frequent times they could not rouse him from death's little cousin, sleep.

He'd been off the juice now for ten years, but still smoked like a fiend, maybe two packs of Marlboro's and half a lid a day.

"I tell ya, I'm lucky to be alive. That last time they brought me in, they thunk I was a goner, and I thunk so, too. I was in too bad a shape to make out any kind of will or something, then I realized I had spit to give and nobody to give it to. There's death in that bottle, I know that now—pure death. I'm a lucky man to be here at all to tell you that," he had told Chat at the same spot last year.

"Hey there, boys! Check out the new rig!" he said happily this day, and of course the boys piled in, "ooohing" and "aahing" at the brand-spanking new camper, a sweet 38 footer with AC and a shower, comfy captain chairs in the dining section and a bedroom that looked like a 5-star hotel. The boys were all atwitter, and Red was mighty proud, too, showing the rig off, twisting up a fat joint and bragging about how little it had cost him—only fools would buy a new camper; you waited until somebody died or got too sick to go anymore, then bought it out from under 'em.

"How the hell could you afford this rig, if you don't mind my asking," Sterling asked him, and Chat winced. For an Ivy League guy, Sterling could be pretty crude, he thought.

"I been putting money by the last ten years or so. Hell, now that I don't booze no more, I don't need much money. I spend all my time just camping and picking anyhow."

"Still, must have set you back a good deal," Sterling persisted.

"Couldn't afford a liver, so I bought this," Red said, a trace too loud, and the boys all looked at each other first, then at Red to see if they should laugh. But Red wasn't laughing, just looking at them with pot-reddened eyes.

Johnny finally broke the silence.

"Geeze, Red. You need a *liver*?"

"What they say. I figure, if I gotta go, I'll go in style. No sense waiting around to do the things you dream about doing, right?"

"Yeah, I *guess* so," Chat murmured. "But, well, shoot, Red. I'm so sorry to *hear* that."

In the awkward lapse of silence they could hear the Lost Ramblers next door teasing out the harmonies to an Everly Brother's tune, "Bye Bye Love."

"We all gotta go sometime, Chat ole friend. I got no regrets. I done more in 55 years than any six guys I know, screwed more women and got drunk as a lord, seen the world, all 50 states, Europe and Mexico, played a thousand tunes."

"A thousand? Hell, Red, you played that many last *year*," Chat said, mock-cheerful.

"Well, let's make that a thousand and one then, my friend," Red said.

The boys walked into the crystalline sunlight, picked up their instruments and were soon back in the only world that seemed real at a time like that, a world where an idea turns into a vibration that makes chords that become riffs and then songs and then universes of songs about the real world. They were songs with more weight and muscle, more blood and bone, more hope and more misery than the world the music was supposed to represent, the music soaring above the summer goodness like joyful birds against a landscape of greens so rich and blues so deep they made all the other colors jealous, weaving skeins of faith that held and lifted them all up like Ezekiel's wheel.

Chat paused in between the songs, thinking of the place without Red in it, wondering, and he could tell the others were thinking that, too. He looked at the snug campsite with new appreciation, perhaps trying hard to burn the moment into his mind, and played out the weekend the way he thought it would go.

He knew that the woods edge where they were camped would keep the sun off until at least eleven the next morning, and that was important. They would be lucky to get ten hours sleep over the next three days, reason enough to have taken the following Monday off.

Up until this year, Chat had taken only four days off a year, besides Sundays: first day of buck season, first day of trout season, and the Mondays following the two festivals they always played. Homer was too happy to fill in at the pumps and could repair a flat or tune a carburetor if the need arose, although he invariable wound up getting somebody riled over some trifle.

But, people had come to expect it, like Christmas or the first snow, and so Chat figured it wasn't all bad.

"Hey. Lets get jammin' here," Sterling said, anxious.

"Relax old son. We have all *weekend*. You know you're fingers are gonna be sore when we're done anyways," Chat said.

Johnny sat silently and smiled, sipping the first of five-dozen beers he would drink that weekend. *That was the way,* he thought. *One an hour wouldn't hurt a fly.*

He stopped for a moment and sat in one of the folding captain's chairs, took a long pull on the Yuengling and looked out over the festival grounds. The sun was touching the trees on the ridge opposite, throwing long shadows that stretched themselves towards him. Johnny half-remembered his grandma, she was Acadian, singing a song:

Quand les cieux sont bleus

que je suis un homme corageux

Je ris et chante, je travaille sans un soin

Mais quand le soir est pres de

Les onmbres me reclament

La nuit tourne le rhome et je frissonne

Seul pensant de l'une qui est alle avant

His mind translated the words with ease. "When skies are blue I am a brave man, I laugh and sing, I work without a care. But when evening is near, the shadows claim me, the night turns cold and I shiver alone, thinking of the ones who have gone before." He gave a little shiver; surprised at the memory, then also remembered what she would say whenever that happened: *l'oie marche sur la tombe*: goose walked on my grave. He took a pull on his beer and looked for a pleasant thought to put that all out of his mind. Too morbid, that was.

This was one of his favorite times, after all, sitting and listening to all the faint sounds of picking, a fragment of a banjo, laughter from a group of friends in the hollow, the evening like silk or a ripe peach, smooth, delicious, the smell of a good steak cooking over wood smoke, pinpoints of fires leaping into view as the sun began to hug the horizon and the halflight of dusk smoothed all the ragged edges. The small and twisted trees in the forest opposite melted into a dark, solid sentinel against the pinks and oranges of the sunset, the gray and rutted road became a silver ribbon, the unkempt midfield, hastily mown and raked out with clumps of grass and hay sticking up like cowlicks in the light of day now became a field of incredibly smooth greenness in the moment just before all color ceased and the world was made into a black-and-white photo.

Johnny had seen that happen once. They were driving through the Water Gap, the Delaware River running high after a heavy rain that had first melted the snowpack and had itself turned to snow, coating all the branches, trees and rocks of the Indian Head and Mount Minsi on the opposite side of the river, and both mountains were clothed in white. They had been driving through the dusky light to a bar job they had over the border, and Johnny couldn't put his finger on what was odd about the beauty in front of him until he realized that the land was in black and white and the sky, a deep indigo, was very much in color.

Yes, Johnny saw things like that, and, once in awhile, if the boys weren't too frisky and prone to making fun, he'd point it out, although he knew pretty much when they felt it, too. He just didn't want to be thought stupid. Sure, he hadn't been the best at school, but part of that, he reasoned, had to do with being made fun of. After all, the teachers had to get him a special desk when he was in the fourth grade, because he was so big. And he wasn't much for reading like Sterling and Chat, and he certainly wasn't much for clever talk and the ladies like Jo-Jo.

That didn't mean he had a heart of stone, as the song went, especially for things of beauty, which there was more of now that girls were coming to the festivals and listening to the music. In the early days, there might be some women at a festival; some guy's old lady, maybe with a couple four kids running around while Dad picked and drank and joked with the boys.

But now? There were young girls in halter tops, barefoot, with small toes like pink sausages and chipped red nailpolish, silver bracelets around trim ankles, or the new woven friendship bracelets with wooden beads, long golden hair, or spiked green hair that surprised Johnny now when he saw it because some of them actually looked pretty good that way. He particularly liked the curve of their young cheeks, laying on blankets and kissing a little bit with some lucky buck or catching the rays after being up all night camp-hopping.

The kids liked sliding from one atom of music to the next, a center of musicians circled, playing and laughing and singing, looking at each other and smiling as if they were in on some secret joke, the listeners coming and going, surrounding them from song to song. And then came the time Johnny almost hated: walking from one campsite to another had been getting harder and harder as the beers went down and the clock ran on, and now suddenly it was getting easier to get around. It always took a minute for him to figure it out: the sun was getting ready to rise, and the hidden ruts and holes that had grabbed at his feet for the hours prior were now slowly revealed.

It was then that a man had better rush to get to bed or risk another day and night without sleep. The whole weekend would be a blur and the music would suffer.

He took another sip—empty—and heaved to his feet. He still had an hour of light left, time enough to get the stew on the stove and the lanterns lit, the fire set and his own bed made, so that later all he had to do was fall into it. He couldn't think of anything better than when they would be jamming, maybe the night being a little cold, they would have the sides down on the cabana, he would leave to relieve himself, and then, coming back towards his temporary home, he'd see the cabana lit from within with shadows of the musicians inside made huge on the walls like the champagne scene from Dumbo.

How could a man worry in a place like this? It was the reunion of a family who knew how to love, who cared about its members, a campground full of people almost all of whom were delighted to see each other and bask in the music one more time. Johnny went to get his bass out of the truck, ready for the evening and the night like the small child he once was getting ready for Christmas or the best birthday ever.

_20_

≋ CHAPTER TWENTY ≋

Ted watched in the last part of the afternoon as the big machines tore up the green hillside, ripping up the tall pines and the remains of the Hertz's place. When he was done, the hill would be as flat as a table, and the fill carted over to the "wetlands" that he had gotten re-zoned on the QT by the state boys. That had cost a couple hundred thou, but it was going to be worth it.

The epiphany had come while he was bathing, soaking in his hot tub and staring at his silk bathroom. He was trying to remember where he had gotten the robe, and how much it had cost. The habit of appraisal was one he had acquired even before his dad had begun getting rich. He finally remembered that he had picked up the rich red robe across the state line at one of his favorite specialty stores, and it came back to him that he was a bit annoyed at the price tag. He begrudged himself nothing, but paying too much—well, that always bugged him. And the worst part was the *tax*, which of course in this state didn't apply to wearing apparel.

He didn't jump out of the bathtub like that lame Greek guy had, or even shout. But, suppose he could get some top clothing manufacturers to set up some outlets. With sale prices all year and factoring in the ten percent or so that city pukes would save on taxes, the customer would be looking at a 40% savings on clothing, a good 1/3 off most other stuff.

How about that? And with the interstate in, he could run buses, maybe make a few bucks on that as well. He forgot the robe and the bath and began to make some calls. Who could he reach out to that had an in with the big-name clothiers? It was such a simple idea. He had to be careful about this, or someone with better connections might scoop him. That would fry his butt big time. He was still mulling that over when the phone rang, and he was delighted to hear Dalton's laconic drawl on the other end, asking him what on earth he thought he was doing. Oh, that was delicious!

"Why, Chat, I'm developing my land. You know, making it worth more to me and to the community?" he'd said happily, and then, when Dalton had threatened to have "something done about it," Ted had told him exactly what was happening.

"Whatever else you may think about me, Chat, you have to admit that I have never been one to lie about my intentions, not when it comes to business. So *now*, I think we're even."

That had been a week before, but in that week, Ted had some rude shocks. He was a construction guy, and he knew where to get the best deals on shiploads of lumber, 'dozers, even how to shake down labor. But garments? Good Lord, it was all Jews, and he had to admit it was out of his league. He could build the buildings—that was a snap. Although he knew in advance that the sewage was going to be a problem—the plot was either bedrock or swampland, neither of them good for sewage beds, although he might be able to sneak some French drains out towards the little Sambo. Bad for the fish, maybe, and the toads, but good for the bottom line. Besides, that was all the county had, for the love of Pete, fish and toads and crap like that.

That was when he remembered Hugh McAdam, a guy he had met a few times buying used cranes. He was from the city, and he seemed to know his way around.

Ted thought back to the last time they had met for lunch, some swanky place in the city that Hugh had flown them to from his building. Turned out that it was only a few blocks away, really a short stroll, but McAdam was a showoff about his money and his toys, just the opposite of Ted, who always downplayed what he had to keep the jealous eyes away and to avoid talk about how he had gotten it.

He had called, thinking that he would have to eat a little crow before he could make any headway with the guy: the last piece of heavy equipment he'd bought from him, he'd had to take two days off, stroking the guy. Pathetic. But when he had called, Hugh answered with alacrity, bought in to the whole idea without even seeming to think about it, and set up a meeting for the next day, not near the property at all, but back in the city.

It was almost like he was expecting the call. Ted dismissed the thought. He'd have to work on the way he handled other big fish. He just wasn't used to not being the top of the heap.

"Ted, Ted, Ted," McAdam had said, like he was talking to a younger brother, "You're a builder, same as me. This idea you have is a very good one, very good! But the last thing you want is for everybody and their brother to know who you're in bed with, you know? And we're not the guys to set this up, either. You're dead right about that one. We need some heavy industry representation to make this work. I mean, hell, you have the Outlets down in Reading, and that could be considered close. We need to convince them that this is a new market, no overlap and no competition. So let's have a meeting, we'll get some game plans set up, I'll make some calls, and meanwhile you'll need a couple of months to get even the first part of that parcel ready to build. Sound right?"

Ted had to admit that it did, and, at the meeting, he had already roughed out in his head some ways to make his end of the deal unshakable. If he didn't really know McAdam, he knew people like him, and he'd be damned to do all this work and then have it all stripped away like a ball on the one-yard line.

So on the drive back home with his team of lawyers—after only one day of meetings with smooth guys who looked like kids but had some serious leverage—he still was bemused and puzzled. McAdam had taken the limited partner's role, agreed to all the covenants Ted's lawyers had drawn up, even offered a few tidbits like buyout options that Ted had asked for, mainly so he had something to give up if he asked.

"He wants to make money, same as me," he tried to tell himself, and "You can't be entirely crooked in this business and still get along," and also "He needs a local guy to get this going."

But in his gut he was not as confident as he would have preferred. Again he had that feeling that he was just missing something, a flick of motion, a glimmer of light, like the name of someone that is right on the tip of your tongue, while a friend spewed suggestions until you knew you couldn't think. He needed to know more about McAdam than he did, and there was still time to learn it—a few months at least before they had the plans drawn up and the footers in. It would all move pretty fast once they got the engineering done—steel buildings were quick and dirty, although Ted pined for the days when the Bethlehem Steel was up and running and you could get material for much, much less. He breathed in the smell of diesel and dust, turning it over once again. He'd get his number one guy on it—do a 'net search, make some calls. McAdam wasn't the sort to be squeaky clean, unless he missed his guess.

It took a few weeks to get things set up at work, coupled with weeks of listening to Nan bitching about the idea, which made the move easier and more attractive to Tony by the day. So, on a hot day in June, he kissed her good-bye and drove the two hours to his new home.

"Pigeon Forge," he smirked. "Land of Opportunity."

The first thing Tony did when he got into town was to stop by the local diner and grab a paper. He'd checked into the Sunset Motel in Fiesterville that morning then drove up to Charmers County to get the lay of the land. An older waitress stopped, asked, "Coffee?" then left him to consider the menu and the scene. Tony felt like he had never left. When he was younger and his Dad would take him on the job, the first thing they would do would be to stop at the nearest diner. Tony thought it was just to shoot the breeze and relax, but of course he realized now that his old man was there to get business contacts, or networking, as the stiffs called it now.

Things hadn't changed much, to look at the clientele: fat men in gray work shirts with a quarter barrel under their shirts or little scrawny ones with yellow teeth and a wife who was 500 pounds and probably beat the crap out of the little guy on weekends just for fun; the silver-haired retired set, for whom this was the day's high point; and maybe one or two younger kids from the high school. Never any good-looking babes, not if the waitress wasn't one, and this dame, "Ellie," he gathered from the folks there, certainly wasn't in danger of winning any beauty contests.

He was actually enjoying being back in Smallville, although Nan hadn't liked it much when he told her the plan.

"A paid vacation *where?*" she said when he told her. What he couldn't stand was the crying when she found out he was going to go ahead of her to "find a place" and then send for her.

It was a sweet deal: two months to cruise chicks, drink beer, shoot the shit with the locals, and dig for dirt. Being in the garbage business had its advantages.

"So, what are you doing after your shift?" he joked with Ellie.

"You're a fresh one!" she laughed. "You'll get more action out at the Bennykill, bucko."

"And where would that be? You wanna come with, after?" Tony said, winking and, lapsing without thinking, into the dialect.

"You couldn't handle me, you young whippersnapper. You from Fiesterville, then?"

"Umm, close. Coplay?"

"Still coal country. What's your name? What brings you up here, then?"

"Name's Tony. Thinking of moving up maybe," he said, unconsciously editing Nan out of the statement. Might be some nice tail around town after all, and they would all be talking about him when he left. He knew that much, for sure.

"What do you do, Tony? You'll be looking for work then?"

"I'm, well, I can do lots of things. Carpentry, drive truck, tile work."

"This place'll suit ya, then. You can't get by just doing one thing here, unless you can do a lot of it."

"So that includes you?" Tony said, laughing. He liked this old biddy.

"Honey, I work from five a.m. 'til we close. That's nine at night. And I do that six days a week."

"The seventh?"

"We're closed. I make like God and rest," she said.

"Well, Ellie, thanks for the coffee and the conversation. So just where is this Bennykill anyway?"

"You just go on down the hill. It's right before you turn off to go either to town or the highway," she said, smiling at the two bucks he left on the bill. Anything more would be a red flag, and they'd all have him being some rich or dangerous guy, not at all what he wanted.

What he wanted was to plug in to the underside of this little prissy town, and he suspected the only bar for twenty miles was the place to do it.

The weather was turning again. The sun had come up all pinks and purples, a pretty sky that Layton knew spelled rain. He checked his freezer and fridge for wings and burgers. At the first drops, the construction guys would be in for an early lunch, and they would stay until he closed the doors at two. He had four boxes of wings and two Tupperware containers full of fresh ground meat, more than enough to last.

Sure enough, at a little past ten, the first raindrops hit the back windows, a light spattering at first, and then a peal of thunder and sheets of water fell. Ten minutes later, Jo-Jo and his crew pulled up in the white cab Chevy he drove, and by eleven the place was as busy as a Friday afternoon. Even the spacklers and sheetrockers snuck in as soon as the bulk of the workers had left the work site.

He was glad to see the door open and Katie come in. *Must be Wednesday. Her day off,* he thought.

"Morning, Layton," she said. "Figured I'd come in and give you a hand. You want it?"

Jo-Jo saw her and waved negligently, went on talking to his crew of three guys. She stifled the urge to smack him on the back of his head, Italian style.

"I do. You look a bit tired, Katie. Sure you're feeling all right?" Layton said. She nodded absently.

"Ah, just a little indigestion is all. 'Sides, it's only a couple hours. Might make enough for those new rings today, huh? Couple newbies here, I see," she trailed off and nodded her head towards a table with a young buck sitting and *writing,* of all things. Not a little notebook, like some guys used for calculating board feet of lumber or sheets of ¾ plywood, but a journal-looking thing. She walked over to his table and smiled, peeking over her shoulder to gauge Jo-Jo's reaction. He was in the middle of a story that involved his favorite subject: Jo-Jo and things Jo-Jo.

She walked up to the new guy and asked cheerily, "Can I get you something to eat?"

"Hmm. Thanks. Not just now. Although you could get me another beer, I guess," he said. He was eyeing her up and smiling diffidently, and Katie didn't mind it a bit.

On her way back to the bar, she took a few more orders, waiting perhaps a beat too long at Jo-Jo's table to see if they needed anything, and then put the orders up in the kitchen.

On the way back to the stranger's table, she snuck a peek at the notebook, lying open.

"Poetry?" She said, quietly, amused. He snapped the book shut.

"Shh. Our little secret, right? Not something these manly men might like to see, you know?" He winked at her.

"Oh, then. My lips are sealed. But, umm. Maybe I could see? I write a little myself."

She put the beer in front of him and raised her eyebrow, questioning. Behind her she could feel someone close, and turned to see Jo-Jo standing, smiling.

"Hey, Katie. New friend?"

"Stranger in this town, I guess," she shrugged. The new guy stood and extended his hand.

"Tony DiAntonio," he said, sticking out his hand. Jo-Jo grabbed it and shook it, perhaps a bit more firmly than would be comfortable for the average Joe. Tony didn't wince.

"Jo-Jo. That's a good grip you got there, Tony. What's your work?"

"Ah, you know, I do whatever. Brick, block. Tile."

"No shit. You any good?"

Katie moved away from the two to take another order, miffed a little. Just like him, the prick. Had to get in the way. Before she was at the bar, Jo-Jo had the new guy at his table, all introduced and acting like he'd been there his whole damned life.

Katie was bugged—bugged by the casual way Jo-Jo had moved in on her, bugged by the morning sickness, and especially bugged by the crappy grade she'd gotten that morning from that pissant communications prof—I mean, a C in communications when she was pulling straight A's in all her academics? The guy just didn't like women with spines, that was all. And he had to prove that his course was sooooo hard and he was sooooo smart. As if. And when Tony signaled for his check because he was ready to leave, ignoring Jo-Jo's imprecations to stay, that inexplicably bugged her even more. Maybe that was why she scrawled her phone number on the check she gave Tony, giving him back his little wink.

Two could play this game.

21

⇒ Chapter Twenty-One ⇐

Chat sat quietly at his desk, squinting through the new 10 x 50s he picked up at the sporting goods shop down in Fiesterville. He hadn't been obsessed with the idea of an interloper, exactly, but it was always in the back of his mind, so he always kept his eye on the road near the top of the hill, and unconsciously listened for the sound of an engine, which he was sure he would be able to hear from that distance. At the first wink of sun off a windshield he would wait for the car to pass his garage on the way down the road. With no turnoff between there and here except for the old tow road, whatever came down the hill had to go by Chat's front door.

He'd been at it for a week or two and hadn't seen or heard anything unusual. The leaves were out now, so he had all but given up any hope of finding out who was using his spread as a farm for that crap, at least until this particular morning, when, in the damp quiet before the rain, he had heard the faint sound of car wheels on the gravel road up above the swamp.

He could barely make out the outline of the car, a dark-colored one, parked at the brow of the hill. And he could see, through the soft greens of the new shoots and leaves, quick and sporadic movement.

What to do? He wondered how long whoever it was would be at the task. He thought for a moment, jumped up, locked the bay doors and climbed into his truck.

Minutes later he was edged into a turnoff just past the opening of the tow road, facing towards the top of the hill, and he canted the mirror and slouched down in his seat to scan the opening of the tow road behind him. He was betting that whoever it was would head back the way he had come.

Was it a he? Maybe a girl? He smiled at that. Women's rights aside, this kind of stuff was almost always a guy, and he'd bet money on it.

He hadn't been there long enough to even get a crick in his neck before he saw the front end of an old Dodge plow out onto the paved road, and as he suspected, the car blew past him, the taillights winking on for a second as whoever it was caught sight of his truck at the last minute. He had puzzled over how to ID the car. Should he sit up quickly and get as much of the plate as he could, or just content himself with a look at the vehicle? But even before the taillights had come on, he slouched even further into his seat.

It was Mrs. Jerman's car. That made sense. The kid was rumored to be a pothead, and Chat had idly wondered a time or two how he kept body and soul together, as the old folks said, seeing has how he had never done an honest job of work that anybody could tell.

He waited a few minutes before he backed out into the road and headed back to the garage as a few fat drops of rain spattered on his windshield. Then the sky opened up with torrents and lightning.

"Fertilizer. That's what he was doing. Fertilizing," Chat said to no one, and wondered what to do.

A little knowledge is a dangerous thing, Chat thought. *Knowledge puffs one up*, and, *Judge not, lest ye be judged.*

He'd talk with Sue about it, and then decide.

Tony hadn't intended to do anything more than hang around the town and chill, but when Jo-Jo asked him if he wanted to work, he thought about it for a minute and decided it might not be such a bad idea after all. Small towns didn't like you not to work, and, truth be told, he was already a bit bored when he showed up at the Bennykill. His protests about lack of tools hadn't stopped Jo-Jo, who said he had all the tools Tony needed, and a bunch of tile work that just wasn't getting done fast enough to suit him or the customers.

And, judging from what he had seen, Jo-Jo knew everybody around—even Katie—and wasn't shy about what he knew, either.

"A freakin' *tileman?*"

That's all Nan had to say about it when he had called her with the news, just after agreeing to meet Jo-Jo at the diner the next day.

"Listen, Nan. Uncle Guido wants this done, and we go nowhere without Uncle Guido. The house out in the Hamptons you want? Your Cadillac? It's all from him. And just what is so bad about tilework? Doesn't stink like garbage; it's no harder on your back than driving truck all day. And it's just for a few months until whatever is going on goes on."

After a long pause on the other end, he heard Nan's voice, cold and thin.

"You never ask him. You never ask me. And you never listen. You never listened to your old man, and you never listen to me. You just do. Just exactly what is 'going to go on?' It could be anything, and you never even *ask*. That's what gets me, Tony. What about what I think? Doesn't that count for anything?"

"You shounta brought my old man into this, Nan. That's not even fair."

She said nothing. He said nothing as well, and they each listened to the other's nothing, all across those wires or waves. What an odd thought: to be tied to someone a hundred miles past the ends of loving arms by a wire or a wave, imagining her face, the way it scrunches up on one side of her mouth and her eyes roll to the right when she's unhappy, like at that moment. She knew he would not be back for months. It was possible, and he was happy about it except for Nan, who he thought he might really love.

He had expected tears, maybe a shouting match. Oh, they'd had some beauties there, boy oh boy. But this was something new for Nan. Ordinarily, this would be where Tony turned on the charm to smooth things out. Let her go bitch to her girlfriends, get it off her chest. But instinctively, Tony avoided the first three glib things he was going to say. He was feeling poetical, and that always screwed him up.

"Hon. Listen, I know this is hard on you. This guy, Jo-Jo? He says he knows a couple places for rent, nice ones. You could have a garden, maybe. Hey, I'm still getting paid from the shop, and with the tile money, maybe we could go someplace nice later on, like France or something. Hon?"

The silence roared in his ear so long that he thought maybe she had hung up. He watched Katie absently. Maybe he'd better not. He was beginning to believe what he had told Nan.

"So when do I come down there?" she finally said.

"Soon, honey. Just let me get settled in, work a bit and get the place set up for us. Imagine it, huh? Now we have that summer house you've been thinking about so long."

"It's you I want more than that stuff. You understand that, don't you? Tony?"

He was watching Katie laughing with some fat guy in a Hawaiian shirt.

"And I want you too, baby. So let's not fight, huh? I'll call you later, 'kay?"

"Just you, Tony. All for me. That's all I want, " she said.

And to himself he said, "What every woman wants, sooner or later. Like the Wife of Bath said."

Jimmy had almost blown old man Dalton off that morning. He was already blasted, for one thing, and it was drizzling out, for another. A good morning to watch Springer and think about what to do with the money this fall. Dalton had piqued his interest when he mentioned a business proposition. So Jimmy had sauntered into the diner and gruffly greeted Ellie and Chat. He walked in with a shoulder-hunched swagger he imagined looked tough, like Clint Eastwood or somebody.

He certainly hadn't expected the too-firm hand on his elbow, steering him over to one of the back booths, nor could he seem to catch Ellie's eye so he could order. And then the old shit had commenced to bust on him about his patch. Oh, he had others. He couldn't put all his dope in one basket. But the way Chat had brought it up made Jimmy mad as hell.

"Stay out of that swamp or you'll wish you had," he had snapped at Jimmy, like he was some little kid or something. He didn't even pay attention when Jimmy tried to deny it all.

"Listen, I saw you in there, and I saw you drive off. You just think back to when you saw that truck parked at the pull-off the other week. You remember, Jimmy? How you put your brakes on for a second, trying to figure what to do about it? What I should do is just call the cops. But out of respect for my wife, that you're kin to, I won't. But don't try my patience, Jimmy. I suspect what you're doing on my piece, you're doing other places, too. So be smart and stay out."

And the bastard just got up and walked out like King Shit. So who could blame him for going down to the Bennykill and getting bombed? His best patch, and his own damn uncle to boot. He got pretty drunk, all right, and the next day he awoke with garbage-breath, wondering who the hell he had been talking to half the night. He had vague memories of saying perhaps more than he should have, but he couldn't imagine anyone he would've felt comfortable enough around to be blabbing. Oh, well. What can't be remembered will not bother, he figured, and cracked a beer and rolled a big fat spliff up for breakfast.

Tony's future seemed bright, so much so that the place together in the country he had promised Nan kept receding, day by day, like the shimmery patches of water on pavement that dissolve when approached. He and Kate had been out a few times to see a movie and get some dinner. Then last night she was content to simply take a walk down by the river. It was odd, how his mind worked. To the guys at the garage, he would have said, "Great knockers!" and of course they were. He could tell that even through the thick sweaters she seemed to favor. In fact—and he knew this was impossible, maybe just a case of his wanting something so much that it began to look better and better—he could swear they were getting bigger as the days went on. When he was with her, well, that was hard to explain, but maybe he had some kind of personality disorder like that chick Sybil he had read about. It became poetical then, her breasts were as soft as silk, her mouth like berries dappled with fresh dew.

He never told anyone about the poetry before, but when he had gotten around to calling Kate the day after he had met both her and Jo-Jo, that was the first thing she asked about after they had settled into a booth at the Bennykill. Maybe it was why she'd given him the come-on to begin with—some chicks dug the sensitive artist types.

"I read this book, Spoon River Anthology, about all these dead people who like, gossip about each other? So sometimes I play around with that when the mood strikes me."

He watched her gray eyes considering him, as if deciding something.

"Say one for me," she said, and he recited the one he wrote about a girl he had known that died when he was still in high school.

"This is called 'Honorie VanVliet':

I never asked to be beautiful

Green eyes and silken hair, the body of a colt

To run dappled in the sunlight,

Chased by boys who knew less than colts.

How I longed for one to see beyond

The green eyes and silken hair

To see the innocence, the shyness

Or even the mutinous cells that turned on me

And sent me home before I turned

Old enough to know better."

She liked that one. She praised it and made him read it again, her hair now hiding her face as she bowed her head and said once more, "Again!"

Then she raised it suddenly, and became the sunrise, her smile, her clear eyes, the skin glowing healthy—he had never seen such skin!

He was so distracted by the thought of her, night and day for the last week, that he had almost missed the chance to do what he had been sent to do.

Sure, he had been sending the faxes right along to the address they gave him: all the land transfers every week, police blotter, and top local stories from the paper. Some nights, he even had to go straight to his place, a nice little pad down by the Wyansock—good trout, he'd heard—and he'd clip and dial until seven or eight in the evening. This sometimes pissed people like Jo-Jo off, when he needed Tony to stay late, or Katie, once, because she thought he was playing her—he was very sure of that assessment—or Nan when she couldn't get through, a few times a week. Hey, Guido was giving him a flat fee, and what he didn't spend, he got to keep, so what was they sense of two phone lines? He had done what they had sent him to do.

This was an extra effort. Guido hadn't actually told him to do anything other than what he had been doing, but he heard some talk around about Dalton that maybe Guido's guy could use. *That would make Guido look smart and me look smart too, and who does it hurt?* He thought. Tony could remember the few names on the list Guido had given him that this McAdam wanted dirt on. Chat's wasn't the only name on that list—not by a long shot!—but it was the first one. If he decided to not say anything, who would know? Maybe nobody. Or maybe Guido or McAdam had other people in their pocket, and his not saying would be a bad thing.

So some kid blown out of his skull started talking to him down at the Bennykil, talking trash about Chat Dalton and some pot plants and being descriptive about the whys and wherefores of it all, too.

He had almost hesitated to make the call, having figured out that Dalton and Kate were close, but then, everybody seemed to be close down here, including Kate and Jo-Jo, which Tony thought ironic and amusing. Something about someone else's woman made him hot as hell, and he planned on keeping his thing with Kate quiet: he had plans for the two of them, sooner or later, and the less the world knew, the better.

Tony finally decided to make the call, dialing the number he had been given and telling the voice that answered that Dalton had a problem that might be of some use. When he finally dialed the guy up, he could tell by his tone of voice that he was a scum bucket, from the very first word he said, and that made Tony feel unaccountably bad. The flat way he responded to what Tony had told him meant, he guessed, that it would not be long before Chat Dalton began to have a run of bad luck. He'd seen it happen before. A few years back, a rash of pizzeria fires sizzled. The shops were owned by these two Greek guys who thought that the price of pizza dough and cheese the boys in the "Pizza Club" wanted was too high, and so they passed on joining the club, a little association run by one of the families. The next week—Boop!—every single pizza shop they owned burned to the ground.

He had been to hear Dalton's band. What else was there to do around here? Of course, he got to check Kate out at the same time, so it made him feel bad for the guy. *But I mean, be reasonable,* he told himself. *Haven't you slept with any woman you can for the last five years or so, wives, sisters, whomever? So it couldn't be scruples all of a sudden, right?* It was just that he was actually getting to like it here—easy-going pace, the people all so friendly to a displaced Pennsylvania boy like him, and Nan not there to nag him about every little thing.

Well, not to worry. If it hadn't been him, it would have been somebody else. And he'd be seeing Kate again tonight.

22

≋ CHAPTER TWENTY-TWO ≋

Chat was surprised at the number of people who had come to the festival, considering there were no big names there. No matter what time of year, it was generally cold in Lopez. Last year, it had been down in the twenties at night, and the cabana and the tent heater were mighty welcome when the sun went down. But this evening was gorgeous, fat and silky, something that washed over the soul and made a body feel happy to be alive, proud to be whatever the Good Lord had willed.

They were playing "Old Dangerfield," one of Bill's trickier pieces, a three- part song that really could stretch a guy out, it was that quick. Right before Jo-Jo's break, Chat heard the most awful sounds coming out of Jo-Jo's fiddle, just for a moment, and he looked over, thinking Jo-Jo was making some kind of his not-so-funny jokes, when he saw the look on Jo-Jo's face and watched in fascination as the bow tumbled out of his hand and clattered on the ground at Sterling's feet. Sterling had heard it, too, and had opened his eyes—he often played with eyes shut, as if he was imagining the notes, Chat had always thought, and when he got drunk, the eyes stayed closed for longer and longer pieces of time until the poor old boy was asleep on his feet. They all stopped vamping, looking at Jo-Jo, who was looking at his hand as if it had betrayed him.

They had all struggled with what Chat called "Sunday hands," when a musician's hand refuses to behave from numb fatigue. Picking twenty hours a day for three days and then sleeping on cramped cots or on the ground would do that to a fellow. However, this was the beginning of the weekend, and Chat took that as a bad sign.

"Geeze. I guess I musta pushed the afternoon too hard trying to get here," Jo-Jo said, trying to laugh it off. He bent over to pick up the bow, gave a tentative lick at the fiddle, which gave up the same rich tones and deep movement that had become his signature—not really Kenny Baker, nor quite Mark O'Connor—something in between, with a whole lot of Vassar in the margins for good measure.

"Hmmm. Well, sorry about that. Maybe a touch of carpel tunnel, is all," Jo-Jo said, shrugging.

"Not too many beers?" Sterling said, in what Chat could see was a meant to be a friendly voice.

"Hell, I had only six or so all afternoon. You had twice as many. I'm *fine*. Pick it up at the end of Sterling's break and I'll show ya."

They did, and so did he. The last vestiges of worry left Chat when they finally hit the stage at 8:30, and Chat could see that almost everyone in the campground had come out—lawn chairs, coolers and all—to catch the show. They had smoked that set—bitter-sweet vocals like "Hold Back the Rushin' Minutes" and "Aragon Mills," irreverent tunes like "They Go Wild, Simply Wild Over Me," thoughtful songs like "Blackjack County Chains" and "High On the Mountain," and of course the train songs: "Train 49," "Rubin's Train," "Midnight Train," "Long Lonesome Rail," a couple of originals that Chat had written over the last year or two, all stitched together with their gentle banter and comfortable-as-an-old-slipper stage chatter. Then, as a finale, they ripped into "Old Dangerfield," as hot and smooth as molten metal, fast as a lightning bolt, with an "awe-shucks" ending, a bow and a wave, and they were suddenly backstage again in what seemed only an instant, stirred, energized, lifted up, converted—real, true believers.

"Day-um!" Sterling said, when they got off the stage. A knot of people were waiting backstage to pat them on the back—saying, "Great show!" and "You boys did great!" and "Nice job" and offering a beer and an offer to "stop by the red camper—see it over there under the trees?—I got some good shine I'd like for you to have." As the icing on the cake, a promoter named Buck said he was interested in backing them "somewhat," maybe to do some touring if it fit into their schedule.

"See? Nothing to worry about, preach," Sterling had whispered to Chat as they talked to their fans.

"What, me worry?" Chat said, cross-eyed and smiling. Of course they wouldn't be going on tour. With their work, that would be impossible. But it was the thought of the possibility that struck Chat then. He could feel the worries about the family drifting away from him, and the night stretched before them as wide and inviting as a drift down a summer river with the stars overhead, the rich smell of camp smoke and the thin tinkling of strings in the forests, the utter luxury of lots of time and a thing you loved to fill it.

On Monday morning, they awoke late—ten or so—and lolled around camp, cooking up some bacon and eggs and breaking camp in a desultory fashion. One would amble over to the truck with the bedding and the tents, or sweep out the pop-up, another put away the lamps and heaters, disassembled the fire ring, or drained the cooler and stashed whatever food was left for the trip home.

By lunchtime, they had the gear stashed and the pop-up stowed, all but Sterling's army-issue pup tent, and they broke out the instruments again for another hour and played. Soon enough the music was replaced by the doleful sounds created as they began to strike the cabana. The poles and knuckles clanged against themselves and the metallic sounds echoed up into the woods opposite as the boys folded and refolded the white nylon tarps, which spewed the road dust from three days of pretty much non-stop partying. *And what,* Chat thought, *was wrong with that?* They did one final sweep of the grounds to make sure they hadn't left anything more than the partial pile of firewood: good for the next guy!

The grass on the ground where the cabana had been was beaten flat, and paths led to where the tents had been and to where the pop-up still stood. Chat always hated this time. Although he knew the fun had to end, he had never liked endings much. He backed the truck up and dropped the pop-up on the hitch expertly, then pulled forward and rolled down his window. The sun was shining brightly, and it was warm again. Maybe no need for heat the rest of the season, he hoped.

"Well, here's to you boys," he said, and drove out, waving to Sterling and the few stragglers left in the park. Sterling waved back, walked three steps, plunked himself down in his seven dollar green fabric rocking captain's chair with the beverage holder in the arm, and picked up his book.

As he rocked, he read:

> The point where ferocious spring melds into languid summer is impossible to pin-point—another border of sorts—just as the eruption of leaves in the months prior seemingly happen when backs are turned or eyes are closed: are they ever truly opened? Eventually the gray and naked hills are swathed in rich greens and the night air caresses. Imagine the land sensuous, fulsome, disquieting, with a million fireflies dotting the silken air above the verdant meadows. It makes what was once a barren field of mud and broken growth a vibrant, effervescent, swirling, mesmerizing miasma of light and silent song.
>
> This is the season in which all things are possible. Now the days stretch towards fourteen and fifteen hours, the air just chill enough to make a fleece or thick sweater a soft womb against the gentle tug of reality, the weather perfect for the campfires of the festivals and campgrounds. Back-packers scale the Indian Head or perch high up on the Appalachian Trail away above the Delaware, listening to the scream of the wildcat, the barks of the fox and coyote and the rustling of the nocturnal prowlers, the coon, the possum and the skunk. The sudden snort and brush-busting flight of the whitetails in the darkness is enough to make the hairs stand up on every inch of a person's body until nervous laughter almost quells the fears.
>
> Then Aurora, the rosy-fingered dawn, quells those nighttime fears with the soft blush of sunlight. The quality of that light was written in yesterday's portents. The streaks of cirrus clouds called "mare's-tails" at sunset spoke of impending rain; the flawless over-vaulting blue of today's crystal clear sky was revealed in last night's heavy dew. Smart country boys or girls would know that. And in the latter days of summer, the first night of the katydids marks the beginning of the end—only six more weeks till the first frost. Time doesn't allow a person to think of that now. Sweet corn is knee-high, the best of the trout season is over, and the folks spend their evenings by the river. They sit with a lantern on a forked stick, rods propped up similarly,

waiting for the big catties to bite—and savor the night like a snifter of the finest old brandy on a cold winter's night.

"Hey Sterling!" one of the Ramblers shouted, leaving in a van with zoo animal contact paper covering the sides and hood. "You take care, now!"

"And you do the same, my friend!" Sterling hollered back, waving slowly. When the plume of dust had settled, he took a swallow of beer and resumed:

Now is the season to play ball, double-headers in the heat of the late afternoon and early evening, sweat-stained ball-players hollering at each other and at the ump—*Are you blind? His foot was off the bag!*—tempers rising as the heat rises.

Not all days are delightful; they can be dreadfully hot, even here in the mountains. It is often sweltering from first light, making the skin damp and the sheets twisted. The sun is a dull orb whose light seems not to illuminate, but to bleach out and remove, till the outline of things are dull and fuzzy, not the bright and harsh lines of the desert, but muted by the water being sucked out of root and leaf, away from ponds and streams, and out of the soil in the garden which gets baked hard. Not hard enough to slow the growth of crab-grass, deadly nightshade and jewelweed, though, which stay amazingly succulent in the midst of bone-dry weather, and which the farmer, enervated, has not the strength or gumption to deal with. Not today, at least.

It is the time for swimming, planning a time when the municipal pool is not over-run with day-care groups and when the block building—put in after the big flood—will cast some shade for parents as their kids dive for pennies or use the slides. No more diving boards, God forbid! Somebody might get hurt! Kids clamor up the ladders and out of the pool to hop, one foot to the next, on the baking concrete and ask—*please please please!*—for a quarter or a dollar for the best of summer foods, a slurpie, some Nachos and a big handful of Swedish fish (Thanks, Puerto Rico! And thanks to you, too, Sweden!).

Or maybe this is the time to spurn the pool and find a place on the river. Better yet, find a couple days and a canoe, and sail down the river like the old raftsmen would sail down her waters, the mists in the morning softening the outlines between bank and water, between mountain and sky, until you can't tell where one leaves off and the next begins, the whole universe melting together for a minute or an hour until the sun burns through: time to load up and paddle. The river is pure glass, the banks and sky reprised in reflection, the paddler listens to the small sounds of the paddle, sees the rings where it has entered and left the water and the green herons or deer on the banks. A bald eagle sits in a dead tree, and just around the point of the next cove the traveler might hear the incredibly loud *spat!* of a beaver disturbed as the canoe rounds the bend, or hear the raucous cry of the great blue heron —fishing-long legs, the Lenape called him.

The islands stand downriver like huge ships in the middle of the channel. Often, as a canoe passes beneath the bluffs on a foggy morning, it is as though the river stands still and the islands are steaming forward.

At such a time, on a quiet summer morning, the water slips past the towhead at the top of the island and the purple loosestrife in the backwaters, with the new sun making golden streaks on a hammered silver background, like some old serving tray. Suddenly a million shad fry obey some unheard call and begin jumping out of the water in the dusk, as far as the eye can see, making the surface a shimmering, boiling sheet of translucent color and motion.

Sterling stopped rocking, finished his beer and opened another. In the woods he saw the small lights of some of the regulars being lit. Most of them were retired guys who would spend one more night and leave in the morning. How nice that must be. Sterling tried to content himself by rumbling his way through the book, feeling and seeing the weekend as it had just happened, and trying to hear some of the notes and chords that they had created, as if they were still floating in some other dimension that he could tap into if he were just smart or talented or persistent enough.

The Yuengling still tasted good as he settled back in, rocking slowly and reading:

This is the season also for torrential rains, trees as big around as a barrel that are snapped in half like twigs, mountainsides of leaves showing silver and shivering madly in winds of gale force. Weather leaves long swathes of trees uprooted, a jumbled chaos marking the passage of the occasional tornado. Lightning splits the sky in an afternoon almost as dark as night, or rattles far away on some other section of river, which will soon run brown and muddy.

Humbling to watch tranquil riffles become standing waves, powerful haystacks three and four feet high that can peel a canoe like a banana.

It's not all greens and browns this time of year. What began as the yellow splashes of forsythia and daffodils has erupted into splashes of purple bergamot or the gaudy red of fireweed. In the uplands where fire reigns, the burgundy cones of the staghorn sumac and the fairy-sprinkling of the bluets, clover and viper's bugloss in the meadows and fields are every possible shade from red to violet. In the forests, the ground is a carpet of lady's slippers and trout lilies, or is strewn with May apples and johnny-in-the-pulpits—strange and wonderful organs of procreation!

Thousands of honeybees work the large flowers of catalpa to make a honey that is almost clear and sweeter than any other. Later in the season the tree makes large bean-like strands that spread everywhere, another transplant that has thrived here in the loamy soils of the bottomlands and the rocky, thin soil of the mountainsides. Many other plants have thrived, too. The native species have been pushed out: the brown trout taking the place of the mottled brookie, chicory crowding out the delicate colt's foot, and crown vetch covering the ground where ground cedar and Indian pipes once flourished. The first people, making their way across the Bering Land Bridge and finding the east coast as congenial a place as could be expected also carried the small burrs and seeds of new plants, a natural version of musical chairs that left some species out.

Pennsylvania. It's a state of firsts, all right: first in covered bridges, sausage production, rural population and pretzels; first because of this season, season of mad growth and possibilities, of new blood, hot and rich, and an aching to create; to sculpt and shape, a season in which everything might be improved, God willing and the creeks don't rise.

"Amen to that, brother," Sterling said, heaving to his feet and crushing the last can of beer into a thin, round, metal wafer. He tossed the chair into the back of his Nova through the open window and settled into the driver's seat, not looking back as he revved up the engine and finally drove away.

23

≒ Chapter Twenty-Three ≒

The four-hour ride home took Chat across Route 6, perched high above the greening valleys and the lush woods. The whole time, Irish reels were dancing through Chat's head: O'Rourke's, Larry Redican's, Miss Ramsay's, although that last was more a strathspeys, really. The crisp fiddle notes that Jo-Jo had been playing of Leinster Buttermilk seemed to cascade down like the wavering reflection of the budding trees in his windshield, but when Chat pulled into the dusky shade near his house and saw the white of the patrol car and the flashing lights, his heart skipped a beat and his breath caught in his throat like he had fallen into the ice-choked river in the dead of winter would snatch the breath clean out of a body. He was out of the cab and running towards the worn stone steps in the front of the house, seeing Sue's figure rising out of the door, flying down the stairs and across the small lawn to him, trying to reassure Chat with her look and failing. She was upset, mad as hell—relieved?—but definitely mostly mad. He ran up to her anyway, caught her at the waist, an almost hug.

"Your son was nowhere to be found, and I was...*frantic*. So I called the only ones I could, in the circumstances," she whispered, disengaging herself from his touch and walking back towards the steps. The door opened then, and Hildebrandt came out, tipping his hat to Chat and saying, "Sorry about the fuss, Chat. The boy was fine. Said he wanted to hike to the top of Minsi and back, and when he had, he came back home."

As Hildebrandt said this, his eyes were snapping and his head was bowed so that Sue would not see what he thought so funny: overprotective, hysterical female. How droll.

"Sorry to take you out on a nice night like this. You could've been bass fishing or something," Chat joked. His chest still hurt from the shock, and his throat ached from his struggle to breath. He managed a smile. Sue looked at them both, and walked inside, her face flat: a look Chat could not cipher.

"You know bass doesn't open for another week, Dalton, you old shit. You trying to get me in trouble with the law?"

"The *law*? The *law*? The law is a *human* institution," Chat quoted, deep-voiced, deadpan.

"Just remember. The policeman is your friend," Hildebrandt said, fingering his gun comically.

"Let's hope so! Thanks for coming out so quick. Sorry for the trouble, too."

"Forget about that this minute. You just take care, now, and tell Sue I said so, too. Both of you, don't be such dumb bunnies, eh?" He pronounced it "dump-unnies."

"Next time you call, call to invite me to dinner, say?" Hildebrandt had lapsed, thick for a moment, into his native "Dutchie" talk.

"Yeah, well, constue?" Chat laughed quietly.

"And me what?" Hildebrandt said, chuckling.

He and Herb went way back. He hoped the guy would live forever, and then he thought, *there was that trooper gunned down on the big road last year by those crack-heads from the city.* And he thought, *Thank You Lord for delivering my child.* He realized that all those thoughts must have been written on his face, and he bowed his head downwards for a moment, as if considering his shoes, then looked up again to wave goodbye.

"Be well, Herb. You take care," Chat said, turning to walk towards the house. He turned again, to wave, slowly, as the cruiser swept away, lights on to illuminate the warming buds of spring. Chat watched as the lights scribed a fiery bright line up the hill and towards the Bennykill hidden around the side of Godfrey's Ridge. He realized that he had yet to unpack, and had to ready himself for work the next day. And he had to deal with an errant child and an angry wife this night, too.

Had she cause for anger? Is there such a thing? He wanted to be able to say there was, but then he thought of scripture. Jonah was angry, Chat remembered, and the remembrance did not assuage him any. Jonah was angry—who wouldn't be? What a trip! He was angry and chastised the Lord for his plight—some nerve there, Chat thought.

"But the Lord replied, 'Have you any right to be angry?'"

Rights or wrongs didn't much matter. He heard it once in high school.

"I don't believe in violence," one of them said, and the other one punched him real hard and said back, "That's okay. It's still real."

The headlights dotted their way back into view, going up the hill to Ellie's. Chat walked back into the house, with fences to mend the best he could and the issue of Jimmy very much on his mind suddenly. Seems Jimmy had been spilling some spleen and a lot of loose talk down at the Bennykill, and Sue hadn't taken to *that* much, had blamed Chat for the way he had handled it, and Chat had just pooh-poohed it all, waving it away as if Sue's words had been the uttering of a mad woman instead of the real true feelings of his wife, whom he loved more than life itself.

Hugh thought for only a moment before he made two calls: one to Malchio to give him the heads up, and second call that would push the boulder down the hill and flatten that bastard Dalton like the bug he was. He told the girl to get Meade on the line and told him what was what.

"You *knew?* Oh, sitting on it, huh? Well, I'd like to move the timetable up. Like today. I know it's a pain. But I'm sure I could get something out of the gombas here that would be a nice hit, later on. All the numbers, you know? Sure, listen, Meade, just consider this as a favor for me, okay? And of course, that *would* be your job description, too, right? My girl'll fax over the tax map and the rest of the information so you can get right on it. Then later, say, Thursday next, let's get together. Usual place. I'll buy. Sure thing. See you then."

That was all it took.

Chat had just skinned the crap out of his knuckles trying to break loose a rusted bolt that he knew he should've used the torch on, and it was almost enough to make him cuss. So he was fuming and trying to get the damned bleeding stopped when the cop cars pulled in. He wasn't really paying close attention. *Just Hildebrandt back again to bust my shoes,* he thought.

A short muscular state trooper flashed his badge as he walked up to Chat.

"You John Wesley Dalton?"

"Where's Hildebrandt? I've never seen you around here," Chat said, intentionally ignoring the strange trooper, walking over to the sink to rinse his hand.

"I said, sir, to please identify yourself. Are you John Wesley Dalton?"

"I am. So what?"

"Please stop where you are and turn around, sir," the trooper said, fingering his weapon, "You're under arrest for conspiracy to produce and distribute marijuana."

"What the *hell* are you talking about? Lemme wash my hands and we'll talk."

Another man, tall and blond with a good suit, had gotten out of an unmarked car behind the cruiser, flashed a badge—Feds?—and the second cop turned on the cruiser lights and got out as well.

Chat saw Marv Atbie pass the garage and slow down to see what was what, then slowly pick up speed and head up the hill towards town. Chat was unaccountably embarrassed.

"Sir, please stop where you are. You have the right to remain silent," the trooper said, starting towards him.

"What *the, the, Sam Hill* are you all *talking* about? Where the *blazes* is Hildebrandt? He'll tell you! Distribute marijuana? Geeze, I don't even *smoke* the stuff. This must be some kind of mistake," Chat said, finally getting the sink to operate and sticking his hand under the water. He half-watched the cascade of red, thin vermillion ribbons inside the stream of water, just a blush of death. Chat again had to struggle to catch his breath.

"Hildebrandt was removed from this district, hadn't you heard?" the stocky one said, obviously pleased with himself and happy with his job. He proceeded to drone out the rest of the Miranda warning, waving a sheaf of papers with the State Seal on the top at Chat , who could only stand numb and mesmerized, while scarlet drops of blood spattered on the floor.

"Turn around, sir, or I'll have to use this," he said, patting his nightstick.

"Please, sir. Give me your hands and get in the cruiser. Herb said you'd behave yourself. You'll have plenty of opportunity to give your side of the story."

"But, but," Chat said, but the cop was waving the papers in Chat's face and pushing him with the nightstick, trying to get him to turn around so he could cuff him. In one moment the insistent prodding made Chat suddenly understand the phrase "seeing red." He had the cop laid out almost before the second uniformed officer and the suited one could react. In another second, they had Chat down on the ground, face pressed in the gravel, smacking him hard in the ribs with the nightsticks. Chat felt the fear and struggled like a man possessed, and they cuffed him—unbelievable violation of his dignity—with him shouting at the top of his lungs *"This is America, gosh darn it,"* and *"I have my rights!"*

In the puke-green cell, Chat tried sorting it all out. The way he felt, he could have sat there without moving for another day or two, or a week, or a month. He could have just sat there to consider the pain in his left cheek, the bruises under his ribs where the truncheon had done its work, and the raw wound on his wrists where they had clamped the cuffs on too tight, even the skinned knuckles he had given himself just when the world turned over and became some bizarre fantasy, like a bad dream from which he could almost convince himself he would awaken. He asked for an attorney—obviously he was in over his head. Before anyone else showed, he was visited by another DEA man, a guy named Gormley, a stocky, bow-legged, pock-marked man with a bad suit and one eye that seemed just out of focus to Chat. Gormley happily intoned that Chat's land and property were "under the control and jurisdiction of the United States Government until or if this is all resolved."

"I'd love to know what the hell you all are yammering about. Pot this and pot that. I don't smoke, and I'm a law-abiding citizen. You ask Hildebrandt. He'll tell you."

Gormley flipped open his briefcase and flashed a half-dozen pictures: Jimmy's plants with Chat's building in the background. Even "Chat's garage" and the "No Parking" sign were legible, the pictures were that good. Chat had a strong urge to tell them whose plants those were, but he said nothing.

That might do some good at some point, or it might not, but he wasn't the one to decide that. He wasn't going to say a word to those bastards before his lawyer got there.

"That's your land. So these are your plants."

"They most certainly are *not!* Geeze. Even if they were, the *Feds?* For a half-dozen lousy pot plants? What kind of sense does that make? This can't be legal," Chat said, stung.

"Conspiracy to distribute, Mr. Dalton. That's a federal case, right there."

"And you can just waltz in and take a man's property, then? That can't be right!"

"There's more, Mr. Dalton. Plenty more. So you can help yourself here by telling us who your contacts are, who buys this stuff."

"You've got it all wrong," Chat said, suddenly realizing how lame that sounded; *I been framed!*

"Sure, you're going to say you didn't know anything about this, right? Must be somebody else's, you're going to tell me. I'm disappointed. You seem like an intelligent man. You think I'd be here if we didn't have more than a half-dozen pictures?"

"You can tell all that to my attorney. Unless I died and woke up in freakin' Red China, none of this is gonna stick, and I'll have your badge if it's the last thing I do." Gormley just smirked as he left the room, and Chat thought he was on pretty firm ground, upset as he was.

It was all just a bureaucratic screw up, and he'd get it straightened out. This situation was like the gremlins he was famous for fixing in these parts, those car problems that came and went and made diagnosis danged hard. If he was careful and patient, he had no problem flushing out the problem. The fixing was the easy part, really.

But his heart sank when he saw who his free lawyer was going to be: Hank "Chooney" Wilmore, one of his schoolmates from the old days, known then for his thick glasses and always-running nose, and now renowned for several things: not wearing socks ever, drinking early in the day, and consistently losing cases, all of which made him politically popular for his job. After all, where there's smoke, there's fire, and weren't the so-and-sos all guilty anyway? A body might as well lock them all up, save the cost of a long trial, they figured.

He and Chat conferred only long enough for Chat to find out that, yes indeed, they could "confiscate any and all properties and apportunatures or some such used in the production or distribution of class two controlled substances," Chooney said.

"Man, Chooney, you seem to be right on top of this case. How's that, anyhow?" Chat asked, seething.

"They have to lay that stuff out when they charge you, you know. So I took a minute to look that up before I came over. You know, old time's sake, and all."

"Well, thanks, Chooney. Not that knowing is going to do me much good," Chat said morosely.

"Well, that's the least I could do. You never were on me like the others, back in school." Chat noticed a little shudder in Chooney, who was possibly remembering the years of teasing and bullying. But Chooney shook it off. He always had, even when the taunts and getting tossed out of the boy's locker room naked and having to run around the classroom building to get back in seemed to Chat to have been the worst kid of evil. The administration had dismissed it all as good clean fun, which it maybe was for anybody but Chooney.

"But, anyway, that's gonna make it hard to make bail," he said.

"What? Sorry. I was someplace else for a second," Chat apologized.

"Prolly 'cause you're wishing you were someplace else. Anyhow, what I was saying is that there's a lien on all the property now."

"Shit." Chat had almost taken the Lord's name in vain at that moment, and he remembered himself.

"Thy will, I guess," he muttered to himself darkly. Then, "So how do I get out? They brought me to Reister for the arraignment, and the bastard set bail at a quarter million. A quarter million. Can you believe that shit?"

"I see that," Chooney replied. "That's high, no doubt about it, seeing they have all your property tied up, too. I wonder why. Maybe the assault charges? That one is gonna be tough to get out of."

"Well, I don't regret that for one instant. Wait, that's not exactly true. I wished I had got another couple licks in on that cop. Maybe because Reister can't stand Aunt Jenna anymore? He tried to make a pass at her at the Republican rally a couple years back — he was drunk as a lord. Jenna threatened to have him arrested for sexual harassment in front of about a hundred of the high muckety-mucks."

"Oh, that's right. I remember that. Reister was mortified. They were cracking jokes about that one for months. But somehow, well, I called over to the Fiesterville barracks to talk to Hildebrandt, and he's on assignment in Pittsburgh, for crissakes. Oh, sorry about the language. But anyway, I thought that one was odd. How about your uncle? Think he can raise the cash?"

"Dunno. Guess we'll find out. He should be able to, all that land and all. So. Anyhow, thanks again, Chooney. It's nice to see a friendly face after all those dicks," Chat said, sputtering to a halt. He had no idea how to fix this, none whatsoever. So of course that had to be just as hard on Sue.

"You sit tight. We'll have you out first thing in the morning, as soon as the banks open, and we can get the paperwork moving."

Chat shook Chooney's hand and tried to compose himself for the call home. Best to be matter-of-fact about it all when he got Sue on the phone, that he was being "processed" as if he was some side of beef or something. And the whole time he was struggling to make himself believe that he was going to spend that night in jail, at least.

He waited while the phone rang. He heard in the small distance between himself and the cellblocks the clinking and clanking of an iron and steel world, cell doors ramming home, and the locks. A lock would go off every three minutes at this time of day. As sore as he was—and he was plenty sore, for those cops had thoroughly enjoyed their little tap dance on his butt—he was even more mortified. He knew he was innocent, and he knew that he had always been a stand-up guy, honest, helpful, and not full of himself that people could notice, but he knew people well enough to know that tongues were wagging. He also knew that he was not universally loved. Some folks found him abrasive, self-absorbed, and many of the heathens didn't care for his faith as if it was some kind of embarrassment they found vile and disturbing.

Maybe it was the end days, like some of those snake-handlers back in the hills of Paulenkill maintained.

"Further along, we'll know all about it," Chat half-sang under his breath, and then he heard Sue's irritated voice at the other end.

The phone surprised Sue in the middle of a bath, and she muttered under her breath while she hoisted herself out of the tub, grabbed a towel and trailed soap-sudsey water into the kitchen to answer it.

Her "Hello" was the last word she could utter, faintly hearing the click on the other end, and she stood, irresolute, while a puddle of water gathered beneath her feet.

"I'll be go-to-hell," was all she could get out eventually, and then she hung up the phone and quickly punched in Homer and Thelma's number. She hoped she would get her, and not him, but, crazy or not, he was the only kin she could think of. Right now she needed more than anything to hear a voice she knew would be on her side.

Thelma answered, and for a moment Sue almost laughed at her own inability to say anything but Thelma's name over and over, but, once she started, she found the words gushing out like a torrent, a nonsensical stream of words with only one clear meaning to Thelma. She and Sue would be taking a trip down to the police barracks at Fiesterville, and she'd have to figure out a way to scrape up the bail that the asshole Reister had set for Chat.

"Where are we going to get that kind of money, Thelma?" Sue said, crying uncontrollably.

"There, there, honey. You just take it easy. Homer and I have some put by. We'll figure this out somehow. This is bound to just be a mix-up. Everybody knows Chat didn't know nothing about no pot plants, land sakes!"

And that just made Sue cry all the harder. By the time they had reached the barracks, she was in better control of herself. She knew Chat like the back of her hand, like she knew herself, but this was something so bizarre that she had no idea how he'd be taking it. The assault charge, well, that part she could imagine.

She and Thelma sat in the waiting area, one wall dominated by vending machines. Plain-clothes cops, secretaries and troopers walked in and out of the place. It was business as usual. Finally one cop came out and indicated that Sue was to come with him.

In a sterile room with a table and three chairs, they sat her down, shivering. *Did they keep it so cold on purpose?* She wondered.

A second door opened and a trooper brought Chat out and said, "Ten minutes." He then stood to one side, impassive.

All she could blurt out when she saw Chat brought out in cuffs was, "It was all my fault!"

Chat shook his head slowly.

"No, Sue. No. I should have listened to you about Jimmy, but I was so danged pigheaded. Dang. *Dang!*"

"But, Chat. Darlin'. They're not gonna make this stick. You know that. You're an innocent man, and, well, if it has to be between you and Jimmy, that's not a hard choice for me to make. So we spend some money, get a good lawyer. We'll take out a loan against the house. We can beat this," she said, anxious to be positive about it. "Right? Chat?"

He didn't answer for a minute.

"Chat?"

"They want the house, too. They want to confiscate the land, everything on it. The shop. There was a DEA guy there. He said it was all theirs "until or if this is over." That was what he said—those words. "Until or if.""

"What do you want me to do? Homer and Thelma can help. Thelma said so."

"I guess you'll have to ask for them to get a mortgage on their place—a bail bondsman, I guess. Shit, I don't even know if there is one around here. I don't know anything about how to do this."

They sat there in silence, a silence so complete they could hear the trooper breathing—Sue heard a little congestion there. She could also hear the traffic noise outside, ever so faintly, and in between, boots on metal grating and the sound of locks.

And just like that, the trooper said, "Time." He was guiding Sue with a hand under her arm to the door, which shut behind her and left Chat sitting, stunned.

Suddenly Chat felt something he had denied was even there, his own equivalent to the evil little imp Sterling had once told him sat upon his shoulder late some nights. Sitting there in the Fiesterville Jail, he tried not to remember.

24

$\Longrightarrow$ CHAPTER TWENTY-FOUR $\Longleftarrow$

He thinks about that spring. It had been bone-chilling cold and rainy for weeks, but that day dawns delightful and balmy. They lounge about for a time, and then it's the most natural thing to head on down to the river. They all go on down in three vehicles, the aunts, the uncles, and a couple of the cousins. Chat remembers that the Hodgeden twins were there, and a couple other kids, too. Pa and Homer are the two tall trees in the forest, and off they go, with a whole lot of food and some beverages. They slide and slither down the steep cut bank as best they can. The clay on the river banks is still wet from the thaw, and it's next to impossible to get down there without getting a little smudged up. Chat sees that his mother has managed somehow to do that. Had old Dutch lifted her when he wasn't looking?

They all get down fairly near the river and spread the blanket on the sandy shore. Some of the aunts stand for a moment and do what Chat always does. He looks upstream to see the sights. He tells himself he is looking into the next day, the next week, the next month, perhaps the rest of his life. He read that in a cowboy book, only the cowboy had been looking at the sky and thinking that. To young Chat, making the river do the bidding of the sky makes sense somehow.

Looking upriver, Chat thinks, is the closest a man can come to looking into the maw of the great beyond. On that day, things seem as clear as a bell. Chat doesn't heed the grown-ups much, always talking as they are. He is a reticent boy, then, and listens far more than he speaks. He looks at the river, and he notices that, for not having had any rain, she seems a tad muddy. And, after an hour or so of eating and laughing with the other kids, throwing sticks in the current, and watching the scoters and the black ducks splashing down, eating, and taking off again, he hears, above the casual buzz of conversation, a worried murmur. He looks up to his old man, wondering if he has heard it as well.

It's the river with bad blood on her mind. Chat sees that the old man hears her, too. And he looks at his old man, and he thinks he sees the old man wink, except the old man never does that. So he relaxes.

"Well, time to be going, I guess," the old man says, perky.

Chat stands there, looking at the river, and the sun getting towards the horizon in the afternoon. He looks back to his old man. The relatives all stop their jabbering and ask, all at once, *Why, Dutch, why do you want to run off like that so soon?* There are still a few hours of daylight left. Dutch answers *You'll see!* and he smiles broadly as he and Homer help the older aunts to their feet. Then Dutch says to Chat, "You scurry on up to the top of the bank, there, and help the ladies up that last little bit."

Chat looks again, to make sure, and he notices that Homer and Thelma, and Dutch and his Ma are all deadly focused like they know something. Chat does as he's told—he always does as he's told—and one by one they get the oldsters up the bank, and Dutch gets Homer to bully the little ones up to the top of the bank until there is only Dutch and Madge down there and Chat and Homer up top. They are reaching for Madge's hand, with Dutch steadying her from behind, when the murmur becomes a terrible roar, and before anyone knows it there is five feet of water swirling around them, and logs as thick as a man's leg spinning around in a backwater that appears from nowhere as fast as the water rises.

Homer and Chat have Madge by the wrists, and Dutch is behind her, up to his chest in swirling brown murk. Chat still thinks it's only a damn inconvenience, that his mom's dress is soiled for sure, now, and that Dutch is going to bitch about this for the next four years. Up above, the oldsters are clucking like hens, and it is then that the universe, which had been hiding like a shy bride on her wedding night, disrobes and reveals herself to Chat.

In one second, the bank washes away. In the next, Homer and Chat lose their grip on Chat's ma. In the third, Dutch and his bride are swept out into the current, and Homer wastes no time. He's into the water, head first, and the fourth second has him brained by a log and floating near the bank. Chat plunges in, feet first, and he grabs Homer, and he never bothers trying to get back to the cut bank. He drags Homer in the dead-man's carry that he learned in Scouts downstream towards the woods below the point, where there will be quieter water. More than once he thinks he will drown, now, beaten by the flotsam like cudgels from hell, and he kicks frantically until he is suddenly in the backwater, and Homer is coming to—none too happy, either.

Chat thinks, *well, if this won't make a topic for conversation this evening, after we get it all sorted out.* He knows Dutch will have done just what he did, although they might be a bit downstream before they make land. He knows his Ma and Pa are his betters. They'll be all right. He feels his arms and legs—pounded by some floating trash—an arm-sized branch packs quite a wallop going twenty miles an hour, and the water had been thick with lumber of all sizes. He's bleeding in a couple places; he must be, because the water they're sitting in is turning a dirty ashes of roses color from the crimson ring that surrounds Chat.

He sits with Homer for a minute until he comes to all the way, and then Chat gets him to walk himself further up the bank away from the river. Chat is having a hard time taking this all in. The river has gone from calm to manic in a few heartbeats, and he wants to look at Homer but he's afraid to because Homer is bleeding too. He looks back over his shoulder at the shoreline. The leaves aren't quite out near the river, and he would see his parents if they rose.

"The paper mill dam. The old dam. It went out. That's what it was," Homer wheezed.

And that *was* what it was. Chat wanders back up to the vehicles with Homer, dripping and sore, and Homer's head is bleeding in great vermilion drops that spatter on the pavement as he staggers towards the cars. Chat supports him, feeling the thin fingers clutching his strong arm until it hurts. He says nothing. The oldsters are crying, Thelma especially, until she actually has Homer in her arms, and then she buries her face in his chest and bawls some more, and the oldsters are weeping, quiet, quiet. The twins stand there, amazed, watching trees the size of a truck rushing by, and Chat is watching, too, still watching. Didn't the servant who watched get rewarded, while the one who slept was chastised? He keeps watching downstream, for Dutch and Madge to emerge from some part of the bank, while the maelstrom carves out half acres of land at a time, and tree after tree tumbles into the flood, flipping upright for a moment, then slamming downwards, the fine branches whipping the water into a brown froth while the tree shudders its way over the rocky bottom. The biggest branches snap with a force he can feel in his chest, until the tree is stripped bare enough to float, and then it careens down with the rest of what had been, moments before, forest.

"Jesus," Chat says. And then, once more, "Jesus."

That is when he knows he is not going to see Dutch and Madge again alive. And, in that little twist and turn, he becomes himself.

Thirty years later, Chat remembers that the next three days are like looking into a deep pool of clear water. The things that are closest to him are scribed in eerie clarity, scarcely affected by the translucent matter that only hints that it is there. As he gets deeper, it all begins to fade, until the clear water somehow completely obscures the picture, the solid rubbed away by the ethereal.

Chat remembers everything, the smell of the hospital, the ride back to Homer's, the wallpaper there, the smell of the woodstove, the lumpy sofa, the scuffed linoleum in the kitchen. He remembers sitting in the overstuffed chair at Homer's after they return from the hospital, and it is late. He remembers only the ticking of the clock on the mantle, and the murmurs and moans that come from the bedroom, the soft keening. Homer has no other brothers or sisters left. He has no one now except Chat and Thelma. After a time, it becomes silent, the sounds falling away like the leaves at the end of autumn flutter down silently, and Chat waits for the dawn. He waits for some feeling. Even as the sun rises, the silence continues, like going over the mountain used to make his ears plug up, then pop. But this time, there is no pop.

The next day, Homer seems to be begging him to stay behind. He is obstinate; he mouths the words that he will ride with the Civil Defense people in the Army-green boat. Sporting soiled bandages, they ride down to the landing, jump in the boat and begin the tedious search, stopping at the head of every island to look. For three days, they search each towhead, and the larger islands as well. Chat is surprised at how many islands remain, and the water is still nasty high, making a landfall dangerous, and the simple act of floating downstream is a gut-wrenching tedium. After the first day, Homer and Chat go back to Homer's place.

That first night, Thelma has the meal waiting. From what Chat can see, there is little speaking, and just as little eating. At sundown, Homer doesn't bother with the lights, and Chat is happy to scurry over to the overstuffed chair to wait. The next day is the same, and the third also. The warmth has sharpened the smell of drying river mud and death. Every island is the same: huge logjams have formed, and interspersed with the maze of shattered trees are dead leaves, straw and twigs, and the flotsam of humanity. Bottles, faded tennis balls, shredded plastic, light bulbs and tin cans are embedded in the logjams like plums in a pudding. By the third day, the cattle that have been swept down are bloating, and the flies are shimmering in the sunlight around this great good fortune. More than once Chat sees the searchers heads snap around, and it soon dawns on Chat that they are listening for the buzz of a thousand flies like some bizarre Geiger counter of death. All that day long, they follow the same pattern: land and disembark, fan out from the head of each island to the foot of it, a distance of a few hundred yards on the small islands, better than a mile on the larger ones. On several of the big ones, they cannot even see the other searchers on the other side, and Chat waits impatiently for the rendezvous at the other end. He wants this to be over. They are halfway down to Fiesterville, and the sun is waning, as a chill settles in the hollows of the river. Three more islands left before the river cuts through the mountain, and none below it. There, the river rips along right nasty below bluff banks for thirty miles, all the way down to Houser's Eddy. Chat begins to doubt they will ever find his Ma and Pa.

The head of Bennykill Island is in the cold dark shadows of the ridge above, and he sees one of the firemen waving his arm. Chat's heart stops for an instant. He leans against a tree, ready to puke. How can he look? How can he not look? Homer is there, looking at him with eyes that Chat has never remembered as being that large. Chat can tell by the way they work it is not his parents. The sideways look is missing, so this is someone else.

They walk down to the small point where they see the search party standing about. Turns out it is old man Peters stuck in the logjam. Zane Peters, a kind of famous fellow in these parts, the great-great grandchild of Zane Grey, who loved nature and thought nature should be preserved. His farm is ten miles upstream from where Chat and the others had been the day before when the river, with a negligent swipe, had torn apart Chat's life.

They bring the boat up and tie it fast to a tree. Already the river is back down to a normal level, although it is still muddy. It will be for days, Chat knows.

The body is entwined in the logjam, and the men begin to slice the logs that embrace it with chainsaws, taking care to avoid getting brained by limbs that, suddenly released from the tension that holds them like a coiled viper, might whip free with a sound like a rapier and the force of a battering ram. As they work, those coiled springs fling mud and leaves dozens of yards in the air, spattering all of them with dirt.

Chat and Homer don't offer to help. Instead, they slump exhausted on a jumble of logs nearby. It is late in the afternoon, and the nearest landing is a good hour away. The men finally free the body and carefully carry it to the boat, laying it on musty canvas and covering it up. They all climb back on board, avoiding the load in the middle. The last two days, this time of day would be a signal to finish the lunches the Red Cross ladies had packed them up with, but today, the last few white cardboard boxes sit in plain view, and no one bothers with them. They swing back into the current, running downstream towards the next takeout. The sun is deep gold, and a marvelous streak runs towards it, broken into a thousand facets of light where the wake of the boat shatters the water.

Chat knows he will not be going out again tomorrow to search. He knows they are not going to find Dutch and Madge.

Chat can't really remember anything else except the eerie silence at church that next Sunday, where everyone gives him all the room he needs and perhaps a bit more than he wants. At old man Peters' funeral, the damp clay dropped in small clods into the grave, and Chat found himself filling in the sounds like a mental soundtrack of a silent movie.

So now he is sixteen, and he moves in with Homer, who buys him the brand new red Chevy pick-up with the 8-track player in it, that Chat blasts as loudly as the dial will go, waiting for his ears to pop.

Later that week, Chat figures it will all settle in when he finally goes back to where he was raised, in the shadow of the Blue Ridge, near the water that he had heard, night and day, boy and man. Dutch was no dummy, and the house used to stand well above the flood plain, but even Dutch had not counted on the dam breaking. Below the house, where the boathouse stood, nothing is left. The river has scoured out the flat below the house and the bank above, and the only things left are three steps that would have led to the boat ramp. Chat looks at an alien landscape, trying to remember where his Pa had tickled him, or where they had stood to clean a nice mess of catfish after a good day's fishing in the fall, when the air was crisp and wisps of ice clung to the reeds near the river. He can't even see it anymore, and so he waits for the reality of the loss to sink in, for the inevitable pain and the sadness.

Thirty years later, perhaps he is still waiting.

If Sue had lived through a bleaker night, she couldn't remember when. She couldn't hide her eyes from the kids, all puffed up as they were. What was that song Chat sang? "Such sad, sad eyes/ they seem to go/ from misty to a river of tears." She went about her business with deadly attention to detail: leave no stone unturned. The kids were all eyes, watching. *That's what they do*, she said to herself, and she got the dinner on the table at the appointed time, dishing out the kid's fav, hot dogs and mac 'n cheese. But something in her heart was just the tiniest bit bruised, and she had to think to quell the quiver of her lower lip. She tended to get stern when she was feeling pushed, and she knew that she and all the family around had been shoved in a mighty way. *Try and put up the best front you can, no amount of gumption is going to carry you over that; no "hold-your head-up" routine would convince anybody with half an eye and a third less brain. Of course the kids were curious and frightened.*

"Mommy. What's wrong? Is Daddy hurt?" Megan had asked. Jesse had said nothing. He simply pounded his wooden mallet against the wall again and again until Sue grabbed him and took it away.

"Everything is going to be fine," Sue said, thinking of the statement as a white lie. "Daddy had to go away for a day or two."

"See? He went to a festival like I told you," Meg gloated to Jesse, who was still pouting about the hammer.

"Mommy doesn't cry like that about festivals," Jesse said.

"Does too."

"She does not! She swears when she cries about festivals," Jesse said.

Oh my God, thinks Sue. *And what else have they been learning without my knowing it?*

"Listen, kids, Daddy had a little misunderstanding with a policeman, and they want him to stay to clear it up. That's all. And I do *not* swear!"

The phone rang: Marge Atbie calling "to see if there is anything I can do." *Fishing for dirt,* Sue thought bitterly. That was the first of a dozen calls, not all of them unwelcome. Sterling, Johnny, Meg and Kate all called. Sterling commiserated and offered financial help, or just to be a go-fer if she needed. Meg offered to baby-sit. Johnny asked if they wanted to come over for dinner. Kate called to see if they wanted dinner brought to them, to which Sue had surprised herself by saying, "That would be wonderful."

An hour later, the whole bunch had descended on the house, each carrying a covered dish.

"What is this, a wake?" she had joked, near tears.

After a few minutes of awkward shuffling and muttering, Sue convinced Meg to take the kids out to the edge of the meadow to see who could catch the most fireflies, and of course every stitch of a child was out the door to take the prize in a moment, leaving the adults standing, slightly shocked by the sudden silence.

In the next moment, Sue began to bawl like a child. Johnny remembered he had to check his "bat-ree floo-ud," and excused himself, and Sterling muttered about making a phone call about the bail, leaving Kate to sit with Sue over the next half hour to listen uncomfortably to her litany of confusion, anger, and guilt.

My God, Sue thought, *she's not the person I've always made her out to be, listening to me like this, like she cares what's to become of us all. Is this something new?* But listen Kate did, right up until Sue gave a shuddery laugh and said, "Guess we better get supper on."

"Things will be fine. Anybody would feel the way you do, Sue. Chat'll land on his feet. You know he always does. Just remember, the darkest hour is just before the dawn, so if you want to steal your neighbor's newspaper, that's the time to do it." She smiled, almost patted Sue on the arm, and picked up a casserole—tuna, she thought she smelled—and carried it into the kitchen.

Sue picked up another dish and followed her, pausing at the sink and looking her in the eye.

"I guess I was always a little pissed about Jo-Jo," Sue admitted, blushing red.

"I'm sorry," Kate said, and Sue could tell she meant it. "It wasn't my fault Jo-Jo picked me. And, plus, look at all the good it did me," Kate said, making a silent, ironic "yuk-yuk" with her mouth. Then Kate said, "Speaking of which, I have something I'd like your advice about, seeing as how you're a mother and all, and you know Jo-Jo."

For a few moments, listening, Sue forgot her own troubles, and then, as if it had all been scripted, in dribs and drabs the rest came back, first the kids, then Meg, face flushed and eyes laughing, then Sterling and finally Johnny, all looking the better for a small spell off on their own.

They sat to dinner as if they had eaten that way all their lives, passing the gravy and potatoes to each other like the were the infield of the '67 Mets, like they had always been doing this, like they were the two halves of a rower, like the rich coal in the ground, like the quiet sound of a good engine, or the sound of wind on sail and rigging, like they loved one another, which of course was exactly the case.

They sat around the kitchen table after dinner, talking about what the next step was. Sterling knew a bail bondsman in Fiesterville. Johnny could take a day or three to help round up Chat's tools or replacements for them and maybe find a place to work. He knew a guy that had a garage out on the old Dark Horse Pike—he was getting older and maybe didn't need the bays a few days a week. Meg and Kate sat and listened, or murmured with each other, nodding, or helped with the dishes or with watching the kids, who were busy playing and talking. "There's a new kid in my class, and she talks funny!" "There's two new kids in *my* class, and one of 'em *looks* funny!"

And when the company finally left, Sue breathed a sigh of relief; welcome as it was, she needed to get the kids settled down and her thoughts in order. She got them in bed—to them, the evening was just an unexpected play-date, and they were both fast asleep before she could get halfway through "Good Night Moon." She tiptoed out of the bedroom at the head of the stairs. She had been uplifted by love, and between that and the emotional violence of the past twenty-four hours, she doubted she would get much sleep this night either, and decided to bake some banana bread. What if they were thrown out of the house? Wasn't it part of the same parcel that the shop is on?

Mash four well-ripened bananas and add 3/4 cup of white sugar.
She needs to call the bail bondsman first thing.
Add one egg and blend well.
She needs to talk to the kids before school about what not to say.
Add 1 ½ cup white flour, 1- teaspoon salt and 1-teaspoon baking powder.

She needs to get a grip. She wants to shoot her cousin Jimmy.
Bake at 375 for 35 minutes or until brown.

She couldn't believe she walked out of the station without finding out if there were visiting hours, how and when to get in touch with Chooney, if Chat was going to need stitches for his cheek, how she didn't even ask how he got those scratches, how she was alone now without him, or how alone he must be there in that jail cell.

There was the bread to be made, and a house to clean—God knew when she'd be able to do it all later. She pushed herself from chore to chore. If they were to be dispossessed, they would return to a home that was spotless and welcoming, at least. When the dawn broke, lavender pinks and deep yellow golds, and the birds saluted the coming of day, it did not surprise her. She was exhausted, but thankful that the darkness, which seemed eternal, was over. At least now she could begin to do something to straighten out this horrible mess.

25

≡ CHAPTER TWENTY-FIVE ≡

The next day was a blur of phone calls and hurried trips to town to talk with Chooney, Sterling and Homer, then out to Fiesterville, to see Chat again—*Ten minutes! No more!*—where Sue could see he had not slept either. At least she had some help, and she answered some of his questions: Homer and Sterling were working on the bail. She would know more details at lunchtime, although she guessed that there would be no way to get a message to him.

"But," she said, "I hope that we won't even need to. I hope you will be walking out with me and home by supper."

"You always were hopeful. What about the house? Are we going to have to stay with Homer?"

"Chooney has a request for a stay on eviction, so maybe we'll luck out," she said.

Then the cop was saying, "Time!" and Sue kissed Chat like she realized she hadn't kissed him in a long, long time.

She left teary-eyed for an afternoon of meetings and waiting for word from the DA's office, the cops, Sterling, Chooney, dealing with Homer at the bail-bondsman's place. Homer was saying, "Highway robbery is what it is! Ten percent! If you wasn't the only one around here, I'd have a half a mind to beat the living crap outta ya!" and the guy, six three and silver-haired, himself an ex-cop and reputed to be a bit on the crooked side even when he was on the force, just laughing at that, said that nobody had a gun up to Homer's head.

She ran back to get the kids from school, and finally heard from Chooney that Chat was being sprung at four p.m., and she could come over and get him, but to be sure they didn't leave town until the arraignment was finished.

"And what about all this, Chooney? There's no way they can make this stick, right?" Sue said.

"Well, maybe not. But they're not known for moving with lightning speed, the Feds. Case could take a couple years, as it stands now."

"Years?" Sue had repeated, dumbfounded. Dumbfounded was what they both were after she had walked Chat out of the Fiesterville Police barracks, and the shock stayed with them as they took 511 down from Fiesterville. They drove past the huge scars and scabs on the Blue Ridge from rockslides, gas and power lines, fires—even, Chat pointed out, the metallic glint of metal fabric still lodged in small bits on the Indian Head from the twin engine Cessna that had a little too much faith in late '60s instrumentation. The wreckage was visible only at that time of day and from that viewpoint, although the glimmers of metal grew a little dimmer each year: it was easier to see when he and she were younger. Perhaps someday it would be just a legend: a flying machine that forgot how to fly, a time when flying took bravery and courage, when not just anyone would risk life and limb soaring in the airy heights, with their lives in someone else's hands.

Homecoming was bliss, even with all that was and all that might be: a delightful but somber returning. Even the kids sensed it, being good as little angels and even going to bed on their own—Meg's idea, Sue knew, having overheard the conversation. And so passed the first day of the storm.

Kate had a lot to chew on when she left Sue's place. She was used to toughing it out, being Little Miss Independent, and she did just fine. Well, she *had* been doing okay until this. What Sue told her made sense. Jo-Jo wasn't ever going to change on his own, and it would be a mistake to count on him changing at all. But she had to at least give him the chance, and so she steeled herself to call him—something she never did, something she studiously avoided. She could hear the surprise and sudden guardedness about his voice, all tight and proper like he was talking to somebody about a sale.

"I'll meet you at the Bennykill," he said, and she contradicted him.

"No, Jo-Jo. I need to see you someplace else. I'll meet you down at the park. It's nice out yet."

"The park. Okay, the park," he said and hung up.

She guessed he would take his sweet time getting there, so she sat on the swings and began to pump, slowly at first, then with more vigor, getting the chain to go just a little slack at the top of each swing. Her red sneakers stuck out, pigeon-toed, framing the ball field where they used to play pick-up softball games and where a half dozen teens were taking batting practice in the twilight. It was a gorgeous evening, as luck would have it, a nice, warm seventy, and the light breeze carried with it the smell of newly cut grass and burgers from somebody's barbeque. Kate leaned backwards, watched the ground rush up at her and then saw the sky and the trees upside-down. They didn't make much sense that way, like objects she had never seen before, time after inverted time.

She was listening for his hog, since it was the perfect night to ride. Instead she saw his crew cab pick-up swinging into the parking lot, narrowly missing the bike racks in the front of the park. She stopped pumping, scuffing her feet in the dirt to slow herself down, the swing twisting back and forth as it came to a halt. Jo-Jo had parked, but he was slow to get out, and Kate would've bet money that he had had a few beers already. He walked stiffly towards her, but the grin of beer origin was missing. He was sober, then.

"So. What's going on that's so important?" he snapped at her, leaning against the galvanized metal pipe that held up the swings. Even though he didn't have a trace of booze on his breath, he was still disheveled and ill shaven, not like him at all. She resisted the urge to ask him if he was okay straight off.

"Where's the hog? It seems a nice night to ride," she said.

"Forget that. Never mind about the bike."

"Are you alright? You look, like, sick or something."

"Never mind that either. I just been working too hard, too many hours, that's all. Now tell me what was so important it couldn't wait for a day or two. You know I hate drama."

She took a deep breath and began.

"Have you ever thought about being with me for good? I mean, being a real couple? I mean, I know what you've always said about it, but a person might have doubts, or maybe change his mind, getting older and all that. So, how about it? Any changes at all? Even an inkling?"

"An inkling? Freakin' college courses got you sounding like some kinda goddam perfesser. Listen," he paused, changed hands on the swing set, "Why are you bringing all this up *now*, huh? Why can't you just enjoy what we have, go with the flow?"

"Well, Jo-Jo, I just figured I'd ask because my situation has changed. Somewhat." She looked at him with what she hoped were kind and understanding eyes, and he looked back with the briefest hint of defiant hurt in his.

"Is it that Tony? I mean, I can fix that little problem quick enough, if that's got you confused."

He gave a short, harsh laugh and glared at her.

She hated the belligerent tone he took when he was close to being emotional, but that was the way he was. Only two emotions worked in his world: happiness and anger. She got ready for the anger.

"I enjoy Tony's company, same as I know you enjoy other people's, other women. I'm not blind, either, you know. But this has nothing much to do with him. I need to know for sure that you haven't ever thought about us that way."

"No. No, I never have. When did I ever give the impression I had?" he spun on his heel and faced away from her towards the ball field, and Kate noticed that his knuckles were white from gripping the metal pole.

"You never have, Jo-Jo. And you've never lied to me, and you've always been nice, as far as that went. But, like I said, things have changed for me, and I thought I'd better give you the chance to change your mind."

"Or else what?" he snarled. His hand shook as he wiped his mouth.

"Jo-Jo. Or else nothing. But it's not just me, now. I'm pregnant. So I thought you should know."

He stared at her as if he had never seen her before. Kate was grateful that there were no tears in her eyes. She felt nothing, really. Plenty of time for that later.

"Pregnant. Shit. I mean," he said, shaking his head slowly from side to side three times. He came over and grabbed the swing next to hers, had some difficulty sitting down, and just looked at her with a confused stare.

"Jo-Jo. There's no pressure. I mean, it would be great if you were to help out financially, but beyond that, nothing."

"It's mine? You're sure it's mine?"

She had anticipated that question. He really was that clueless about her. She guessed she had always known that, but it was enough to make her almost lose it. She didn't say a word. *As if he had to ask.*

"Shit. Goddam, Katie. Couldn't you just, you know."

"No. No matter what, that's not happening. And really, Jo-Jo, I don't want to feel like you're going to do something because you feel sorry for me. If this is something you can't do, I understand. I haven't been with you for this long without knowing that much about you. I just had to be sure. If you change your mind, you can let me know, 'kay?"

She got up, kissed him on the forehead, and walked away. He looked like he was ready to ask for a hand up at the moment she turned, as if it were him and not her that were saddled with a burden that couldn't be borne alone.

Or maybe the burden was more like a miracle. Katie remembered Sue's words as she climbed into the Buick and let it rumble to life—she was only getting maybe ten miles to the gallon. Maybe she could talk a better ride out of Jo-Jo. Severance pay, kinda.

"They've saved my life a hundred times, the kids," Sue had told her. "Right now I feel like they're the only thing holding me up. And I bet that's true for Chat, too. Sure, you're scared. Who isn't? But that's the way things are meant to be, and I bet you a buck that this time next year you'll wonder why you even doubted."

Kate looked in her rear-view as she pulled away. The kids were still smacking the ball into the outfield, running and snagging flies, laughing and shouting, and Jo-Jo was still sitting there like a statue. Sue wasn't prone to be troubled by doubt. She had that much faith, and so did Chat.

How nice that must be in times like these.

26

"Josh! Come on! Wake up. I want to get moving here," Sarah said, poking the lump of teen buried under heaps of pillows and comforters. Deep within, a moan of assent, a stirring, and then a soft snore.

Sarah ripped the comforter off the bed and Josh recoiled from the cool air, simultaneously baying protest and curling tightly into the fetal position.

"Come on, please. I want to get out there in time for lunch. Mmmmmmm. Scrapple," she said, waving the comforter and licking her lips lasciviously.

Josh said, "Mom! Gross!" He sat up suddenly, grabbed back the comforter, and settled it like a king's robe over his shoulders.

"Mom. Why can't *you* just go and leave me here? I'll be fine. I can stay over at Howie's for the night if you want me to."

"You don't want to keep me company," Sarah said, mock-pouting.

He murmured a happy assent and flopped over, comforter-camoflaged once again. Front wise or backwards, Sarah couldn't guess.

Well, she could understand that. What would she have thought if her mom had been like that, had blurted out, "Oh, come on, let's hang out together. It'll be a blast!"

Seriously! She'd have been kind of ambivalent about that, even with the whole mother-daughter thing, so of course she could understand the limit to a teenage son's patience. Besides, maybe it wouldn't be a bad thing to be on her own for a little spell. Maybe she'd have a fling! Hey, why not? It could happen.

"You'll call me, then?" she said sternly.

"Yes, Mom," the muffled lump said.

"At dinner and before bedtime?"

"*Yes,* mom." A leg and an arm popped out.

"And no going out?"

"Awwww. Mom." With this plea, his full face was in view, apparently awake and ready to negotiate.

"Say it, and I can leave you without worrying about what trouble is going to find you, okay, sweetheart?"

"Okay, *okay.* Can I go back to sleep now?"

Before she could answer, he had pulled the comforter back over his head, tucked his arm and leg back in his comforter shell, and was snoring blissfully again.

Sarah shrugged, went downstairs to brush her hair—ponytail, this time!—picked a sweater that accentuated her still-pretty-damn-good figure, picked her favorite ball cap—*Duke Racing!*—then bounced down the stairs. She was on her way out of the city while the sun still hovered over the waterfront. The sky was clear, and the air was comfortable and warm. She cranked back the sunroof and smiled, thinking, *two days with people who don't make my flesh crawl, in a place made for humans, not like the city, built for animals.*

Then she thought of Ty. Was he *finally* coming around? She knew he was interested. She hadn't been out of action so long that she couldn't tell *that.* Besides, hell, her ex hadn't been around in months. That worried her a little, though; it wasn't like him to leave them alone for long, unless he had found somebody new to abuse. It had happened before, but not for years. After a few weeks, Josh had started asking if she had heard from him, and at first, when she said she hadn't, he looked forlorn and sad like a whipped puppy dog. But the last time, she could tell he was getting angry with her, as if she was keeping something from him. And her asshole boss? Man, this project involved some pretty mean stuff, even for him.

Oh, she'd heard all about it. McAdam treated her like she wasn't even there, and never watched what he said, so she knew that this wasn't just about making money anymore. It was a personal thing. That had surprised her a little. She hadn't thought him capable of passion like that, for or against anyone or anything.

Forget that, girlfriend. Get involved in something else, someone else besides you and what's left of your life. Long strings of Canada geese flew overhead, heading north again to nest, and she could hear, faint but clear, their honking above the road noise.

She powered the Beemer up to eighty and weaved in and out of the traffic: cars full of moms and dads, and buddies and sissies, stuff crammed into nooks and crannies visible in the rear windows: lawn chairs, pillows, duffel bags, water skis, stuffed animals, coolers, all the tools of leisure. Dour-faced businessmen drove, and women navigated in well-kept Acuras. Oldsters pottered along in Mercedes and Cadillacs, and kids raced off to class at the local community college in old little red cars. Construction workers in twos and threes rode in pick-up trucks spattered with concrete and mud and loaded with wheelbarrows, picks and shovels, lumber and pipe and carpet hanging out the tailgate, laughing, smoking butts and drinking coffee. Families were off to a week or a weekend of camping and swimming—too early to swim for her—or folks were off to go hiking, doing all those country things she had always read about.

She passed tractor trailers hauling milk, garbage, potato chips, gravel, construction debris, computers for Timmy, makeup for Tricia, medical waste, toothbrushes, flatbeds with strange metal contraptions she couldn't even begin to guess, lowboys with 'dozers, and the occasional orange truck full of orange cones and hard-hatted road workers, getting ready to lean on their shovels or signs and watch her pass them by, blue water jug at their feet, walkie talkie in hand, boredom all over their faces.

What a life *that* must be. As if she had room to talk.

When she finally pulled up in front of the Bennykill, she wondered if her memory had been faulty. The lopsided inn, nestled in the curve of the mountain and overlooking the stream, was not in the state of casual disrepair she had pictured a dozen times in her mind's eye—odd phrase, that. Was there such a thing as a mind's eye?

It was hard to put her finger on it, exactly, but then she saw the difference: flowers cascaded out of spackle buckets that had been painted green, blooming in the narrow strip of dirt between the parking lot and the side of the inn. At first she thought that it was simply the time of year for that, but on closer inspection, she could see the telltale marks of a rake on the mulch that had been lovingly spread, marking the plantings as new ones. The window boxes had been freshly painted, and the flowers in them were also new.

The place looked tidy now, with no piles of cigarette butts in the parking lot or gum wrappers littering the ground. *Was this a woman's touch?* she wondered.

Layton saw her before she saw him, making her yelp when he came around behind her from the far side of the building and greeting her with a "Hello again, miss."

"Hi, Layton! It's," Sarah started to say.

"Sarah," Layton finished. "How many bee-you-tee-ful young wimmin you think I get in here on the average day, huh? You come to stay again, I hope?"

"Tonight and tomorrow, yes, if you have a room."

"Never fear there, missy. I haven't been full up since the flood back in '55."

"People stayed here during *a flood?*" Sarah asked, eyeing the bank-full stream with a puzzled look.

"Didn't say I was full up with people," Layton laughed. "Water was up over the porch roof, there. Wonder the place didn't just wash away. But I guess they built it right, back in the day."

"When was that?"

"Oh, 1740s, or thereabouts. Used to be an old stagecoach stop, then a post office, and for awhile, so they say, a, umm, well, " said Layton, stopping awkwardly and kicking dirt.

"You're blushing!" Sarah said. "No! A *brothel?*"

"Yes ma'am. Not a thing I'm proud of. I guess, Civil War time and all, and Gettysburg not too far off, there was more than a fair share of soldiers through here, and, times being what they were," he said, trailing off, looking over his shoulder and waving his hands.

She laughed and patted him on the forearm.

"Place looks great, Layton. You hire a landscaper?"

"No, one of my new tenants. And let me tell you, I was madder than a wet hen to have to rent to her. That damn Ellie set me up. But the woman has done some little bit of good here, I have to say that."

"Mad?" Sarah said.

"Well, oh, hell. You ask Ellie about it when you see her. She's probably still laughing at getting one over on me."

"Layton. You're blushing. You're sweet on this woman, aren't you?"

"Sweet on a, um, on her? That would be the day. Well. Pretty soon you can be ready for me to start speaking French, then. Humph." Layton stopped speaking, walked a little towards the small gravestone on the hilly side of the road, and stopped, stock still for a moment, then walked back to Sarah.

"Sorry, Miss Sarah. Your room is ready and open—help yourself—make yourself comfortable. I'm glad you came back. Pretty girls are good for business, I say. Then come on downstairs, and I'll fix you a nice burger."

"Nothing low fat?"

"Next you'll be after sushi or some stuff like that."

"I'm joking, Layton. Remember? My little joke on thee?" she said, smiling. "Oh, that band going to be here again tonight? 'Cold...cold' something?"

"Spring. Cold Spring. Well, maybe. You know the guitar player, Chat? He had a run of bad luck a day or two ago. So we'll see."

"Bad luck? Hope it works out okay for him and his family. They seem really nice. So. I'm going to get my stuff unpacked, Layton. I'll be down in a few minutes."

"I'll start the burger, then. Beat the regular lunch crowd that way."

Sarah popped the trunk, smiled to herself at the prospect of love, and took out her overnight bag. She walked back up the familiar harlequin stairs to her room, all the same except for a new picture hung on one wall and the faint odor of flowers. Roses? Lilac? She couldn't decide for a moment, then remembered as a girl the scent of wild roses in an abandoned lot next door to her's.

She softly closed the door and stood in the dappled shade of the balcony overlooking the stream, imagining a torrent of brown and angry water washing at her feet instead of "this clear, this limpid stream/ In deft small voices greeting/ Or murmuring/ Farewell/ Farewell." Tennyson? Wordsworth?

Her grumbling stomach interrupted, compelling her downstairs, and it took a moment for her eyes to adjust from the bright sun to the cool darkness of the inn. Layton was alone, and he straightened from the paper he was reading, held his finger up—just a minute!—scurried back into the kitchen, emerging with a steaming platter of hamburger and fries.

She sat down at the bar, relishing the savor of the smells, asked for a beer. *What, a Yuengling? Sure thing!* How decadent at 11:30 in the morning, but she supposed the fresh air and the travel had given her a huge hunger. She happily ate and chatted with Layton, who seemed to be content to sit and talk instead of pretending to be working at something.

"I see your new help hasn't gotten down here," Sarah said, waving her free arm to indicate the head rails and shelves above, full of Layton's collection.

"Odd thing. She never comes in here. She'll wait at the door for an hour before she'll come in. Odd, her kind."

"Her kind?"

"Never mind. Sometimes I say too much."

"Those ice tongs? I saw a pair of them go for a couple hundred bucks last week at an auction upstate," she said, eager to change the subject. She took a large bite of the hamburger, which was juicy and delicious.

"Two hundred bucks? Man. What? Were the people on drugs or something? For a pair of ice tongs?"

Layton shook his head: flatlanders. No figuring them. Both of them turned when the door opened, and Sarah immediately recognized Chat and Sue, standing and blinking just inside the door.

"Chat! Susie! Come on in, now! Take a load off! How about a little something?" Layton shouted out to them.

They came in and sat, or rather sagged, Sarah thought, into two seats, murmuring "Hello" to Sarah, who nodded back and smiled, lips closed, mouth still full.

"How are you doing, Chat?" Layton asked. His voice turned serious.

"I don't want to burden our new friend here with sad stories," Chat sighed. "But things don't look good at all."

"Sorry, I'll take my food over there by the window?" Sarah said swallowing, and then getting up to leave.

"You just sit tight," Sue said, putting her hand over Sarah's arm. "We've met, right? Down on the road by the church that Sunday?"

"Yes. With your kids, the very nice-looking pair," Sarah said.

Sarah stifled the urge to ask how they were. Perhaps that was the problem. She thought of Josh and hoped not.

"Thank you. Chat and I have had a spot of trouble lately," Sue said, irony in her voice.

"I'm sorry to hear that. Seems like a good place to have a problem, though, with friends like Layton here," she said, patting his hand, raising a blush beneath Layton's thinning white hair.

"You're a smooth talker, aren't you now?" he said and chuckled. Then to Chat he said, "So, no help down at the bank, then?"

"They only loan if you don't need it. And we sure as *hell* need it," Chat said.

Sue said, "Chat!" and slapped him on the hand for swearing.

"Sorry, pumpkin, but I don't know, I don't know. Layton, give me a beer."

"One for me, too," Sue said.

"My treat," Sarah said, draining the last of hers and putting the bottle near the far edge of the bar.

"We couldn't," Chat muttered, draining his glass in one swallow.

"You must!" Sarah said.

And before she knew it, as the regulars shuffled in for lunch, Sarah Percelli became a confidant to the world of trouble that had come down on Chat and Sue in the form of the *law*, of all things, when she could tell that this pair was honest to a fault. Chat was locked out of his garage with no way to make a living as the *feds*, for crying out loud, attended a round-the-clock watch on his house. Lucky for them all that Homer hadn't sworn over the deed to his piece a year or two prior like he had thought to do in order to save the estate taxes. All because of the way things were going with the law. Ha! There was a laugh. How the government could just waltz right in like that and take someone's place, made him feel a little something for those Indians after all. And there was no prospect of things getting better, either, because he had no cash for a crack attorney, not that Chooney wasn't doing all he could.

Chooney had the same 168 hours a week as everybody else, and then suddenly the DA wanted him to review the law in all the past cases involving third-degree felonies—that was like *all* of them, something like 200 cases. Chat had even talked to his Aunt Jenna, hoping she could finagle some change and get him some real help, but she had called back to say that somehow or another the DA just wasn't cooperating in the least.

"Almost like they have it in for you, I'd say, if it made any sense to say that," she had said.

"Oh, that doesn't seem fair at all," Sarah said.

"Fair's a place you take your cows. This here is life," Chat said.

"So you need money for a lawyer, and you say your uncle hasn't any more?" Sarah asked, taking another small bite out of the burger.

"So he claims," Sue said and sipped her beer.

"Sue."

"I'm sorry, Chat. You have to wonder. Or at least, I do. He's kin to you, so maybe you don't ever wonder. But he's my kin, too, and I *do* wonder."

She looked frankly at Chat, Sarah, and Layton.

"Well, I'm awfully sorry to hear about all this. It sounds complicated," Sarah said. She was beginning to feel the beers now, or she would never have said, "Maybe you could have a fund-raiser?"

All three stopped at that one for a minute. The idea was so ludicrous that Chat laughed, and soon they were *all* sharing a good laugh.

"A fund-raiser! What? Sell baked goods or something?" Sue said, wiping her eyes.

"Yeah. How many brownies do you have to sell to hire out a law dog?" Chat snorted to Layton. But Layton had stopped laughing and was gazing at an old deer head with a Santa hat and sunglasses.

"Hey? Say! Layton!" Chat said.

"Oh, sorry," he said, coming too. "But I was thinking about something Miss Sarah said. Didn't you say that them ice tongs sold for a big bunch of money?"

"Two hundred bucks. Right. "

"So then all this clutter might be worth something?" Layton asked, pointing to a stuffed beaver.

"Well, maybe not all. But I bet you'd be surprised at what this stuff brings. City folks love to play country with the plows and the milk cans."

"Milk cans! Hell, I have a couple dozen of them out in one of the sheds," Layton said, getting excited.

"You think this would work?" Chat asked, trying not to get his hopes up too far.

"Leastways, I could get a clean couple sheds. Maybe even a place to park my car."

"Layton. You don't *have* a car," Sue said.

"Maybe there's one buried out there under all that trash—or rather—them valuable antiques here. Lemme call old man Coulter to see if he'd be interested in running an auction."

"They take time to set up, auctions," Sue said. She'd seen them auction off her old man's stuff. That hadn't been a good day for her.

Chat said, "Well, that's one thing I have, time. Maybe working on something with Johnny's buddy to use one of his bays a couple days a week. At least they let me take most of my tools out of my place."

"Here's to that!" Sarah said, and they all hoisted their glasses.

Turns out that Chat was not the only one with time on his hands. The next pair to be disgorged by the swinging door was a couple of stiffs with bad suits and blood in their eye, a tall fat one and a smaller one. Sarah watched as they both rushed the bar with their badges out. *Good thing they don't give these bastards guns*, Sarah thought. And then came a tentative barking of orders, not the serious kind with violence behind it that Chat had already known. As if orchestrated, they all suddenly saw the blue strobe lights of a cruiser outside, and Laurel and Hardy redux simply walked behind the bar. Behind the bar, Layton backed up in astonishment. *No man* walked behind another man's bar! Not in *this* state! They all listened as the fat one ordered— ordered!—Layton from behind the bar, saying that this establishment was closed until further notice by order of the Liquor Control Board, and all the occupants of the building must vacate the property immediately and forthwith, upon penalty of law.

"What the Sam hill you talking about? Where's the charges? Or the warrant? Or even the due process?"

Chat could tell Layton was scared for real this time as he backed up against the Bud cooler, leaning against the sloping shiny stainless steel door. His face was like it must have been when he was five, and he realized that people don't live forever.

"Hey. Why don't you just take it easy? Layton hasn't done a wrong thing in his life," Chat said.

"You shut up, mister. This is none of your business," the almost-thin bastard snarled to Chat. "I don't even have to tell you why we're closing you down. That'll come at the hearing, up at Scranton. All occupants of this building must immediately vacate the premises until *we* direct otherwise. Understood?"

Layton stood, or rather leaned against the cooler, irresolute, confused, scared witless.

"Understood?" the fat one asked.

They all waited for Layton to just slump into nothing. Layton whispered, "No, I don't understand. We done nothing wrong, never started no problems. We sponsor the *Little Leaguers*, for gosh sakes! Nobody ever gets hurt here, no wrecks on the highway from *us*. Look it up! And you know how much money we donate every year to the homeless and the people who need it when the rich churches around here won't even pick their heads up from their prayers? Do you? *Do you?*"

Layton was breathing hard, but he was really standing now. *If he had his Louisville in his hand, those two would get their ass kicked*, Chat thought, but then he began to catch the same tightness in his chest, the same woozy feeling he had had the one year he had gone out for football and had been beaned by a helmet on the square part of his head.

"The staties call you sir, buddy," the fat one snarled. "They're out there waiting. I'm just going to say it one more time. All the occupants of this building must immediately vacate the premises, or you will all be arrested."

Chat tried to say something more and failed. The plumbers, framers and bikers, the two college kids there in the corner, just getting into some meaningful talk about Kant or Kafka, the bleached blond at the end of the bar, nursing her vodka and coke, even the old fuddy-duddy perfessor at the last stool, who sat and smoked his pipe and sometimes settled everybody's hash, he knew so much—they all sat there dumbfounded and silent, and watched as Layton, clad in his gray farmer's work pants and gnarled fingers, his old slouch flannel shirt showing a thin crescent moon of his red neck, pushed himself off the stainless steel of the cooler and tottered towards the end of the bar.

Sarah, Chat and Sue sat as still as stone, their eyes darting first to each other, then to the putrid pair at the bar, then finally at Layton, who looked, Sarah thought, as if he was one foot out of the grave. Then suddenly remembering her manners, she stood and began to leave; it would not be seemly to let him walk out in front of them.

"You just wait one minute, there, Mr. Big-shot state man. We have a right to finish our drinks, and he has a right to rest for a minute before you toss him out of this place like he *has* no place," she said, her cheeks flaming.

"And who the hell are you?" the almost-thin one smirked at her.

"I'm a human being. And so is this man. Least you can do is act as if you are, too, don't you think? Oh, and if that isn't enough incentive—can you understand that word, little man?— how about we tack on theft of services and infringement of constitutional rights?"

"What the hell are you talking about? This place is shut, and you have to go. And that's the long and short of it," the fat man said, his voice rising, a fleck of foam at the corner of his mouth. Outside they could all hear the crackle and squawk of the police radio, and the sound of doors being slammed.

"And I bought this burger and this beer with cash money in a legal establishment, you gave no probable cause and showed no writ of any kind, you hit this man without provocation, and," Sarah was shouting now.

"*Hit* this man? What the *hell* are you talking about?" the fat one said.

Sarah stood and shouted, "You saw them hit Layton, didn't you? First the fat one and then the thin one?"

The cops burst in the door to hear choruses of, "yeah, we did!" and "I thought it was the *thin* one first and then the *fat* one!" Layton was leaning against the bar again, still leaning instead of standing, like the poem Sarah had once read about "Not Waving but Drowning."

"Let's go, folks. Show's over," was what the cop said, and it was only then that Chat realized that it was the same one who had cuffed him and smirked the whole time. Both he and Sarah were standing and ready to fight. While Sue and Layton watched in shock, Chat realized something, maybe like his daddy Dutch had realized those many years ago, and he could see Sarah knew it, too. The best thing to do was to get the loved ones who couldn't do for themselves out of danger first, and to think about the rest later.

Silently, Chat took Sue by the elbow and helped her up, while Sarah took hold of Layton and stood there by the corner of the bar. Both of them motioned for the rest to leave. They motioned by way of holding up the still-juicy burger and still-cold beer—this was Sarah—to take what they had bought with them as they left, and if motions were not enough, then Sarah's strident call:

"Take your food and drink! There's way more of us then there are of them!"

It was relief the fat man and the thin one and the cop felt as they all filed out, leaving Chat, Sue, Sarah, and Layton, like a wedding party, to walk out last, while the LCB men locked the liquor cabinets—Layton followed the LCB rules and had a cabinet with locks on it for his booze!—with their own locks, and the cop poked here and there, just in case, then all three paused a moment to gloat. *These punks are the same all over, all blow and no go.* Told a few jokes, checked the till. *What kind of guy leaves the money when he walks out? He isn't seeing this for a while!* Then they strolled out into the bright sunlight, more big padlocks in their hands and ready to shut this place down.

It was then that the smug officers were treated to a shower of beer, burgers and fries, just exactly like a wedding party, except the only ones running to the cars were the two-dozen barflies, laughing and hooting. The cop and his LCB buddies stood there, drenched and bespattered with beer, mustard, ketchup, and burger juice, while Chat, Sue, Sarah and Layton watched, their faces four dour masks.

"Let the record reflect, your honors, there are two dozen witnesses that will swear that none of us four had anything to do with your wardrobe malfunction," Sarah said, fighting laughter.

27

≈ CHAPTER TWENTY-SEVEN ≈

When the dust had settled, Sarah was out a place to stay.

"What the hell do you mean, nobody can stay upstairs? You guys are the bar guys!" Layton had screamed, but it turned out the place had a hotel license and shut down meant the whole thing.

Sarah spent the night with Chat and Sue—at Sue's insistence!—and a trip up to Scranton the next day turned up the following facts: the Chester boys had been carded leaving the place the night prior, and of course, Layton knew that they weren't but eighteen and twenty. In exchange for not being charged, they dimed Layton out in a heartbeat, telling the LCB how they had been drinking every day for lunch and again after work for a few years maybe, and recounting all the times the boys had used the grinder or the slicer for a nice haunch of venison, which, strictly speaking, wasn't legal either.

The total damage? Two weeks closure and a ten grand fine. Layton couldn't open until he paid the fine, which was money he didn't have. As Chat drove back, all Layton did was just sit there and sigh every three minutes, until Chat couldn't stand it anymore and began to talk, quietly and with conviction, about how they would get through this all. Maybe they might even laugh about it in a year or two.

"I'll bust the mouth of the man that I hear laughing about this, by Jesus I will!" Layton shouted, and Chat smiled.

"That's more like it, ole bean! Stand up for your rights, by gum, and give 'em hell!"

"Hmph. You sounded like Homer there for a second. Anyhow, that's easy for you to say. Ten grand! Where am I gonna get that kind of money? I'd almost have to sell the place to do that."

"You talked to the guy about the auction, right? Well, use some of the money for all this screw-up, why don't ya?"

"That money is for you and Sue, Chat."

"Let's just see what's what with *that*, then. But I say we split it. Heck, the stuff is all *yours*, after all."

"I suppose. This whole thing has got me jumping mad, though. And the, the *maid* went and moved out when this trouble started, rented a place down from you, so I guess I'm out a, a *housekeeper*, too."

"She had to go someplace. Besides, you never had one before," Chat shrugged.

"I got spoiled. Now she's up and gone, got her name on the list for those low-income houses Malchio's putting up over near your place. Sorry to bring it up. You been over there?"

"I have not."

"They tell me they're going right along with it. Maybe my piece here is next, huh? Sold for taxes, so they build more houses for more kids so they need more schools so more houses get built so taxes go up and every last farm here in the county is all a dream."

Chat held the image of his home in his mind for a long moment before he said, "Come on, Layton. It's not all that bad. We'll be fine. We always have been before. Why expect that to change now?"

"Just feels like the end of something, all this bad luck. We'll see. We'll see," Layton said, and wearily got out of Chat's truck.

Chat watched Layton's stooped figure walk up the long drive that led to his house, another one that had been in the family for a few hundred years. *Maybe he was right*, Chat thought. Maybe this wasn't a new beginning as much as it was the end of an era. All good things must come to an end, he guessed. But knowing it was so didn't mean believing it was so. And if Layton was right, now was the time: they could both use all the company they could get. Chat rolled down his window and shouted to Layton just before he disappeared behind the row of cedars that lined the outside of the drive.

"Hey, Layton! Whyn't you come over to my place and let me buy *you* a beer for a change, ay?"

Layton stopped where he was, stock still for a long moment.

Then he turned and gave a wan little smile.

"Sure I will. 'Bout time someone else bought, huh?"

They rode back towards Chat's place, sunk in their own thoughts.

We could at least try and get some money together, so Layton wouldn't have to lose anything more than the two weeks worth of sales and some rents, Chat thought.

"What in the world did I do to deserve *this*?" Layton asked himself out loud.

And when he and Chat had gotten home to Chat's, and Sue had called Homer and Thelma up and they had all sat down to the dinner, fried chicken and fluffy mashed potatoes, green beans from the garden and a nice bottle of Dago red Chat had gotten from a music buddy up in Ransom, and Sarah had asked about the whys and wherefores, Chat had to say that it was just the dangest run of bad luck he had ever seen for a couple country boys. He added in his mind a little list: the raid on Layton, Jimmy, the DEA thing, the projects by his house, the screw-up with that helicopter guy.

"Hugh McAdam Enterprises," Sarah said.

Chat jumped up, a shiver running down his spine.

"You read minds?" Chat yelped.

"What?" Sarah said, laughing. But she could tell by the look on Chat's face that he was spooked badly.

"Are you okay?"

"I was trying to remember the name of that helicopter guy that set down in my lot a couple months back. Then you said his name."

"Oh my God. Oh my *God*! You're Chat *Dalton*. How on earth could I have been so dense? Oh, you poor, poor man."

Chat looked at her dumbfounded.

"I know I don't have lots of money, but we're not that bad off. What *are* you talking about, anyhow?"

"McAdam has been working his butt off, calling senators and everybody you can name and think of, Prescott at DEA, hell, I think he was even talking to the governor the other day, not sure, but, anyhow, all that was about *you*."

"Wait. Wait. Are you saying that this whole pot thing and the bust at Layton's was all a *setup*? You've got to be *kidding* me."

Sue stared with her mouth open for a moment.

"Why would he even bother? Because of that whole helicopter thing? Nobody is that bored or vindictive," Sue said.

"That was the same guy said he'd buy my place and burn it down," Layton interrupted. "And there's been three offers in the last week and half alone. One was for a quarter million."

"A quarter million? Layton, you could live real nicely on that," Sarah said.

"Well, and do what with the rest of my life? Sit on the porch in a rocking chair and die? Not for me, thanks. I'll work until I keel over, and while I'm down there on the floor, maybe I'll do some of that yoga stuff—the barking dog or something," he said, squatting to grab the back of his ankle with his hand and arching his back comically.

"Wow, Layton. Aren't you the picture of Hindu health," Chat said, shaking his head. "Sarah. This whole thing is to achieve—what?"

"McAdam is talking about putting in cluster housing and a huge mall with some guy from around here, Ted Malchio? 'Just a matter of squashing that bug Dalton' is what he said, pardon my French there."

Chat sat there, stymied and stumped. To think that anyone could be that low-down. "How does a man come to this?" Chat asked Sarah.

"Thing with him is," Sarah said, "from what Ty tells me, his family was from Lexington, dirt poor, and McAdam got some kind of patent from one of his childhood buddies. Something about blood plasma, stole it from that guy like it was a purse and made about a zillion bucks. He bought a bunch of thoroughbreds and a big-ass ranch—excuse me—but then couldn't get into the Breeders Club. Too common, they told him. So from what Ty said, he's been like this ever since. He can't be controlled when he feels snubbed, and he's always out to prove how much a big shot he is."

"That's those Lexington bastards all over," Homer muttered.

"Umm. Should you be telling me all this? Isn't this, umm, confidential and all that?" Chat asked, still puzzling.

"I'm not a priest or a doctor, ya know. I'm just 'the girl' from what he says. I bet he can't even remember my last name most days. And, guess what? I've been saving, and, well. Maybe yesterday was my last day at work. The bastard."

"Nice of you to say, or, well, not nice, really, but I appreciate that," Sue said, confused.

"Oh, hey. It's not just this thing. He's so rude and pushy, thinks he owns the world. I could get a job around here, maybe, just hang out with my man Layton."

She patted him on the hand and smiled, and he began blushing again, a deep, deep red.

"You're a hussy, young lady. And where would you work? The McDonalds out to Fiesterville? Why do you think half the world is moving here and then leaving their kids to be drug addicts and thieves while they make the big bucks in the city?"

"Layton," Chat said, dragging his finger across his throat.

"Well, what would I say if she wasn't here, huh? So that's what I think and you're welcome to it," Layton said, nodding, still red behind the ears.

"Don't hold back, now, Layton. Let 'er rip!" Homer said, giving a dry laugh.

"Yeah, like you have room to talk, Homer, sending letters to the president complaining about taxes and wiretaps," Layton drawled.

"My phone *was* tapped, dammit!" Homer sat down by the fireplace, arms crossed and glaring at Layton, while Thelma clucked over him.

"Don't mind him, folks. The bail money has got him all steamed up," Thelma said, only loud enough for Chat to hear.

"We'll talk about that later, then, Thel," Chat whispered to her. He had an idea about that.

"We're all a little cranky, I guess," Layton offered. "Up early, and all this, this *excitement*."

"But how is he doing all this? The bail, Jimmy's pot. He must have a way of finding out what's going on around here," Sue asked Sarah.

"He has somebody's been sending him faxes, no signature or anything. Just signs the papers 'T'…for what that's worth."

They all looked at each other for a beat.

"Could be anybody," Chat and Sue both said in unison.

"That would explain the pot thing, the high bail…even Hildebrandt being shuffled off so we can't figure what's going on at the barracks," Chat said. "Seems like a powerful lot of trouble to go through just to get even with some poor cracker like me."

"Well, you've got to think like him, though," Sarah said. "Nothing he loves better than winning, except making a ton of money. And from what

I've heard about his plans, tons is about going to be the size of it. He has twenty-three retailers foaming at the mouth to get into this complex Malchio is building."

"The little shit. He still owes me a thousand for that 'vette."

"Well, he's going to have a surprise coming to him, too, Malchio. McAdam was gloating to his lawyer yesterday about some papers Malchio signed the day they cobbled this all together. He's going to be out of business before the first dollar hits the till, somehow, according to McAdam. Something about sticking him with the construction and having all the rents go to 'costs' the first year. I don't know."

"Brr. This guy is reptilian," Sue said, shivering.

"I hear they taste like chicken," Layton said. "Makes me wonder, though."

"Oh?" Sarah asked.

"Everything tastes like chicken, they say. So how come eggs don't?"

Chat almost spewed his mouthful, and began choking, coughing and laughing simultaneously.

"Goofball!" he finally said.

"Takes one to know one. So, what do we do next?" Chat asked Layton, who didn't hear him. Layton, having seldom drank wine, was staring at Sarah's strong chin and her direct eyes, except he had to squint into the sunlight that was blasting through the kitchen window. That finally made him sneeze.

"God bless you," Sarah said, finishing her glass and smiling, affirmed.

"God bless us all," Chat said, then muttered the puzzle to himself again: "A false witness that pours out lies and a man that stirs up dissention among his neighbors."

The auction was scheduled quickly, and not a moment too soon. Chat met Chooney up at Ellie's, and she busted on Chat as soon as she saw him.

"That any way to treat the woman who loves you best?" she needled. "Don't come in for a couple years at a clip and then just *waltz* in here like you were some kinda swell?"

"We're glad to see you, too," Chooney said to Ellie, laughing. She slapped him on the arm hard, and he winced.

"How about the best seats in the house, then, boys? Sorry, Chooney, dint mean to hurt ya!"

"Like hell. That's one mean punch you got there, sister."

"I didn't even give you my roundhouse. Here, sit and relax. I'll get you some coffee."

And she led them over to the corner booth, where she knew they would be talking serious business, a business she heartily wished was over and done with.

Chooney began to bring Chat up to speed. What he had to say didn't make Chat feel much like eating. The Public Defender's office had given Chooney's secretary a bunch of extra work from some other cases, "just as a temporary thing—we have all these new cases from the move-ins down at the projects in Fiesterville." After talking with some folks, Chooney pretty much chalked it up to somebody that had it in for Chat.

"Oh, you don't know how right you are," Chat said, then filled him in on what Sarah had told them. Chooney sat, eyes wide and nodding. It was all beginning to make sense. Telling the story got Chat in a bit of a lather. Chooney could tell: that little muscle near the corner of Chat's jaw started jumping around. Back in grade school that meant somebody was going to get a licking.

"Try to not take it so personal, Chat. He'd have screwed anybody if it got him something. Just some guy out there that makes big bucks being a bastard."

"That would be a good name for a bluegrass band, bub."

"What?"

"The Big Bucks Being Bastards Bluegrass Band. Five B fever. I can see it now," Chat said, trying to laugh.

"But, listen, seriously, the paperwork isn't what I came over here to talk to you about. At discovery, I found out that you knew about that patch in there this *whole time*. That's not too good," he said. He was trying hard, Chat could tell, to be non-judgmental about it all.

"What do you mean? How could they know I knew about it?"

"So you *did* know about it!"

"Dammit, Chooney, stop trying to foul me up here."

"Better hope they never get you in front of a jury, Chat," Chooney shook his head. "Motion-activated cameras. Those ones you can use for whitetails, to scout? Cops love them things now. Seems they've been watching our little buddy Jimmy for some time now. Kid's got a big mouth, and they were laying for him the whole time. You just walked right into this one, buddy. One of the shots I saw this morning shows you in there, doing some little thing—kinda bending over, pulling a weed or something, you pick something up, kinda look at it, like maybe a seed? Then you smoothing out the place, putting it back to the way it was."

"Oh, crap. Crap. I'm gonna kill that little shit. I should have when I had the chance. Bastard didn't listen to me when I told him to take that shit off my land, pardon my vulgarity."

"Well, maybe you should have killed him, then. Because he's swearing up and down you not only knew about it, you were in on the action."

Chat almost sprang up, wanted to pitch his cup against the wall, imagined the splinters of porcelain flying all over, and the foamy stain of his coffee running in streams to the floor. He heard Chooney from far away, calling to him.

"Chat. Chat! Helloooooooo! This will go up for preliminary hearing in about two weeks, unless you want a continuance on it, a delay to get ready," Chooney said.

"Homer is already mighty unhappy about the mortgage—first payment is due in a few days, and it's a doozy. Something like 2,500 bucks," Chat said, trying to stay focused.

It was hard when you were mad, harder when you were tired. When you were tired and mad? It was like a test from God.

"Chat, all I can tell you is that we're not going to be ready to do much at the prelim, even with the extra help I wanted to get. What they have is enough to bind this over for trial, and I suggest you concentrate on that aspect of it all. What I think we need to do, though, is try and get that bail reduced, so Homer doesn't have to foot such a big bill. Where's he getting the money to pay this off, anyhow?"

"I know he's got some put by. But hell, his piece doesn't make *that* much, few thousand from cattle, some from the corn and soy. I don't know."

"Well, least ways you have friends, and Jimmy or not, you tell the whole story at the trial and you've got a damned good shot at getting off on all but the assault charges. Not much we can do about that, I think. But Jimmy has no credibility that I can see, and doesn't matter how stupid the jury is. They'll see that, too."

"Like all those famous trials? Like Michael Jackson or OJ?" Chat said.

"This is different. Nobody likes Jimmy," Chooney said.

"Same as saying they have a chance to make it stick. No offense, but who can you find to help on this?" Chat answered.

"None taken, Chat. They're just not going to let me work on this case the way I need to and I'd be doing you a disservice to pretend that just me working with a half a secretary is going to get you the traction you need. Soon as you hire somebody else officially, I'm done. That's not me talking, Chat. You know that. There is a hotshot from Fiesterville—Younts? Makes his living defending crackheads with lots of money, and he's deadly good. And really, you're better off with a guy like that, Chat. You know I'll give you as much time as I can afford, so the office doesn't know about it."

"So they cut back your hours, and then if I try to take up the slack, they pull you altogether. Some system. Don't mind me, Chooney. I'm not a bitter man, but this has really got me down," Chat said, eyeing the spot on the wall where he had not thrown his cup.

"Hey. I understand. You'll call if you need any help from the inside, huh? I'll get us through the prelim, talk with Younts to make the transition easier, fill him in on what's what. That's what I would do if I were you."

"Well, thanks, Chooney. That's very much appreciated. Another cup of coffee?"

"Naw. Makes me piss too much. Bad for my prostate, the doc says. I better get to work on the bail thing for you, though. See what I can do there, maybe get Homer's payment down a little."

"Any chance I can get a mortgage out on the Meadows, take the heat off Homer a little? Oh, and Layton, too, 'til the auction is over?"

"Isn't that all on the same piece your house is on, too?"

"Naw. The Meadows was part of Homer's great uncle Birch's piece, gave it to my Dad's dad to spite Homer's pop, Emil."

"Why on earth for?"

"Seems they made a bet on something. I don't even know what it was, the World Series or something. Birch told Emil he'd bet him a hundred potatoes. That was slang for dollars back then. Then Birch won, and didn't Emil show up the next day with a peck of seed potatoes, laughing his ass off, and Birch told him he'd have the last laugh, and so he did."

"I'm sure you could get a bank to give you paper on that. That's a nice flat piece, too. Anyhow, you take care of yourself. Guess you'll have some time on your hands now 'til this is all finished, huh?"

"Well, there are a couple tunes I've been meaning to work out, and there's some housework I could always do. Maybe I could take up knitting. Knife throwing. Umm, bocce. Anyhow, I'll see you around. Anything I need to do in the meantime?"

"I'll set up a meeting with you and Younts for next week. Other than that, try to stay calm. Things will work out."

"Thanks. They always do," Chat agreed somberly, and thought, *just not always the way we like 'em.* He shook Chooney's hand again and walked back outside. Time. Wasn't that the most important thing? The only thing you could not make more of? Time to enjoy a day like today, the sun up, birds singing in the trees, his wife and kids happy and healthy. The rest of it was merely detail.

He got in his truck and drove slowly and thoughtfully towards town, parked and went into bank, the one that used to be First Commonwealth but was now owned by some outfit in Boston or someplace. Liberty First, it was now, and the officers who he had grown up with were switched to new banks or transferred out of state. He signed the card to get into his safety deposit box. He noted his signature, over and over again, and the dates that stretched back to the '80s. The first ones were neat, childish, somehow, perhaps from lack of practice. *Living will whittle away all the curlicues,* Chat thought. His signature now had the hard and angular look of maturity, of facing life, which is often crueler than it needs to be.

Chat idly looked through the Indian Head cent collection that he supposed was worth something, and the three gold pieces left from the five he had been given by his Grandpa back when he was a little shaver. He paged through the various deeds and papers until he found the one for the Meadows, tidied up the box, called the girl to lock it back up, and walked over to the customer service desk. He exchanged pleasantries with the girl, asked for a loan officer and was unaccountably annoyed when a fat Hispanic woman called him into her office.

It was business, after all.

"There is loan origination fee of one hundred dollars, and then we appraise the land. This will take several weeks."

"*Weeks?* I really need this sooner than that. There was a guy that worked here—Sam? You know him? Anyhow, can I take out a loan, a personal loan, with this as collateral?"

"One hundred seventy acres. How much a loan?" she said.

He had thought that through, at least. *Figure ten or fifteen hours for Younts, Layton's ten grand, and living expenses.* "Fifteen thousand dollars," he said, confidently.

"You can wait here, please? I have to ask about this all," she said, and then left Chat for a good twenty minutes. He idly read all the plaques and signs hanging on the walls: "Get a great rate at Freedom First!" "Freedom First—for all the things you want!"

Then he tried to read the papers on her desk, upside down, and the inexplicably neat hand-written notes in the margin of some applications. Hey! Old man Foster was applying for a mortgage on the Outhouse Steak House, and this woman had inked in, next to income, "Denied!" As if Foster wasn't to be trusted! Chat began to fume. True, he had nothing pressing to do, but he *might* have been busy. They didn't even ask him.

So he was surprised to learn that the only emotion he could recognize when the woman came back in and smiled at him was one of relief. He wouldn't have to deal with the humiliation of being denied by her. And, rather than feeling burdened by debt as he walked out into the sunshine, which he now was—first time for everything, ole son!—he felt instead a kind of giddy hope that any action was better than inaction, that boldness would somehow lead to resolution.

Leastways it would pay the bills for the next few weeks and get Layton back in business—Maybe they could hold a benefit, too, help raise some cash that way. And of course he didn't approve, but he had heard though the grapevine that the Chester boys couldn't get any work all of a sudden, and no place to have a beer if they did find it.

Served them right for acting like that.

28

⇒ Chapter Twenty-Eight ⇐

Two weeks passed like a dream for Layton, who spent every morning going through old papers at his place instead of cleaning the bar. He went down there a few times a week over that long fortnight, just to dust and clean. They let him do that much, at least, and to make sure the place was still in one piece. One morning, he found scratches around the big dead bolt near the back door. Somebody had been trying to bust in, and it was only two-inch oak doors and the massive homemade cast-iron lock that had kept them out, much like it had kept out the marauding Indians back in '57 when the damn French had gotten them all stirred up.

Up in Milford, Layton had heard, the Lenape were all up in arms now about the Tom Quick memorial. Tom Quick, the famous—or infamous—Indian Slayer, who had watched his dad murdered in his bed and went on to kill either one or 99 Lenape, depending on the legend, was a kind of cult hero up around there, back in 1889. The people of Milford, good xenophobes all, had then erected an obelisk in the towns square with some memorabilia from the time and some of Tom's remains: the odd phalanges and so forth. The Lenape—who Layton had always found reasonable—cried foul.

After that it got complicated. Layton thought he remembered that the Cree Indians were called in to broker a deal, and that they told the Lenape that the memorial was a grave that should be revered, not reviled. Then somebody took a sledge hammer and busted the hell out of the monument, and now the town fathers were trying to appease the history nuts *and* the Indians—the white bigots and the red ones—and it was dead draw which bunch was more clueless.

But of course Layton didn't expect that he had gotten any of that correct, so he allowed himself to forget and went back to dusting and tidying.

The Saturday of the auction dawned fair and clear. Birds sang in the trees, the stream by the Bennykill purled over rocks that had been underwater just a month before, and already the parking lot was full of cars. The road that led to the abandoned post office and the dead end that used to be the bridge over the Wyansock Creek was lined with vans, pick-up trucks, trailers, BMWs and Mercedes. Some serious money was walking around, and the auctioneer was taking care of last-minute items that had been unearthed in the crawl space under the kitchen or in the attic above the rooms upstairs.

Chat and Sterling were there, directing traffic so the road stayed open, and to act as runners as the auction began, which it did at the crack of nine. Old boxes with *FLIT* and *QUAKERSTATE* and *GOLD MEDAL FLOUR* were snapped up at *ten do I hear twelve, let's go here folks, you'll need a good stout box for the all them treasures, 15 and 20, 25, 30*, or *fifty bucks the beginning bid for the milk cans*, or *three hundred for the old plow*—somebody's new mailbox post.

The ice tongs went for two and a quarter, the feed sacks for five bucks apiece. The auctioneer would joust with the crowd, "Come on, come *on*, let those moths outta your *wallet*, folks! You know these items are only going up in price. Best investment you'll make today, I betcha. Seventy-five bucks to number 347 for the old Coke sign, a hundred and a half to the lady over there in the bee-you-tee-ful hat for this hex sign. Keep them devils away from your door, you betcha!"

By lunch they had moved all the items from the bar, and Chat was beginning to get wheezy from running the items to the folks that bought them, or taking it out to their cars—getting tips!—until by five p.m. he and Sterling were bone-tired and hungry. Just before they broke, the LCB boys showed up to argue that they weren't allowed to sell *anything*, but they all just denied that anything had been sold.

"This here was a potlatch," Layton said, nodding sagely.

"A what?" the dumpy one asked.

"Forget it. You can go look it up. Now beat it before I call the cops on account of harassment."

Ragged as they were from running product all day, Chat, Sue, Sterling and Amy B., Johnny, Megan and all the kids burst into a nice round of applause on that note. After they watched the LCB guys out of the area, they all sat back at the bar, munching on bar snacks while Layton whipped up some burgers—"Seventy pounds of burger, I went through!" he crowed. They drank the icy beer with gusto.

Layton came out of the kitchen with the platter, cordless phone to his ear, saying, "Umm hmm. Yeah. Good!" then hanging up and giving Chat the thumbs up.

"That was Coulter. Not counting the bigger stuff they'll sell tomorrow, we made better than twenty grand. Imagine that. Twenty thousand bucks."

"Place looks great, too," Meg offered, waving her hands at the shelves and head rails.

"Kinda naked looking to me," Layton said, but then he shrugged. He'd have more stuff before anyone knew it. Old lady Turner was sick, and the Horsts were getting on. Layton knew what they had stuffed in their garages and cellars.

"Layton, I don't know how to thank you. I mean, really, it's a humbling thing to be helped like this, in this time of trouble," Chat said, suddenly close to tears.

"Hey, hey, hey. None of that stuff, now. You'd do the same for me. Have done things like this all your life. Can't go turning our back on you now, huh?" Layton said.

Chat gave a shuddery smile.

"Least I can pay that Younts. Man, he wants 200 bucks an *hour*. And the bank and all. It doesn't take long to add up that way, spending like I have been. But what I'd really like is to freakin' *kill* Jimmy, the little *shit*."

"You'd have to find him first. They took him off someplace. Witness protection, the bastards," Layton said.

"He'll come back sooner or later," Sterling said, wondering if he was up to that kind of job. He could leastways smack him around good and proper some night after Layton got him drunk. He smiled at that thought. He liked vengeance, Bible be damned.

"So, where are you guys next weekend, then?" Layton said.

"Down near Galax. Big concert down there, and we're opening for *Del*. I heard rumors Country Music Television is gonna be there, too."

"Wow. You guys are getting famous. I saw Johnny on the cover of Bluegrass Now last month!"

"Well, just the back of his head, really," Meg said, laughing, "So, you're driving down, then?"

"Yeah. Good thing we have a good mechanic, hehe," Sterling said.

"Surprised Jo-Jo wasn't here today," Layton said.

"Said he had some appointment up in Scranton."

"I don't know what's up with him lately. I mean, I know he's pissed about Kate and that new guy, but he seems to me like he's losing it. Doesn't hardly come around here anymores, and when he does, he doesn't say much. Why'd he go on up to Scranton, then?" Sterling said.

"Seeing about more building stuff, I bet. That's what we all need, huh? They got that low-income thing just about done, and that, um, woman who was living upstairs is gonna be one of the first in. How do you like them apples? She moves here from the city, gets all kind of help, and a few months later she's in a house my own money built," Layton said, bitterly.

"She's still working here and up at Ellie's?"

"Naw. Maybe why I'm so ticked off. Got a job as a cleaning woman in Fiesterville and plunks her two kids in school here. I was talking to one of the teachers out there at the grade school. They got seven new students last week alone. *Seven!* Classes of thirty kids? And that's just the one school. I got my tax bill last week, went up almost three hundred bucks. Teachers are what they need, they say. And where do they expect the old folks to come up with an extra three hundred a year, and with it going up all the time like that?"

Layton swiped at the already-clean bar with a towel, shaking his head.

"Place is going to the dogs. Maybe I'll move to Wyoming."

"You've been saying that for ten years, Layton. Guess we have to take the bitter with the batter."

"Batter? Reminds me of a joke," Sue said. "What do you do to an elephant with three balls?"

"What?" Sterling said, astounded.

"Walk him and pitch to the giraffe."

"Essh. That's bad," Chat said.

The group fell silent for a moment as the door opened and disgorged a knot of strangers with Yankee hats on backwards, pumping money in the jukebox, swearing, shouting over one another, until Layton had to walk over and point out the new sign he had put up recently: "No swearing or foul language permitted! Yes, I mean YOU!"

Chat, meanwhile, was getting on his own last nerve. It wasn't just him, and it wasn't just the whole DEA and lawyer LCB thing, either. Sue was cranky and tired, and the kids were all riled up. He would ride with the band, and he would suffer when somebody got a bug up their butt about something. Sterling would never let things rest where they were, always moving stuff around "on account of because." Finally Chat lost his patience for once with Sterling, blasting him for a good ten minutes while they rode down roads which would not see another human for perhaps days.

Sterling missed two beats and said, "So you don't ever get the feeling that there's an evil imp on your shoulder like when things get really bad?" Sterling said to Chat. They were on the way back from a pig roast up near Tafton, the real heart of the Poconos: all Pike County diamonds and scrub oaks.

In the rear seat, Jo-Jo and Johnny were both sleeping, so Chat responded quietly, "Oh, no doubt about that, my friend. That there is the devil. Then you got another lil' imp on your other shoulder, that's the angel. You know, like 'The Emperor's New Groove.'"

"Dammit, I'm serious. Wait. I never saw that movie. Don't tell me what happens. But—seriously—there really are times like that I swear I can *feel* it," Sterling said.

"You just don't have *faith*, that's all. 'Course death is all around us. Only the hand of the Lord is holding us *up*, you know."

"God helps those who help themselves, I say. Trust in Allah, but tie your camels, huh?"

"What's the word? Hubris? You got some of that going on, Sterling ole buddy," Chat spat out.

"I'm not all that proud. And P.S.—people in glass houses, my friend."

Sterling stopped speaking for a moment, and on the outside, they could hear the katydids and the swish of the tires on the road. Sterling remembered when he was little, and hot summer days would draw pools of tar from the roadway by his house in the sticks of the Eastern Shore.

He'd love to go down there, pop the little bubbles that would form on them in places, kind of goo around with a stick, drop some pebbles in. He'd pretend they were dinosaurs, being really really careful to keep the tar off his hands, and always failing, and having to ask his mom to get the rag, and then having to get all those things himself after awhile. It wasn't so easy to get clean without someone's help. Eventually, he stopped playing with the enchanting black goo at last.

Finally Sterling said, "You know, back when I was a little guy and they sent me off to Catholic school because my older brother was screwing up, the nuns used to yammer about that faith thing all the time. So I asked one, once. I think this was pretty brave, because you just didn't dare to talk to them. If they wanted your opinion, they'd give it to you. I asked what someone would do if they didn't have any faith. I mean, *I* wanted to get to heaven. The nun got mad as hell at me. One of the priests heard the commotion and came into the classroom, heard what the question was, and then he said that it was a *damn good question*. Well, not really those words or anything, but, you know. He said that little boy should go home and pray to God for faith. So like a dimwit I tried that, every night on my knees for what seemed like weeks. And one night it hit me."

"What, a brick?"

"Hehe, no. Here I was praying to an entity I didn't believe in so that I *could* believe in it. That was the end of the road right there, buddy. I never prayed a second after that, I can tell you."

Outside the window the telephone poles whizzed by, and once or twice they saw eyes of deer shining back from the fringes of the road. Chat sat silent so long that Sterling was beginning to think he hadn't really spoken.

Finally Chat said, "So, what, then? You saying faith is some kind of gift? I don't buy it, Sterling. The ones I see that don't have it, why, they're the ones have too big an opinion of themselves, you know? No offense meant."

Sterling wanted to be able to say, "None taken," but he couldn't.

"Preacher Dalton. Life sure has to be easy for you, huh? No questions, no doubts."

"Yeah, sure. Spent all my retirement money and then some on a freakin' lawyer, out of work, mostly, and traveling with a bunch of godless pagans. My wife is at the end of her rope for some danged reason or another, I see Jo-Jo coming unglued before my very eyes, and my best friend is a guy who would make Madeline Murray O'Hare look like Mother Teresa. But what the hell, I still love ya, man."

"Well. Small comfort in a cold world," Sterling huffed. "I mean, I really understand how nice it is to say you have all the answers."

"Just annoys somebody like you who knows everything, right?" Chat said.

"Now listen. This is what I was thinking the other day. You know they say the universe is infinite?"

"That's what they say. I don't understand that at all. Somebody once said that if one sparrow carried one grain of sand at a time across the ocean, and he managed to get all the sand on one side to the other, that would only be the *first second of eternity.* And I can't get my little mind around that one, so I guess I'm no expert," Chat said.

"Well, not about this. Suppose the universe really *is* infinite. If it were infinite, there should actually be separate parallel universes, all a little bit different."

"Like there's one where you make sense?"

"Yuk yuk. Lemme finish. So each universe would have to have a CEO, you could call 'em 'God.' So maybe all these 'Gods' have to get trained, have seminars, you know, learning about omniscience and predestination and all that."

"Sterling, that's blasphemous. It's funny, too! So, oh. Double blasphemy!" Chat said, more softly.

"No, here we have but one God. But, see, what *I* was thinking was that maybe these gods are kind of like us, some of them are really studious, and some are, well, maybe not so much so. Then I was thinking about how it would be if one of 'em had ADD or something, and couldn't even really pay attention, not that his intentions weren't good, necessarily, but he would miss stuff in class, and then later, like at a convention or something, one of the other gods would walk up to ours and say, 'Hey, Yahweh! How's it goin' in *your* universe?' And he'd say, 'Well, not so hot, people are always *praying* to me to make myself known to them, and it really takes up a lot of my *day,'* and then the other one says, 'You mean you created sentient life and you didn't tell them you *exist?*' Then Yahweh says, 'Well, I didn't know I was *supposed* to!' The other one says, 'Well, you've got to *tell* them, then!' Yahweh says, "I can't do that! I can't just *tell* 'em! What about all those people for the first 15,000 years? I mean, it wouldn't be *right!*' What would that be like, huh?"

"You're a twisted unit!" Chat said, but he was laughing a little.

"Yeah, and then maybe Yahweh is also a little compulsive. Say, like he can't resist any sport that begins with a 'b.' So he's on his way to prevent a disaster, and he sees a god basketball game, and then starts playing and forgets to go and do whatever, and *bango*! Earthquakes and horrors! Then he'd feel all bad and stuff, mope around for a few god days, try to so some real good, and maybe pull it off, too, until," Sterling said, pausing, searching.

Chat said, "Until he saw a dart game!"

"*Darts*? That doesn't start with a 'b!'

"So maybe he's dyslexic, too," Chat said, with a deadpan tone.

"We're both going to hell," Sterling said, croaking.

"No, my friend, only you are. But I'll miss you, I really will. ADD. Sheesh!"

"Watch out! There's some deer over there! I mean, somebody needs to pay attention, right?"

"I'm not the Director of the Universe, but I am a good driver. And, just so you know, I do pray for you all the time, my friend. Thanks for being here for me."

Then Chat gave Sterling a gentle tap on the shoulder and they drove on into the night.

Homer and Thelma spent more than their share of time worrying about the way things were going with the kids. Chat was a proud bugger, and he'd die before he admitted things were looking bad. At the preliminary hearing, the magistrate refused a reduction in bail, set the court date for late September, and just glared at Homer when he asked—nicely, Homer thought—when they were going to come to their senses and who was going to pay for all this when they finally decided they had their heads up their own nether regions.

"Fifteen hundred bucks! Contempt, my ass!" Homer said afterwards, fuming, while Thelma straightened up in the kitchen.

"Homer, every single person that loves you tells you to keep your damned trap shut, and you never listen one inch. Then you wonder why you have such luck. It's Chat should be asking the 'Whys' about things."

"Speak of the devil," Homer said, when Chat's truck appeared at the bottom of the driveway. Thelma stopped what she was doing, put on the pot of coffee, went out to the porch and waved hello as Chat parked and hopped out of the truck.

"You seem perky enough today," Thelma hollered to him.

"Getting ready to go down to Galax for the fiddle contest, but I just wanted to stop by and tell you a thought I had about this whole mortgage thing."

"Fifteen hundred. The bastards," Homer howled.

"And a good morning to you too, uncle."

"Coffee?" Thelma said.

"Love some. Here's what I was thinking. Layton gave me half of what he got off the auction, so I'll be able to square up with Younts for what I owe so far."

"And how much is that parasitic worm asking for seven minutes of work?" Homer said.

"So far, six grand. Six! And we're not even to trial yet. He's saying that he's confident that the whole thing will get thrown out, but that they intend to appeal if it does go to court. Already have that set up, he says, and that was more than half what he charged, getting ready for that part of it, " Chat said.

"I wonder who McAdam is paying off. Should've killed him when we had the chance, buried his body in the swamp," Homer said, almost under his breath.

Thelma came out with a tray of some homemade chocolate chip cookies and three steaming mugs of coffee, thick fresh cream in a blue stoneware pitcher and sugar bowl. The sun glinted off the cut crystal of the sugar bowl, which used to be his folks', Chat suddenly realized.

"Who you killing now?" Thelma asked Homer.

"Nobody. Never you mind. This way, you can't testify when they grill you about it later," he snorted.

"I'll testify that you're a *nut* case," Thelma said.

"He's *our* nut case, then," Chat said, smiling.

"What the hell you so all happy about, anyhow? Sunk in debt, no way to make a decent buck for yourself, your wife is at her wits end with all this nonsense, and here you are as happy as a clam. What are you on?"

"Well, I'm on my way to Galax, for one. And this is what I did down at Fiesterville. I got the mortgage on the Meadows this morning, and later today Sue and you need to settle out your note on this piece."

"Where'd you get the loan? First Freedom?" Homer snorted.

"Where else? Only game in town. I was kinda surprised, though, at the rate they gave me. Seemed low."

"They're bastards. How low?"

"Six percent. Anyhow, that'll square us up, and when the case gets tossed, I'll have to be working overtime to get caught up."

"Music money'll help, I guess," Thelma said, almost hopeful.

"Well, cash spends best, Thelma. Worse comes to worse, I guess I could sell the Hofstetter piece, or part of it. Right on the road like that, it'd make a good commercial piece. Hate to say it, but," he said, stopping before finishing his thought.

"Well, with that scene Malchio's got going down there, don't guess it'll be good for much else. Throw in another fast-food joint for all the fat flatlanders."

"Good name for a band, maybe."

"Frankie Furter and his Fat Flatlanders," Homer said.

"Like that band from Colorado you were talking about. What was it?" Thelma said.

"The Bad Livers?" Chat said.

"Hooo! No, Special Ed and," Homer said, stuck.

"Ah! The Short Bus Bluegrass Band! They're actually pretty good, those boys. Well, there's a girl in there, too," Chat said.

"Seeing more and more of that these days. Good thing, I guess," Thelma said, and Homer snorted again.

Thelma said, "Fer the love of Ned! Why'ncha blow yer damn nose, snorting like that all the time. Bout time we women get some credit. Lillie May and Olabelle and June and Mother Maybelle."

"There is *no* place in bluegrass for women. That's the only damn thing that low-down Rosine snake Monroe and I ever agreed to," Homer huffed.

"Well, Allison is making the big splash, and the Dixie Chicks," Chat said, sipping coffee and watching Homer's little red rooster dusting itself in the driveway.

"Traitorous Hollywood whores. That's what they are. And that's not even bluegrass, not the way it was put together."

"Homer. We're having a nice morning, now."

"Just means he's back to his cantankerous self, Thelma. Anyway, I'm excited to be playing this job. Might get scouted for some of the big festivals for next year, maybe."

"Well, far as I'm concerned, you boys are just as good as any of them out there. You sing like all them Paisleys—or are they the Lundys? Sterling's solid, no star, but his vocals make up for that."

"Well, just I worry a little about Jo-Jo. He's been a little off his feed, and this thing with Kate has him more upset than he's letting on, new boyfriend and all that."

"Oh? I hadn't heard about that one? Who is it?"

"Some guy named Tony. Tile man. He seems nice enough."

"Where's he from?" Homer asked, sitting forward and squinting into the light a bit, down towards the garden.

"Dunno. You see something?" Chat asked, gawking now also.

"Down there by the garden. Couple turkeys."

"Where? Oh, yeah, I see 'em. Yeah boy. Few weeks, they'll be in the oven, huh?"

"Couple weeks and they'll be invisible. Damned birds."

"Next thing he'll be calling the Fish and Game Commission, complaining about the droppings," Thelma said.

"Hey, didn't that guy over in Minisink have to drill a new well on account of the duck crap from all those ducks and geese? Well, he got what he deserved, feeding 'em like that. Those implants. They never learn, do they?" Homer said.

Chat hoisted himself out of the rocker and onto his feet.

"Well, Unc, I'm on the road. I'll see you in a few days, then."

"You take care of yourself. We'll do what we can for Sue."

And they watched Chat drive off, blue tarp covering the bed of his pickup, a couple steel poles poking out the back, and the pop-up bouncing along behind, rattling and clanking down the hill.

The fresh dew was gone now, and the sun was up high enough to make short sleeves a welcome thing.

"July. Almost August. Winter before you know it," Homer said.

"Sitting there, sweating, and worried about the cold. Men," Thelma shook her head, clearing plates and shaking her head.

29

≡ CHAPTER TWENTY-NINE ≡

Kate spent her day off day from Atbie's cleaning her apartment, did some grocery shopping—don't forget the crackers for the morning sickness—and made her way down to Ellie's, where the construction guys were substituting tea and coffee for shots and beers. After the scene with Jo-Jo, she made up her mind to give that Tony guy a better shot, young as he was. Hey, what's ten years among friends? Part of her knew she was doing that for spite: Jo-Jo was oddly possessive, and it would bug him. But the idea of having some support, someone to spend time with, well, that appealed to her, too.

Sure enough, there they were at the corner booth. Tony was there with the crew. Mercifully Jo-Jo was missing today, although she had made up her mind she wasn't going to let him being there stop her. Tony was laughing and telling jokes, enjoying the center of attention for a change. He did have a way with words, she had to admit, and, from the looks of things, he was moving right in with the boys, no doubt about it. It took a minute to get him off to the side and let him know that she was free later if he wanted to grab a bite to eat out to Fiesterville, maybe a movie afterwards.

"Yo, I'd like that, seriously!" he said.

"Yo? What's *that* all about? So, been writing any more poems?" she whispered.

"I have a couple new ones. I'll bring 'em," he said, pole-axed.

"Pick me up at six?"

"I'll be there with *bells* on," he said.

"Knock it off, goofball!" she said, shaking her head, and gave him a peck on the cheek she was sure would get the rumor mill going. That made her smile. After all these years, she was still a rebel.

He watched her leave, the sunlight streaming around her as she opened the door—what an ass!—and went back to finish his sandwich.

"Hey, Tony! Messing with the boss's girlfriend, there, huh?" one of them taunted.

"We're just *friends* is all," he said, waving his hands.

"Sure, sure. Whatever you say, Tony," they all agreed.

So later, when Tony picked Katie up, he had just picked up some new slacks and a fresh shirt, broken out his pinkie ring with the diamond, and dusted off a few of what he thought were his better poems.

After an indifferent dinner and an equally forgettable movie, he drove her down to the river again, down to the Onadaga Inn, where the lawns were nicely manicured and he could almost imagine how it must have been like in all the stories he had heard from the boys here. During the forties and fifties, Don Ameche and Jackie Gleason were regular guests, the great one getting drunk and running golf-carts over little old ladies' flower beds, his man coming around the next day with the checkbook to pay the damages, or some little part of them. Back then Gleason was close with a dollar, as most rich folk were; Mr. Greenjeans would prank the rich folks, afterwards playing for a time with some old-timey band, the Lost Ramblers. The stretch limos would bring all the families from New York, from Pittston and from Philly.

Poker games lasted for three and four days, and maybe ended with somebody getting whacked, and somebody laughing and saying "Yeah, drunk whacked, maybe!" And then more laughter. They weren't butchers—as long as they had their steak, they'd say in Italian, and laugh and laugh some more. *Those Dutchies never got it,* Tony thought now. *This girl seems different.*

They found a spot just opposite the head of the big island, spread the blanket near the park-style bench, and plopped down in silence for a moment.

"I brought some wine. Los Voscos. It's a very nice red," Tony said. As he spoke he was inadvertently reading the river, the water running silvery over the gravel on the near-shore side.

"No, thanks very much, Tony. None for me."

"I didn't know you were a teetotaler?"

"No. Just, sort of a, diet thing," she said.

"Oh, well. I can wait, too, I guess."

"I love this river," Kate said.

He waited a moment and said, " You ever canoe here?"

"Some. Sure. Why?"

"Does it get deep down below on this side, just before the end of the island?"

"It does. Is the next question going to involve my birth sign, repugnant political conversations, or why nobody ever figured out the whole Clark Kent/Superman thing?" Kate said, smirking.

Tony laughed.

"No, I was just remembering the Susquehanna, how the up side of an island always had shoal water on one side and deep on the other, but then nine times our of ten, the down side of the island was the other way around, deep on the shallow side and shallow on the other side. If that makes any sense."

"Naw. It really doesn't," Kate laughed. "But, at the end of the island is where my cousin dumped three years ago—lost our brand-new Grumman canoe. We spent three days looking for that sucker. Never found it."

"A most grievous loss. Maybe someday we could go."

"Maybe," she said, and moved closer to him, the warmth of his body welcome now in the dusky air. A faint evening breeze raised goose bumps on her arms and gave her a slight shiver.

He finally hugged her properly.

She had to admit, he had good hands and he was warm, too. Those Italians!

"Did you bring the poems? Is it light enough yet?"

"Here's one I like pretty well. There was a guy I went to school with, always in trouble, getting into fights, but that son-of-a-bitch could write. I mean, _I_ always thought he was really good. And eventually he went away to college and came back as a teacher at the same high school, which was pretty cool, because you can bet he never let anybody pick on anybody else in _his_ classes."

Tony took a breath before he began. He'd rather strip in front of strangers than read poetry. He said, "So, here it is—I call it Tom Bonhomme."

I was cudgeled
    as a child
Like my brothers.
My father worked ten hours
    Drank eight
        slept four
My mom
    Tried her best.
        She made the school plays
The band concerts, too
–once
She dragged the old man to one
    He passed out,
           pissed his pants…
That was his last concert
    It was a piece by Bach…
        My poor mom–too much testosterone for her!
She taught me well.
Though fists and shoves
    may have scribed my life,
I never complained!
    The muse lived in me–
Anything of art
    Was the shape of my heart
Dare to laugh!
    I'd knock your block off!
Never had money
    Spend it before it's gone

How odd to think I'd get to teach my kids–
My students and my sons,
My daughter!
All of whom I truly love!–
That a place there is for anyone
Who makes a place
    With fists and shoves
        And an art-shaped heart.

When he was finished, Katie gave him a small kiss on the cheek, and then sat silently. Small cat's-paws of wind just were chilling her, and here was the welcome warmth of his arms. The river basked in the last light, a ripple on the far shore where a muskrat was looking for dinner, the shore-bound flight of the green heron or the stately one of the piliated woodpecker, going from one shore to another in just two or three broad swoops of flight.

She remembered how she felt the one time she had done a solo on the river—all her friends were against it. They were going on about the risks and whatnot, but Kate was free, white and twenty-one, and she did what she wanted.

Solo wasn't enough. She picked the dead of winter, too.

It was almost prehistoric and scary to share an island with a piliated woodpecker in the dead of winter alone, as Katie had done not four miles from where they stood. Bitter cold: teens in the day, sub-zero at night.

She had a system for the cold that involved two tents. She first put up a small pup tent, then put up another over the first, and stuffed the space between them with what was left of the saw grass from the year prior. As the thin sun set, she spread out the down mummy bag, got the stove going and supper made—mac and cheese with a can of sardines—and had just changed out of her day clothes and then climbed into her dry silks, then into the wool long johns and finally into sweats and two pairs of thick socks. How delightful!

She was snuggled just like she was snuggling now when that big bird had swooped in from his day's hunt at last light and landed on a dead beech just up the cove from her—maybe fifty feet away. She was way too close for that bird's comfort, she remembered, and he gave her hell for the whole time the light held, cawing and hammering on the tree with a power she imagined would really put the hurt on mere human flesh. Finally, when her lantern was the only light left, he retreated into his cavity. She admired the way he had carved out a space in time, and how he had stayed alive, although the air was bitter and snow flew often in the fitful winds.

Kate thought, *No! Now the storm of fireflies on the Jersey shore winks, the river is made of gold, and I have made up my mind.*

"I think I'd like for you to take me home," she said, and almost laughed at his obvious disappointment. He had misunderstood what she meant. She waited.

Men. How on earth could they be so blind? How on earth could women *love* them?

"When I get to heaven, I'm going to have a few questions," Kate muttered, kissing him full on the mouth as she rose, and watched the light finally dawn in his eyes, the smile blossom on his face.

30

≡ CHAPTER THIRTY ≡

Chat tried not to dwell on the whole situation, but he was a man who knew how to count. Sue, the band, the money, and the trial? It was almost more than a man could bear. Besides, it was in the hands of the Lord, anyway. Meanwhile, the band had gotten together on the sly and agreed that playing a lot was the way to keep Chat's mind off his troubles. Besides, it might put a few dollars away in the bargain.

Sterling had three month's worth of personal days, days he had never used before. Bobby had given him hell the first long weekend, and so the next time, Sterling made sure to bring him a large Hershey's bar and a hat that read "High Lonesome," which Bobby wore proudly until the next weekend, when it was replaced with another that read "Horseshoe Curve" and then still another that said "Grand Canyon of PA." Long as Bobby got his hat and his candy, he was all good.

"Norty Lue!" Bobby would say happily, putting the hat on cockeyed and eating his chocolate, looking at the green boughs and saying "bare."

Johnny had figured it out, too. Making a hundred a day was a hundred a day, and the coal he didn't dig this year was there for next, so he didn't mind not going. His partner would just use day help and give them half as much as Johnny would have taken when he had to dig. And nobody could dig like Johnny, so it was a wash, money wise. But of course it was a lot more fun to be drinking beer and playing than digging in the ground.

Jo-Jo had a tougher time with it; he and Tony were on the outs, all business, and it was hard being with a guy day in and day out with that stuff going on in the background. Jo-Jo had found somebody to replace the Polack kid, an old guy who had been in business for himself and just got tired of all the phone calls and problems. All he had to do was show up and read prints, get the houses framed out, and holler at the help from time to time—all things he was good at doing.

As soon as the CD was done, they were busier than Chat could believe. The splash it made locally had gotten them into the Big Valley Bluegrass Festival and attracted Buck's interest.

Thin and intense, with a love of incredibly sweetened coffee, Buck got ten percent off the top wherever he booked, and he booked a lot. Like a boulder rolling downhill, he found the Cold Springs a spate of invitations to play other venues.

Even this late in the booking season, bands were breaking up, lead singers were dying, fights erupted, and Buck was all over it, wheeling and dealing to get them in to festivals they couldn't have touched a year prior.

At least they could do without the sound engineers and equipment that the newgrass groups needed, with drum kits, electric fiddles, and amps. Shit, why not just play rock and roll, then, or, the so-called "country?"

So they were on the road in earnest. Chat strained the limits of trust with Sue and his friendship with his customers, leaving early enough to make the twelve o'clock stage times when they had to take them. New kids on the block always got beat stage times, at least for one season. They flew a few times, gigs that netted them no real money after expenses.

"Sure, but Buck gets his ten percent, you can bet your ass on that one," Jo-Jo had complained. They all ignored him, worrying about the instruments the whole way, and trying hard to joke about it when the topic came up.

They flew over mountains that looked like postcards, to places like Cheyenne and Laramie, where the flat, hard ground made Johnny gape for the lack of trees and the blue skies opened up a man's head. Johnny felt like the clouds were getting rid of a bad cold that he didn't even know he had. The air made Sterling's nose so dry that he began to have nosebleeds, and Jo-Jo's hair would not sit the way he liked it but stood up in a way that Chat found amusing.

They drove to places like Moline and Memphis, when they could get stage times that allowed it. Chat quickly came to love those green spots near the Mississippi. They sat at rest areas and ate peanut-butter sandwiches on their way to or from a festival, while the barges churned their way up the chocolate waters. The thrum of the engines was oddly settling.

Then they penetrated even deeper into the mountains, passing through pockets where the general store could have been Atbies, except everybody stopped talking when they walked in, and the locals did not always return a hello right away, or even sometimes at all.

They were stunned by thousands of listeners, including large men with suspenders or kids with tie-die shirts, and white-haired, glove-wearing ladies who sat in their lawn chairs and politely listened, and applauded warmly when they were through. The stages were tractor-trailer beds with blue tarps over them, or permanent buildings with murals of mountains painted on the back walls that looked like saw teeth or green bumps, or fields that were inevitably autumn fields, with golden corn stubble and shocks of corn stacked like teepees, and a split-rail fence that ran gallywhoompus across the scene.

Chat had never ever seen a fence like that in his neighborhoods or in any of the new places he was seeing either.

They slept in motels when they flew, or camped out when they drove in Jo-Jo's huge motor home. It actually turned out to be a sight better than the ones owned by some of the big names they played with, who had this to do and nothing more. They felt pain watching one of the world's best fiddlers huddled inside the bottom door of a bus, with a continuity meter, trying to get an AC unit working, all while the world's second best banjo player stood outside with a flashlight, offering suggestions on what might be wrong.

"Man, we'd be rich if Nashville'd let us," one well-known player had groused when learning his bus had thrown a rod. No one argued that point.

Here the hat singers were knocking down the big bucks for banging out three chords and singing songs as flat as a cereal box, with as little heart in them as you would find in a kiddie songbook.

Meanwhile, pickers with blazing fingers and songs about death and the hereafter or about the love of a woman and the pain of separation were *pay*ing to play, almost. Players who could pick two and three and four instruments as mean as a three-day drunk or as sweet as the spring rain, quiet and calm like the moment evening started or as raucous as a close ballgame, wandered around from one small knot of pickers to the next.

They traded licks and showed how *this run* or *that run* could be achieved if the listener had hands and heart and head quick enough for it. Chat himself wondered about the wisdom of chasing all over the country, mostly for the love of the music, although even Jo-Jo was happy with the money they managed to make out of a three-day-a-week thing.

One night, on a dog-tired ride back from Morgantown, Sterling finally said, "You want to be sitting there on your porch wondering what it might have been like to go for this?" At that time, driving through dense fog near Morgantown, Chat had muttered something less than tolerant about the hour and the conditions.

"I want to be sitting on my porch all right," Chat said glumly. He sported a three-day beard on his face and a tinny road taste in his mouth. He continued, "I'd rather be sitting with a cold beer and my Sue."

"Can't really argue with that," Johnny agreed. "I mean, not with Sue, you know, but with the beer. And Meg. Boy, though. I never thunk we'd be playing with some of these bands regular enough that they call a man by his name and all," Johnny said, dreaming.

Chat had to admit that the notoriety had him beguiled a little bit. The local paper had done a big spread on the band after the CD, followed by the parade of smaller articles about Winterhawk and Asheville when they played, and more frequent mention in Bluegrass Unlimited, who called them "refreshingly authentic" and "true to tradition without being bound by it."

Those were quotes that even Sterling thought refined enough to acknowledge. And they were selling their share of recordings, sometimes several dozen a show. At one show, Jo-Jo spotted a home-made T-shirt with the band's name on it, a bootleg version with a mountain that looked like a big green golf tee, cliffs falling into nothing, and a little cabin perched on top with a white-washed chimney on the end and the vines growing up by the door. Quarter notes poured out of a chimney and tumbled through the air, turning into birds or getting lost in the clouds.

They began to see the same listeners in Tennessee and Rhode Island and Montana. These people made a bluegrass pilgrimage every weekend. They were computer programmers and mechanics and doctors by day, or toothless factory workers with '23 Lloyd Loar's on their backs or Martin's with "New York" stamped on them, instruments worth more than the vehicles that carried them. They toted Yamaha and Guild guitars, or unmarked instruments with holes worn in the tops, homemade fiddles shaped like boxes, triangles, even spaceships. These folks would never fail to come up after their show to say hello and tell the boys how much they liked to hear their particular brand of the music.

Work was another thing, though. More than once Chat could feel himself dragging, and he very nearly stayed home a few drizzly mornings. The drive out to Fiesterville was almost an hour now, with traffic, and it wasn't his shop. The old man he was renting from was nice enough to let him have the run of the place, but it was foreign, and often his mind would wander away from the bearing he would be packing or the timing belt that had gone south. He took to drinking coffee in the afternoon, three and four cups of it, and he still struggled some days to keep his eyes open on the ride home. He would have to pinch himself to stay awake, or even pull over and close his eyes until the beginnings of his snoring would awake him enough so that he could make it the last five minutes.

"You look mighty peaked," Sterling said to him during one of their weekly rehearsals. Their practices had taken on a more somber tone now, because at the bottom of it all was a new promise of success, an implied agenda and a race to be run.

"I don't have sick days to use at will like you do," Chat snapped back, regretting it instantly.

Chat could tell the road grind was beginning to tell on them all, even Johnny, whose knuckles seemed more skinned than usual, and who would lapse into a vague state in between songs without a smile or even the quiet stare he used to wear that said he was ready to go again. Instead his eyes were more often thin slits that could not be seen until he shook himself awake at the sound of his own name. Then they would fly more open than they needed to be. It gave Johnny a startled look that bothered Chat for some reason. He could not put his finger on it exactly: Johnny was a big boy and had as much say as any of them, but for all of that, Chat still held a secret feeling that he was partially responsible for Johnny, as a brother would be, and that he was letting him down.

Even Jo-Jo had begun to show signs of unraveling. He had always been the first to arrive and the last to leave a party, and could drink for two days straight—beer, wine or shine, anything really that came to hand—and then go out on the job site at seven in the morning and walk the rafters like they were as broad as a cakewalk, swinging the twenty-ounce framing hammer as light and easy as a diner wielded his fork. But now there was an afternoon or two when Chat saw him and couldn't help but notice the gaunt circles under his eyes. At practice, Jo-Jo would zone out and forget the key signature, even once the words to one of his favorite songs, and Chat began to wonder if maybe they hadn't bitten off more than they could chew, if they weren't perhaps ignoring something vital.

"Maybe we should rethink some of those later dates, Jo-Jo. You look like you could use the rest, son," he had murmured to Jo-Jo, quietly so the other two couldn't hear. Jo-Jo had transferred the bow to his left hand and reached for his beer, and Chat noticed a faint tremor.

Jo-Jo forced a laugh and said, "Yeah, you just say that because of that valve job you buggered up on Wesley's truck yesterday that cost ya a half a day." He said it louder than he had to, but Chat noticed he was doing the same thing Chat was, eyeing his hand that was shaking like a man with the DTs.

"A man is allowed to change his mind, if it's for the best," Chat said, laying his hand over Jo-Jo's, but Jo-Jo pulled away from the light touch with a glower that surprised all four of them.

"Man's sweet on me, I think," Jo-Jo joked to the other two, and they proceeded with the practice, with Jo-Jo going a bit beyond on his fiddle break as if to say that things were as right as rain.

The worm of worry had begun to gnaw at Sterling's gut now as well, like the faint sound of angry water, the unnamed worry that kept a body up at night. Sterling got a fluttery feeling in the pit of his stomach sometimes because it felt for all the world like death was sitting on his right shoulder. He could almost feel little feet bumping against the hollow that was up there by his clavicle, just as he had confessed to Chat one night.

He hadn't ever told Chat about his Grandmother, though, or the stories she always told. He'd been so taken with her talk as a child that it never went away, even when he wished it would. All the schooling, the course work, and the books, they never could make those little feet stop bumping. You couldn't think that away, that was the problem.

At times like that, he could feel his shallow breathing, perhaps faint-headed tinges of hyperventilation. He couldn't do anything but grit his teeth and bear down, 'til his bowels cramped. Every time, just before it was too late, at that very last second, he would break a sweat.

Sterling had this conversation with himself on two occasions. One was when he let Jo-Jo talk him into taking a few puffs on the way out to a job, and he was driving, being steady-Eddie on the outside, acting like everything was under control, while on the inside he was just sure he was going over the shoulder, about to lose it completely, to lose control and to wreck, to allow the entire known universe to be destroyed in one careless moment. It was, he knew, just another case of drug-induced paranoia that always made him promise himself that he was going to swear off the weed, although the next time Jo-Jo gave him a nod and a wink, he was right out the door behind him.

The other time was a time like now, when he had been out too late and had to get up too early. *White knuckle it, buddy.* That's what a coach might have said. *Can't go on? Ready to lose it? Grab the sonofabitch and hang on.*

Wear death out? What a stupid idea, Sterling thought. *Man, a person could never get any practice for it, either, when death wanted to show how stupid that idea was. Up it would ride, big old grin, the same old story, only this time, perhaps one could just zig at the last minute, just jump right before the elevator hits, and there won't be any harm done.*

Man. The incredible machine.

Sterling was thinking about all that one night, coming back from a festival organized by a group that inexplicably called themselves the Bluegrass Oyster Cult. The were a strange and lively bunch that befriended lonely bluegrassers and specialized in strange theme parties. This week it was pajama party night, and they were all running around in skimpy negligees or PJs, eating and drinking and playing a bluegrass version of "Mustang Sally" too loud and out of key, whooping it up, celebrating no rain and a decent gate.

Jo-Jo was snoring in the back and Johnny was slumped against the window asleep, both dead to the world. Sterling could feel the beginning of a memory, a picture of the cabin on the deep-water canal and the spicy crabs dumped on newspaper with a bunch of friends and many cold beers. He knew where that train was leading, and tried hard to think of something to say while Chat was driving down the road in late night silence.

"How you doing?" Sterling said finally, and Chat just grunted a little at first, then said, "These drives are getting harder every week."

"You remember coming through here last winter in that snow?"

"That was a bitch. Um, sorry."

"Hey—you mind if I read out loud some?"

Chat grunted again, then said," You aren't gonna use the dome light, are you?"

"No. Amy bought me this clip-on light. I was just asking because there's a whole section in here about where we are now, more or less."

"Somebody *wrote* about that? Why?"

"I dunno. But listen, once. You might get a kick out of this."

While they rode, he read,

Drive deep into the heart of Pennsylvania, past the fringe of the Lehigh, across the first branch of the Susquehanna, a mile wide and an inch deep, with the land all open after the hedgerow thickness of the Pocono Plateau. The trees there are all fifteen feet high, four inches thick and eighty years old, just waiting for the blast of wind or the fire that will perhaps level their neighbor but leave their roots in the ground and a piece of the sky open to their leafy arms—outstretched to Sol, giver of heat, light, and life. Go out to the broad and fertile valleys of the Allegany Mountains. Dairy farms as far as the eye can see on that big Route 80, the Eisenhower Highway, the first link in the system that would eventually rewrite, erase, rework, eradicate, defile, improve, dissolve or implode some of the world it was meant to merely traverse. Another first—Thanks, Pennsylvania!

Of course, every ending must have had a new beginning at some distant juncture in space and time, that led to the change that made the present reality the only thinkable one. Good thing humans can only pay attention to one or two things at a clip, or they might actually see all those possibilities converging all at a point in space: the point being them.

Frightening thought.

None of that today. The sun shines bright on our ole Pennsylvania home, the farms stretch out to the horizon, the highway stretches out to infinity, or Columbia County, or Elk, or maybe even Potter. Maybe they're all the same. The hills roll on, an earthly tide, frozen like a snap-shot for just a geologic moment—*Smile!*—with the distant church steeples or farm silos thrusting into heaven. Contented cows litter the fields, and every field is scribed neatly with the attendant hedgerow or stone-course, a practice in this heartland that has not been abandoned yet. Economy of scale is something that makes sense only when you have disposable humans, and humans, oddly enough, are in short supply here in the heartland of the East. This place might have been the blueprint for the heartland of America, Pennsylvania being a land of firsts.

Take Route 44 north, sweeping through the hills, all bearing the mark of their labor this year past, corn stalks sticking through the shiny crust of snow—what a shame for the deer! —a few busted bails of hay, round now and not the rectangular icons of youth. The timothy or alfalfa looks like an ancient beard in search of an old and wise face, finding instead only the earth, immutable, stubborn, fertile, and inconstant; wonderfully surprising.

A traveler will pass a small hardware store about eight to twelve miles out, with a bar on the corner opposite. Folks get together in the old schoolhouse just past that corner. The good folks of Jerseytown have that little schoolhouse in their hearts, and they open the building up to the community and the whole world, getting some good jams going out there in the country.

"Man. That's Jerseytown to a 'T,'" Chat said. "Read on, old boy."

Outside, it's a brilliantly cold day. Cows stand stoically, waiting for the magic door to open and bring them food or leave them in to the warm stalls they can almost remember. Horses with winter coats stand in their paddock, breath steaming from their nostrils—lazy like old cigarette smokers when they are still, then blasting great blasts of vaporized, roiled clouds when they have a mind to caper, not as rare as one might think: they are animals, after all!

Every house has a plume of white smoke wending its way towards heaven, all those eons and generations of trilobites and fern trees having found their way into a cozy home at last, the warmest spot in the house, thence to be reduced to a rolling pillar of whiteness, perhaps like Lot's wife. To think, all those millions and billions of life-forms now acting as just the hard clinkers and ash in the bottom of the furnace—did the smoke turn and look to see the earth, the old home place, before passing away into the sky so blue?

The walls of the little school house are covered with the detritus of the past, decades of classes pictured in snapshots now yellowed, corners curling slightly, small classes with eager-looking faces. They are all smiling except the one boy in the back, who looks surprised or worried. Twelve and fourteen and twenty kids, with teachers so young-looking, hair neatly combed and suits and ties (the men) or flowery dresses that cover the knees (women). Sarah Jones not pictured. These are now the gray-clad matrons at the truck stop or the fat old men who, when they drive by, give even a stranger the two-fingered farmer's salute as you pass, the other three still on the wheel.

"That's the picture, all right," Chat said. "I loved looking at all those pictures last time I was there."

"Sure! Listen to this!"

On the wall by the kitchen are pictures of every house in Jerseytown, all twenty-three of them: the Geat's place, Shannon's, Dougherty's, Fiester's, or the Banks' houses. They're all neat and tidy, not too pretentious, even though there are bound to be a couple millionaires out here, the money not leaving the unwilling hands. Buy right and you'll never go hungry: a grain elevator for 300 bucks when the guy next door goes out of business and the kids don't want the farm.

How can you keep 'em down on the farm, after they've seen MTV? So it goes from one generation to the next, until something breaks the strand of continuity, and—improbable in that landscape—the fields and woodlots begin to sprout McMansions like perverted mushrooms. The dark soil that once said "soy" and "corn" and "wheat" now shouts or murmurs, "Hummer, swimming pool, fences, trespass notices, cul de sacs and light stanchions." The old simple and direct ways are gone now, and the intemperate generation of boomers or gen-Xers carve up the landscape like it was a block of cheese. Just like the commercials: *Eat all you want, we'll make more.*

The Mennonites in their black carriages know better. *Buy land,* as Twain said. *They don't make it anymore.* They do stick together, those folks, so that when Zeigenfus or Borger has a set of preemies at the local hospital, and the bill is fifty grand, the young farmer walks in, blue bib overalls, and pulls out a stack of hundreds. "Here's 25,000. I'll have the rest tomorrow for you," and the girl at the counter with face of white calls security all worried and in a lather. After all, she's "never seen so much cash in one place!" Every cent is gathered from the families around the county for young Jedidiah and Rachel.

"Well, when you go to bed at eight and you don't drink, smoke, mess with women or gamble, and you're not allowed to buy any toys, you're bound to save some bucks," Chat said, interested.

"Well, there's more. Here:"

But that's the country way. Neighbors help one another even if they can't stand each other. Perhaps a fellow brags too much. Maybe he drinks too many beers, which is one or two more than what is generally seen. Maybe he didn't give permission for an access road across his lower forty so the next fellow can get into the lower field a little earlier in the season, the old road being all steep slope and prone to washouts and mud. But if his barn burns or his daughter gets sick, a neighbor will house his cattle or fix a large pot of chicken soup for him and especially for the kids, who should never be put into the position of having to pay for the sins of the father. Not, at least, until they are twenty-one.

Flags fly everywhere out here. Not the rainbow flag or the confederate flag, like farther east where the country mouse and the city mouse have been forced to rub elbows. Nor the Puerto Rican flag either. There might be a P.O.W. flag right under the American one, a not-so-gentle reminder that 10,000 Pennsylvania boys sleep in their graves from 'Nam, another 10,000 from the Civil War.

"Really? That many?" Chat said.

"I'm not convinced the numbers in this are right," Sterling said. "But it's interesting, kind of."

"More interesting than a late night road trip, anyway. What else does it say?"

Not that anyone would confuse folks in this heartland as liberals in their taste for company. Nobody out here understands the whole Negro question, because there are no Negroes here, at least not yet. The idea of welfare and aid to foreign countries are dirty words out here in the heartland, too, where a man is expected to make his own way and work hard, go to church every Sunday and join the fire company because it's the right thing to do.

What person in his right mind can expect anyone out here to give one good thought to Washington, New York, Dallas, San Francisco, or what concerns those metrosexual folks? Gay rights? Please. "Me and my wife want to get married, say—to our son, daughter and dog. How do you like them apples?" they say, "It's Adam and Eve, not Adam and Steve, thanks very much. It's a free country. But be polite. The whole neighborhood doesn't need to know every little thing."

In all fifty states, these heartlands endure, ignored by the millions who are tethered to a city, the folks either from Dallas, LA, New York, Miami, Cleveland or Chicago, or who were once from there. The heartland is especially ignored by Hollywood and Madison Avenue, the denizens of which realize that they will never make a nickel on country folk.

Those folks know about how to rebuild a carburetor, skin a deer, or put the magnet in the stomach of a cow so she doesn't cut herself to ribbons from rusted strands of barbed wire and the metal trash that gets thrown out of windows.

"Ellie was complaining a little about business since Malchio put the Biggie Burger in, and I was thinking about the trash from there and how people just pitch the damn stuff out the window. Good thing we have those convicts in the orange jumpsuits to pick it up. Just back aways, I saw a sign that said the Rotarians have adopted this little chunk of interstate to 'beautify.' I mean, can you really make a strip of concrete and steel pretty?" Sterling said.

"You read odd books and think odd thoughts, my friend. *I* was starting to think of a nice cup of coffee at Ellie's."

"Nice thought, that. How much longer, you figure?"

"'Nother hour puts us back in the county."

"Not a second too soon."

"Amy waiting for you?"

Sterling smiled to himself and sighed contentedly.

"Yeah. Lucky Sterling," he said.

"Lucky Sterling is right," Chat murmured, looking at the dark stripe of unburned oil running down the right lane in his headlights and the banks scathed clean of all vegetation except unkempt grass and crown vetch.

"Get me a cup of that day old coffee down there in the thermos, Lucky," Chat said, rubbing his eyes and bearing down on the road.

31

≈ CHAPTER THIRTY-ONE ≈

McAdam reflected on the beautiful unfolding of events around him.
Malchio gave *him* a call that was like offering him the keys to the city: all
the supervisors' names, the fire companies they belonged to, their party of
choice, what and where they liked to hunt. All this McAdam got over the
next few weeks at the edges and margins of meetings. It cracked McAdam up
when Malchio thought he had just nailed McAdam for something that was
of value, like that puke outlet thing or the Section XIII money that Congress
had passed and was anxious to funnel into the county.

McAdam was surprised to learn from the legal beagles that the "little
things" would be worth ten times what Malchio was thinking, making a large
outlay in redirecting the legal landscape not only feasible but imperative. In
short order, McAdam gained the ear of every decision maker in the county
that mattered. Better yet, none of them knew his name. They only knew
his gifts—the ten grand to the Wyansock fire company that would finally
buy the new pumper that will protect the land and buildings which would
eventually be McAdam's.

The new bank, First Freedom? They had some serious leverage problems.
Apparently they didn't have enough cash to deliver on their mission statement,
so what could they say to a quiet, shy and soon-to-be-retiring executive
thinking of maybe settling down here with some serious assets?

That's what makes me a tour de force, Hugh thought. The little lines on the
map made one thing happen over here, and another thing happen over there.
Those little lines were generated by primitive technology: one man's hand,
and in it a pen with ink to draw. That's all it took, to move a line over—just
one inch—and history winds itself out in a different pathway. Don't think

so? Ask the Jews; ask any East Berliner; ask somebody in Kosovo trying to get just over that little rise in the hills, there, where he might be safe.

He wasn't really a mindless bastard. He just saw the bigger picture. Wasn't a ballgame better than no ballgame? So build a stadium! Wasn't a house better than no house? So build houses to contain consumers that will support the infrastructure that he'd own—got that abandoned rail-bed!—and then sell 'em what they need, and with that cable thing he's got going, tell then what to think. Eventually he would own them.

Life was good, except for that secretary who was already late twice this month.

Twice! Proof of his benevolence!

It wasn't the lateness as much as the fact that Hugh could really tell she had enjoyed herself someplace. But then, they had to have some little fun if they were going to pull the wagon. So the girl could stay, for now. She was useful.

With Tony's missives, and the Web-searches, and with Malchio calling—every two days, for crissakes!—McAdam had a mental map on his mental wall that made Malchio's real one look like a fourth-grade project of "The Lost Colony" made with two colors of Play Dough and some Popsicle sticks. All this would be his; it was the golden rule, the prime directive, no matter what the bleeding heart and swells said.

Chat found himself spending more time at the new garage and less time at his own house, because the air was thick there with almost-stated recriminations, and Chat had no idea what to do about it all.

Talking about Sue to Sterling, Chat said, "Marriage isn't a word, my friend. It's a sentence."

Sue definitely found no humor in the situation. She had stopped coming to festivals when the kids were small; it was too much of a hassle, and, unless you were a picker, there wasn't really that much to do, or for that matter many people to do it with. In those days, there wasn't much of a family thing going on either. No other kids to play with, so in the end it was enough to decide Sue to stay at home.

But now, with the boys on the road the better part of each week, Sue had to face facts: she was at the end of her rope. She tried to hold up and be brave, like the singer in that *Circle*, cleaned house as if her life depended on it, suffered through an invasion of mice towards the middle of the summer, and declared war on the little vermin, which gave her purpose and something meaningful to do with herself.

She began to feel like she was winning, too, buying traps and cheap peanut butter, the kind that used some lard in there to make it stick to the roof of the mouth. Stuck good to the traps, too. Sue took better than a dozen mice in three days, no more mouse turds on the bottom of the drawers, and then suddenly no more working toilet, either. The line between the house and the cesspool was clogged with dead mice, and she had to call Homer, who told her they didn't have a snake, and then she had to blow 200 bucks to get a man with a snake in there to blast out the expired fur balls.

Much as she hated to do it, she picked the day and waited.

"And I want to tell you, she went at me like a house afire for about an hour and a half," Chat told Sterling afterwards, doleful and resentful as well.

"Well. Amy hasn't been too pleased about it either, us on the road all the time, " Sterling half-grunted.

"You still seeing her?"

"You sound surprised, Preach. We're quite the item, doncha know."

"Well, that's a nice thing for you, then. 'Bout time, of course."

"Of course. Listen, Sue'll be right as rain in a few months, soon as you get that bullshit with the law straightened out," Sterling said hopefully.

"Younts is gonna bust me, Sterling. I went through that ten grand from the auction in three weeks. Three weeks! And now I got that note on the Meadows, and I just don't know how these things are supposed to all come together at the end except as one big mess."

"Man. You are *down*. So take whatever you're saying and cut it in *half*, then take a spoonful of *that* and throw the rest away. That's all that worry stuff will *do* for you," Sterling chanted it like a mantra and sawed the air with his hands in time, one of them with the mason jar in it, half full or half empty, whichever.

Sterling gave him the cool-cat words and then handed him the jar. Chat took a swig, feeling the fire go down and his ears begin to burn.

"Yeah, what they say. Worry doesn't save tomorrow's tears. It just sucks the life out of today!"

Even Jo-Jo was offering helpful hints about "how to mollify."

"That's a big word, and I woulda never learnt it except it is so handy. It describes me to a T so," Jo-Jo said, and fluttered his long lashes, belched and took a swallow of beer.

That was the talk as they were leaving Peaceful Valley up in the great state of New York, arching down towards Pennsylvania, joking about the family that thought they had the system beat. That weekend they nabbed the best campsite ever—even the boys were a little jealous, the way they were right there on the banks of Delaware. Then on Friday night the heavens opened up and turned most of the campsites into muddy messes, and there those folks were, stranded on what was now a little island, looking all comfy except that they had figured on going here or there with the car, which was stuck on the island with them, so of course, their sight-seeing hopes were dashed, at least for a couple days. The good news was that some of the folks there had slung a rope over to them and had made it fast to two trees so that they could wade through the thigh-deep torrent and use the port-a-potties. The boys laughed at that one more than once on the way home.

But then, after dropping the boys off, Chat walked up the back steps and into waiting Sue.

She began her speech by saying that she had always loved him, sometimes as one thing and sometimes as another, although that did not get in the way of her getting pissed as hell about the things he did or did not do, and that she had always assumed to be the meaning of the words "for better or for worse." These long absences, the legal and financial things, now suddenly the problems with Jesse at school getting into fights and sassing back the staff just as if he had been raised a heathen was all too much. Her considered opinion was that it was all because Chat was on the road too much and had let the music beguile him.

"Beguile me! *You* were what beguiled me, for the love of Pete! What do you want me to do? Stock shelves at Atbie's with Kate?"

"Shows how much you know about the people you were born and raised with, the ones that care about the real you, not just the music you. Kate gave her notice. She's preggers with Jo-Jo's kid. I guess they have some understanding, seems to me."

"Jo-Jo? Kate? A *kid?*"

"Chat, I love you more than it's wise to love somebody, especially somebody like you."

"Somebody like *me*? What kind of crack is that?"

"Please go off the road. We can sell the Meadows. Malchio has the back half of the road all screwed up anyway, and that's bound to spread. I know it has been keeping you busy, maybe not letting you get down and all, but, Chat, you have to, for the kids and me."

"Dang it, Sue. We're three weeks away from the Big Ass, umm, the big festival. If we do well there, we can still play four times a summer, places it would be good to have the kids see, Colorado and Wyoming, maybe make a few dollars at this."

He stood, hands palm up, shoulders shrugged, trying out a sheepish grin, feeling a little like a used car salesman and realizing it wasn't going over at all.

"Weren't you the one that I found deaf as a post? And wasn't it you that I hauled his sorry ass all over the county and then the state getting you looked at, all without your freakin' uncle Homer suspecting, because that was what I knew you wanted, even then, keeping it all out of sight, your little faults, your peccadilloes and your ways. We all have our ways, and I know you haven't been all that pleased with me lately, being a little short the way I've been. But for the love of God, Chat, remember what it's like to live in silence, then think whether it's right for you all to go leave me here and go on down to Pennsville to play Labor Day. Hell, 'scuse me, they're starting school the week before, Chat!"

"The week before Labor Day? What genius came up with *that* one?" Chat asked, unwilling to fight.

"School board did. Said they had no choice," Sue said, tired of the fighting herself.

"So why they have to shorten it now, change everything? School before Labor Day. What next?"

"The flatlanders come up here and buy one of those worthless SUVs and then think that because they have four-wheel drive, they can stop better, too. Then they slam into some school bus full of other kids from the city and the parents all sue the district for pain and suffering."

She looked at Chat, her eyes red rimmed and the hazel a faded green, tired, tired almost to death. She decided for the third time that day that she did still love him, despite. He was being the good listener, behaving, anxious to please if he could without losing something dear to him.

"Remember how the bus drivers used to just throw the chains on, and most folks would stay at home? Then the buses were fine, but when there was six or eight inches and they called school off—wasn't that magical?" Chat said quietly.

It was late, late at night, and Chat could hear the thrum of machinery from over the last rise before the river came into view. He needed to block that out, make things right with Sue.

"Remember that time we got let out of school early, and there was already a half a foot down and we were coming down the hill into Pigeon Forge and the bus started," she said, taking a breath.

"Sliding towards the edge and there was no guardrail there," Chat said, finishing her words.

"At the last minute the tires bit."

"And bumped you into me."

"That was the first time you kissed me, waiting for my old man to get out of his driveway so he could pick us up."

"That Jeep was always freezing," Chat said, even shivering for a second now. He was once again a fifteen year old with his world in one piece, and he was remembering his breath that hung like ragged clouds for moments as he propped himself up backwards on an old milk box, the really old kind that were made of wood, or later of insulated corrugated aluminum.

Sue's dad, Chester, had taken the back seats out because he needed the space for all the junk he always carted around to make a buck. That was something he seemed good at until, when he died, they found that he had not a cent to his name, and Sue was ironic about when Chat had finally gone to the therapist Sue had found before the Internet, in the days of only three TV channels!

He had gotten his hearing back with apparently something added, and just in time for the funeral. Chat listened to himself complain because they had unplugged the freezer after Chester died and all the meat in it was shot, even the last ten pans of scrapple Chat and Chester had put up together. That much was well-known: the best way to a farmer's heart was to help with the chores while you talked—helpful if one was after the guy's daughter.

32

≡ CHAPTER THIRTY-TWO ≡

They were gone on the road for two weeks, swinging down through Baltimore and Pokemoke City, then out to Smith Island and back over to Crisfield for the crab festival—Sterling was in seventh heaven—then south to Durham and Charlotte before coming back up to end in D.C. There, Sterling got word that they had been booked at the Beacon Theatre for the Down from the Mountain Tour with Allison and Jerry Douglas—and Ralph. Only the producer wanted a five piece, so they called the Ice-Cream Man and asked for Sue the fiddler to fill in. The idea was that then Jo-Jo could double up on fiddle or play mandolin as he liked.

It was an idea no more welcome to Jo-Jo now than it was when they cut the CD, and he did what he always did when he didn't get his own way, just shut down and glared for the first day or two, or until he had seven beers. After that, he would mutter comments that the boys had long ago learned to ignore.

While they drove, Chat gave the boys the news of what his Sue had told him.

"She wants me to stay off the road," he said.

"But why? I mean, we worked all these years, and you know how it goes. You get your foot in the door and you're all good, but take a year off and try to get back in the ring then, buddy, that's a hard thing," Sterling said, nodding sagely.

"Hell, I understand why, but seems like she's going overboard on me."

"You have to go, Chat. You know that," Sterling said, sure of himself. "We're depending on you, and I know you won't turn your back on us, your old buddies."

"Yeah, yeah. What I know is that, either way, I'm in a tight spot. I think she means to leave me if I don't slow it up some."

"She won't leave. That's not her way. Winter's right around the corner, and we can all rest then," Johnny said, thinking that there was plenty of time to rest later on.

Little birdie, little birdie, such a short time to be here and a long time to be gone.

Friday morning put them on the road again, Jo-Jo driving, with a stop in Maryland for a private party at some yacht club. They had gotten the job for big bucks from some guy they met playing the CrabFest the week prior. Next, they went on to Charleston to play at a "Block-head" party for a bunch of Dodge Hemi fans with cars that cost as much as a nice house, maybe two or three nice houses.

"Just think of it as income reallocation," Jo-Jo crowed as they left, sitting in comfort in his Suburban's cushy leather seats. He was making more money than Carter had little liver pills, whether or not he was around—hell, his other business was almost on automatic pilot with the old guy and Tony in there, Jo-Jo had to admit, gloating.

"Pass me that bottle back there in the cooler, Johnny, ole boy. From here on up, it's all downhill!" Jo-Jo chortled.

Ada was among the first to move into "Birch Hollow," as the building man had named the place. The snubs and cold shoulders she got from the others who were already there didn't surprise her. America! Land of the free, home of brave. But every family had one, and in a family like this? Plenty of trouble and strife, plenty!

"Implants," the fat matrons would say on the bus that took them all home from Fiesterville. They would talk as if she weren't there, with seldom a kind or Christian word. Ada felt confused and angry. She saw the way they stretched their feet and rubbed their ankles, swollen from too much time on their feet, she saw their hands, gnarled like the old oak she had climbed as a child. *Aren't my hands too like yours after all? Are we not sisters?*

If they were, they were not close sisters. So Ada kept her mouth shut and looked straight ahead. "Spic," they whispered, or worse yet, "Nigger!"

She went back and forth to her full job four or five days during the week and returned by six on three of those days. Two evenings, she stayed to clean an extra pair of offices next door to where she worked. In both her jobs, the people seemed very nice. *A little more going on in the upstairs*, she thought. It was only the bus ride home that was the trouble, at least at first.

She still thought about Ellie, made a point to come to the diner and eat at least once a week or so with the kids. The stools that spun and the clinking of spoons against coffee cups made her feel at home. They visited the horses that Angelina had named the second time they stopped and had learned to feed by the time after that. They even learned to like that terrible grey mush that all the locals loved so much. Scrapple. Phew! And every time they came, Ellie asked if she had been back to see Layton, and she said nothing, hanging her head. The potted plants were all weeds, she had seen that, and it made her sad.

She had no room for more sadness just now.

"You should just march right back there and tell that old polecat he's taking you back and that's the end of it!" Ellie said on one visit.

"Via con Dios, Ellie. You are a good woman. We will be happy to come again next week."

"Yeah, thanks for the extra fries, Ellie! They're awesome," Rico said.

That was what he called himself now. What a change! She was ready for the troubles. They had them every time they had moved, and always it was Rico who had been at the front of the trouble, and, oh, he had some tough times, on the bus. She was so pleased and proud when he came home one night—always on time now—and asked if he might go out to the movies with some guys, and when she had poked just a little bit, then he said, "Yeah, maybe a couple girls might go along, just pizza and a movie. It's no biggie. Can I go, then?"

And what mother wouldn't chase him out and smile and perhaps cry just a little, if la Nina wasn't watching.

She thought back to the second day at the projects. She had gotten up very early, without waking the children. She took the bus to Fiesterville. She did not want to spend the money, but she needed to know the limits of this world to see if it was large enough to hold her.

She walked to the library. She had studied the map when she was still at Layton's, asked about it when she could without being a bother to him, and planned. Not such a wonderful thing for someone who had traveled 6,000 miles, but she never made any new trip without her heart beating like a little girl. Nothing happened, except what she had planned. At nine in the morning, she arrived in Fiesterville and went straight to the library to sign the forms so she could have free books. She had planned well, stopped in a small restaurant and had a steaming cup of coffee and some toast beforehand. She was excited to see the books, the quiet tables and the papers most of all. What she found she could not believe at first.

The library was in a house on the main drag of town. It was an old building with uneven floors and wavy glass windows, a porch that had no flowers and needed to be painted. Inside, books were stacked everywhere, in corners, on filing cabinets and on mismatched shelves. A half dozen old chairs filled one room for those that wanted to stay and read, although no one was there this morning. The librarian looked at her curiously, asked if she could help, and Ada hesitated for a moment. She wanted to know if they had any Spanish papers, but the woman shook her head "no."

"You have eyes," she said. "We can't even get papers in English here some months, and there is no chance the voters are going to approve a new tax for *books*."

Ada nodded, smiled and said her thanks. She picked up the daily newspaper, read, as best she could, about the growth in the county, and the trouble the schools were having. Was she really so strange to them? How hard a time the natives were having about the new ways. She read no words about how the new people were having troubles finding their way.

She was not the only one from the city now in the new low-income housing units named after beautiful trees. To Ada they were ugly boxes in the country, not at all like the beautiful things they were named after. The man who named them liked cruel jokes, she was sure of that. Would it have killed the builder to put in a few flowers or a swing set for the children?

One of the families there had also moved from the city, and Ada had learned their story from the mother one Saturday as they sat on the lone bench and watched the construction continue. She was a mulatto, half Puerto-Rican and half black, and she had moved there for the same reason Ada had—to get her kids out of a bad neighborhood.

"Oh, there was crack all 'round that place. Shootings, oh Lord. And then I sees this ad says, 'Why you makin' the landlord rich? Own your own'.

So I go down there to the office they got, man ax me, 'How much money you spend on rent?' and I tells him. He say they could work it, and I ax him how, with me only making so-and-so and my old man not doing no better. And he say, 'You leave that to *us*—you just pick your dream house and we see what we can do.'"

"When it comes to the money, they say whatever they like to us. We are the dirt under their feet to them," Ada said quietly.

"True that! That man say he gone get that house for us, and goes and get us a mortgage for the ever'thing we owes, says you can forget that down payment and all that, we just write that in and you pay that all the last year then we forget to charge you. All some stuff I don't get. Few months later, we all moved in, but the bus it cost 400 a month and the car break down then, and pretty soon the cards maxed out and we say 'Ain't no *way* we goin' to be able to pay that mortgage, we better *sell* that house,'" she said, starting to cry.

Ada heard then that when they put the house up for sale, they found it was worth fifty thousand less than they were told, and the house didn't even cover the mortgage at all. The only thing left was bankruptcy, and here she and the old man were, still taking the bus into the city, though, leaving at five in the morning.

"Oh lordy, we don't get back until almost nine, and the kids they not doing so good in the new school, on account they don't like blacks at all here and they's always picking on them."

"Why do they?" Ada asked.

"Just because they get to class late or talk loud or some other such stuff, want to wear the dew-rags for they hair. Stupid little stuff," the woman said.

Ada was polite, and secretly proud and glad that Rico and Angelina were doing so well. So soon, too! The first days of school had been anxious, a couple incidents here and there when the local kids had made fun of the accent and the dark skin, the name-calling, and what was worse were the stares and whispers and the giggling that meant they were being mocked. And them with Spanish Lords and Inca kings in their bloodline. They were cowards, Ada told her children many times, and they know what they do is wrong before God, but they do it anyway because their souls are twisted and they have lost the way.

"Be proud of who you are. They are only peasants, as their fathers before them."

The women Ada talked to that Saturday wasn't the only one working fifteen hours a day. Many families in the projects like that left their kids to go to work, trusting them to get themselves to school. One of them, a boy of Rico's age, stayed at home as often as he went to school. On those days, getting ready for work or returning from her job, Ada could hear the dull thud of that music, cruel words of anger and hopelessness, *whore, pimp, bling-bling*. What did it all mean? She knew how it *felt*, like doom and the end of all things beautiful.

She missed Layton's place, expensive as it was. On the mornings when la holgazan was home, she thought of going back there, if Layton would take her back—far from certain—to be near the stream at the foot of the mountain, and to see the quiet valley stretch out before her. Then she remembered Layton's ways, how he let her in only because Ellie had insisted, even how he stayed away from them all because, Ada suspected, he was growing to like her, or at least the kids. They were good kids, wonderful kids! God protect them.

She swallowed her pride and stayed where she was, ignoring the drunken fights that happened near the first of each month after the checks in the mail had arrived, ignoring the comments and stares of the locals. Perhaps they might change some day, God be willing. Then they could all live as God had intended in peace and with love, and see her for what she was: a daughter of God.

On Sundays, she walked to the Catholic church with the children because the bus did not run by there, a far walk with two children at such an early hour. She would kneel, wishing the mass was still in Latin. Somehow she understood that better than the English they used, or perhaps it was that it was the feeling she missed, the chants that went from the priest to the choir and back, stately feeling of the high Mass and the strong smell of incense that had upset her stomach in the days when they had to fast before communion. All that was done now, and some even went to church on Saturday evening so they could sleep late the next day. Not Ada. Each Sunday, she prayed to the Virgin to deliver her from evil, and especially her children, and for the souls of those who snubbed her. Thefts were becoming more common lately—small things— and Ada had spent a good day's pay to buy strong locks for her doors and windows. So many of the things she had fled seemed to follow her. Perhaps these things could not be avoided.

She had the day off and a long list of things to do. It was difficult to live here without a car, tying her to the buses and their routes. She had laundry and cleaning to do and an afternoon trip to the grocery—where was one to get good Spanish food?—and that made the loud music from the apartment on the end all the more annoying. No relaxation that day for her. All morning, she heard the teen howling to the records. The noise only got louder as one or two of the braver neighbors pounded on the door and shouted, "TURN! IT! DOWN!"

It was useless. The smell of smoke and the noise continued, and everyone knew better than to call the police. The last person who had done that had the tires of his car slashed and paint dumped on it—thousands of dollars damage to a car that was only worth hundreds, on paper he said, although it was his only way to work.

Mercifully, the noise ended abruptly just after noon, and she saw the ruffian leaving. He wore torn jeans, a dirty white sweatshirt, and a hat over his face although it was eighty degrees out. He was laughing and swearing, singing bits of the filthy music he was always playing as he staggered up the walkway. She made the sign of the cross. God deliver them all, she prayed.

She was glad for the sudden quiet—all quiet except the muffled din of the earthmovers. She was just getting ready to go to the grocery when she heard a scream from outside and the sound of footsteps running up the walkway towards her front door, which she thrust open just in time to see a young boy run past her, wild-eyed and out of breath, pleading "Hide me! Hide me!" She grabbed him and tossed him into her bedroom, not before she had thrown the bolts home in the door and all the windows.

Through the crack in her curtain she could see the beast pacing back and forth like an animal, bleeding from his cheek and lip. Ada recognized ugly nail-marks! She made the sign of the cross and tried to say an Ave Maria, but she lost track of where she was and had to be content to simply cross herself again. Madre Mia, she had no phone to call for help. Who would she call anyhow?

Outside, the beast was shouting vile obscenities. He was not drunk, Ada realized. Drugs? Very strong ones, it seemed. Now he was peering into windows, scanning the stoops to see if any trace or track of the boy was there.

He had been muddy, and the door might be marked. She crept into the back bedroom. Empty!

"Chico! Psst!" she whispered. A dirty face peered out from underneath the bed. They could both hear him out there, the walls were so thin. Ada looked at the boy.

"You are the son of the guitar player," Ada said softly, to sooth him. "He is very good. I listen to him when he played at the inn, and I was living upstairs. I used to listen in the evening, when the stars were out and the air was smooth and warm. The heart of the music. It had such a big heart! It is not like the zuls and drums I have grown up with, but I feel know these songs," Ada whispered, trying to cover the sound of screaming outside.

"Who are *you*?" the boy said, hissing. She ignored the tough-guy act. Pah! Big men acted bad, and the little men wanted to be bad also.

"I'm your neighbor. Can you tell me what happened? Why is that, that bad man chasing you? Did you break something of his? Get him mad?"

"You talk funny. I dint do nothing. I was out in the woods, and he come after me. Grabbed me. He had his wiener out, and he was grabbin' me, and," he cried. The sobs flowed forth, too loudly!

"Shh! Shhhh! He'll hear," Ada said. But she spoke too late. He had heard. Or perhaps it was just chance that made him start pounding on her door, screaming at the top of his lungs. Suddenly they heard the sound of breaking glass.

"We got to get out of here!" the boy said.

"We go out the back window. Quiet! Quiet! Here," she said, and the next minute they were running, afraid to look back. Ada followed the boy. The road was on the front side of the building, and they might be seen. He quickly ran into a small gully behind the building, a thin river of muddy water trickling at the bottom, then shimmied into the culvert that led underneath the road. Madre Mia! She hated tight spaces ever since the truck ride back in Texas from Mexico with the heat, the quiet groans and the stench of the people packed so closely she could feel every bone and fleshy part of those nearest her, so demeaning! Thank the Lord she had been on that one instead of the one that followed. All but five souls dead when the driver thought he spotted an INS checkpoint, had pulled onto the chaparral and had left them all to cook to death somewhere near Brownsville. Ada gagged at the thought,

"Come on. Come ON!" the boy hissed, and she took a deep breath and followed. The corrugated pipe was rough against her knees, and the mud, sticks and gravel ripped through her pants legs. The sound of their labored breathing and movement was amplified in the pipe until she was certain a deaf man could hear them. He would find them and they would be trapped like dogs. She stopped for a moment. The boy was a silhouette ahead of her in the round light that was the end of the pipe, pausing also to listen. Above them, she could hear the muffled screaming. It did not seem very close. Then the boy disappeared, and Ada scurried out as well. They came out on the other side of the road in a small ravine she hadn't even noticed, running as if el diablo was at their heels and realizing that behind them there was now a sudden silence. What was he doing? Was he in her home? Where would she go now? And what of Rico and Angelina? They would soon be getting off the bus, walking home, laughing about the day at school and opening the door.

33

≈ Chapter Thirty-Three ≈

For Sue, the day began like any other, but when the school called again, her shoulders slumped. What now?

"We're very sorry to bother you, Mrs. Dalton, but Jesse left the school grounds just a few minutes ago, and we thought you should know. We took the liberty of calling the police as well."

"The *police?* What the *hell* were you thinking? What *happened* there, anyway?"

"Mrs. Dalton, of course you're upset, but let me assure you we are as concerned as you are about this pattern of behavior."

"Pattern of *behavior?* Just whose behavior are we talking about here? Those lame-brained monitors you hire? I want to know what *happened!*"

"There was an altercation with the lunch lady, and Jesse bolted out the back door."

"He'll come home. He always does," Sue said, tears welling in her eyes. She knew it was rude, but she couldn't talk anymore. She hung the phone up gently, as if it was an act of kindness.

She was pissed when the cruiser showed up, more upset when she remembered that it was not going to be Hildebrandt, and finally incensed with herself for failing to control the tears.

The cop was grilling her like she was guilty of something, asking about fights she might have had with Jesse, if he had been on-line at all, if she had hired anybody out to do work, where he might be going, and what about the last time he didn't show up and *she* had called for their help to find him? Sue sobbed out her answers as anger and fear grew like two twisted flowers in her heart. She finally willed the anger to overshadow the fear, sniffed one last time and asked what the cops intended to do to help her.

"That is your job, isn't it? To *help?*"

Sue was almost relieved to hear him say that they had dispatched some men to check the area around the school and towards the mountain although Sue doubted Jesse was heading far away. More likely he was trying to find a place to hide until he could calm down about whatever it was that made him mad enough to bolt.

For the next half-hour, Sue endured the questions, the insinuations from this little worm—who asked no fewer than four times where Chat was—and if she had noticed anything unusual about the relationship between her husband and her son.

"Just what the *hell* are you implying, Mister?"

The cop said nothing to that, merely shrugged his shoulders and offered a smug smile that made Sue want to choke him to death.

She held her mad long enough to get through the last of his questions. What was Jesse wearing? How tall was he? Any friend's houses nearby? And as he got back into the cruiser and drove down the drive, Sue went back inside and finally let herself go, screaming and sobbing and throwing whatever came to hand—pots, plates, chairs—until she collapsed on the sofa whimpering. Her child was gone! *Oh, God,* she pleaded, *don't let him be hurt! Don't let him be hurt or I will never believe in you again for one instant!*

Ada was numb. In shock, she followed the boy through the woods, and they approached the boy's house a few minutes later. Jesse began shouting, and a woman ran out of the neat little house, grabbed the boy and stroked his hair, rocking slightly. She riveted Ada with her gaze, nostrils flared—she was mad!—as the boy buried his head in her belly.

"What have you done? What have you *done!*" the woman screamed.

Ada found herself angry. She had delivered the child, as was right and just, and now her own children were in danger. Suddenly, Ada remembered what Paco had told her about the green cards. They looked okay, he told her. He loved the American ways of saying things. "Okay!" he would say, or "Damn right!" Now, with the woman screaming at Ada, she remembered what Paco had told her time and time again.

"Don't get involved with the policia, not ever!" And now she was going to be involved. She resorted to an old trick, when the English she heard was not what she wished or deserved.

"No hablo Ingles! No comprendo! Via con Dios!"

Then she sprinted down the path back into the woods as she had as a child in the Andes, her heart heaving with worry, back to protect her own. The boy was "okay," and so there was no need to trouble La Senora. She knew she could not remain where she was. The foul pestilence of her neighbor was too dangerous. *One day*, Ada thought as she slowed to a jog and began to weep, *he will kill. Can I go to my savior, knowing and not saying?*

There was no Spanish priest to speak with her, only Anglos, and they would never understand. She rubbed her cheeks raw with her sleeve trying to get the mud off and crawled up the embankment to the level of the parking lot, pausing before she rose, watching the front of her home. There her window was, broken out, the curtains licking outwards in the faint summer breeze, but there was dead quiet. No sound came from her apartment, no vile sounds of murderous music swelled from his, and between them, no door or window opened. The neighbors were all too scared to go out just now, out in the country where it was supposed to be safe. Her neighbors did not understand the way Ada did. Many of them had been born here, and they thought that danger was always in a crowded city, never in the country.

She remembered the death squads and the sounds they made as they approached a village. That was a good night when they could hear and see them all at once. But they seldom did their work with a noise and a shout. It was the quiet nights when, one after another, they had all retired, only to awaken to the news that Condalita's man had been kidnapped, and they would all go to their homes to begin grinding the grain that would sustain them all while they mourned for a man whose body would never be found.

Who to call? And how long might it take for them to get there?

In the country, time was sometimes all a person had. She took that time and she jumped up and dashed to the wall nearest the door she had to open, just as Paco had taught her when they had been caught in the trouble in Bogotá. She pressed herself to the wall, watched the face of a driver looking at her as his car went past, saw the look of disdain on his ignorant face, red with drink and being in the sun stupidly, saw him spit out the window and laugh to himself, and even while she watched this all, and his taillights disappearing up towards the boy's home, she still listened deeply.

No sound. She pushed on the front door, and it swung open. Ada ducked back to the wall, ready to run, but still she heard nothing. But Ada did not go in. She would wait on the one bench they had been given, sitting there out near the bus stop, and she would wait for her children and take them all somewhere safe, until they could find their way.

Today—Thank the Saints!—Rico was to come straight home to get ready for a dance, and Angelina would be home soon as well. It would not get dark soon enough for Ada. There was her home and here she was covered in filth. She could not sit here, covered with dirt, and greet her neighbors.

Ada prayed to every saint and stood, walked back to her home and entered it as God intended, walked through every room, seeing the destruction, ignored it all, and went into the shower and cleaned herself. Deliberately she dressed in her traveling suit, found the luggage, and packed it all with whatever she could find of her things and the things of her children. Madre Mia! Where had the two gotten all these things? Trophies, plaques, stacks of cards—they must go now! She walked, sore and burdened with her luggage, back up to the bench to wait for her children and to try to begin again.

She avoided the mud-stained half of the bench she had been sitting in just a blink of time away and waited for her children, always looking back at the building behind her to make sure there was no movement and no life.

Sue could not move from the spot for a moment, watching the receding figure of the woman who looked vaguely familiar, and she watched the path into the woods long after there was nothing further to be seen, watched until Jesse's tears had changed to muffled squirming bleats of indignation.

"You're squeezing me too tight!"

She let him go, and he flew into the house and up the stairs. She could hear he was crying again, then heard the slam of his bedroom door.

Chat was somewhere in Maryland with no cell phone, no way to get in touch with him at all until Sunday night, not unless he called, and he had mostly stopped doing that. Neither of them could stand the long awkward pauses and the hints of guilt and blame. How could there be so much of that for both of them?

She walked back inside, slowly mounted the stairs, and pushed his door open. Jesse was in a heap on the bed, covers over his head, still sobbing quietly.

"Jesse, hon. You're home. You're safe. It's going to be all right. You don't even have to tell me anything. You're going to be fine. Everything is going to be fine."

She hadn't even convinced herself. From deep within the mound of blankets she heard Jesse's response.

"He knows where we live, mom. The bad man."

"What bad man, hon? Can you tell me what happened?" Can you be a big boy and tell me?"

"He grabbed me. He had his wiener out. I got away, and I ran as fast as I could. I ran towards here, and then he saw the house, and he was hollering about how I couldn't hide here, how he was going to come back here. I thought you'd hear him, and I was hoping you would come out with the twelve gauge and kill him. Then I ran over the hill and I went down to where they're putting up the buildings and I was screaming and he was chasing me, and I got around the building. This lady let me in and then he was pounding on her door and we ran again, back towards here. I know it was a wrong thing to run away from school but the lunch lady made me throw my lunch away and I got mad. I'm sorry, Mom. Sorry. He's going to come back here, Mommy. We can't stay here. We've got to get away from here."

Sue knew that he was right.

"Hon, I'll call the police. They're out looking for you right now, so we better let them know you're okay, huh?"

"They gonna let me ride in the car, mom?"

Sue smiled through glimmering tears.

"I bet they will, hon," she said.

Hold up! she thought. *Be strong!*

But when the cops came back and heard what Jesse had to say, they bundled both of them in the cruiser and brought them both immediately to the hospital at Fiesterville, where a screaming Jesse was brought in for examination despite Sue's protests. The doc came out—a very tall woman, thank God—and tried to comfort Sue. *Just because he said nothing happened didn't mean he was telling the truth,* she told Sue. It was common for rape victims to make up stories about what had happened or didn't happen, so they could handle it, especially youngsters like Jesse.

Sue only heard the one word she had said, and it wasn't until the doc gently shook her arm and asked her about Meg that Sue realized she didn't have the luxury of falling apart right now. Sue had to get Megan from school, and while she thought of what she had to do, she was trying to place the woman. Suddenly it clicked: she had been staying at Layton's. Sue remembered his talk when she had moved. She called Thelma, asked her to pick Meg up after school, telling her that she would go on up there after they were done here. The Sexual Abuse Response Team said before they began that they would be wrapping up in an hour or so, and Jesse would only have to tell his story once to the docs and the DA and cops, instead of the three times it used to take.

Sue shuddered at the thought of telling anything like that even once.

Instinctively, she decided to keep this to herself if it were humanly possible. Old lady Atbie would be pleased as punch to discuss the fall of the Daltons and the reasons thereof, and Sue intended to deny her the pleasure, at least for a time. Until at least Chat got back.

She thought, *I can't do this alone.*

The sun was going down when Jesse finally left the hospital room where he had been examined, and the doc called her over to let her know they would be releasing him in a few minutes, but not before Sue overheard the cop saying to the DA that it all sounded like the kid was just trying to get back at his old man for not being around or maybe just trying to get out of trouble for bolting from school like that.

The doc rolled her eyes.

"I miss Hildebrant," she said, and Sue couldn't help but agree.

"That cop is a jerk. If I find out any of this is real—why would he doubt it, with that woman with him and all?—I swear I'll have his badge!" Sue said, near tears.

"I understand what you're saying," the doc offered, patting her on the arm, but then she said, "Maybe right now you'll want to just take care of Jesse. I believe him, and so does the DA. And you'll need to take care of yourself. Here's the number of Women's Resources, if you like."

"Women's Resources? Jesse isn't a woman," Sue said, her voice tailing off.

"They've had plenty of experience counseling folks, though. But, if you're not comfortable with them, here's the card of a child psychologist. He's pretty good, too. And you'll need to think about someone you can talk with yourself, you and your husband."

"Maybe this same guy? If Chat wants to," Sue said, then thanked the doc for her time and kindness. Would a man be so patient? She thinks, *I sure don't think so, not right now.*

Then Jesse was flying out the door and into her arms, and she was saying, "Shh. It's going to be fine. We'll take the car and go get Meg, and we'll go out to dinner. Not to Ellie's, we'll go to Fiesterville. We can eat at the cheesey chip place, and you can have all the soda you want, hon. Shhh. It's going to be okay."

Although how it would all turn out okay was, like the ways of God, a mystery.

34

⇒ CHAPTER THIRTY-FOUR ⇐

Layton sat idly by the front door in the late afternoon, with his chair propped up against the worn wooden siding, watching the occasional car slowing on the turn and then accelerating out towards the highway. He felt the chill of the evening and noticed the first hints of color on the leaves, seeing the rank growth of jewelweed and nightshade in the planters she had put there, and hearing very little but the sporadic chirp of a cricket near his feet. He had read somewhere that the Chinese kept crickets for good luck in some places, and in others, that they were fighters and could make a man a lot of money. It was too cold for katydids now, a good time of day to catch grasshoppers for trout fishing. He had learned to put them in a mason jar with a nylon stocking tugged over the top when he was a kid, like the man in that Hemingway story, "Big Two-Hearted River." Rose had always liked a fresh trout cooked on the charcoal with a little butter and some salt and pepper.

Layton blinked into the setting sun, now touching the treetops at the top of the hill, and saw the woman walking down towards him, away up on the hill. She had her children behind her, all three loaded down with luggage and backpacks. It would be a few minutes before they reached the inn. In his mind, Layton felt a little glimmer, a thrill of anger and revenge, and then he shook his head, got up and began to weed out the planter nearest the doorway.

Marge Atbie was the first to hear the news on the scanner, two bits of news, really. First, Dalton's wild child had run off from school, but that turned out to be nothing, she guessed, because then she heard the call canceled a little while later. Then, a youngster had been *abducted* from his home near town, new people from the city that had left them *latch-keyed*, and of course she had her thoughts about all of that. The world was going to the dogs, with all those perverts and pedophiles and people with that damned accent, though their money was green and the past year had been a good one for her and Marve. She couldn't *wait* to phone him up to see what he had heard.

"I heard the mother—you know her, the one that's always going on at the school board meetings about mold in the schools and all that trash? I heard her on the radio, crying and begging for information, and there's a big offer, a reward. I think she said ten thousand. It was ten thousand, I think, or twenty? Anyhow, she should be ashamed of herself, leaving a twelve-year-old alone like that," Madge told Marve.

He said, "I heard they was both home at the time and asleep when that all happened. Heard it from the Scobles that live down near there."

"Something wrong there, *I* say. A man just walks into your house like that? I bet it was somebody they knew, or the kid just ran away, probably, the way kids are these days. Say, did you hear that the Dodson girl is pregnant?"

"No! The father?"

"They say it's some nigger from the city."

Madge heard Marve snort in disgust, and heard a crinkling sound up close to the receiver.

Marve said, "What is the world coming to? Decent folks can't feel safe in their own homes with all that trash coming in with their airs, and you can't even keep track of 'em there's so many new ones. So I heard from Charlie up at the station house that they're treating this like the real thing, fishy as it sounds."

"Twenty thousand dollars? That's a lot of money. What are you eating there?"

"Oh, jus' open a bag of chips," Marve said, chewing. "Just like OJ, id'nit? Good way to throw off the scent. I bet there was insurance money. You mark my words, Madge. There's something fishy going on here. More than they told on the radio."

"TV will be all full of it by suppertime. That poor boy is dead, sure as shooting. They always are."

"What about that Smart girl? She was okay," Madge said.

"One in a million. And that lightning already struck. Oh, wait. I got a call coming in, Madge. I'll call ya back."

It was going to be a busy afternoon. She was glad she was off work. Things like this just didn't happen everyday.

Chat almost forgot his troubles, driving up to the Beacon Theatre, the last stop on this road trip. He had a glimmer of an idea to call home, but he squashed the thought. Nothing he could say on the phone was as good as what he could do in person, and their last job had been canceled, so he would be coming back tomorrow anyway, two days early.

They took the George Washington Bridge to the Henry Hudson just at dusk, with the evening traffic heavy. On their right, the Hudson river was choppy and leaden in the failing light, small whitecaps foaming and driven under a hard north wind, banks of cumulous clouds almost obscuring the setting sun until they parted just enough to let radiant beams of golden light cascade outwards from a notch at the top of one of the clouds. The water in one slant spot became iridescent and alive, and the cloud above, with the bright notch in the middle and two symmetric wings of light above the dark gray clouds, was the Paraclete descending on them all.

The beauty in that cityscape was a surprise to Chat, and the number of cars on the streets was a surprise too, at least to Chat. He was glad of Jo-Jo's offer to drive, as the big Suburban dodged taxis, slammed over metal plates and changed lanes like bumper-cars. Ill kempt, bearded men with stained pants and seven layers of coats stood on curbs hollering at the cars, and gorgeous women with thousand dollar coats—ten thousand dollar coats? What did he know?—strolled confidently across streets that seemed like certain death to Chat.

"How the blazes do you know where you're *going?*" Chat asked Jo-Jo. Whether on purpose or because he didn't hear, Jo-Jo said nothing, gripping the wheel and horsing the vehicle around stopped delivery trucks, off-duty cabs, piles of dirt and orange cones, or a cop car with lights flashing in front of small knots of people.

They arrived in plenty of time, and there on the marquee, right below Ralph's, which was below Allison's, was their name: The Cold Spring Band!

Hundreds of people stood around the entrance, waiting for the doors to open. They parked by the stage doors—it would cost them twenty bucks to park anywhere else—and unloaded instruments and a few soft coolers with water and sandwiches, just in case the hospitality people were negligent. "Put some beer in there," Jo-Jo had complained, but this time Chat was adamant. No drinking before this show, not one beer after Jo-Jo blew the ending of El Comenchero last week, buddy.

They collected their neck tags and guest passes, and wandered up a set of stairs to the ballroom that was set for a thousand listeners.

"Damn. Lookit this!" Jo-Jo had called, and, sure enough, they had all peeked through the curtains like little kids. Even empty, the auditorium was impressive: rounded shoulders where the walls met the ceiling, valence lighting all around, and Georgian scrollwork covering the chair rails that ran the length of the deep golden wooden wainscoting. The soundmen were still wringing out the system, with the tech watching banks of lights and LED displays, where the sound was reduced to a code on a machine. He twisted the knobs and slid the faders against the high squeal of feedback.

"4K spike there. Yeah, turn it up. Now 1.2, right, right," he said to his counterpart on stage until the feedback disappeared, and then resolved into a higher squeal.

They got the instruments into the warm-up room. It was set up nicely, with a big cooler full of water, soda and iced tea; a few bowls of fruit and another couple bowls of chips; and finger sandwiches of tuna, beef, turkey and—Johnny was happy to note—PB&J, too. They opened the cases, letting the instruments warm up a bit, and Chat peeked outside to the band parking area. No sign of Ralph's bus yet, but they were two hours early, thinking to run over some tunes with Sue, who had agreed to meet them there. She was coming up from someplace in Kentucky, because the promoters of the concert were insistent—the same personnel as on the album, no substitutions.

"I wonder if they say that crap to Ralph or Del. 'No substitutions!'" Jo-Jo had groused, and Chat was amused to hear Sterling explain it all, as if it were the most reasonable thing in the world.

"They have to market us, you know. Brand recognition. Nobody cares who plays with Del, well maybe except Ronnie. They know he's gonna be packing big guns. But us? Well, they just want to make sure."

"You're a regular Henry Clay, you know that? She was a pain in the ass to work with on that record, far as I was concerned."

"Look, Jo-Jo, not our fault the Ice-Cream Man wanted harmonies on those two fiddle tunes or thought mandolin would sound good in that one slow tune. I think he was right. Which song was that?"

"The one we played so much we played it to death and none of us can stand playing it now," Johnny drawled. "More Often Than Once in Awhile."

"Hey!" It was fiddler Sue, case in hand, bags under her eyes and that faraway look she had until she started to play. Sterling, sitting and changing his strings, smiled up at her.

"Sue. How was the ride up?" Chat said.

"Fine, this time. Muffler wants to fall off, but other than that, fine." She stood there, passive and watching.

"Glad you're here."

"Thanks for asking me."

She was one of the few Chat could not chat up, but still, she had come.

"So let's run a few tunes, and then we can take a break and eat some before the show." Chat suggested.

"You won't mind if I pop out and get some calamari, right?" Jo-Jo said, but Chat just ignored that and got the 28 out. He tuned it perfectly, strumming out "Rain and Snow" while he waited for the rest to get ready. They were below stage here, and they could here the footsteps of the techs, and then the sound of voices. They were letting the people in, and it would soon be showtime, to play before a crowd who loved bluegrass the way they loved it and who weren't afraid to plunk some serious cash down to just listen.

Although she said little, Sue had a good long bow and a good ear, too—she was an animal on the fiddle!—and they ran through the set, just the beginnings and endings of the vocals where she played back-ups, the whole tune where she had breaks with Jo-Jo on the twin fiddles. How the notes soared, there in the little room under the stage, with the world impatient above them! Chat listened where Jo-Jo was to take the mandolin breaks. They were simple, Monroe-style with the heavy right hand on the downbeat at one point or the more elegant, melodic runs akin to Sam's at another.

They ran the whole "Big Mon" down without a hitch, and Chat said that he thought they were ready. After a few moments of munching chips and sandwiches, a young girl with elfin bangs and jeans with holes in the knees, red sneakers and a tie-dyed t-shirt came bouncing in and told them, "Five minutes." It seemed mere seconds before they were walking out on stage, to the last strains of the words, "Ladies and Gentleman, fans of bluegrass and lovers of Old-timey music. Please welcome to the stage, The...Cold... Spring...Band!"

All the lights washed away the audience that they could hear but not see, screaming and clapping. One or two of them hollered out the names of the originals on the CD: "Blue Dawn," one man shouted, and another woman countered with "Play the Pigeon Forge Rag!" They launched into "Blue Moon of Kentucky." The notes were all crisp and swirling around each other, and even the girl was smiling a little as they got the first thing exactly right, which meant that it was only going to get better as they went.

That trip was perhaps a bridge too far, Chat thought when he returned. Sue was gone with no hint where she had gone, and that was a slap in Chat's face, all right. No note, nothing, and the mail all piled in the mailbox, two days worth of it, like she had just driven off on the spur of the moment.

He considered it. Perhaps there was a logical explanation. He was back a day early, after all, and maybe she had gone off to visit her sister down in Carlyle, although they weren't what you'd call close.

He stomped inside, legs aching from sitting too long, and the tin taste of the road in his mouth. He cracked a beer—he was drinking regular now— and began to go through the piles of mail. He found mostly bills. Younts wanted another five grand, and he grimaced when he opened the some tax bills—taxes were up another four mills. That made the tag on his property seven hundred more than it had been last year, and him with exactly no money left in the bank. Then the one from Freedom First, a bulky piece that took several minutes to decode.

Even then he wasn't sure he understood what he was reading, and he called Chooney up immediately to get his read on it.

"Meet me down at Ellie's, and bring that with you, lemme see what's what. And bring a copy of the mortgage, too, can ya?"

"Sure thing," Chat said. Ten minutes later was sipping coffee and looking at Chooney hopefully.

"There's no doubt. They sold the mortgage two weeks ago, and this is all legal."

"Sold it? Sold it to *who*? And what difference does it make, anyhow, who I pay?"

"Maybe none. Maybe you get some outfit that's all a bunch of pricks, too. And this also says that the mortgage was in arrears. That's why they sold it."

"Arrears? Well, maybe I missed last month's payment by a few days, but Lordy, they're lucky I can pay it at all, and Younts has continued this thing twice already, saying he needs more time. I think he's just playing me, is all."

"You miss again and they take the Meadows, Chat."

"What? What did you say?"

"You're not hard of hearing, are you? You really should have talked to me before you signed this note, Chat. It all but gives them your firstborn, here."

"I miss one more and they take the Meadows? How in the hell is that supposed to work?"

"It's all here, Chat. I'm sorry, buddy, but maybe you can get this note paid off, although it looks like there's a pre-payment penalty, too." He shook his head slowly and said, "Whatever you do, make that payment early. I can lend you a few bucks if you need it."

Chat tried smiling, but failed. He shook his head.

"Thanks, Chooney. I'll be fine. Something'll come up. It always does."

When Chat finally returned to the house, he figured that now was the time to take that short walk to see what Malchio had gotten around to doing down below the place. He thought he was ready for the worst, but once glance told him he could never truly have prepared himself for what he saw.

Chat had been avoiding the neighborhood in the interim; he didn't want to be reminded of the injustice of it all. He did what he always did when confronted with unpleasantness: he turned, not his other cheek, but his whole head around so he didn't have to see it.

That made what confronted him all the more stupefying. The entire lovely field and the quiet stream that had always been almost a part of his kitchen, his home, and his life were all gone. Hell, this was only a few hundred yards down from his piece. The part nearest the property line had been 'dozed. Not a tree nor a blade of grass was left; all Chat saw was a hundred acres of mud, pickup trucks spinning wheels and workers milling all over the place. Instead of birdsong and rippling waters, all he heard was the clang of pipes and ladders and the roar of generators and graders.

Half a dozen foundations were already in, and surveyors with transits were shooting elevations. Roads of crusher-run ran through the place that had been a field where he could always count on pushing out a pheasant or rabbit in the season. They ran through the swale that had been covered in wild grapes—a sure-fire place to kick out grouse or woodcock; they arched around the knoll that had the nicest stand of white oak for a mile in any direction and a sunny south face to it. That made it a spot the deer favored in the late fall and early winter.

Chat could see one of his tree stands at the very edge of his land, now overlooking a scene of carnage and destruction, a sad and empty sentinel that had not saved a thing. Thick rivulets of muddy water ran down to a holding basin that was already overflowing into the small creek that led to the Sambo, and gullies three-feet deep were scribed into some of the steeper slopes, as if land and the topsoil on it were a cheap commodity. Well, they would never grow anything here again, that was for sure.

He eyed the scene closely, shaking. He blinked four or five times as if to clear his eyes. Nothing changed. Chat could see Malchio's work trailer. Inside Chat imagined a drafting table covered with blueprints, a desk and phone, a coffeepot and two or three filing cabinets, a couple of cardboard boxes full of stakes or white PVC fittings for the drains and sewer lines, and some mud on the floor and smeared on the wall closest to the door.

Next to it was the temporary electric service with a pole that hadn't been upright, ever. On the outside, he could see the stamped metal steps leading to the door with a building permit taped fast to it, a cracked pane of window glass, the trailer itself jacked up off the ground at one end a good five feet, leaving one end sticking out into the air like it would tumble down at the slightest wind. Nearer the road and Chat's house, two buildings had been built, and a parking lot covered the ground where Jesse had shot his first squirrel.

The scene looked like a shot of the Martian landscape, which kept Chat from realizing the size of the buildings right off. Good Lord, they must have been a hundred feet long, and each one had five front doors on each side.

Twenty units, just in those two! He counted, three, four, eight, ten! Ten of them! What in the world would Malchio do with 200 units? That was more units then anyone had in the whole county, Chat thought.

Chat felt sick to his stomach. On the side lot line, they had planted arbor vitae, one every three feet, maybe four feet high. At the rate they grew, it would be ten years before they shielded anything. Ten years. He felt like he would never last that long.

He knew it was wrong, and weak, and a sin against God, but he finally wandered back up the hill to his place and sat down on his back door stoop, out where the light from his kitchen had once lit a warm yellow rectangle of hope in the greening lawn. He sat there and considered his life, the suddenly almost-famous Cold Spring Band, Homer sick, Jo-Jo acting strange and cranky, Younts spending money like there was no tomorrow, and Sue being brave and strong. He suddenly feared that she didn't really love him, perhaps, and the carnage he saw was all too much. He began to cry, great racking sobs, moaning and keening, tears a grateful interruption of his vision. He'd seen enough. What was that Jackson Brown song about seeing too much?

Chat had arrived at noon, wept through the lunch hour—if the workers saw him, they gave no inclination—and was still sitting there at dusk, as the fog rolled in and softened the harsh outlines of the place. Headlights made an eerie glow like aliens landing from behind the hills as, one by one, the pick-ups left and the sudden silence boomed in his ears like a tidal wave of despair.

35

≡ Chapter Thirty-Five ≡

Sue found Chat on the porch, long after dark, bent over now and utterly still—how could things get any worse?—and when he looked into her eyes, saw that there was another human there, another soul tortured and tormented, one who had been ill at ease with the world these last ten or twenty years, and here he was just glad-handing it all over the place without the slightest clue. He steeled himself for the moment in which she would say that she needed to tell him something that he did not want to hear, that she was going away and it was all a dream, all over.

Maybe he got it now. Just a little whiff of the stink of wet clay and diesel brought it all back: the complete possibility of the army-issue john boat that had ferried him and Homer over 27 islands, the fifty miles they walked, the stink of it all and the silence that had descended on him afterwards.

For almost a year, Chat had not been able to hear a word, a sound: the chirp of a bird, the swish of tires on a wet pavement, rattle of halyard on the flagpole in an empty schoolyard, mew of a cat or the barking of the next neighbor's dog. He couldn't hear the heart-stopping flight of a grouse flushed when the leaves were aflame and the world was a study in the possibilities of gorgeous color, or the equally manic, catatonic sound of whitetails in the November woods. No noise of the swish and murmur of the canoe paddle in the morning quiet, or the eerie sound of geese on a foggy spring night, the fog like velvet on eager skin, the sound of snow in the deep woods, or the crash and roar of thunder, the skies a belching flame of light and noise. Not even the very small sound of a child's wonder, or the larger one of his satisfaction.

None of these sounds had penetrated the silent gloom of Chat's mind in that time. He had to imagine the grinding scrape of the road plow and the shouts and hollers of the ball game. He had filled in the riffs of Homer's guitar that rang and rang in silence for the year that followed Dutch and Madge's death—had he ever really said those words? The church ladies wanted to have a memorial service, but even then, Homer wasn't having any of that.

"You bury bodies," he had said.

Then he sang, "I...I...I...I...I ain't got no bodies."

And laughed.

When Chat saw Sue, really saw her for the first time, she had put that Martin in his hands at Jo-Jo's first big barn party, and he had just blinked. That was pretty much what he had been doing for the last year, anyway— deaf as a post and nobody even knew it. Chat could talk, and he did that sparingly, using nods and laughs instead of words to get along. Sue was the only one who ever suspected that the 8-track was all a ruse. She was the only one that had ever called Chat on it, and of course, he had no choice but to begin again to hear.

Maybe because he had been making up the sounds in his head that whole time, Chat began to hear songs, just like he was listening to the radio, except *he* was the radio. So when Sue found him there, soaked to the skin in the fog and the mist of late afternoon, she could not know he was listening to a new song, a straight-ahead bluegrass song, key of G, with a lopey kind of rhythm that began in the chorus and then told the story:

No more deer,
No leaping spring
Happy voices no longer ring
No strength of mind, or force of will
Can mend this land, nor comfort bring.

Oh, the sight, that crushed the man!
The earth is raw, a twisted land!
Tall trees broken, broke and tossed aside
If this world should fail
What can abide?

Over the land
The west wind sighs
Longing for the trees,
A lover's touch
Whis-per-ing sad-ly, o'er the rock and the clay
Where------------------ have they gone?

And then the song would hold on the G with a kind of break on the fiddle. Then a reprise after the last line and a modulation up into A. Then to the minor:

Where have they gone?
Do they abide?
Do they abide?
Please---------------don't tell me that they're gone.

And repeat that once more, after a break, and then modulate once more into B minor and reprise:

Where are the deer, the leaping spring?
Youthful voices no more will ring
No strength of mind, nor force of will
Can mend this land, nor comfort bring.

Then hold the last word in singing and resolve to the B major.

Resolve.

"Chat! Come on, we've got to get back to Homer's. Something's come up, now. Come on, honey, please," she said, tugging on his sleeve as if she was just a little girl and he was the daddy. Ironic, since he was looking at her again with the blank look that said he heard not a word of what she was saying. She felt the hairs on the nape of her neck stand up. *Now? Again?*

She slapped the palm of one hand with the other, the sign for "Let's go!" and he stood up, unsteady, looking towards the Meadows and the curve of the road that hid the nightmare Malchio had made of the piece down below. She put her forefinger below her nose as if to sneeze and rotated her hand: *the kids.* Then she stabbed her forehead with one forefinger and her stomach with the other: *sick,* the only way she could remember to tell him he needed to get his ass moving, before it was dark and the scumbag returned. All those sign classes and what she had learned were gone, as if she had never taken the trouble.

She began speaking to him as she led him back to her car.

"Lucky for you I stopped in at Ellie's and found out you were home early, and she told me you were with Chooney. What she told me didn't sound good, and I can see from the mud on your shoes you went down over the hill and saw what they did, but I don't understand why now, Chat. Because I can't get through this legal mess without you, and there's more, more."

She swept her hand, palm down, away from her mouth: *bad.*

She tried it again, difficult while she drove, grabbing Chat's arm and tugging, making the sign for kid, the sign for bad, one for sad, hands open, palms towards the face, making fake tears with a sweeping motion. Then she added a closed fist sweeping over an open palm: *help!* That was where she almost lost the wheel, the tires skidding in the loose gravel coming down Jap's Hill and Chat banging his head against the doorjamb when she pulled the car back on the road.

He put his hand out as if to shake and ticked his palm with one finger: *what,* then *you* and finally two hands grabbing towards his heart: *want?*

Sue swerved over at the bottom of the hill, fat teardrops spattering on the seat, and then turned and slapped Chat full in the face, grabbed his shirt collar and screamed at him that what she wanted was for him to stop being all about himself, so self-satisfied—how many other words with self were there?—selfish, self-absorbed, self-centered, so full of self-pride, as if he was the second coming.

Sue could not contain herself and began ranting, "Don't sit there as if I'm not here, like you can't hear, when I know damn well you can. You are just being *stubborn.* When I married you, didn't you say that there were two kinds of musicians out there, the kind that say 'Listen to *me* play this song' and the kind that say 'Listen to me play this *song?*' Here I thought you were the second kind, but I see now that that was all a lie. There's only one kind of musician. You're all slaves to the music, and you're blind to every other thing that doesn't touch on music."

She began to cry and Chat looked at her helplessly.

"This does, though, please see that, Chat. Your family needs you so bad and you have to get over this nonsense right now. All over a piece of dirt that isn't going to be worth a second of our time in ten years, the way the place is going. It's me and the kids you need to care about now."

Her voice grew quiet and she said tried to sign as she spoke, "Isn't that in all the songs, how you didn't see the orchid for the rose, how everything passes, and we need to get on with things? Please say you hear me, Chat, because Jesse won't come out of his room because of something that happened that's bad, bad, bad. And I am so pissed—angry—at you for not being there. I know that's not fair, but there it is. And didn't I beg you to stay home? Not that I'm sure that all this wouldn't have happened if you had, but I wouldn't have had to wonder about it all my days, especially if it all comes to a bad end, Chat."

Sue sputtered to silence and began again to drive, tears running down her cheeks, and Chat reached out to place his hand on her arm.

Things were different now than when he was a seventeen-year-old afraid to grieve, denied the pleasure of hearing voices, song, or the thunder of fate in the form of walls and worlds and oceans of water and mud, trees and docks, stove boats and dead cattle. Chat began making some sense of the signs and the now-faint sound of Sue's voice.

He remembered all the sessions up at the Scranton School of the Deaf that Sue had smuggled him to without anybody in Pigeon Forge being the wiser. She took him to a shrink—a nun—about four feet tall with piercing blue eyes that would not let you go and a way with words, or really, signs, and she had hypnotized him. Chat knew that his Pop would have said that it was sinful and that he was toying with the devil to take part in such pagan rituals, but Sue was a modern girl with ideas of her own. And didn't that nun poke and pry and grab Chat by the jaw, squeezing until his mouth puffed out like a fish's? Didn't she force him into the part of his mind or soul—she signed that she believed they were the same—that struck into the memory? Didn't that lead to the sound of death? Didn't that sound lead to his hearing life once again?

Reluctantly he gave up the shield and went deep into the place where the images and demons hide from the light of day and rational thought, where the monsters under the bed are as real as typhus or dysentery after a bad flood, and he saw the doors of perception opening again. He heard her lamentations: "Oh my poor people, put on sackcloth and roll in ashes, make mourning as for an only child, most bitter lamentation, for suddenly the destroyer will come upon us!"

His wailing and keening joined Sue in a song of torment, a song Chat thought they would have to sing past if they wanted to put their family back together again and pretend to be strong.

They made it back to Homer's, Sue talking rapidly to get it all out, ignoring Chat's half-formed murmurs of surprise, rage, and anger. That long string of "selfs" rang in his ears now, and he felt shame, too. What a baby. He put his hand on her arm again as if to beg for her to please stop talking for one minute. She pulled over at the next turn, put the car in park, wiped her eyes with her sleeve. Her nose was running, too—how attractive!—and they said their awkward words of regret and apology, hugging and hugging as the foggy night entombed the car, with headlights that were two cones of brilliance that illuminated nothing more than the air itself, and then they braced themselves for the return to Homer's. Sue guessed that the situation there was bound to be crazy, with her out searching for Chat all afternoon and not coming back.

"Sue," Chat said, minutes from the driveway, "I am so sorry. Really, I am. I wanted to run and hide, and I wasn't thinking about you at all, and Jesse." He trailed off, new tears in his eyes, to think on his child, alone with such evil, scarcely believing it had happened.

"Pride," he said. "That's all that was, only my most secret joyful sin. I was a fool, and if you say 'No,' I'll understand it, anyway. Is there a way for you to forgive me?"

"Maybe if you could think more of yourself and less of yourself. Let's just concentrate on Jesse now, and getting that woman to tell what she knows. She's got to know the creep; Jesse said he had dark skin, was talking half Spanish and half English. That little bastard cop wants to talk to you, too. Wants to know if you and Jesse had any fights, if he's been acting strange or different lately."

"What the hell does *that* mean? What did you tell them, then? About school and all?"

"Let them find out themselves. Hildebrandt wouldn't have let this go on the way that it has. They don't even believe it happened, I don't think, and they won't ever unless we get her to talk. Far as they're concerned, it was our fault, and Jesse is just putting one over on us, trying to get attention."

"Bastards. Sorry. Poor Jesse. If I get my hands on that son of a bitch I will kill him," Chat said, but thought, *How the mighty have fallen!*

"So. What, what are we going to do?" Chat finally asked.

"I already made a call to some guy they gave me the name of up at the hospital. No answer by the time I called. I'll try again tomorrow." They topped the hill and the headlights illuminated the front yard, Homer and Thelma on the porch, wrapped up in Indian blankets against the chill, with the two kids wearing coats and hanging out in the apple tree, munching apples and whispering somberly.

"Christ on a crutch. 'Bout time you get back! These youngsters wear me out!" Homer groused, and Thelma just slapped his hand with a loud *crack*!

"You hush. Listen to me," she said, motioning them in to make a little knot of conspirators in the damp foggy night.

"Another child has been taken, not far from Chat's place, and the parents are on the news, frantic. I turned it off before the kids heard it, but they will certainly hear it when they get back to school."

"Oh my God. Another kid. Jesus," Chat said, wide-eyed. "Car's still warm. Homer, we have to go find that lady, or the cops will be having Jesse traipsing all over the woods, looking," Chat said, his voice almost under control again.

"Wait! Wait just a goddam minute!" Homer protested. "You can't leave them here and go take off like that! You stay here and I'll go talk with that woman. I know how to deal with her kind."

"Homer. You don't know how to deal with *any* kind," Thelma said. "We want her to *talk*. You'd have her on the next boat to wherever. We'll stay, dears. You go and take care of what you need to."

"God bless you, Thelma," Chat said.

"He already has, honey. Even with this old grouch of a reprobate for a husband, he has."

36

⇒ CHAPTER THIRTY-SIX ⇐

Layton had half a mind to tell the woman to go jump in the creek. What did she think, that she could just go and leave him in the lurch like that, then come back nice as she pleased? But the children came too, both looking somber. Something bad had happened, Layton could tell. The boy was saying, "Hello, Mr. Renfroe. How have you been?"

The little girl, who had gotten used to him before, suddenly was shy again, and hid behind the woman and all that luggage. Ada put her bag down, turned to the boy and said something in Spanish, and he took the little one by the hand and walked away, towards the horseshoe pits down by the stream.

"Please, Mr. Renfroe. If you say no, I have to leave this place, but I beg you for the apartment again. For the children. They are doing so good in school now."

She hasn't even put her suitcase down, Layton thought. *She expects me to say, "No".*

"So you can run out again? Get me used to all this cleaning and tidying and then just take off like that?" Layton said, defensively.

"Please. I'm sorry. I try to make a better life for my children. They say the apartments will be cheap and nice, but there are animals living there, cruel people. I, I cannot tell you all the things that bring me here. If you do this thing, God will bless you. I will pray for you every day, clean, I will do what I must do," she said, defiant.

He looked at her. She was keen, her hands competent, her dark hair lustrous, her eyes soulful and honest. Her head was bowed, ready for him to send her away, to deny her. *It's your pride and your humanity having a wrestling match,* he thought, *and I don't know who's going to win this one.* Even before he could force himself to gently tell her it could not happen, that life was too hard to get used to someone only to have them leave, he saw Chat and Sue blasting down the hill, skidding to a halt in front of the inn.

Sue jumped out of the truck and grabbed the woman, pleading with her to tell them something, something that must have been damned important, judging from the blanched look of fear and pain on all three of their faces.

"What the Sam Hill is going on here?" Layton demanded.

"There's been another boy taken," Sue told the woman. "You have to tell the police what you know. Soon. Right now! Please, ma'am, please."

"Another boy? *What* boys? Sue, Jesse is all right, isn't he? Tell me he is! Somebody tell me what the blazes is going on here!" Layton said.

"Another boy? Madre de Dios, " Ada said softly. "Senora, please! I cannot go to the police. My papers, they are not in order. They will send me back, after all these years. The death squads. Please, senora. Your children are safe. I will tell you who it was, with your son, but not the policia. For my children, please."

"Ma'am? Search your soul. You know you have to do this thing. We'll all do whatever we can to help you. The papers will write about your bravery. Maybe we can get the congressman to do something. But right now, time is running out," Chat said, equally quiet.

They heard the sound of a vehicle approaching, a big old blue Buick trailing light wisps of purple smoke. Getting out of the car, Katie knew something was very wrong, but when Layton told her to go ahead and get the place opened, she'd know about it when it was time, she stifled her questions. *Further along,* she reminded herself and left them.

"Ada. Put your stuff upstairs and let me get the cops," Layton said, suddenly firm with her, and she called to the children.

Even before Kate had the bar open, three cop cars rushed in, one of them the same nasty little cop that had tagged Chat, the one that had grilled Sue and Jesse like they were the criminals. It was all Chat could do to keep from grabbing him, even in the midst of all of the regulars. They were now beginning to show up, curious, deferential.

Ada walked down the steps as if to her execution, marched up to the largest cop there and began to speak, still very softly. The cops wrote furiously, as one grabbed a radio from the nearby cruiser, barking numbers and orders. Just like that Ada was guided over to the car, with Layton saying not to worry about a thing. He would get the kids dinner, and she'd be back before she knew it. With one look at him she told him she knew that was a lie and thanked him for caring enough to tell it.

Jo-Jo's arms and legs felt numb and useless, as they had all day. Finally, after lunch, he put Tony in charge of the crew, framing a new CVS out on the Dark Horse Pike, telling him that he had some stuff to take care of in town.

"Losing your stuff there, boss?" Tony had ribbed him, but Jo-Jo nailed him with a look that Tony understood, and he backed off, even said, "Sorry."

Jo-Jo had come back, feeling not much better after trying to rest at home. How could he sleep? He hadn't even had anything to drink the night before, but he was slurring his words. He found himself speaking sparingly, carefully forming his words like he had a mouth full of marshmallows, walking like his legs were asleep. Hell, they *were* asleep, even after dark, when boredom and annoyance finally forced him to take a trip down to the inn.

When he got there, the place was all abuzz. He was ready for a snide remark from Tony, but Tony wasn't there. Everyone was talking about an abduction, an Amber alert for some kid. Katie pulled him aside and let him know what she knew. The "PR" that used to live upstairs was back, and the cops had taken her, Chat and Sue off someplace.

She had left her kids with Layton, who was upstairs with them now, and it all had to do with the missing kid. Then the television suddenly blasted news at them. They watched, courtesy of Eye In the Sky Cam 17, a view of Chat's Meadows down below, and the headlights of ATV's swooping crazy through the woods. They stared at a picture of the road up above the Meadows, with portable light stanchions and ambulances and cop cars all over it, and then—Chat and Sue and the woman by a cop car! They were pointing and saying something. They saw shots of a stretcher with a little body on it, one hand with shreds of duct tape waving weakly to a woman grasping her hands to her heart and crying, running over and kissing the boy.

Then the camera switched to a ground shot of the projects and a wild-eyed punk cuffed and struggling like a man possessed. Each neighbor stood on the four-foot square of concrete that was his or her doorstep, and the regulars kept up a running commentary about how they wouldn't live in a place like that for anything. Then Jo-Jo was looking at a talking head of a fat woman with bad teeth going on about what kind of neighbors they had been, and suddenly the talking stopped and Jo-Jo felt himself drop the beer. He watched with remote interest as his legs folded under him.

Two or three people, Kate included, ran over and asked him over and over if he was all right. He wanted to get up and brush them off, or make a smart remark, but for one instant he could not. His mind was trapped inside, and his body would not listen.

They called and waited for the medics—they were all out at the Meadows still—and by the time they arrived he was up again, mumbling "sorry" about the beer. Kate ran upstairs to get Layton, then got Jo-Jo in the car and drove him home.

"You haven't been drinking," she said to Jo-Jo, after ten long minutes of silence.

"No," which actually came out, "Naaaaaa."

She guided the Buick around a corner, purposefully not looking at him.

"You have to see a doctor, Jo. Or did you already?"

He shook his head "yes," not trusting himself to talk.

"And?"

He put two palms up as if to say, "Who knows?"

"When will you find out? Any idea?"

"Shafer. Tomorrow," was what he hoped he said.

She pulled up in front of the house, let the car run and got out to help him up the stone stairs. She quickly opened the huge front door with her key—she had forgotten to give it back—and guided him into the bedroom, helping him down onto the bed. She took off his shoes thinking, *I've done this before once or twice, after a good night of shine.* Naturally she closed the drapes across the window that overlooked the deck and the lake beyond.

"I'll be back after my shift. I'll put the cordless right here. You call if you need me."

He shook his head weakly. *Yes. If I need you.*

Chat and Sue didn't get home until after midnight, and they both, without speaking to Homer and Thelma much, drifted to the back bedroom to check on the kids, hugging each other and gazing on what they realized should be the most beautiful sight in the world to any parent worth the name.

Chat walked over to Jesse's bed, knelt there for a moment. He almost stroked his hair, but stopped, afraid to wake him. Jesse was tossing a little in his sleep, as his head gave little twitches: a bad dream.

Chat could just imagine those dreams. For him, it was the smell of river mud. Would the woods now be like that for Jesse? At least the bastard had been caught. They found the other boy safe, duct-taped up in an old refrigerator somebody had tossed over the bank near Malchio's.

Chat bent his head in prayer for the first time, he realized, since all this had begun. Sure, he had gone to church, said the responses, sang the hymns, but in his heart, it was all him, that litany of selfs that Sue had chanted at him to bring him around again. So he prayed, first for forgiveness, for his pride and his selfishness, for the protection of Sue and the kids, and to say "thank you" for his little gifts and the wonder of the world, even in the awful moments. Finally he prayed for the wisdom to see the right way and to lose the childish adoration of himself.

They kept to themselves the next day. Chat and Sue slept late for the first time in how many years, and Katie did as she promised, spending the night lying next to Jo-Jo, who she thought had wanted to be amorous halfway through the night, which she ignored, feigning sleep. As if.

The next morning was a study in glory: blue skies and the birds, the few that remained, singing, the air crisp but not cold. Katie got up early, got the coffee on, then, when Jo-Jo awoke, offered to take the day off from work to take him to Shafer's.

"I'm fine," he had insisted. "I was just tired yesterday. Working too hard after that festival in the city."

"Jo-Jo. Please."

"Look, I'll call you as soon as I know something, okay? Really, I feel just fine today. A good night's rest was all I needed. How's, how's the baby?"

Kate patted her belly.

"He's fine. His father's son. He never stops kicking."

"Hehe. Look. I'm gonna go. You can stay here if you want, for a bit."

"Naw. I got to get ready for class. Three more and I have my certification."

"A teacher? Putting up with those kids? Eww."

"I've been trained by the best," was all she said. She kissed him and grabbed her coat. She was out the door with a little wave, elbow on hip, and then she stepped out into the bright air, leaving him to consider the day.

If Jo-Jo had been able to speak the night before, he might have told Kate the whole history of this thing he still hoped was nothing more than too much shine, for he'd heard how a bad batch could screw you up, sometimes weeks or months afterwards, even. It had started with the tremor that was not going away, and the numb hands that had nothing to do with the weather. That would make sense when the mornings were ten below, but not now. Not when the sheets stick to you, it's so hot. So he made the appointment to see Doc Shafer, who ran a bunch of tests, blood work and stuff, couldn't make heads or tails of it all, and had sent him up to the clinic in Scranton.

Today was the day. He had already told Tony he'd be late coming in today, if at all, making sure he understood that if they didn't have the roof on when he got back, there'd be hell to pay. He drove slowly up towards Scranton, the Electric City, coal capital of the world, and capital of polkas and peppermint, too. Johnny had always laughed at him whenever he asked what the two had to do with each other.

The folks in Scranton were the ones that gave Jo-Jo the news. The docs called him into a conference room, of all things, sat there looking uncomfortable, then told him straight up the news was not good.

One of the doctors handed him a pamphlet on this thing they call "ALS." He read aloud:

"'Amyotrophic Lateral Sclerosis?' What?"

Then he read silently, the tremor in his hand making the paper shake:

ALS symptoms may include tripping, stumbling and falling, loss of muscle control and strength in hands and arms, difficulty speaking, swallowing and/ or breathing, chronic fatigue, and muscle twitching and/or cramping. ALS is characterized by both upper and lower motor neuron damage. Symptoms of upper motor neuron damage include stiffness (spasticity), muscle twitching (fasciculations), and muscle shaking (clonus). Symptoms of lower motor neuron damage include muscle weakness and muscle shrinking (atrophy).

Nothing there that sounded promising. But the worst part wasn't the symptoms; it was the prognosis. Less than 20% of the people who had the disease survived for more than a few years. *It's a death sentence, that's what it is. And from what the doctor is saying, the end is not going to be pleasant.* He'd be bedridden, soon begin drooling, and lose his ability to move his hands and legs. The tremors would get worse, and now was the time, they told him, to get his affairs in order, and to do whatever it was he had dreamed of doing, a trip to Europe or hang-gliding. Whatever. Music? "Play as long as you can," they told him, but live with the reality: he'd be lucky to be walking or eating—or breathing—on his own in a few months.

So Jo-Jo drove down the road towards his home as his hand vibrated on the wheel, and tried to get the idea of his own death. He tried to imagine a world without him in it, but his mind refused to create that image. It all seemed so unreal, and yet the tears were streaming down his face.

Almost laughable that, at this stage, the only thing he could think of was his pride. He had never been beholden to any man, woman or dog, and he didn't want to start now. He considered telling the boys, but he couldn't see himself doing that at all. Imagine, an invalid! He wanted to laugh, but he couldn't. And then he found himself pounding the wheel with his fist. What he really wanted to do was to destroy the entire world, just as it has been destroyed for him, even though he was still walking around.

"I'm scared shitless," he muttered, and then dialed Katie as he promised. He thought that she had every right to tell him to take a leap. That's what he expected, and half what he thought he deserved. What he didn't expect was for her to drop what she was doing and rush to him, bounding up the steps like she was still sixteen, open his door and cradle his head in her arms, shushing him while he bawled like a baby.

Kate was half-watching TV and half-reading her Psych homework when the call came, and she did indeed drop what she was doing, speeding over to Jo-Jo's house. Amidst the tears, never before seen, she heard a new Jo-Jo. This was not the charismatic charmer who was almost all-state in football when he was coming up, the boy who was quicker and more ruthless than anybody for miles around. He had been the rebel who was a rocker when that was avant-garde, the anachronism who shocked the old gray-haired train buffs by becoming a long-haired version of them, the young man who surpassed them all as a model-builder, buying the old signs from the railroad station with a picture of a fantastic Victorian stunner called Phoebe Snow, extolling the virtues of her railroad, dressed virginally and declaring:

While some may wait

And hesitate

To bring their stations up to date

They're new and bright

When you alight

From off the Road of Anthracite

And...

Says Phoebe Snow

About to go

Upon a trip to Buffalo

My gown stays white

From morn till night

Upon the Road of Anthracite

She remembered Jo-Jo when he was the first to smoke pot, the kid who pissed the teachers off to no end because he skipped school when he felt like it. That was the Jo-Jo who quit school in tenth grade and was making three times the money the teachers did before he was even twenty-one. That was the same Jo-Jo who had a house and a nice car by the time he *was* twenty-one, who had friends or at least people that were glad to see him, slapping him on the back and telling him jokes: *you hear the one about the one-armed fisherman, hehe?*

It was all coming to an end, now. And she would be there for it, her and his kid—her belly was just starting to bulge the least little bit, although the morning sickness was getting better. She wondered if she had the right stuff to be a caregiver, and, rocking him there, she tried to keep from wondering about Tony, and about how to break this news to him. Of course, Katie knew that he was a player, but she never really cared about that. He was a poet, and a damned good lay, and he made her feel safe and wanted.

Oddly, so did the new Jo-Jo, now. What she had wished for she had gotten, and her tears were silent, running down her cheek and into the thick knit of her sweater. And what about Cold Spring, then? Had he told Chat and the rest yet?

Jo-Jo didn't answer. What was left to say? What he thought of was the saying that "all good things must come to an end." Buddy-boy, this was a bang-up ending: ironically, he learned from the slim little pamphlet of doom that the last things to go on someone stricken with ALS were the mind and the sex drive.

37

⇒ Chapter Thirty-Seven ⇐

Nan was tired of waiting, and the every-other-weekend thing was a joke. She hadn't seen Tony in a month, and it was her *right*, by Jesus, to get him back home where he belonged. She gassed up the car and made the drive through sheets of rain, buckets of water smashing against the windshield when the big rigs passed her and left her in a blind foggy mist for a moment, as the wipers just barely shed the oily water that made the world look all streaky. She found the exit no problem and stopped at a *freakin' general store!*

The racks of penny candies and the pretty, pregnant girl at the counter were something right out of some old movie, and there was an old guy on a ladder putting up rolls of paper towels over a display for work gloves and plumbing fixtures. She looked around for a moment. The walls were covered with traps, nozzles, washers and bolts, flex piping for toilets and even toilet seats, right there next to the Kraft Macaroni and Cheese and the Vienna Sausages—what the hell was in them, anyhow?

"'Scuze me," Nan said to the girl. "Do you happen to know a Tony DiAntonio? Young guy? About this tall, just moved up here?"

The girl snapped her head up quickly, narrowed her eyes.

"And you are?"

"Oh. Sorry. Nan DiAntonio. His wife." She almost-whispered that last little bit.

"Wife. How nice. You'll probably find him at the Bennykill, right down the road from here. Tell him Katie sent you down there."

"You know him, then?" The flat look in her eyes—she was with him! Kate held out her hand, and, after a beat, Nan took it and shook it firmly. No sense getting mad at her. She probably didn't even know Tony was married, Nan thought.

"He's quite the poet. And a nice man." Kate said.

"He's a dick, and I'm going to kill him when I get my hands on him," Nan said, and became furious with this, this, *Kate,* and with herself for breaking down and bawling like a little kid. Kate handed her a tissue and shrugged her shoulders, patting her belly without thinking.

"Oh my God! It's not—you're not!"

"No. Oh, no!" Katie almost laughed at that one. "It's my, um, boyfriend's."

"How nice for you, then. Well. Nice meeting you."

"He has good taste, I think," Katie said, smiling. "Be a shame to waste a perfectly good guy like that."

"I don't think he'll ever change."

"They never do," Kate said as she shrugged again.

"Can't live with 'em, and you go to jail if you kill 'em. Good luck with the baby," Nan said, pulling up her hood and getting her umbrella ready to dash to the car. Outside, the rain was being driven sideways, and great gusts of wind were blowing leaves and branches around. Streams of water were running on both sides of the road.

"Thanks, Nan. And you have good luck with *yours.*"

Outside, it was growing dark, and Nan heard the first peals of thunder. She drove the mile or so to the Bennykill and found the parking lot full. She spotted Tony's Tracker, and the next minute she was in the door and screaming at Tony, who had been in a somber conversation with some other Dago who looked a little rough around the edges.

She couldn't control herself any longer. She was crying and stamping her foot, and some old bald guy had tried to shush her, but she started punching Tony, first on one arm, then the other, then the chest and almost a shot to the head before he pinned her hands—strong!—and then kissed her.

Tony's buddy simply looked on, shaking a little bit, and the whole crowd of workers and tourists and college kids and bikers stopped what they were all doing to watch the floor show that only lasted until Tony walked her out to the parking lot. From the parking lot, they could hear only her side of the conversation, with great long invectives and expletives, then a momentary lull that they guessed was his part, and then minutes worth of ire from her again.

Layton looked at Jo-Jo, who was draining his fourth or fifth beer, and shrugged.

"Must be love."

"A month ago, I'd of said 'I wouldn't know,'" Jo-Jo said. "But I guess you're right about that. Not that we're worthy, you know. But it's lucky for us that they make no sense at all. Otherwise, why would they even bother with us?"

"Life sure is a mystery," Layton agreed.

"So's death. Layton," Jo-Jo whispered. "I'm scared, man."

"Somehow we find the strength. This might be a good time to talk with the Reverend. I mean, not even about religious, God stuff. Just about dealing with it, you know? It really helped me when I lost Rose."

"Thanks, Layton. You know I was never a big fan of being all serious about things—easy come, easy go, I always said. But I'm having a hard time turning this into a joke. You can take that to the bank."

"Thy great big one on me. Keep your chin up. Maybe you'll beat the odds. If there's a man out there lucky enough to do it, it'd be you. Long as you don't lose hope. It's the rule of three."

"What rule of three?" a kid next to Jo-Jo asked.

"You can only last three minutes without air, three days without water, three weeks without food, and three months without hope."

"That's depressing. One more beer. Then I gotta rest," Jo-Jo said, lifting the glass, small droplets of beer clinging to the sides.

Hope. He thought he remembered something from Sunday school. *The greatest of these is hope.*

Chat was in Fiesterville when Sue got the call from Thelma. "Come quick, there's something wrong with Homer and I called the ambulance!"

Sue grabbed her keys and was out there in ten minutes, just after the paramedics had arrived and were working on Homer, as Thelma stood by and wrung her hands, weeping and quietly moaning his name over and over.

The medics moved like dancers, got Homer—a big man—onto the gurney and in the back of the ambulance, and Sue and Thelma followed,

Sue looking back in her rearview at the house, front door still open and the curtains blowing through the open crack of the front window.

"He's dead. He's dead," was all that Thelma could say, over and over, as Sue made shushing sounds and patted her hand while crying herself, keeping the flashing lights of the ambulance in her sight, the sound of the siren a wailing, heart-stabbing sound, a wail of death, fear, defeat, the ultimate surprise.

At the hospital, Sue called Chat first, then went into the receiving area. Homer had been taken to CCU, the docs told Thelma. It was a heart attack.

"He was breathing yet when they took him in," Thelma said to Sue. "He'll be all right in a day or two."

Sue didn't say anything to that, just hugged Thelma tightly, and Thelma thought, *He's strong and stubborn and the love of my life.*

The look on the doctor's face was a telling one, and Chat arrived just in time to hear the news. He did as he promised himself he would do: right there in the waiting room of the ER he knelt and prayed.

Jenna Shultz bid goodnight to her secretary, watched for the second frosted glass door to close, and then opened her desk drawer, second to the last on the left. A small sterling silver flask was what she was after, and after she had beheaded it and poured her teatime libation, she put her feet up on the desk and considered.

She had been around the block, these last twenty years, and just when she thought that she had seen it all, time after time, she found out differently. One might read, think, or watch all one wanted; Jenna was often convinced that Plato was right, and that it made as much sense to try to figure out the world and the people in it as it did to parse the shadows on the wall.

To begin with, the world was rife with far too many heroics. Old Irv Wallers was in front of her two or three years ago, and he had been charged with murder—a stranger lay drilled, Irv with the smoking gun in his hand, and a look like Martin Luther on his face. She knew he was innocent as soon as she saw him, and just as quickly she knew he would be a dead man.

The laws of the state demanded he be put in prison, and Irv wouldn't last a month in there after being in the fields and woods his whole life and being his own man. A week of being bossed by people he knew to be his mental inferiors would be too much for him. Of course it had been self-defense, of a sort. Irv had caught the cretin going through his shed, with a pocketful of tools, and the guy had come at him: *best defense was a good offense*, she supposed was what went through the thief's mind, except that the guy didn't know Irv like she did, and he always had the Colt with him.

Imagine, she thought dourly, a worthless piece of city trash like him, to be the cause of Irv's death and the end of the Waller line—he had only one child, and he had died in 'Nam. Yes, the end of the line, for many things, she guessed, and who would mourn the passing of this way of life? Who mourned for the blacksmith, once the sinewy heart of the village, his clanging clarion the call for everyone to be up and about, milling, selling, growing?

The blacksmith was no more, and no one even remembered what it had been like, never realized the sad lack they called progress. Soon the farmer would be gone, too, and the country ways, scrubbed out by the Internet and cable, bringing trite trash into the homes of the children, sold for a mess of pottage, and the parents so pleased with themselves and their liberality, as if in their heart they did not already know that they were deserving of the millstone around their neck.

Pride, she thought, tossing off the good Rebel Yell in one quick swallow, *was the hallmark of ignorance.*

She wondered why they stopped teaching Greek and Latin myths in school. Those stories would have been such a boon to them, to see what truly great heroes and heroines came to in the end, vis-à-vis Priam and Helen of Troy, not to mention Odysseus.

She had taken this job instead of going to school to learn about plants, which were then and always after had been her love. The old-timers had laughed at that and asked if she were crazy to sit in a classroom and ask questions about a plant. She was sure that they were wrong, and she was not shy about laying it all out for anyone who was interested. But Jenna was practical, too. All that schooling to make a pittance, and then she would be too poor to buy the plants she loved so much and was too busy to study. So she went into this instead. Yes, she was quite sure they were wrong about a great many things. Anyone would know it; all it took was one look in the mirror, unflinchingly, to say the things that were real and to look deeply for the lies that were the heart of man. Yes, and women, too.

She made a mental list of the folks who were clueless about life: cops, first of all, most of whom had tried to date her when she was a middling age, and whose rebuffs made her job dicey the first few years. Thank the Lord she was related to everybody in the county. They'd have to blast her out to get rid of her now. Then there were the defendants—"perps" in the newspeak she detested—against whom Jenna mostly had a decidedly unchristian aversion. Finally, Jenna detested the news media, those beautiful talking heads she had long ago learned to distrust and despise. All sizzle and no steak.

Now here she was, dealing with Chat Dalton's problem, as was right and just. But still, she had to wonder. First off, Chat didn't even know the half of what *his* family was all about, and then, if that all came out, things might be hot for *her,* which of course she was against, both on principle and in practice. On top of that, the odious, faceless new presence was funneling money into the county machine like there was no tomorrow, to an end she could only guess about. She had little use for short-sighted politicians and those who let self-interest alone rule their thoughts, not that she was impractical in her own thoughts.

But whatever was driving the small changes and redirecting the district lines was troubling to her. Hadn't old man Feister sold his big holdings to the Van Dansks back in the early 1800s, leaving the lawless side of what had been one town in one borough, with the wealthy in another? The ones with the money, the means and will to enforce the law found themselves on one side of the bridge hand-tied because their laws stopped at the middle of the creek, and the ones with the fire in their belly just on the other side of the line, who broke into homes and raped and pillaged like Hessians, stood there laughing at the law.

That was something she could not abide. She got up, pulled her Carhartt off the coat rack and shut the lights, carefully locking both doors as she walked down the stairs and out into the blustery, cold night.

It had snowed, and a few flakes spun in the orbs of the streetlights. Small puffs of white swirled along the street in long sinuous waves where the gusts of wind picked up the snow and redeposited it. The katydids had predicted an early winter, and the geese did also. Jenna thought that they were as right as rain once again. Tomorrow she would unseal the will.

She wondered how Chat would take it all.

38

⇒ CHAPTER THIRTY-EIGHT ⇐

The day dawned bright and sunny, and Layton waited impatiently, thinking sadly about Homer and the time they had played hooky from school and hopped a freight out to Mauch Chunk. They had been warned a thousand times, it seemed, but one day they were bored and the train had slowed down right in front of them, the boxcar door was open, and what was a country kid to do? They jumped off the train at a crossing in town, walked out to the countryside and swiped some ripening apples, went swimming, went past a cornfield and tried their hand at making corncob pipes. They didn't know the trick to it, because the cobs began to smoke themselves, and the hollow forsythia stems they used for the pipe stem left a nasty taste in their mouths. They vowed to stick to chew or cigars when they could get them. They hitched a ride back home, didn't get back until ten that night, both with stomach cramps from the apples, and both of them got a hiding that made it hard to sit for a week, which made them the heroes of the day.

It was the best day of their young lives. They talked about that day for years after, and now Homer was due to be six feet under. What was left of the old ways, the old days?

Chat had offered to come with him down to the jail to see about Ada. Both he and Sue had, actually, but Layton knew Thelma needed to have them around to make the arrangements and for company. Besides, Jesse was still a little bit clingy and wanted them near at every moment. They had all been incensed to learn that she would be held pending INS clearance, and they were shocked to learn that there was no bail for unregistered aliens. They weren't even going to get her out so he could talk with her, at first, only the sheaf of school papers Layton carried and his mention of caring for her kids softened them at all.

"I wouldn't get too wrapped up in this, I were you," the little runt of a cop had said. "She'll likely get deported, from what the INS guy was saying. Her and her kids. So you'll have to wait 'til he gets here to talk with her. She's his problem now."

"But this here is *America*. This woman risked all she had so's you could find that pervert you got locked up. If she didn't go down there and tell you what was what, that kid would be dead by now."

"We have no say about it," Runty said. "The INS man will be over here in a couple hours. You can wait if you want to."

Layton often wished he was quicker with the word, like that day in the bar when the LCB had pulled that jackboot crap with him and he had just stood there, doing exactly what he was doing now: sputtering. He shook it off. *This is important,* he told himself. Somebody had to be a man about things.

"I want to see her *now*," he said, licking his lips. Then he remembered Sarah. "'Less you want me to start making calls about holding somebody without charges and without a lawyer. Wonder what the paper would make of *that*, huh?"

He watched as the runt tried to think of a good reason to say "no." Finally he turned and went inside, motioning Layton to the small visitation room while he went to get the woman.

"So," Ada said. "They will send me back. I am a dead woman."

"You saved that kid's life. That counts for something. I got an idea."

"Gracias, Senor, but there is nothing you can do now. I have seen how this will be. Soon I will be on a plane that will land back in my home, and in a few weeks I will be dead, or worse than dead. I cannot go back to the village. If I stay in the city, there is no work like here in America. I have seen the women there. Their eyes are dead, their faces, also dead, because they have been shamed."

"Listen close, now," Layton said, quickly whispering something to her, and her eyes flew open wide, her hands fluttering up to her mouth like a pair of wistful doves, as her head nodded in agreement with something shocking to her.

"Here, that's enough of that. Let's go. No more secrets," the runt barked, and Layton watched as Ada was hustled back inside.

"I'll be back," he promised and hurried out of the door.

Sterling waited for Amy impatiently. He was getting used to having her around, so much so that he felt a thrill of fear that she might go away. And Homer's death had rocked him, it seemed, more than it affected Chat, although Sterling didn't understand how that could be. Today was the funeral, and he was sure he could not have faced it without Amy there at his side, and that made him think seriously about their being together for good.

He had talked to Chat about it a few weeks prior to all the madness, and Chat encouraged him to pop the question, but Sterling was afraid.

"What if she says 'no'?" he said. "I'd be doomed!"

"I don't think she will. But wouldn't you want to know sooner, instead of later?"

"Maybe I'd rather not know at all," Sterling said, trying to joke.

"Been there. Done that. Doesn't work, my friend," Chat had replied.

So now he was sitting on the front steps waiting, and reading:

The autumn is the season of nostalgia, a clamoring for warmth, sucking the last atom of heat from the thinning rays of the sun, the world a wonder of color and of quickening urges: deer scraping large patches of ground bare to leave their odorous calling card for the does, the bucks all crazed with the primal urge, running towards the sound of a scuffle in the leaves or the tinkling of antlers in the brush: two other bucks are fighting over what is mine!

The first thin filigrees of ice cover the mud puddles, apples ripen and the garden takes on a worn and tattered look. There are bare rows where the beans used to be, the broccoli is spindly and topped with splashes of yellow where the errant floret has obeyed the prime directive and flowered. Leafless tomatoe plants are tottering with heavy, red, ripe fruits, and even the weeds look wan and tired, ready to give up the struggle, despite the warm afternoons and the bright sunshine. There's no fooling mother nature, alright, and all the world knows that the days are waning. The time for a mad dash to procreate or put on thick layers of fat is *now*, it must be *now*, for the winds that blow hard in this season, ragged remnants of hurricanes, hold a thin edge of violence in their comings.

It will soon be deep winter, the ground as hard as the facts of life, snow covering the ground and what little food remains, the trees bare, no cover for the hunted, no rest for the hunter, either—eat or be consumed by hunger yourself, soon the season for bone-rattling cold, cold enough for the timber to freeze with a crack like a .44, as the song goes, cold enough to freeze the small ponds clear to the bottom, and then if you are a frog or a turtle, you had better hope that you dug yourself into the mud deeply enough, or there will be no resurrection and no life for you, now just a chunk of flesh to feed the microbes, the most ancient of life, the life-form of choice when the going gets tough. There is that promise of a season with no remorse, the killing season, as if death could be summed up in just a few words: ice and snow, and no where to hide.

"Hey!" Amy called. Sterling had been so entranced that he had not noticed her parking there in front of him.

"Hey yourself! You look beautiful," Sterling blurted, and Amy blushed and murmured "Thanks!"

"So. Almost ready?"

"Funeral's not for another twenty minutes. You want to be early?"

"Ummm. Well, not really."

She turned her car off and got out, walked over and sat beside Sterling, then put her arm around him gently.

"Sterling, I know how bummed you've been about Chat's troubles—and now Homer's dying."

"Well. Yeah." Tears were in his eyes.

"I just want you to know, well, I'll be here for you."

"Amy."

"What?"

"Did I ever tell you how I got this book?"

"Oh. I thought you were going to ask me something else. No. No, you never did."

""Eh he. Well, maybe I will, in a minute. I did tell you about my wife, right?"

"Not so much. Just you were married, that's all I know. Really, if you're not comfortable talking about it, that's cool, too."

"Well, let's just say that I think I secretly thought of going back to Crisfield, like maybe she would die or something."

"You're sure she's still there? I guess it still matters, then."

"I'm not sure she's still there. I'm pretty sure it doesn't matter so much anymore. Here, let me read a minute."

And to calm himself, Sterling shook and read:

It is no accident the Indians called it the moons of the harvest and the hunt, for the imperative is to button things down, tidy things up, and get ready for the snow. There are bikes to be put away, lawns to be raked, screens to be replaced by storm windows in most of the older houses in the towns, coal bins to be filled and the woodshed not nearly as full as it should be, the chainsaw needs sharpened, and gas mix to get for the snow-blower if you're rich enough or young enough to have one.

For the older folks, it is a time to focus worries on exposed pipes, drafty windows, a car with too many miles on it and no good snows, a time to think that maybe this could be the year to go down to Florida like the Wilsons did last year, that seemed so happy about it all back in the springtime, although truth be told, some folks claim that they were mostly miserable down there, worrying about the place up here, and lonely for the few old friends that remain to them, the ones still in this world instead of the other.

The autumn colors are a big draw, the reds, yellows, golds and maroons of the graceful floating orbs from the fall balloon festival almost as good a show as the foliage, the flaming orange of the maples, purple highlights of the dogwoods, shocking yellow of the tulip poplar, and the deep reds of the shadbush and chestnut oaks splattered across the landscape like God was a drunken painter or a child with a new set of celestial crayons.

Of course, in the late fall, after the leaves have fallen, the whole world is naked again, carpet of leaves, still with some color, covering the ground and sounding like walking on corn-flakes on a path a hundred miles long all in the frosty morning, the dog working the pheasant cover with gleeful bliss, the hunter carefully choosing his path to be as silent as the woods allow, scouting for the foot-wide scattering of turkey scratchings that mark the feeding ground of the birds that can range three miles a day, easy, all on foot, and whose drumsticks consequently are not worth cooking, but whose breasts, cooked slowly with a philo dough and some olive oil, make his tame cousin taste like cardboard, the tender flesh shot with the flavor of the toothsome buds the bird had been eating all those months.

"That's almost the end of the book. I think you read the whole thing to me, one time or another," Amy said, still hugging him.

"Hmmm. Maybe I did. I was thinking that the last little bit in here might be good for Homer's service. Thelma called me and asked me to read something, and I know neither of them were church folks, much."

"That would be sweet," Amy said.

"Marry me," Sterling blurted, and by her tears, her kiss and her bear-like hug, Sterling thought that he could finally afford to part with his book.

He had it memorized anyway.

Jenna was just ready to go out to lunch when the phone rang. She let the machine get it and would not have picked it up if she hadn't heard Layton's voice on the other end, sounding rather frantic.

"Layton Renfroe, this had better be pretty damned important to be calling me during lunch. You know how I love my lunchtime."

And when he had delivered his message, she had to agree her lunch could wait. She pulled her briefcase out from beneath the rolltop desk where she had dumped it, opened a few filing cabinets, and got her notary seal out. Twenty minutes later found her at the barracks in Fiesterville, where Layton met her anxiously at the door.

"You are nonpareil, Layton. The clarion call of the village."

"I'm a candy? A clarol call? Well—wait, never mind all that. The INS guy is due here any minute. What are our chances?"

"Better than even, I have a hunch. Would you like to put a fiver on it?"

"I've knowed you since you were a little shaver, I always thought. Times like these makes me wonder what I do really know," Layton said.

"Then you are indeed one of the wisest men on the face of the earth. Come along and let's see how this plays out."

The service for Homer had been short and sweet. Thelma had heard his opinions about long funeral orations enough times to know that she wasn't going to disrespect his memory by having things go on and on. It was a small crowd, just Sterling and Amy, Johnny and Meg, the kids, his Aunt Jenna, Layton and Katie. Homer was never what one would call sociable, and the speech given by the preacher was a simple reminder that Homer was simply going on before them, marking the way that all flesh must follow. Chat barely heard the platitudes: dust to dust, valley of the shadow of death, the way and the life.

But when Sterling stood up to speak, Chat forced himself to listen:

"Thelma asked me to speak a few words, and I know how much Homer loved to farm and fish, and to till the land, so I'd like to read just the last few words of this book. I think Homer would have liked it.

Fall is a season of extremes: a cold frosty morning, and an afternoon of such warmth you cannot imagine why you are burdened with coat or gloves. It is a time of torrential down-pours—the leftovers of Hurricanes like Agnes or Hugo—water washing over roads, carrying sticks and branches and sometimes cars and people to their death, tall tangles of detritus stacked under bridges and around the culverts that bisect the state like arteries, stranded on one side of the Delaware or another because the bridges aren't safe or the road is washed out, the river coming up a foot a minute, the smaller creeks five feet in the same time, not time to do much—Thanks, Ivan!

Then, in a matter of days, sunny spells that last a week or two and bleach every stitch of wood and field to bone-dryness, the husks of corn in the harvested fields as fragile as Chinese paper, the forests waiting for the careless match or odd lightning-bolt to burst into flame. It is the season to lock the summer house and shutter it up, to cast a wistful gaze at the surf and the endless sweep of beach, or bid farewell to the tent nestled under the beech trees out on the island, to enjoy the last cooler full of beer or rack of ribs on the BBQ, a time to shuttle the bikes downstairs, to get the plastic up on the one set of windows by the kitchen, to button up the deck, to get all the tables and chairs in the shed, to clean old rings left from once-cold beverages one last time.

There are tarps to hang or drape over woodpiles, wheelbarrows, canoes and grills, hoses to be drained and stored, the last of the herbs to be hung and dried, the garden mulched and the hunting gear readied, a time to return to school and new friends, struggles, loves, dreams, mostly of the time when burgeoning green and the promise of increase holds sway.

Sterling repeated the last line and sat down crying.

≡ Chapter Thirty-Nine ≡

Chat thought it ironic that Sterling had called him back to his faith, broken as it was, or at least held him up over that long summer with his jokes and his ways and his plotting to put him on the road so he didn't have time to think.

While the preacher went on, Chat remembered the day before when Sterling had shown up looking guilty about something or another, and began to apologize about the way things had turned out, as if he had some evil intent deep in his heart.

"Sterling, you did all that because you're a good man at heart. You were trying to help. And I think maybe you did, too," Chat had said. "But, you know, the best laid plans of mice and men and all that."

"Yeah, but if you all had been home, well. And then I keep feeling it was the shock of all this put Homer down, too." Sterling said.

"Almost put me down, I'll tell you that. Pisses me off something fierce: the stares when we go to town, the way the conversation stops when Sue and I walk into a room. All the wrong people know what happened and can't wait to get the dirty details like this was some kind of made-up TV show, pretending they care even at a time like this with Homer lying there dead. And Jesse, well, we just hope and pray he'll be all right. And then, Jo-Jo. I mean, I haven't even gotten my little brain around *that* one yet. Maybe that's what you get for being selfish in this world. What was that word the dots use about getting what you deserve?" Chat said.

"Karma?"

"Yeah. Karma. Anyhow, it was a good summer."

"It was an awesome summer. It was bluegrass nirvana, something you can hang on to when the times get rough."

"Like now," Chat had said then, frank tears making the sun sparkle.

Now here lay the man that had raised him up from a youngster, wet behind the ears, raised him up to be a man. And what kind of man had he become? Was this death the end of a run of bad luck? They said bad luck came in threes, so Chat counted, or tried to. The trouble with the law, that was definitely one, and then Jesse, then finally Homer. Perhaps God would let him up for a breath now. He remembered the verse: "I will set my face against them, and I will make the land desolate because they have acted faithlessly."

And indeed the land was desolate. What would McAdam say if he knew he had been an agent of God? Chat actually smiled at that thought, but stopped the smiling as soon as he saw Sue watching him with concern.

Chat supposed he would have to get used to confusion, for what had been so clear to him a year ago was now a hopelessly muddled mess. He considered his life. What had he done that was not good, that could have led to all this? Because there must be a plan, a reason, much as Sterling insisted there was none.

At the graveside, of course, he wept. They all did, as each of them placed a flower on the casket, and Sterling, coming last, gently placed his book on the casket as well. Tears blurred the panorama of the valley down below them, and the thin silver thread of the river running through it. Below he could see the head of the island where they had found old man Peters, and in his mind's eye he could also see also the whipsaw of the branches flinging mud and leaves twenty feet into the air, covering them with the rankness of the earth. The numbness was a blessing that would soon enough wear off, he guessed. Even now, flashes of his feelings caused Chat's eyes to swim and his hand to shake, just ever so slightly, and then one of the boys or Sue would pat him on the back. The children were uncharacteristically good. On the way back to the church, he heard the kids talking somberly. They had never seen so many grown-ups crying, Meg's Caitlin said.

"Well, it's a sad thing when someone you love dies," Sue said. "So it's right and proper that we weep for a time. But then we've got our work to do, and our lives to live, too."

"I'm gonna be a cop and catch bad guys like that darkie that was after me," Jesse announced, pouncing with his hand in a pistol shape.

"Jesse. We don't call folks that," Sue scolded.

"There's a picture of one of them up in the attic at home," little Meg said, and Sue shushed her, too.

The big Meg said, "Whyn't you boys go on down to Layton's? Sue, Amy and me'll see to the kids. They've been good as long as you could expect them to be, I guess."

"You all don't mind?" Chat said.

"No. You go on ahead. Maybe we'll catch up to you after we get the kids changed and Thelma back home," Amy said.

"We'll walk down, then."

They continued down the hill, road rutted out by the recent heavy rains that had stripped the leaves of all but the white oaks, the tattoo of their leaves in the late fall woods a mark of a good deer stand when the mast crop was good.

"Not many acorns out this year," Chat said. Sterling and Johnny both paused to look at him for a moment.

"What? Acorns?" Sterling asked.

"Never mind. Just thinking out loud. Those white oaks over there," Chat said, motioning vaguely towards them.

"You're an odd one, Chat," Johnny said, confused.

Sterling chimed in, "In most cases, a person talks to be understood, but I guess that would be too much to ask of you."

"Har har," Chat said to Sterling. Then, to Johnny, "When it comes to my brain, all I can say is that I didn't build it, my friend. I'm just trying to drive it."

"I wish Jo-Jo had come," Johnny said, quietly.

"Maybe just as well he didn't—for him and us. I guess we'll have to get used to digging around for the fourth player this next season."

"There's that girl fiddler from Florida, played with some Hawktown Ramblers or something like that. Sue was talking about her. Carrie something or other."

"Oh, yeah. I met her out at the Benton festival. I don't think she's the staying kind," Chat said.

"It'll sort itself out somehow," Johnny said. "Sue said she'd help any way she could."

"This conversation is getting too serious, buckaroos. I say we get us down to the inn and have a few beers. Homer would've approved, I say," Layton murmured, tears in his eyes now.

They filed off the hilltop in silence as the last remnants of leaves, gold, silver and bronze swirled around them in the fitful winds. They descended the knob. Overhead, the sky darkened with thick clouds, scudding and boiling like an airy hellspot, although further up the valley the sunlight was shining in a small break of clouds that turned into diadems of hammered gold.

Layton removed the sign on the door that read "Closed for Funeral," opened the door, snapped on the lights and walked behind the bar to get some pitchers and glasses.

"You guys have some beer, here. I'll get some burgers on," he said and left them.

They grabbed a corner table, nursing their beers, saying nothing for long moments, staring out the window, and in between times, making desultory stabs at conversation.

"When is the hearing? You hear yet?" Sterling said.

"Tuesday," Chat answered. "Younts is finally done raping me, I guess. We're due to get our day in court. Maybe things are falling back into line," Chat said, doubtfully. "We'll have to sell the Meadows, one way or the other, though. Who would have dreamed any of this a year or even a couple months ago, huh? Ain't life grand?"

"Beats death, anyhow," Sterling said. The little feet were kicking him now, in the hollow of his shoulder down below his clavicle, and he drained his glass in a swallow.

"Jesse seems to be doing okay now," Johnny said. They were all careful about bringing that whole thing up, although they had all heard Chat complaining bitterly over the last couple days about old lady Atbie and the rest of the busybodies in Pigeon Forge, all gossiping to beat the band, even while Sue and Chat were dragging themselves and Jesse to see a shrink, who had turned out to be not so bad.

"We were worried that the whole thing would sit there festering and then bust out ten years from now when he was starting to be of an age, but the guy said not to make trouble where there wasn't any. He's sleeping through the night now. He has the last couple nights, anyhow," Chat said.

"Helps they got the bastard. I hear tell the guy was drummed out of the marines 'cause he was a wanker.'"

"Victim's Support said the case could take a year or two to resolve," Chat said.

"I just hope they never let that son of a sorry something out. It might be too tempting," Sterling said, morosely.

"I was out to Jo-Jo's last night," Johnny said, voice low. "He was really down. You know he never had no religion, nor nothing like that to help him out, and I guess he's feeling pretty rotten. He stopped going to work and all."

"I feel bad I haven't been out there," Chat said, gazing out the window.

"Yeah. We should stop out, all of us," Sterling said.

"Um. Well, he let me know he appreciated that I came out and all. Actually Kate did most of the talking for him. But then he wanted us all to know he'd rather we left him be and talk to him by computer if we would."

"Computer. I guess I could learn one of those," Chat said.

"We could have a benefit," Sterling suggested. "Invite a bunch of bands, charge admission—maybe down at the Legion?"

"A benefit? Hell, Jo-Jo's got more cash than the three of us put together. What sense does it make to have a bennie for him?"

"Well, it would be a nice thing to do," Johnny shrugged, and Chat had to admit, there were other benefits besides money.

"Show him that we care, anyway. Think he'd be up to it?" Chat said, absently watching the sky outside darken.

"I knew he was there with me, even if he didn't say much," Johnny said. "I bet he'd like it."

"Give us something to do, too. Something a little positive, hey?" Sterling said, switching into his manic phase for a minute.

"I swear. Can't you just sit still and relax? You're worse than a little kid when you get like this," Johnny said. The rebuke was so uncharacteristic that the other two stopped and stared at the big man, reddening madly with embarrassment over the outburst.

"And a little child shall lead them," Sterling laughed, and Chat punched his shoulder, hard.

"Oww!"

"Knock that off, willya? As if the wages of sin haven't been obvious enough, all this trouble. Poor Thelma. She was always doing for Homer, keeping him out of trouble. It's not gonna be easy up there for her without him."

"Eh, maybe now she'll get to travel like she was always wanting to—to the Caribbean and like that."

"Good time of year to do it. It's snowing out," Johnny said, and they all got silent, watching as the ground slowly whitened and the icy needles hissed against the glass.

40

⇒ CHAPTER FORTY ⇐

The week passed in a blur. First the news that the case had been tossed out of court prompted Chat to say that perhaps Younts was worth the forty grand it had cost him. Chat had been religious about the mortgage, wiring the money a week before it was due and calling for confirmation of its arrival. But when he and Sue sat down to see where they stood, it was apparent that the Meadows would have to go.

"I just can't stand it, thinking that it'll all be built up and trashy, like as not," Chat said.

Sue replied, "We could put some conditions on the sale, what do they call it? Covenants?"

"Covenants? Where did you hear that one?"

"Looked it up on the 'net. Well, actually, I did that after I talked with Jenna about it when she called to tell me about the case being tossed. I think she had something to do with all this, Chat."

"Jenna? Why wouldn't she call if she was going to help? That doesn't make sense."

"She did call, Chat. I told you that. Or weren't you listening again?" She put her finger to her ear, poked him in the ribs. "I'm sure she had a reason. Anyway, we might could sell the piece as one chunk, no subdividing. Oh, and she said we have to come down there tomorrow with Thelma. I guess there was a will."

"A will? Really? That's a surprise. Homer was always so addle-brained about everything. What time does she want us down there? I have to get my stuff back into the shop sometime tomorrow."

"She said pick a time with Thelma. I called up there and she said anytime, so."

"Let's do that early, then, leave me the rest of the day to get settled back in. You think anybody would buy it that way? The Meadows? It's over a hundred acres, somebody is gonna want to make some big money out of the deal."

"We could try it, talk with Chooney about it. We have a little room, another couple months worth of cash I saved."

"*You* saved? On what I gave you to run the house? How on earth did you manage that?"

"You always laughed at me and the fliers. I saved seventeen bucks the other day at Good-Buys, clipping coupons."

Chat shook his head. Did he even know this woman?

"Let's get to bed. 'Tomorrow and tomorrow and tomorrow...'"

"What? What's this with all the tomorrows?"

"Beats me. Something I keep hearing Sterling say when he's tired."

"I am that. So let's," she said, and they ascended the stairs, both pausing at the children's door to listen with full hearts to the small still sounds of their children asleep.

The runty cop just stood and looked at Layton and Jenna in disbelief. For once he was at a loss for words.

"Don't just stand there. Go get her and get that INS man here too, while you're at it, " Jenna said, barking the order.

"Who died and left you boss?" the cop said, miffed.

"Very clever retort, little man. That would be Lewellen, *your* boss. I got this all straightened out with him. So unless you feature being a road dog for the rest of your life, I'd go and get that woman. Now."

"Is that a *threat*? Are you *threatening* me?"

"Why yes, I believe I am. And I got five grand that says I could just as easily get you drummed off the force. Imagine what a judge or jury would say about your little gambling problem, betting on your own arrests and convictions like it was some kind of football game. Just imagine the field day the paper would have with that kind of story. So do us both a favor and call the INS guy. He's still in town. I checked. And then go get Ada."

Twenty minutes later, Ada walked out of the jail. Not exactly free, but closer now—thanks to two strangers. Merciful God, she was grateful!

She smiled at Layton, who promptly began blushing a deep red.

"You old coot, you. Who'd have ever imagined it?" Jenna said.

"I'll be honorable about it," Layton muttered, unable to look Ada in the eye.

She saved him some little discomfort when she bowed her head and shyly took his hand.

"Let's get back to the office," Jenna said. "Chat and Sue will be down soon for the will. That should be interesting."

Chat was standing by the car, shushing the kids, and Sue was just shutting the back door when they saw the BMW pulling up the drive. Sue walked down to the driveway and stood as Sarah and Ty got out of the car. Sue stood, stock still for a moment, then walked over and gave Sarah a tentative hug. Ty and Chat gave each other a small wave and smiled.

"Did we catch you at a bad time?" Sarah said.

"No. Well, kinda. We're on our way into town. Homer died last week, so," Chat said.

"Oh. Geeze. I'm sorry. Homer. How's Thelma doing?" Sarah asked.

"She's holding up. She said she was ready for this twenty years ago, really, as mad as he used to get about just about everything," Sue said. "But we're on our way to hear the will. What are you guys doing up on a weekday, anyhow? Vacation?"

"Well, sort of. Gave our notice this morning. Two weeks and all. And the bastard fired us on the spot. So we figured to come up here for a while. We both have some cash put by. Ty was talking about buying a piece of land to put an airstrip in here, the way things are growing, and maybe getting a nice house in town."

"How does a hundred acres sound?" Chat said quietly.

"Sounds too good to be true. Who could afford a piece that big?"

"Maybe you. Right now, though, we have to get into town and get this will thing over with. You're both welcome to stay here. We have room if you want."

"Thanks, but no. I think we'll just head down to the Bennykill. How is Layton doing, anyhow?"

"He's fine as frog hairs. Taking care of a couple of kids of that Spanish woman for a spell. She...it...ah, too much to tell you, I'm afraid, for now. That'll have to wait till later. Maybe dinner?" Sue said.

Sarah nodded her head.

"Chat, we better go. Traffic is getting bad down on the 'pike, and it might take us a half an hour to get down there and find a parking place."

"Yes. And it would not do to have Aunt Jenna wait."

They made it to Fiesterville in plenty of time, parked the car and watched from a park bench on the circle near the courthouse as people strolled down the street, stopping to look at the artwork displayed in a few of the windows in stores that used to be retail stores like JC Penney and Woolworth's, Newberry's and Rea & Derrick's. Chat remembered the long cool marble lunch counters all the variety stores had, and the stools of leather on shiny shafts of steel that he used to love to spin back and forth on, legs swinging. After school, when they could catch a ride, they would sit and drink a "Blende" and watch the traffic through huge plate glass windows that were diligently cleaned by what was then Fiesterville's token homeless guy, Flighty. He would show up each morning with bucket and squeegee and make his drink for the day. Those days were so over; the big mall up the way took most of the shoppers, and left the downtown trying to think of some other reason for being. The courthouse and the seeming thousands of law offices made the place busy for a time during the day, but after five, it was only the bars out on Main Street, jammed full of drunken college kids, that saw any action.

"Time to go, kids. And you mind you're polite to Aunt Jenna. Except don't be calling her that. You have to say 'Yes, your honor' and 'No, your honor,' if she asks you a question."

"What if the question isn't a 'yes or no' kind?" Meg said.

"It's the 'your honor' part that's important, hon. Come on, and let's get this thing done."

Jenna's office was a short walk away, and her secretary, Miss Phelps, almost smiled when they entered.

"Miss Phelps, how are you today?" Chat said brightly.

"Her Honor will see you now. Just go right in," she said curtly, and bent her head back down to the task at hand. She made it a rule that she would not fraternize with the people who came in the office, no matter who they were. They were almost always in trouble, and Dorrie Phelps knew about lying down with dogs and the attendant metaphorical fleas.

They were halfway to the inner door of the office when it opened, and Jenna came out to guide them all in.

"Very good. You brought the children."

"Yes, your Honor," Meg piped up, and they all laughed at that one.

"Teach your children in the way, and they will not stray from it," Jenna offered, and she swept them into an office that was draconian in its simplicity: a huge oak desk, four chairs, three filing cabinets and a picture of a prairie that Chat had always wondered about. He could understand mountains and sunsets and boats or even some of those French guys that must have been out of every color that wasn't a pastel, but flat land and grass? Even in a town that treasured eccentricity, Jenna was odd that way.

"Sit down, please. You're early. Thelma will be along in a minute. How have you all been holding up? I see the kids are doing well."

"For which we are grateful, believe me," Chat said. Outside they could hear Thelma greeting Miss Phelps, and a moment later she had joined them, Chat offering her his chair.

Jenna punched a button and said, "Miss Phelps, we need a couple folding chairs in here. Would you take care of that?" Jenna went over to a filing cabinet and withdrew a yellowed letter, still sealed.

"As you may know, Homer was not taken to trusting strangers with his personal business."

"That's an understatement if I ever heard one. He was not taken to trusting anyone, I'd say," Thelma blurted out, and then tittered and blushed.

"As you say, Thelma. Ah, put the chairs right over there, Miss Phelps, and be sure to hold all my calls and visitors for the next hour or so. At any rate, Homer gave me this back when you were still a teen, Chat, and we didn't know for sure how things were going to work out for you after your folks died. I held on to it, and I'm not even sure it is a will as we understand it, but it was something Homer felt very strongly about because he would remind me every chance he got about it. So, as you can see, he mailed it to himself, still sealed and all, then gave it to me to hold."

She put her glasses on and slit the letter open. Inside was a single sheet of yellow legal paper, and Chat could see the writing from the other side, with the words lifting themselves off the lines towards the ends, and a few spots where Homer had had some trouble with the nib of his pen. The text was half a page, more or less. Jenna began:

"'This here piece of paper is my last will and testimony, me being sane as I understand it. First off, to my wife that I love more than anything, I leave the farm and the Darlington piece next to it to do with what she wants. She was always going on about living in town, or closer by to Chat's, so now might be a good time for that. I leave my 28 to Chat, who I probably should have given it to before, but I still like to pick a tune now and again.'"

Then there was a bit of a blot that Jenna had to strain through to read:

"'Or I guess I should say I used to like it, seeing as how you're reading this and I won't be picking many licks in the other place. Thelma—you'll find an old Bisquick tin in the basement lodged up under the floor rafters near the front of the house, right by the stairs. That there is all my cash, and you're welcome to it. And Chat, there's an old Bible and some other stuff I put away up in your attic, years back, after Dutch died. They were my Dad's, your Grandpa's, and I expect you'll be interested in them. I know you all thought I was nuts, going on about Bill Monroe and the music, and the money and the damned government and all that, but you'll see that I wasn't as crazy as you all thought. Course, I'm not stupid enough to believe that I was as sane as I said I was, either. That whack on the head never did me no good. But at least I tried to do what was right. Oh, and there's some instruments up in the attic you'll want to look at, Chat. I bet they're pretty pricey now—a '23 Loar and three prewar Martins—a 28, an 18, and a sweet triple ought from New York gave to me by your Granddaddy. Here's to hoping the good book is right, and we'll all see each other in the great bye and bye. Tell Thelma I love her still. Sincerely, Homer Dalton.'"

They all sat still for a moment—almost like it was another funeral. Somehow, the antique piece of paper made Homer more alive than his own body in the coffin, and Thelma, for one, wished she had been told about the letter before the service, so she could have that to hold fast to. She had spent her life taking care of a man, and now that he was gone, she felt several things at once. Freedom was one of the things, surely, but there was also some little twinge of guilt. What if she had made him go to the doctors? And, of course, she was already missing him deeply, and his tirades and odd ways.

"Well, let's us go and see about the money that he was always going on about," Chat said finally. "And here I thought it was just another one of his dreams, the money."

"I'd be more interested in the personal effects of your grandfather, Chat—that would be my, umm, Great Uncle," Jenna said.

"I know where that stuff is! There's a Bible, and a picture of a darkie with a pipe, and then this little bag of seeds or something, up in the attic!" Meg said proudly. If they were talking about it, it must not have been the secret Megan thought it was.

"That's great, hon. But before we go, Megan—how old are you? Twelve? Do you think you could take this dollar down to the coffee shop on the corner and get a soda for your brother and you?"

"I can get my own darned soda!" Jesse snapped, then, when Chat glared at him, added, "Your honor."

"You two scamper along then. We'll meet you by the cannon on the circle in ten minutes." A moment after they had dashed out of the room, Jenna took a deep breath and faced Chat.

"What's the trouble, Aunt Jenna? There something else?"

"Chat, you know your Grandma and mine were sisters. But there's something I think I better let you in on, now that you're the oldest in your family. Your parents. Ahem. Well, they were not exactly what you might expect."

"What in the Sam Hill are you talking about, Jenna? Not what I might expect?"

"Hold on to your hat, Chat. This is going to be hard to explain. How much did you know about your grandmother, Maudie?"

"Not that much. I heard she was born here, traveled a little, married Grandpa. Heck, they were so old when I was born, and my folks never really said too much about them."

"Well, you know that both your Grandma and mine were a little on the eccentric side, doing things that not everyone accepted or appreciated. It was the twenties, and things were looser than they would be later, during the war and all. So evidently the sisters decided to take a little trip. They saved their egg money and took a passage on a boat in Pittsburgh. That's where Maudie met your Grandpa."

"That can't be right. Homer said his dad had never been out of the county. That much I can remember."

"He was right. His dad *hadn't* ever been out of the county. That was pretty common in those days. Most folks never made it more than twenty or thirty miles from their homes." She waited.

"But, if he didn't leave the county, I don't understand."

"Chat. Have you ever heard of Dutch Shultz?"

"Wasn't he some gangster with Al Capone and that whole bunch?"

"Wrong Dutch Shultz. This one was a guitar and harp player, worked the riverboats between the wars."

"Jenna. What in the world does this have to do with me and my folks?"

"Seems the sisters had quite a bit of fun those few weeks they were gone. Maudie in particular. So when she returned from what was supposed to be a lark, she was in a family way. With your dad."

Chat looked at the people around him blankly. Thelma and Sue were watching him. If Sue was as confused as he was, Thelma obviously was not.

"My dad was a, wasn't born in, he was," Chat said, sputtering to a stop.

"I know this is a lot to digest, Chat. I wanted to tell you after your folks died, but with your hearing problem and all that, we thought it was best not to tell you for a time, and then it was a year, then ten, and, well," Thelma said, shrugging her shoulders apologetically.

"You knew about the hearing thing? Who else knew it, then?"

"Chat, the whole time Sue was bringing you up to the School for the Deaf up in Scranton, how do you think that was all paid for? Didn't you ever wonder about that?"

"I tried not to think about it, really."

"Well, you did an outstanding job, I'll have to say that. I had the papers filled out for you to be an emancipated infant and a ward of the state, and Sue and I took care of all the Medicaid papers."

"Sue?" Chat sat there, incredulous.

"Well, what was I supposed to do? I was only seventeen, for goodness sakes. I asked for help, and Aunt Jenna was good as gold."

"I don't guess I was worth all the trouble, and, um, I guess it's kinda late, Aunt Jenna, Sue, but thanks," Chat sputtered.

"Don't think anything of it, Chat. I've followed your career around here. You never did a body harm that I could see, and some powerful good to many, so I can be proud of you in my own way. Now, about Dutch Schultz," Jenna said.

"Yeah, right! Who the heck is this Dutch Schultz? I mean, what about my Grandpa Harry?"

"Maudie was a beautiful woman. She knew what she had to do, and she picked Harry to do it with—they were married a few weeks later. It was the talk of the town, that was, although back then I guess folks didn't make such a fuss about marriage. You hired out the fire hall and got a couple kegs of beer—well, moonshine punch, during prohibition—and that was that. Far as we could figure, Harry never knew anything much about it, or if he did, he did a good job of pretending he didn't. Couple years later, Homer was borne. Didn't you ever wonder about your eye color?"

"No. Why should I have?"

"Two blue-eyed people can't have a brown-eyed child."

"Homer's eyes were blue. I can't remember my Mom or Dad's."

"Chat—there's more."

"I'm not sure I want to hear more, right now."

"Well, you can't just drive around in a beat-up red Chevy pick-up and pretend, can you? This might have some health implications for your kids," Jenna said sensibly.

"Eeesh. Okay."

"Dutch was a remarkable guitar player, and a good harp player, too. He was originally from around Rosine, and he played with Bill Monroe back when Bill was just coming up."

"So you're saying that my real grandfather was a Bluegrass Boy?"

"No. You know yourself the term wasn't even used until the late '40s. No, he played with Bill and Charlie and Birch, back in the '30s when Bill was trying to decide if he was going to continue with the music or work the oil fields in the mid-west after one of them got hired out. Work was hard to come by, and Bill wasn't having much luck with the music. He tried accordion, drums. Nothing was clicking."

"How do you know all this, then?"

"I remember the older folks talking when I was younger. Seems Dutch made it a point to get Bill to take his tour through the area. They had a ball-team, and they'd set up tents, play ball all day with whatever local team, then at night have a show. It was kind of like vaudeville, but with country music. He was checking up on his boy, like as not. And he took the time and trouble to sit down and show your Dad a few chords on the guitar, and mostly how to finger pick like how you do it. Some say that Dutch taught Merl Travis and Chet Atkins, too. Anyhow, it was Homer, about twelve or fifteen then, I guess, that waltzes up to Bill after one of the shows and tells him to skip the hoedown music, lose the accordion. Made it sound like a damned polka, Homer said. No, his idea was, let the black guy play more—jazz it up, he told him."

"The *black* guy?"

"Dutch was black, Chat."

"This is a joke, right? My grandfather was a—*black* man?"

"He was fairly light, I guess. The technical term would be an octoroon, for you," Jenna said, helpfully. "Now, not many folks know any of this, Chat, and although I suspect I should feel ashamed, I'd prefer to keep it that way. Local folks knew there was a black man in the woodpile, I expect I wouldn't be getting many votes next time around."

"An octoroon," Sue echoed, looking at Chat like she had never seen him.

"Huh. And to think that, just a minute ago, I was a lesbian."

"Chat!"

"Well, Sue, what in the name of all that is good and holy am I supposed to say? The idea that I'm a macaroon or some such stuff! This could have been all made up, Jenna. Tall tales a couple of sisters told," Chat said, hopefully.

But they picked up the kids and drove out to Chat's, and Meg showed them the Bible and the picture and the little bag of seeds with a scrap of what looked like paper in it. "Poa pratensis!" Jenna said and gasped, although what that meant was a mystery to Chat.

"What? Poa what?"

"Poa Pratensis. Bluegrass seed." She unwrapped the ragged bit of what proved to be parchment, put on her glasses, then rocked back on her heels in the small, dark space.

"'Give to me by my great-grandma Omalee Brown.' Signed, 'Dutch Schultz.'"

Chat's head was swimming, too, but he had to admit there must be something there. The Bible had names in it going back into the 1700s, and right there was Dutch Shultz's name, and then his dad's and a blank after that, along with some scribbles that Chat didn't really feel like reading right at the moment.

"The original source of Poa pratensis? Here in Pennsylvania? Oh, a paper I cannot ever write!" Jenna said, mournfully.

"A macaroon, " Chat said miserably.

"*My* macaroon, then," Sue said and kissed him.

"Yuk! Always kissing! Gross!" Jesse offered, and little Meg disagreed, saying, "That's romantic!"

It was sleeting in fits and starts when the service was to begin, and the inside of the church had the smell of damp wool and perfume, tobacco smoke and aftershave, while Chat and his family sat in their pew, Johnny and Meg behind them with the tribe, and Thelma in the first pew, with empty spots for the brides and grooms.

While the organ played some kind of fugue, they chatted quietly.

"So first Malchio loses the outlets to McAdam, and you know how that torqued him out. Although from what I hear, McAdam is getting out, too, selling to some outfit down in Florida, a maintenance guy was telling me, because the profit margin wasn't what he wanted and he can't get his hands on the Meadows like he wanted to. Even worse that you sold it off to Ty— that was insult to injury right there. Then Malchio was out yelling at some worker out near the projects, and the guy gets disgusted and walks off, and doesn't Ted jump up there and try to run the backhoe himself. They were putting lines in for sewers—God knows why, no sewers within five miles of there yet—and, wet as it's been, he rolls the thing and gets squashed like the bug that he was," Johnny half-whispered.

"All that money. Who gets it?" Chat asked.

"That's the really funny part. Seems Homer did better than Malchio. He died without a will. Figured he'd live forever, I guess, and there doesn't seem to be any relatives, so I hear the state gets it all. How do you like them apples? Messes that whole plot up like that, brings in trash, then he goes and dies," Johnny said.

"Not all trash, you know that as well as I do, or we wouldn't be all here today. Macaroon," Sue said.

Chat gave her arm a slap, and they sat silent, half-listening as Liza Jane Jerman strained the definition of music at the organ: "Ode to Joy," this time.

"How's Jo-Jo, Chat?"

"I still can't get used to that computer. And chat rooms. Why on earth would you go in there if you could just walk out your door and talk to a live person? And I type about four words a minute."

"Jo-Jo always was a surprise," Sue said. "All his posts are real positive, about what a good run he had and how much he has to be grateful for. Not what I expected at all. I suspect he's found God, although he isn't admitting it yet. Still a proud sucker yet, he is. And Kate is great to him. That benefit we gave him, they both still talk about it."

"That was one humdinger of a party. Glad we did it while he could still play a little. Man, even Paisley and Mitterholf showed up, and Compton, and, didn't I hear that Del sent something?"

"Yeah, he did. Nice note with one of his guitar picks. Oh, and I guess Jo-Jo has taken to writing some—a lot, actually. He sent something along for the reading."

"Shh! Here they come!"

They all turned to watch as Ada and Amy walked down the aisle with Rico between them, tall and handsome, just a little nervous, but smiling at them all. This was a good day for him, everyone could tell. Angelina, wearing a dress impossibly white, scattered rose petals in front of them.

Outside, the sleet drummed a harsh tattoo on the stained glass windows. From the inside, they looked dull, but Chat knew what the little house of God looked like from the outside. It was warmth in a cold and dismal landscape, a delicious promise.

Then came Layton, his new suit hanging on him awkwardly, as his work-reddened hands looked in vain for the loops to his overalls, and, not finding a roost, fluttered from pocket to pocket, afraid to light, then finally Sterling, with a broad grin.

They had gotten a minister and a priest to preside, although that had caused some small degree of gossip among the elders. A priest! In the church! But in the end they could deny Layton nothing. He had been too good to too many of them for them to say, "No."

Chat really didn't pay any attention until they got to the reading. Ephesians. "Instead, speaking the truth in love, we will in all things grow… built up in love" A simple homily followed, with a few words from Jo-Jo that there was indeed a time for all things under heaven, and the joyous ones must not be darkened by the remembrance of things past.

"The happy man finds happiness, the sad man sadness, and they find those things in the same rooms, in the same towns, in the hearts of the same valleys and on the summits of the same mountains. My advice to you all is to choose happiness," the preacher quoted from Jo-Jo.

And as the ground outside whitened with gusts of snow, Chat dreamt of a stage in the glen, a sea of hats and an ocean of lawn chairs with smiling people sitting, talking, and walking beneath the trees that dappled the sunlight while the notes of "Maiden's Prayer" weaved and soared through trees so green and a sky so faultlessly blue they made the other colors jealous, the soft breezes caressing eager skin, the music, the vastness it implied. One, then two, and then a myriad of poetic thoughts sung and played, all woven into a magical musical tapestry, a safety net to hold a spirit up, a way to paint on the air, to imagine once again the possibility of increase, and to discover hope, the ember that lies in the ashes of the season.

ABOUT THE AUTHOR

Peter Pappalardo has taught science, English and writing for 25 years, and has written articles and stories about local music and the arts for the last ten. An inveterate musician with informal training, he was abducted by bluegrass aliens in 1977 at the height of the great folk scare, and has since become a rabid fan of the genre, which is the only music form ever to be invented by one man named Bill Monroe.

Since then, he has played stand-up bass, guitar, mandolin and nose flute with several different bluegrass, old-timey, gospel and Irish bands, many of which were called the Lost Ramblers. Pappalardo has played with the late Mr. Greenjeans of Captain Kangaroo fame, Bob Dorough, who penned the popular songs for ABC's "School House Rock" and many other fine and famous musicians who make their home in and around the Poconos.

He is an outdoorsman, erstwhile dartshooter, tile mason and woodworker, and the father of four fine sons, all of whom fortunately favor their sainted mother.

Printed in the United States
33638LVS00004B/61-81